CW00418372

ERRANT

Book One of the
Chronicle of the Seer
Series

Florian Armas

OUT NOW:
Book 1 – Errant
Book 2 – Ardent
Book 3 – Ascendant
Book 4 – Respectant

Copyright © 2017 Florian Armas

Second Edition January 2021

All rights reserved. No part of this publication may be reproduced,
stored, distributed, or transmitted in any form or by any means,
without written permission of the author.

Cover design by Fiona Jayde

ISBN 13 9780993977237

For my mother

This novel is a work of fiction. Names, characters, places and incidents are the product of the author's imagination or are used fictitiously. Any resemblance to actual persons, living or dead, events or locales is entirely coincidental.

Table of Contents

Fate

Home

6

Broken Promises

War

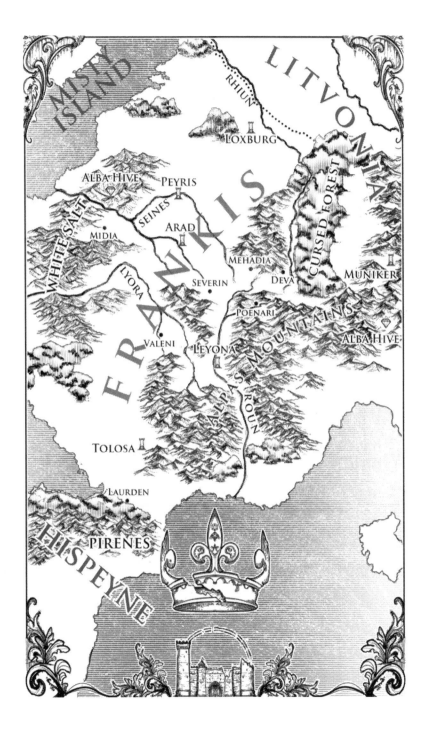

Fate

Slippery Fate plays us, and, having played, slips further.

Prologue

The surge of Light took Ada by surprise. *The Light is too strong for a Vision.* She could feel a hard throbbing in her temples. *It's too strong for a White Trance, and I have already had one. It must be a Prophecy.* A tall, radiant silhouette, vaguely resembling a woman, appeared in her sight. "Goddess." Ada bowed deeply. "I am honored."

Fate nodded at her and raised three radiant fingers. One by one, they morphed slowly, each of them revealing a fresco of people and places. It looked real.

I know the man, Ada thought. *I know the boy. I don't know the woman.* There was a stained-glass window behind the woman, etched wonderfully with the image of a hunting scene. The oldest girl in the woman's arms turned her head, and her green eyes locked with Ada's obsidian. *I am there, but where is there?*

"There will be wars..." The whisper came like the rustling of dead leaves on a cold autumn day. "The man will train the boy. The boy will save the girls." The whispers hastened, each coming at the expense of the previous one, until a blur of sounds and images poured into Ada's mind. There was no way to understand them now; every word and image would come to her later, when needed. It was a long Prophecy.

Fate vanished as abruptly as she had appeared, leaving Ada alone, but the imprint of the goddess was still on her eyelids. She felt tired and lightheaded. *The girls... They are toddlers. Some prophecies span decades. I have to talk to...* Ada was the strongest Wanderer, but she collapsed before finishing her thought.

Light filtered through her eyelids, and Ada opened her eyes gradually. The sun was high over the mountain. "I've slept too much."

"Two nights and the day between them." Eisha, the Queen of the Arenian Wanderers, took Ada's cold hand in hers. "Now, tell me."

"Fate gave me a Prophecy."

"I've never heard of a Prophecy that brought something good."

"This one is no different. I need to find an Assassin. And I need to make him leave their order." Ada stood up like an old woman; her body was weak and slow. Her vision darkened, and she grasped Eisha's arm.

"There are better ways to get killed."

"Yes, there are, but I have no choice."

సౌ

Nine years later.

Tired, Malin blinked the tears of blood from his eyes and grunted against a surge of panic. They were surrounded, fighting for their lives.

Betrayal.

During the first attack, his left wing had left him and joined Orban's army. Swords flashed, and bodies fell under the thrashing hooves. Arrows rained down. Men cried out to Fate. In the fight, Malin had lost his helmet, and he twisted when a longsword arced towards his head. At the last moment, he lifted up his shield to deflect it. The impact ran through his body, but he managed to stay in the saddle. His sword swung, and the man in front of him fell, eyes and mouth wide open. Desperate, he could taste sweat and blood, and yet, even as he fought, Malin thought not of himself, but of his wife and children. That strengthened him. Turning his horse abruptly, he drove away two enemy riders on his right. They almost collided, giving him a moment of respite, and Malin looked west, in the direction from which help might come. The sunset was the color of spilled blood.

"Ah!" he gasped, twisting away as a flying spear pierced through the ring mail and drove deep into his chest. Pain exploded inside him, and he did not realize that he was falling from his horse.

As consciousness faded, he thought again of his wife. *My love, I am sorry to leave you alone.* The noise of the battle vanished together with the pain in his body. Darkness came, then light, and he blinked at this new, peaceful world. A woman walked toward him, her white dress absorbing the light of the sunset. Shadowed, her face remained hidden. *Wife... What are you doing here?* The last of the sunshine, and the translucent glow from her clothes, finally revealed her face. "Who are you?"

"The Last Empress, the Maiden Empress, the White Light of the Wanderers. I have many names."

"You are dead. You died ... six hundred years ago."

"Stand up."

Unwillingly, he obeyed and stared at the woman, then at his own translucent body, then at the corpse in the grass, a dark red gash in its chest. It was his battered body, lying alone on what was a bloody battlefield just moments ago. The valley was silent and peaceful. The grass was green, with no traces of blood. Unable to take his eyes from the body in the grass, he touched the place where the wound should have been in his new body. He found nothing. "I am..."

"Dead."

"Can you send me back? My wife and children need me."

"I can't." The Empress shook her head. "But you still can help them. Dochia, who is my disciple and a friend to your wife, will help them too. I am not saying that they are safe. No one is safe in a failed kingdom ravaged by forty years of civil war."

"And my son?"

"He will survive with them." *And he will betray them.* She raised her translucent hand, and a pearl, its texture an echo of her skin, materialized in her palm. She blew gently, and the pearl flew toward Malin. It touched his chest and vanished inside him.

I wish my son was older and stronger. "How can I help them?" Malin asked, bitterly, touching the place where the pearl had vanished inside him; there was no pain.

We have much to do, but first, you must meet your twin brother. He will die tomorrow, far away from here. The Prophecy is in tatters, and everything now rests on the shoulders of a fifteen-year-old boy and of your daughters, who are even younger. If they fail, there will be only ashes and ruins on the continent. The Serpent God will soon initiate the Fracture and destroy everything. "I have given you enough Light to enter your wife's dreams and guide her. Come now." The last Empress of the Alban Empire, founder of Order of the Wanderers, stretched out her arm and, clasping his hand, she pulled him aloft. Surprised, he did not resist and, below, his prone body became smaller and smaller until it vanished from sight. "From up here, you can see many things."

Far away, toward the west, Malin could see his castle.

"It's too early to go there," the Empress said, gently. *And too dangerous.*

Chapter 1 - Codrin

Under the first sliver of sun eyeing the land, the village woke up slowly. Here and there, people left their houses, ghosts surrounded by shapeless fog patches. The Night of the Full Moon was over. The fear was still there, trailing through the mist, recalling the creatures of the otherworld, beasts able to cross the border of the Realm on nights when the moon is full. A young rooster broke the early silence – it sounded thin and laughably. Pades village stretched along the hairpin bend of the river, between a thin band of forest and water, and there was no way to see the other end of the settlement. It was a hard decision to leave our hiding place, but Strajer and his two sons had not returned in time from the Silvanian King's court.

"They are either dead or traitors," Tudor said in a low voice, looking at me. Strajer was my mother's cousin, but you never know people's loyalties in troubled times.

I patted my stallion, Zor, and took a long taste of the chill air, trying to run from my own past. It did not calm me. I wasn't shocked by the treason; it was the haunting memory of that awful night, almost a year ago, another Night of the Full Moon.

We were in Father's office, the whole family. There was a fireplace and a small fire, its flickering shapes painting shadows on the wall. He was writing at his desk, Mother following him closely. Candles in the chandelier and on table enhanced the shades of dark green and gold on the carpet behind my parents. A hunting scene.

"Are you ready to go?" Mother asked.

"Yes," Radu, my elder brother, answered; we were both fully dressed for night riding and training outside the city. "Tudor is waiting for us."

"Take Ioana with you."

My twin sister smiled, and I realized that she was dressed in one of her elegant riding suits. The dark red one that matched her hair. Elegant but simple. No ribbons and no rainbow colors. She was a good rider, and a good fighter too.

"I don't like to look like a peacock," Ioana used to say to her discouraged dressmaker.

We left the office talking and laughing, anticipating the thrill of the ride. At the stables, Ioana stopped suddenly and hid her hands behind her back. It was a swift movement – she was always fast – and gave me the impression of a ghost, radiant white, but it was just the reflection of my torchlight on her moving hands.

"I have to go back," she whispered, and ran away before we could respond.

That was the last time I saw Ioana. It was the Night of the Full Moon, but those who killed my parents and twin sister were not creatures of the otherworld, they were three cursed men: my uncle and his sons. I will never see her beautiful smile again. I will never hear her laughter again. I will never know why she went back. "She could have been alive," I whispered to myself. "If only I had..."

Down the valley, a horse neighed, then another one. A woman screamed, her wailing cut off abruptly, and I returned from the life I had lost. Radu and our mentor, Tudor, were already on horses.

"Mount!" Tudor ordered.

A girl, dressed in haste with a half-buttoned red shirt over black trousers, burst out of the forest, two riders wearing the colors of the Royal Guards of Arenia following her. Tudor and Radu kicked their horses to confront the soldiers.

The fight was brief, and the girl ran to find some comfort in Petre's embrace, her father and the chief of the village. "They are more than twenty riders like them in the village." She pointed to the dead guards in the grass. Her eyes widened, and her face stiffened. She spoke no more.

"We must run," Tudor said.

Did Strajer betray us? "They will kill everybody in the village."

"I know," he acknowledged, and Petre stared at him, begging. "What's your strategy, Codrin?" Tudor asked, though I was sure he had already planned everything.

Petre's pleading stare moved to me, and I felt my lips parting as my jaw dropped a fraction. It's hard to make life-and-death decisions when you are only fifteen years old. "We should lure them away. There." I pointed to the plain across the shallow river. We could vanish unseen inside the forest, but we owed the villagers who had hosted us for so long. Hoping that Tudor had a better plan, I avoided his eyes and Petre's too.

Tudor nodded, and a little grin flashed across his lips. "Petre, take your family and hide inside the forest. Ride!"

Across the river, Tudor tightened the halter, forcing his horse to paw the ground and neigh, then rose in his saddle to look over the plain, a wide stretch of grassland between river and forest. On our left, a column of twenty riders moved out from the village. In synchronized moves, five more riders appeared from the forest behind the village, and passed the river too, on our right. The village was surrounded; the royal guards knew we were here.

Fate take you, Strajer. Traitor.

"Spread out!" Tudor gestured to the forest in front, pushing his horse into a gallop, on a diagonal path intersecting the five riders' course.

As in our training, we formed a wedge with him at the point, forcing our enemies to break their formation. Slowly, my fingers curled tight around the cold hilt of my sword, and I unsheathed it.

Radu went on the left. I charged on the right. In front of us, Tudor changed direction in a heartbeat, and the first clash happened a few moments later. One rider fell under his long sword – as any Assassin, he was fighting with two curved swords of unequal length. Tudor was a renegade from the Assassins Order, hired nine years ago by Father, to train my brother and me. He put down another rider, but the next soldier was too far from him to engage and came toward me.

There were two riders on my side, and I turned abruptly, even more to the right, hoping to put one rider between me and the other one, praying that Tudor would come and help. It was my first fight. The closest rider loomed up beside me, enormous on his horse. His grin was large too. I bit my lip to stifle a cry. Or I cried. I could not remember. There was not time for this. Perhaps that cold fear gnawing at me made me see him taller and stronger than he really was, but he was tall and sturdy. I ducked, leaning down on my right. His sword sliced air. His body leaned forward. I cut upward, in a diagonal, with all my strength. My sword cleaved through the frail armor under his armpit. A curse followed me, and the wind-rush of his sword, slicing again. Too far from me. A useless move. I may be weaker, but I am bloody fast. I turned left suddenly, making him lose a few precious moments. He had no idea what happened to him when Tudor's sword chopped off his head with a single hard stroke. Blood sprayed out from a headless body still riding until the horse reared. The head bounced off a boulder and rolled further.

The last rider followed me, and we rode in parallel. I recognized my cousin, Jan. *Murderer...* Our eyes met, and a wicked smile spread on his lips.

"Little rat, meet your dead father!" Jan gloated – he was four years older – and pushed his horse on a colliding path. I reined the horse abruptly, almost to a stop. Jan did the same, just one second later, and I was behind him. My sword fell on his neck. I did not have enough force to chop his head off, but it was not needed. Jan screamed, a bubbling sound. Slowly, he slid back on his mount until I saw his wide, white eyes. He brought one hand to his mouth in a strange childlike gesture. He was silent now. Or he was still babbling. I was not sure, and I did not care. *For my parents*, I saluted his death. *My first kill*. Wrath and bitterness, and longing for my dead parents and sister. His body went sideway and vanished from my sight. The wind still blew, as cold as before.

When the fight ended, we yelled to encourage ourselves, swords up, riding further toward the forest. The pack of riders in front tried to cut off our road but, having horses of uneven speed, they started to spread across the meadow.

"I killed Jan," I bragged, yet my voice trembled. Then my hands gripping the halter. I gripped harder. There was a sort of turmoil, something new, something that I did not desire, and I felt drained, almost numb. I avoided to understand it. I looked compulsively back, wanting to go and see Jan. There was no time. And I was not really sure that I wanted it.

"One usurper less." My brother grinned coldly.

Ten minutes later, we turned in haste on the west road, toward Litvonia. I could rejoice at the beauty of the land described by many books and songs, as the road entered the gorge of the Cerina River, but not that day. I surprised Tudor glancing at the tall sides; under his composed expression, something was wrong. I questioned him with a gesture.

"We need a way out, to ride hidden. Another Arenian band may be in front of us," he said.

A large opening appeared on the right, but the meadow was blocked by a soaring cliff, difficult to climb even on foot, and we had to take the road again. The sound of hooves echoed down the gorge, clattering around us in the shadow that looked almost like dusk. Strangely, the rivulet, which had shaped the canyon, vanished into the underground. A horse nickered softly. It took me a while to realize that it was mine, and I patted Zor, speaking in a low voice. Scarred with black cracks and slick with damp, the sheer sides pressed on us, and my heart beat faster than the harsh rhythm of the horseshoes hitting the stones. The gorge could be our grave. A beautiful one, indeed. With every step, it had been feeling more and more like a trap. I breathed in and out, slowly and at measured times, the Assassin Cool. On our left, nature had shaped a stone giant. Water trickled over smooth rock, dripped from the long beard of hanging grass, and from rotten arms that looked amputated at the elbow.

Behind a steep curve, a horse neighed, and we turned abruptly, riding back on the straight road for about four hundred paces. The riders appeared at that moment: around twenty, and wearing the Arenian Royal Guard's colors. At a full gallop, we returned to the meadow that had given us false hope before and climbed in haste to the small ridge in front of the cliff blocking the exit. In the crags high above, some crows flapped and cawed, protesting our intrusion. The sky was clear and intense above the mountains, a few shreds of white-purple clouds stretched out almost still. Here and there, lonely trees loomed up, dark green and tall.

Dismounted, we walked slowly through the scree toward the ridge which was thirty feet long and just one foot high at its lower point. A small plateau sat behind the ridge, meeting the cliff some twenty-five paces back. On its sides, the hard roots of the mountains blocked the lateral paths. The only way to attack us was from the front, through the scree, studded with many boulders, some larger than a bull's head. Nervous, our horses skittered, trying to move onto the plateau, and we freed them.

"Here we stand." Tudor hit the ground with his boot, and the rock answered back with the sound of a healthy land. "I will take this side." He moved to the lower half of the ridge. "Radu, take the other one." That half was a foot higher and better protected. "Codrin, stay back, in the middle. Take your bow and prune their rows before they arrive. You are one of the best *gardeners* I know."

The first column entered the meadow, a compact wave of horses, climbing fast on the easy slope, and the land trembled to the infernal rhythm of many hooves hitting the ground. There was no harmony in the soaring sound. Behind us, the cliff echoed back in angry tones. With the second column, the noise became louder. A burst of fear gnawed at me like nothing before.

"Codrin, take down the spearmen." Confident, Tudor unsheathed his curved swords and balanced them for a few moments. "Flame and Shadow are ready." He smiled to encourage us, saluting with the blades crossed above his head. Each Assassin blade is unique and named by its own shape and color at the summer equinox, baptized in the cold, bitter, red water of the Blood Spring. Shorter, the light blue Flame had traces of iridescent golden vines in the sunlight – there was a sparkling spirit in it, meant for defense. With its dark hues, Shadow was the night shadow meant to kill. Tall and dressed all in black, like any Assassin, Tudor seemed a knight born from an old legend. Gleaming in the sun, his auburn hair contrasted vividly with the rest of him.

I raised my bow in a stiff salute. Radu did the same with his longsword, yet he was not smiling. Neither was I; more than forty royal guards were attacking us.

I aimed at the fourth rider on the left, the closest spearman. Released, the arrow hissed softly. I did not follow it; my hands were already nocking the bow, my eyes searching for the next target. *The seventh, on the right.* I released the arrow again. On the left, a body was hanging on its horse, which moved away from the column, neighing loudly. The echo answered back, and the second rider fell.

"For the King!" Tudor and Radu yelled, raising their swords. It was a weird irony how my brother did not realize that formally he was the King of Arenia; their shouts were meant for our slain father. We just needed an army to remove our treacherous uncle from the throne, and to make him pay for killing our parents and sister.

I missed the third shot. In front of the scree, the first column stopped abruptly, sixty paces from us. The riders dismounted and arranged themselves, line after line, ready to attack. The Royal Guard was the best-trained regiment in the Arenian kingdom. They touched amulets, kissed cold blades, raised their hands, fingers large spread, to attract one of Fate's many eyes. It makes sense to be in touch with her before the battle; when it ends, only the dead stir her attention. You won't want that. A strange stillness fell over the meadow. That cold stillness which comes before a battle, when both sides know and don't know what to expect. Even the wind felt dead.

"Baraki!" Tudor broke the unnatural silence. "You are attacking the King."

"The King is on his throne," Baraki, the Chief of the Royal Guard, answered coldly. He was Jan's father-in-law and the Usurper's right hand.

"The legitimate King is here." Tudor pointed to Radu. "Don't betray the kingdom." This time he addressed the soldiers, measuring them with his blue stare.

"The King offers one thousand galbeni and Knighthood for anyone who kills a traitor," Baraki countered. "Kill them!" His sword rose swiftly, toward us.

Baraki's most trusted men charged, and the others followed in haste; the mirage of gold and privileges was stronger than any sense of justice. I aimed and shot at Baraki. One soldier moving fast to claim his prize got the arrow in his place. In a swift sequence, I released three more arrows, and two attackers from the first line fell on the scree, their heads knocking the boulders with a dull sound.

More determined, one enemy left the line and reached the ridge alone, trying to climb in the middle. Tudor sprang with a speed that defied the eye, his long sword reaching the soldier's neck, leaving a bloody line behind. The soldier fell as if he were asleep. Everything around me felt odd, the images coming in flashes as if I were half asleep too.

In deadly silence, you see blood. Dark red as spilled wine. It spreads on the rocks. It spreads on a yellow flower. It spreads.

The first line arrived, trying to climb the ridge at several points, and I released my arrow. *Just four spearmen left*, I counted fast, looking back and forth across the meadow in front, registering everything. In flashes.

Grass. The blue sky. Tudor's long sword was splitting the sky in two – steely reflection, cold and warm at the same time. Then it split a skull through the helmet, there was nothing better than an Assassin's sword in a battle. A black bird flew low somewhere in front. It vanished behind a prancing horse. A dead man was still hanging, one leg caught in the stirrup. The horse ran away. The dead's head hit each boulder on the way with muffled sounds. The smell of blood came to me, and the perfume of an unknown flower.

A spear flew over us – the soldier threw it at the same time my arrow pierced his neck – and a neigh sounded behind me. At the corner of my eye, I saw my horse, Zor, wounded, yet the spear was down, in the grass. Radu stopped an attack on his side. His sword turned and cut, in a blur and rush of time, the instinctive product of many years of training with a blade in hand. An arm fell on the rocks. Still attached to it, a piece of cloth waved the beautiful red, yellow and blue colors of the Royal Guard.

My eyes recorded everything, flash after flash. Spasmodically, fingers that will be dead soon gripped the stone under them. The stone became red. The fingers moved no more.

My last arrow killed the man trying to sneak behind my brother. *There are no more spearmen alive*, I encouraged myself and unsheathed my sword. I was breathing in gasps, tried to slow my breaths and couldn't. That cold fear was gnawing at me again; I did not have enough strength to fight blow for blow. His eyes wide and dark, a guard moved against me. I turned right. He stepped left, a moment later. My sword moved in a swift arc. It cut a leg to the bone. He howled like an animal, and I ducked to avoid the strong blow. Hard steel crashed on stone, just a few inches from me. I reacted in a split second.

Attacked by four guards, Radu stumbled; a sword caught him from the side. With a last effort, he turned and killed his attacker.

"No!" Tudor cried and moved closer to Radu, his swords slaughtering two enemies in a swift succession. My knife flew in the face of another soldier; they had understood that Radu was not as strong as Tudor and tried to surround him and take us one by one. Another sword crashed on his head, and Radu fell. Sensing the right time, Baraki attacked Tudor from behind, piercing his ring-mail.

"You are dead!" Baraki shouted, his sword up for the final blow. Too soon, in a quick turn, Tudor sliced his neck, a moment later, Baraki's last words lost in the gurgling of blood.

Tudor fell too, and the remaining two soldiers attacked me at the same time; Tudor's skills were still projecting fear in their mind, making me an equal to them.

One sword came down toward my head; the second one made a horizontal wheel, trying to cut me in two. I stepped back. Unopposed, the blade moving down hit the ground, striking red sparks on the stones, and got stuck. The man bent forward, touching a rock with his left hand. The wheeling blade met my ring-mail. Cutting through the rings, it produced a rasping sequence of quick sounds. A burn passed through my flesh. The sword moved further right, hitting the hilt of the blade stuck point down in the ground. A strong metallic clang. A human curse. From its own inertia, the soldier's body followed the sword, half-turning. I cut and dodged the second sword. Pirouette. Slash. Anger. I turned again, and I turned, and I cut, and I turned, my sword whooshing softly. There was no one left standing. My mind realized it slowly, still pushing me to move, though less and less until I stood motionless. Silence. In my head. There were many ugly sounds around, and patches of red color.

The color of spilled blood defines us…

I gasped spasmodically, in short sequences, unequal and rasping in that illusory silence, and my lungs felt like the whole world was void of air. The crisp air was strangely still. My eyes flicked around, between my dead brother and Tudor. Lying on the ridge, Tudor was breathing heavily, and I took him in my arms, resting his head on my knees.

"Go west, Codrin. That's the only chance you have. The King of Silvania is no longer your friend. Remember that you were the best apprentice I ever had, and a friend to me. Make me proud." Tudor smiled tiredly, and I still hoped for him. "One more thing. Your sister... Her hands... They glowed. White. She was a..." Slowly, his head slipped aside, that gentle smile freezing on his lips.

"She was?" I breathed and touched his face, hoping to keep him alive. "Don't leave me…" I whispered, but there was no way he could hear me again.

Fate, I curse your broken world, world of men and women having no honor, world of filth and spilled blood. I curse you all. There is nothing left for me.

The sun was getting down behind the mountains, slitting the clouds with bright crimson lines. The shadows grew longer. Mechanically, I covered my ears to escape the weak moaning of the wounded that would soon be dead, and I do not know how long I stayed like a stone, unfeeling, as if I were dead myself – not even a tear left my eyes – staring at the dusking sun until I could see it even with my eyes closed. White. *Ioana's hands glowed white. Why?* Somewhere in the forest, a wolf howled, heralding the coming of the night. Through the cut in the ring-mail, I could see a five-inches-long wound, there was not much blood, but I had to make two stiches and put a bandage. On weak legs, I stood up like an old man, taking in the carnage around me until I stared at my dead brother. I would have liked to say that his face was serene and at peace. It was not. Contracted, and cut in two by a stream of blood that was almost dried, there was nothing serene in it. Tightened in a menacing fist, his hand was challenging Fate for the game it had played on him. One long-dead philosopher stated that people like to see death. It reminds them that at least they survived the fight. Perhaps he never lost a brother or a friend. Perhaps he never fought in a battle. Perhaps he was just stupid.

Eyes set on my brother's face, I wanted to be sure I would remember this day for the rest of my life. His white face and the red stream of blood imprinted my mind. I did not know what I was doing, and countless nights after that, I just desired to forget everything. *Why?* I asked a question that no one could answer, not even Fate. The forest sent its howling again, two wolves this time, and my blood flowed faster. *I have to bury them. More guards may come... I can't let them... I can't...*

When the graves were covered, I stuck three swords in the ground, and knelt in front of them, gripping their hilts with both hands.

"This child swears before your graves that he will hunt down the Usurper and take back what was ours by right. I owe it to you, to my parents and to my sister. I owe it to myself." Through gritted teeth, I swore the sacraments, the Oath of Justice, upon the field of death around me. Three deadly swords were silent witnesses in front of me: mine, the one that once belonged to my brother and Shadow, Tudor's long sword. I touched them all, feeling their coldness, to give me resolve. "Justice shall be served. I am now a Knight Errant on a quest for justice." Filled with grief, my voice broke off toward the end, and my own silence engulfed me. I slid my thumb across Shadow's edge and let some blood fall in drops on their graves. "My oath is now sacred."

Staring at the graves, I forced myself to breathe long and slow, the Assassin Cool. A silent white lightning blinded me, and I closed my eyes while a strange flash passed through my mind: a merchants' caravan. I was leading it through Frankis. It felt so disturbing to see yourself, and stare in your own eyes. It felt real too. *So, shall it be,* I encouraged myself; no one prepared me for such Visions. In the long winter nights, I heard weird stories about the Wanderers being able to see into the future, through their Visions, but I was not one of them, and maybe they were only stories for children. *My Vision felt so real.* I shook my head and stood up.

I left the place without looking back, riding a horse that was not mine. Zor followed us after I'd cleaned his wound, talking, knowing that my voice would calm him. Knowing that our enemies would desecrate the graves, I took the swords with me.

"An Assassin's sword is his twin soul," Tudor had told us the day we left the Arenian Royal Palace, our home that was no longer ours. "If I die, don't leave my swords to my enemies. Take them with you."

Was it a premonition? I never thought that Tudor could die in a battle; he was too strong and skilled. We do not have the same tradition in Arenia, but alien feelings made me take my brother's sword too. *At least they would not parade it as a trophy...*

The darkness stopped me sooner than I wanted; I was not far enough to be safe and not tired enough to sleep, yet I was away from that bloody gorge that I now hated, despite its stunning beauty. In a ravine, far from the road, I sat down, leaning against an old tree, and pulled my hood over my head – the silent night around was more alive than I was. Under the full moon, my haunted eyes perceived the trees in a strange way, ghostly outgrowths of the darkness, like the noiseless landscape of a dark dream. *My sister's hands glowed white.* The flash of a singing bird came back to me. Unaware of the spilled blood, an innocent skylark was singing during the fight, its trills rhyming in a strange way with the clanging swords. I did not remember it until that midnight.

Death came to me with my first dream. Everything was drowned in blackness, only my brother's face was white, a bright stream of blood cutting it in two. I woke, howling at the whole world, and did not dare to sleep again. *Under the endless sky, each man shall learn he is the one who chooses his own future... Another useless philosopher. We can't choose. Tudor did not choose to die, neither did it my family.* From that night, my brother's bloodied face and Tudor's gentle last smile became parched landmarks of all my nightmares. Dawn came both too soon and too late. Tired, after a night without sleep, I left in the morning, riding without respite all day, through the forest and ravines, avoiding the road. Filtered by a layer of thin clouds and the foliage overhead, the sunlight was not bright. It suited my mood. Close to sunset, I fell from my horse. All that I could do was to roll and hide behind some hardened roots. And I slept. And I dreamt. The same white face, red stream of blood and gentle smile, again and again. The rain woke me in the morning, surrounded by a cold that went deep into my bones. It was not yet autumn, yet the first signs of the winter were already visible on the white, high peaks. Half of the sky was covered, the other blue and clear, illuminating the snow.

I must think... For two days, I was just a headless body riding a horse. *I need a shelter for the winter.* During the last one we had stayed in Pades, but now I was alone and too young to be safe anywhere. *Sixteen galbeni...* I checked my purse. *Two months of lodging and food. And then what? Just move through the desert of my life.* Absently keeping one galben between my fingers, I remembered that most of our money was with Tudor. Reflected by the polished gold of the coin, sunshine flashed in my eyes, stirring unwanted memories. With all that pain, I could not help rebuking myself that I should have been wiser, and that was enough to refresh my mind, restoring whatever little fragment of mental coherence I could muster. There were so many riches left to the dead, more than enough to buy a house somewhere. *Next time, I will use the Winner's Right, and take anything of value. I am no longer a King's son. I am a vagrant. I need to leave the mountains just to survive the winter. Then I will see.*

I changed the bandage over my wound and mounted slowly, with a raw sense of futility. Touching the horse brought me a sense of warmth and life that I desperately needed. Down in the valley, a column of riders was galloping west like a storm. *Twenty*, I counted, sadness and anger filling my mind while the colors of the Royal Guard vanished further away. *Fate take you, traitors.*

Now that my brother is dead, I am the legitimate King of Arenia. I laughed like a mad man, staring at the riders searching for me: the last nuisance for my bastard uncle. *I am nothing. Just nothing...*

The small path rose steeply, and in a few days, the hooves of my horse moved through fallen, blood-red leaves. I forced myself to ignore that cursed color.

From the high road, I faced the sunset and the huge plains of Litvonia. Half of the sky was clear and pale blue above the plain, a few shreds of white clouds stretched out almost still. The view was enchanting, like a carpet observed far from above, forests, rivers and villages, painted in a myriad of colors – I took the highest and least used passage through the mountains, ten thousand feet in altitude. *Freedom. Can you feel it?* the wind seemed to say, but only loneliness came to me.

Tudor's plans were to go into the far west, an area of anarchy after the Frankis Kingdom had been destroyed in a civil war, and in troubled times hard men can go far. He had some links, from his Assassin's past in the southern city of Tolosa, and he taught us all the Frankis words he remembered. They were not many.

"Let's go," I patted the horse, dismounting; the path down was steep and potholed. Zor was still following us. I stared back at the high, white-peaked mountains without seeing them.

One day I will return.

Chapter 2 – Jara

"They are opening the gate." There was no sound. I recalled the old iron screeching like a dying animal. The open space was growing, and I could do nothing but stare through the window, mesmerized by the sliding gate: enemy soldiers waiting to enter the castle. Disciplined and steady, like bronze statues, they looked so small at this distance; their spears resembling inoffensive toys. "The guards have betrayed us." *Orban S'Arad will capture me… He has waited sixteen years for this.*

"No, Jara. I ordered the surrender," Father said. The first enemies were creeping inside, stirring a low stretch of mist that made them look footless, disproportionate creatures sliding tensely through the open gate. "We are too few to defend the castle for more than a month. And the consequences would be far worse if…"

A ray of sunshine pierced the high clouds, dancing with crimson sparks through the mist. The soldiers hesitated, then marched on, their spears glimmering in the sun.

Bad omen. Blood will be spilled today. "Why? Malin will return soon." It was a futile question; nothing in the world could wipe out the soldiers and close the gate.

"He lost the battle two days ago." Father turned me slowly, away from the window. Facing him, I felt like a child again, and he shook his head, holding me tighter.

between his benevolent appearance and the meaning of his words.

Drained and stiff, I closed the door behind me. On weak legs, I leaned on the door, slipping down until a strong hand gripped my arm.

"Let's go, Jara," Father said gently, raising me up, and we walked together in silence.

"I am afraid," I whispered when he closed the door of my new room behind me — an illusory protection in a castle that was no longer mine. *I am more than afraid.*

"Stejara," Father also used my full name, for a different reason, though. "We signed an agreement with Orban and his allies, but one wrong step and everything crashes. We need to survive. Your children need to survive. Think of them. Dress yourself in an armor that does not let your thoughts out. Three days will pass quickly." He held my head until the warmth of his hands moved inside me. "We still have the garrison and the towers, and our soldiers will guard the door when you dine with Orban. One cry and they will act. He will not risk a wrong step. This time, Cantemir, the Master Sage of the Circle, helped us in the negotiations. Orban's allies are content to avoid a siege; they spared many soldiers with the treaty and will not accept a fight now just because he can't handle his pants."

The Circle always worked against us. I nodded, pressing my palm over his, in a closeness that sent me far, into a past without pain and danger.

"Please, have a seat." Orban spoke so politely that it would have tricked any person not knowing him and pulled the chair out from the table to let me sit. We were alone in the room. "Not hungry?" He picked a piece of meat, in a silence that lingered. Absently, I did the same. "Your father is a good negotiator. I wished to have some more liberty in treating you in the best way possible." He stared at my breasts, and a little grin flashed across his mouth. "Maybe we can rearrange some things."

"I can ask the servants to rearrange the table."

"Jara, you are a good host." He pointed at the table. "But you could be even better." His mouth curved up, and his thick eyelids narrowed in satisfaction. "I plan to stay in your ... hmm, my castle, for a month. To take over, you know... Such things are so boring. Would you stay to help me?" His palm hovered over the table, ready for a friendly handshake, his eyes wide open in a show of sincerity. "One month passes quickly, and your children will benefit."

Bastard! I can suffer a month in your bed for my children, but the moment my last soldiers leave the castle, we are in your bloody hands.

"I can give some more land to your son."

The only land you want to give us is our graves. "How is Celine?"

"She is well. Wine?" Orban asked in a pleasant, conversational tone. "I brought something special, just for you and me." He left the table and came back with a bottle that looked old. "Sixteen years old. The year you married. A very good year. For the wine, I mean." At leisure, he filled the goblets. Through the crystal, the wine's blood-red color flashed in my eyes like a curse, and Malin's image filled my mind. "Salute!" He raised his glass, drinking half of it.

Die! I cursed, waiting for him to finish; you are never careful enough with Orban.

"Drink with me, princess of my heart," he said in his most persuasive voice. His lips parted, then tightened again in a crooked smile.

Malin's words... My hand holding the glass sprang toward his face. I should have controlled myself better, but Orban's evil lips had no right to taint those words. As fast as it sprang, my hand stopped. Wine droplets landed on the white tablecloth, like spilled blood. Orban didn't flinch, keeping his obstinate wicked eyes on me. Stiffly, I raised my glass in silence, afraid that my voice would betray me, and took a small sip, forcing my mind to focus on the drinking act.

"Excellent, isn't it?" he said with evident self-satisfaction. "I would be disappointed if you didn't like it."

"Yes, a good wine."

"I have four bottles. We can have a special evening each week. Well, all evenings will be special if you stay."

"Your daughter is now eleven."

"She may be a good match for Veres. Don't you think? I can let my Secretary arrange the details with your father while we enjoy the late spring together."

Before speaking, I felt nausea, and my eyes became muddled. It was so quick. He cocked one brow up, and a mischievous grin crossed his wide mouth.

I tried to reach the water, but my hand betrayed me. "Orban," I breathed and tried to stand. "I am not feeling well. I have to leave."

He jumped and grabbed me by the arm. "You need help. That's what I am here for." He passed his arm over my shoulders, and I walked with drunken steps, leaning on his body. Slowly, he pushed me toward his bedroom.

"Not here, Orban."

"Of course, not here, my dear. It will happen in our bed. Much more comfortable, isn't it?"

I collapsed, and he raised me in his arms, carrying me further. The last thing I remember.

In the morning, our guards inclined their heads in contempt when I left Orban's apartment. That reaction men have when a woman is caught sleeping with someone she is not married to. There was scorn too. A woman spent the night with the man who killed her husband. I glared at them, and their smiles vanished. That strengthened me, and I walked further, speaking the names of my children, with each painful step I took. "Vio". One step. "Saliné." Another one. Everything repeated in a cadence that went faster and faster until I entered my room, where Father was waiting.

"He drugged me," I said, my voice loud and cracked, and threw myself into a chair. *The wine was clean; Orban drank it too. What was wrong? The glass? Did he put the drug in it?* Trembling, my hands gripped the chair. It didn't help. *Ignore the night. Ignore everything. For my children...* My head throbbed and, eyes closed, I tried to feel nothing. It did not work. Heavy breaths mingled in the room, in a strange rhythm, as if our lungs were linked together by two cornered minds. I opened my eyes on Father's marbled face, his mouth tightened in a stiff rictus of confusion and guilt, his sunken eyes dark around the edges. "It's not your fault, Father." I waited for him to say something, yet his lips stayed lifeless. "We must leave today. He wants to keep me here for one month."

Father nodded slowly and left the room, leaving me in a silence that did not really leave me alone. With a muffled cry, I leaned my head on my hands over the table. *Please, Fate, don't let me become pregnant.* When Father came back, my tears were already dry, and I caught his deep, blue eyes. *Clear.*

"Lenard will let us go today. Aurelian, the Sage of the Circle, pressed for our release too. I told them Orban plans to spend a few months here with you and your daughters, before returning to Arad. One carriage and four horses are already prepared. Horia and Mugur will come with us, and Veres is almost fifteen, old enough to ride. We will take the northern road. It's less safe, but shorter, and we are three swordsmen."

"Five horses. I will ride too, disguised as a Knight. I cannot match a man with the sword, but I am better than most of our archers."

Without a King for more than thirty years, and lawless, Frankis was unsafe in general, but we were not fearing only some petty robbers.

The gate closed behind us, screeching hard. *Orban's place now...* Afraid of crumbling, I could not turn for a last look at Midia, our lost home, yet somehow, I remembered that Lenard was the last one to vanish from sight. Maybe I was dreaming. All our soldiers who wanted to leave the garrison separated from us and went their way; the treaty we had signed with Orban allowed us to take only two guards. Up on the hills, I could not avoid embracing the castle with one last glance: the white towers of Midia were gleaming in the sun.

One day I will return, and Orban will pay.

With the sun almost gone behind the hills, we stopped at The Long Road, an isolated inn that Father knew from his past travels. My daughters forced themselves not to cry in front of me, yet they unconsciously curled in my arms until they fell asleep. Now and then, a suppressed sob shook their small bodies – no other sound disturbed the unnatural silence of the night. When their breathing became smooth and even, I went to my bed, where I could mourn Malin alone. The roosters were announcing the morning when my tears dried, and an uneasy sleep, filled with invisible marching boots pounding on the stones, came to me.

"Jara, we have to go." Father woke me up when all I wanted was to sleep forever, and I crept out of my bed clumsily.

There was a sliver of sun shining brightly above the hills. It should have felt warm and enchanting. It didn't. We ate fast, in a heavy silence, and left the inn in a hurry. Too tired to ride, I joined the girls in the carriage, falling asleep as soon as I could sit. Instinctively, I embraced my little Vio when she tried to find some comfort in my body. Saliné was more composed, but she always had an understanding that went above her age.

"Jara," Father woke me again, leaving the impression that everything was just a string of repeated dreams.

No, it's not a dream. We are running. The carriage was uphill, at the edge of the forest, hidden inside. Down in the valley, Orban's soldiers were swarming the inn, searching for us, and I let out a breath that I hadn't realized I had been holding.

Slippery Fate plays us, and, having played, slips further...

Chapter 3 – Jara

Every forest has a different feel. This one felt gloomy, like a silent storm, the fall of light between the leaves resembling a line of spears thrown down by an angry goddess. Deep inside, a fork split the road in two, and we hurried toward it. Both roads went to Severin, and that worked to our advantage; the area was an expanse of dense forests and broken hills.

"Daniel, we separate now," Father said to the coach driver. "Take the carriage on the left road, and conceal it in the forest, two thousand paces from here. The horses are yours." They were worth more than a hundred galbeni, four years of the coachman's wages.

Father took Saliné on his horse. Vio came with me. Well trained soldiers, Mugur and Horia grabbed two small bags of food from the back of the carriage. Our ride for life started on the right path. Cold, the wind flushed my face, and I felt both tired and refreshed. Between my arms, little Vio was absorbed by the ride, overcoming for the moment all the pain in her mind. I glanced at Saliné. Her face had a measured calm. Veres seemed calm too. The road turned east, and we saw again the fork, and the carriage returning slowly. *Daniel betrayed us.*

"Follow me." Father pushed his horse through the rivulet on the right – the water was just under the horse's knees. We turned back for a short time, then went on the left. Two meanders later, the road was no longer in sight, and we moved out of the water through a narrow rocky path. Sunshine flashed on and off our faces under a row of old oaks that lined the trail curving up its way up to the hill like a giant snake. Our speed increased again in the forest, and we rode in parallel with the valley. It took a while until the sound of trotting horses reached us. The sound grew slowly, with no rider yet in sight.

"They are coming," Vio said, half-scared, for her our run was almost a game – she was not even ten years old.

"Do you see the road?" I pointed to the sinuous white-gray line three hundred paces below us. "They will follow it, and never find us. We are safe." At the corner of my eye, I caught Saliné and Veres listening too.

We stopped behind the tall bushes at the edge of the forest bordering the meadow - there was only grass for the next thousand paces, and nowhere to hide. Down, on the road, the trotting became louder, and we waited. Orban's riders burst into view, and they seemed to glide like the ghosts from my last nightmare. After a while, the trotting sound moved in reverse, getting quieter.

"Ride!" Father ordered when they vanished from sight, and we pushed the horses, letting them choose the speed; the path was full of potholes.

Swallowed by the forest again, we stopped nervously, listening for any sound coming from the valley. There was only the whispering wind, and my heart thudding in my chest, strong and alert. We moved slowly, deeper into the forest. It was a better place to hide, or to fight and die. Hard trotting filled the valley again, almost underneath us, the riders partially visible through the forest, galloping back even faster than before.

"They will try to figure where we have left the road," Father said, a trace of mockery in his voice. "Let's move down."

"There might be some riders left behind," I said, staring back at the vanishing soldiers, as if they were a strange illusion.

"Maybe, but there is no other choice, and we can handle the few in front of us." It was not an ambiguous statement, and Father picked a path that moved toward the road climbing down leisurely. With the trotting gradually dissipating far behind us, we urged our horses faster, and by the time we hit the road, they were already galloping.

We met Orban's four soldiers in the middle of a steep curve flanked by tall sides. I stopped my horse abruptly and looked around. A few curled-up leaves fell on a sudden gust of wind and fluttered gently on the road. *We are nothing but leaves in the wind.*

"Veres, take Saliné." Father threw her onto his horse. Handled like a bag, Saliné did not complain, and embraced him from behind the moment she was seated. The men unsheathed their swords, and I nocked my bow, telling Vio to lean forward on the horse and stay still. "Calm," Father whispered, weighing the sword in his hand like weighing our own fate. "I don't want blood between us and Orban right now." It took us a few moments to evaluate the soldiers. They looked as nervous as I was. "Captain Feher! We mean no harm to you; we just want to pass. Can we make an agreement?"

"Sir Cernat," Feher said reluctantly, his eyes probing all of us, swords and arrow. "We were searching for you. Sir Orban needs you back. I apologize, but it's my duty."

"There was an agreement regarding our departure. You were there when it was signed. Aurelian the Sage of the Circle was there too, as guarantor of the agreement." Aurelian was the Primus Itinerant Sage of the Circle, but Father never used his full title. The Sage was worse than a snake.

Unable to decide, the captain kept his horse in place, trotting slowly. One soldier startled as a bird flapped up from a rock behind him. The young man on Feher's left lost his temper and charged Father.

"Stop!" Feher shouted too late; the young man was writhing in the dust, and looking at him, I recognized a face that resembled Feher's.

"I did not harm him," Father said calmly, lowering his sword. That was a masterly move to answer with the hilt against a sword attack, but even at fifty-four, Father was still one of the best swordsmen in the former Frankis Kingdom, and the young man was inexperienced.

"Your son is young and full of temper," I said to Feher. Father glanced at me, then at the young man, and smiled briefly.

"Thank you, Sir Cernat," Feher said, with great relief in his voice. "You can pass," he added, hesitantly.

Moving forward through Orban's riders, my mare became uneasy and tossed her head. Tightening the halter, I spoke softly, stroking her neck to calm her. Father was the last one to pass, and he did it with calculated leisure. Nervous trotting came from behind and, glancing back, I saw the enemies vanishing like a storm. I kicked the mare's flanks, and she burst into a gallop.

We took a passage between two peaks to pass on the other side of the mountain chain and did not stop until the darkness came. Filled with many noises, the night had a vile smell of fear, yet there were just animal snarls or growls. That bloody fear kept my grief away, but each time I fell asleep, the footless soldiers marched through my nightmares again. Early in the morning, the careless cawing of crows somewhere in the forest seemed ridiculously loud in the quiet place. The grass was heavy with cold dew, and the trees loomed over us, almost dark, their leaves singing in the soft wind. The sky was crisp and clear. It felt both gloomy and hopeful.

We took the road before the sun would come in sight, riding until Father pushed us back into the forest running from one hill to another. A short gorge forced us on the road again. Soon, the road narrowed between the steep sides of the gorge, and the curves multiplied. Every sound above made me spin around in my saddle, clutching at my bow, fearing an ambush, which turned out to be a frightened bird. Here, I feared more some hidden robbers than Orban's soldiers. The sun was a yellow ghost over the peaks, the sky thick with streaks of ash-like clouds, darker bruises hanging over the eastern ridge. They resembled my own wounds. There was a mindless tension in the air, and the long trail of slow minutes was hard to bear. There was no choice. There was not much talk either. At noon, we left Orban's lands, and from then on, we stayed on the road. The next afternoon, we were already in our old hunting house.

Meline, our servant keeping the house, opened the sculpted heavy door, brown wood studded with iron. *Last time I came here... I was just married.* She was a child at that time, but I still recognized her. *Now I am a widow.* I coughed, trying to press the sobs down into my chest and stop them drowning my voice.

On the road, my mind was bent on survival, and the first days in our new house kept me in a state of continuous agitation. The fifth day came with the confirmation that I was not pregnant, and the safety and relatively calm that followed allowed my mind to drift and dream, and all my dreams invariably involved Malin: being with him, speaking to him, touching each other. So real in dreams. When you wake up, everything is gone. You are alone in a cold bed, drained of life. And you cry. I clutched the pillow with a desperation that refused to leave me alone. It brought a small level of comfort, but a pillow would never be Malin.

৵৩

"Riders!" Mugur entered the house, and grabbed a sword, flexing it expertly, his way of encouraging himself. I knew it well, and he was a good swordsman, trained for many years by Father. By necessity, our weapons hung on hooks close to the main door, not in the Weapons Room. In a minute, we were all armed, even the girls, small as they were; Saliné with a dagger and Vio with a long stick, having an arrow point at an end – it looked like a spear toy, yet it was not a toy. In some critical situations, Saliné could help, as she had already started to train, but Vio had her stick just to avoid a delaying outburst. It was the seventh day in our new house.

You never know, I glanced at Vio moving her spear back and forth, piercing her *enemy* with surprising speed, her eyes focused, her lips tight. Even in the hands of such a young girl, it could do some damage.

"We wait in the house," Father said. "It's easier to defend. Veres, take the girls upstairs. Meline, you go with them."

"I want to fight here," Veres protested.

"Don't comment on an order in a battle," Father snapped, his forefinger pointing at Veres, who was too childish for his age. "From upstairs, you have a good shooting position for your bow." This time Father spoke calmly, as if his outburst was just an illusion.

I moved behind the window, on the left side of the door, and opened it slowly; my bow already nocked, ready to shoot. Horia did the same on the right. We were the best archers. Father and Mugur blocked the door, their longswords unsheathed.

The riders appeared in a cloud of dust, galloping in a long arc that passed through the entire backyard – the normal assessment of the battlefield. Shielding my eyes against the bright sun with one hand, I began to make out of them. *Six. Not enough for a frontal attack on the house.* They stopped suddenly, not far from the entry, and I recognized Mohor, the Seigneur of Severin. He dismounted at a safe distance, followed by a huge Knight, towering over everyone, and came straight toward our door. "It's Mohor, and he has only five soldiers."

Father came to my window and looked outside. "It doesn't look like an attack. And why would Mohor attack us anyway?"

"We've settled close to his castle. He is afraid of Orban, and wants to clear things up, but you are right, he will not attack us." *I hope.* Down in the valley, Severin could be seen from my window.

"I'll open the door. Mugur, Horia, hide in the next room, and stay ready, just in case." Looking once more through the window, Father moved away from it.

I breathed deeply while he took out the heavy piece of wood that was blocking the door. We went out together.

"Lady Jara, Sir Cernat," Mohor saluted – he was an elegant Seigneur.

The tall Knight said nothing.

Impolite... I thought, annoyed by his brutish way of assessing my body. Trying to anchor Mohor's tone to our previous encounters in Midia, I could not find anything alarming, but he was a cautious and introspective man, able to hide well his thoughts. "Mohor," I said with a calculated dose of effusiveness. "We were thinking to visit you one of these days but arranging the house has eaten up all of our time." I had an agreement with Father, that in times with no physical challenges in sight, I should lead the conversation with men of certain value, and Mohor was not a brute; it was one of the few hard times when it was helpful to be a woman. "Please enter," I invited him, forcing a charming smile onto my lips; even if we were unable to appreciate the situation, he would be easy prey inside the house. Mohor and Father followed me, and the arrogant Knight arrived at the door too.

"Yes?" Father asked in a casual tone.

"I apologize," Mohor said. "I should have made the introductions before. Aron, my Spatar." He pointed to the tall man, then looked at me, with a quick, apologetic smile. "Would it be possible for him to join us?" Being the chief of the army, the Spatar competed with the Secretary for the highest position in any Seigneury. It all depended on the quality of people occupying the position and the troubles of the times.

"Your Spatar is welcome in our house. It was just difficult to realize that he was a Spatar from his silent courtesy." Father underlined that the position and not the man was invited; he was good at putting people in their place graciously, and Aron's face stretched tight, skin turning red, muscle standing rigid.

"How is Senal?" I asked, just to stop the arrogant man speaking. It was also a way to renew some links with Mohor; Senal had been his Secretary for many years and always involved in our negotiations. When the two left us, six months ago, we were almost sure that Mohor would join our alliance against Orban. A month later, we received a letter that he would remain neutral. *Was this Spatar the cause?*

"Getting older," Mohor answered, with concern and fondness in his voice. "He sends his greetings to both of you, and we all feel sorry for what happened." Once seated, Mohor had a brief look around, and after some mandatory comments about how nice everything looked, he stated what was troubling him. "You just moved in Severin," he said in a thoughtful tone, as if we had not realized it yet.

"In our lands," Aron interjected, with his peculiar arrogance, and cocked one thick eyebrow.

"We can see your large castle from here, and I hope that you will find us pleasant neighbors." I ignored the brutish man, and the castle was not so large, but why should I not make Mohor feel good?

"It's just that we might have a political inconvenience from this neighborhood thing," Mohor said.

"Orban," the arrogant Spatar added.

"And what would that be?" I asked, innocently.

"Your relations with Orban are not the most cordial," Mohor said calmly, but there was firmness in his voice. I said nothing. "He might stir some trouble." Our eyes met briefly, and he let a short-lived smile cross his lips.

"Would this help to alleviate your worries?" I handed Mohor the treaty Father had signed with Orban, where he recognized our title over the house and the four hundred fifty hectares of land we owned here, while we renounced in his favor anything else we had. Any defeat has its price. That kept us Knights – at least two hundred hectares were needed for Knighthood and two thousand to be recognized as Seigneur. For anyone having some political knowledge, it was just a temporary truce.

"In theory, yes." Mohor scratched his tight-cropped beard with his free hand. "Things may change," he said in a soft voice, avoiding to look at any of us. "I am ready to make a good offer for your..." His forefinger rotated a few times, pointing in general at the house and whatever else we owned in his lands.

"You are very kind, Mohor," I said icily. "But we hope to be your long-term neighbors."

He made an indefinite gesture that in an optimistic assessment could have been taken as approval.

"We have some long-term common interests. The Dukes in the north signed a three-year armistice treaty. That ties Orban's hands for the *moment*. The Dukes in the north are too strong, the east and west are hard to take too, and that leaves the south. You and the Mehadins. Any of you has enough land to make him a Duke, and just three years to..." I let their imagination to fill my phrase with their own fears.

"Orban is a difficult man," Mohor agreed, scratching his beard again, a gesture which seemed to calm him.

"Difficult... You know his vassal, Barta." I looked at Mohor until he acknowledged. "He is dead. You did not know that. One month ago, Barta refused to *donate* the fortress of Sopron. Orban killed all the family, just to give a lesson to those who may be interested." There was a dose of irritation and perhaps fear in Mohor, while the arrogant Spatar seemed to have an interest in such abject exercises of power. "We know the north well, Mohor." *That's our value... And you need allies, like we needed them once.*

"When you've made all your arrangements," Mohor said after a while, looking thoughtful, and used the same gesture toward the house with his forefinger as before, "you are welcome to visit us. We can talk more about your settlement."

"Thank you," I said, and everybody seemed to agree that there was nothing more to discuss for the moment.

Aron was the last one to leave. From the door, he looked at my breasts long enough to be sure that I caught him, and his burning eyes remembered me of Orban. In plain sight, I gripped the handle of my dagger.

'Aron hates you.' The thought came abruptly, and I understood that the Light had spoken to me. It had never happened before, and I struggled to keep my composure under his stare. He smiled maliciously and left the house.

"It wasn't a bad start," Father said, looking at the departing riders, unaware of my silent interaction with Aron. The sound of the trotting was decreasing in a metronome-like cadence.

"Aron feels like trouble." *Why would he hate me? We've never met.*

"Yes, but Mohor is the Seigneur. As you said, we have three years left to prepare our last fight. Orban will not allow us to run again."

Far in the valley, Severin castle was the sole proof of Mohor's power; it wasn't much.

"We have three years to raise a new army and build an alliance strong enough to defeat Orban," I repeated, mesmerized by the fading trotting. *The sound of moments ticking away.* "We win or die, Father. There is no other choice. I don't want my children in Orban's hands." *Veres will be killed fast, but Saliné and Vio...*

Ah, how I wish Malin were here.

Chapter 4 – Maud / Aron

Porto wine. Sweet and strong, rich with the faraway flavors of a bright hot sun and parched land. The Porto Clan of Hispeyne was the only one that knew how to make it. Maud had heard rumors about the wine being kept in oak barrels in grottos open to the sea. The waves rocked the barrels for a year or two. It could be true, or it might just be a legend meant to enhance the price of the merchandise. The wine was expensive. Absently, she picked up a slice of cozonac, a refined cake, half dough with egg yolks, half a creamy walnut paste peppered with raisins, baked slowly in the oven. The famous cake came from Arenia; it had traveled west with the colonists, as they moved into Frankis. Four thousand years ago, the west coast of the continent was the worst affected in the White Salt War, which had destroyed the Talant Empire. Many things had been erased from collective memory, but one thing remained: large swathes of land had been transformed into poisoned, white salt pans by powerful weapons. Frankis was now fully healed, but south of it, Hispeyne still bore the marks of that war. There were rumors that the Misty Islands, north-west of Frankis, were even worse affected, but for most people, they were only a legend; no ship had sailed that way for many centuries to confirm or deny their existence. The eastern colonists brought names like Arad,

Severin, Debretin, Seged or Deva into Frankis, names to help them feel at home.

So many things happened in Frankis during the last months, Maud worried, an old habit of the third Secretary of Leyona. A bad habit, she could agree on that. *We have three years to prepare the next Candidate King; Orban will have no chance to get another term.*

"You look tense," Drusila, the Second Light of the Wanderers and her older sister, said.

"We may be able to heal the rift between our orders..." Her words suspended, Maud gestured loosely at her sister. "Even with his latest victory, Orban's position is weak, and I don't think that Cantemir will be able to propose him for a third term."

"Cantemir wants to remain Master Sage of the Circle, so he will suggest Bernd, Orban's son. The young man has inherited some of his father's intelligence and only half of his sins. In fact, he has only one serious failing; he can't keep it in his pants when he sees a beautiful woman."

"Do you see such a man becoming the King of Frankis?"

"Being kind is not really necessary for a king, and the son is a better choice than the father." *Except that he will die before the election takes place. Unfortunately, I can't share my Vision with you.* The particularity of that strange Vision made it even more important to Drusila, one of the most powerful Wanderers; her Visions were accurate. She liked to think of herself as the second most powerful Wanderer in Frankis, but all things considered, she was the third. There was a difference between ranking and power. The first was acquired by age; the power came during the Rite of Passage. Eyes closed, she recalled the Vision Fate had sent to her just a day after Orban's victory against Malin: in some unknown place, Bernd tried to rape a woman whose face was not revealed. He was killed by the woman's champion, whose face was half blurred. Drusila was sure that she would recognize the man if she met him, and she memorized everything, including the thin scar on his chin. He was young and unknown to her, at least she was sure of that, but she had the strong feeling that they would meet in some future. There was a meaning in the Visions Fate sent to the Wanderers, not always visible at first. "Cantemir started this war just to force the marriage between Bernd and Saliné, but with Malin's death... Even after losing Midia, I doubt that Jara wants a wedding between her daughter and the son of the man who killed her husband. It may even be that Bernd killed Malin in battle." She looked at her sister, and her lips twitched in a dry humor. "That gives you a free hand to arrange something for your granddaughter."

"Marie is intelligent, and she was marked by the Circle as a good prospect for the next Candidate Queen." Maud's daughter was married to the son of Leon, the Duke of Tolosa.

"So is Saliné," Drusila teased her.

"Saliné is not my granddaughter. If we are able to find a new Candidate King..." Maud looked thoughtfully at her sister.

"What kind of man do you have in mind?"

"Someone less bloody than Orban and easier to handle."

"That will make the next Master Sage the real ruler of Frankis." Drusila laughed, and Maud smiled sheepishly. The Sage who imposed its protégé as Candidate King would become the Master Sage of the Circle. "You will have an unexpected visit today. Aron will be here soon. I had a Vision about him in the morning."

"I still don't know why Aron is our Hidden Sage in Severin. He is the Spatar, commander of the army. Usually, our Sage is the Secretary." She wouldn't say so, but Maud, the third Secretary of Leyona and member of the Circle's Council, was another anomaly, the place in the Council usually belonged to the first Secretary.

"Aron has a powerful guardian."

"Only a Duke can be a guardian. It can't be Tolosa, and that leaves only Peyris and Loxburg. Why would any of them protect Aron?"

"He is Duke Stefan's bastard."

"The Duke of Peyris has a bastard..." Maud rubbed her chin, pensive, without looking at her sister. "This could be a game changer. Now that I know it, I can recall some resemblance between Aron and Stefan. The father is more intelligent tough and has some integrity."

"Aron is not stupid, and I don't think that it's his integrity what you need now."

"There are limits. Why is he coming here?"

"Our Visions don't reveal motives, but I suppose that it's related to Cernat's and Jara's settlement in Severin. Malin's death disturbed the balance of power in central Frankis. Now that Orban has taken Midia, he may become a Duke in a year or two. Or never." Drusila made a face of silent mockery.

"We shall see." Maud sipped from her glass absently, trying to put together some disparate strings of thought. She recovered, only to perceive that Drusila was now frowning, drowned in her own absence. "A new Vision?"

"Yes and no. I had it twice before. A Vision that makes no sense. At least not yet. It was a short thing, merely seconds, a giant serpent hissing at me. And even stranger, Valera had the same Vision. I hate snakes," Drusila snapped, shaking her head, then took a sip to calm herself. She was only thirteen years old when a snake had bitten her. A mildly venomous one, and she stayed in her bed for a week, being delirious with fever, for most of the time. Her mind recorded with unwanted level of detail everything that happened in that peaceful afternoon; the two holes in her wrist, and the blood pouring out slowly. A long red stream, and a short red stream. Strange as it was, that old incident revealed Drusila's strong Light, and made her a

Wanderer, a few years later. That did not stop her to hate all the snakes, venomous or not.

In her naming day, the same day she had passed the Wanderer's Rite of Passage, Drusila was presented to the Council of Seven. "From this day on, your name is Drusila, and this is your mark," the First Light said, revealing the small scars on the girl's wrist. "We don't know why, but they *are* important. I may not live long enough to learn why. You will."

Twenty First Lights have passed away since my naming day, and I still don't know. In a few years, I will become the First Light of the Frankis Wanderers, Drusila thought, nostalgia lingering in her mind, she was no longer that young woman. *If I consider those three Visions, I may learn it soon. I may not like what I learn.*

"Most people hate snakes." Maud shrugged, knowing well her sister's phobia. "There must be something of a great importance if both the First and the Second Light of Frankis had the same Vision."

"Perhaps. We pray to Fate for enlightenment. Aron is coming." *Dochia, the Fifth Light, was marked by a serpent too. Why?*

"Knight Aron of Seged and Spatar of Severin requests audience," Maud's secretary announced.

"What a pompous man," Drusila said tartly and, half amused, Maud nodded at her secretary.

"Have a seat," Maud said before Aron could speak, kindness in her voice, not a great deal. Not a great deal of interest, either. "Wine." She pointed at the bottle.

"Maud, Drusila. Long roads make a man thirsty." Aron filled his glass, then drank it in one shot.

Savage, both women thought; Porto wine was a delicacy meant to be enjoyed slowly, sip by sip. Silent, Maud looked away through the window. Drusila admired the bouquet of flowers on the table. Unaffected by the lack of attention, Aron filled his glass again.

"Too sweet for my taste," he said and looked at Maud, waiting. He waited a little longer, his fingers playing with the glass. His patience broke. "We have a kind of situation in Severin."

"Situation?" Drusila smiled, innocently. "I was ready to praise you and Mohor for being kind and allowing Cernat and Jara to settle in Severin. Of course, Cantemir's blessing and Orban's letter helped you make the right decision. So, what do you mean by having a situation?"

"Who can guarantee their safety?" Aron frowned harshly, his thick brows drawing together. "And if something happens to them, who will pay the price? Orban may attack Severin."

"Do you have a solution to this *hypothetical* situation?" Maud asked, her elbows set on the table, resting her chin on her clasped hands, her eyes fixed on Aron.

Don't play games with me. I am offering you a hand against Cantemir. You want his place as Master Sage. "Maybe a more isolated place would better guarantee their safety."

"Maybe, but who would convince Cernat about that?"

"What if Cernat has no say in this?"

"You will need strong men to ... avoid Cernat."

"My eldest son, Raul, can take over. As the war between Peyris and Loxburg has ended, he will come home. Nicolas, the Spatar of Peyris, has trained him for the last three years."

"Nicolas is a skilled Knight, and he had good things to say about Raul." Drusila looked through Aron as if he was not there. A moment later, he grinned; she had been more or less expecting that, and her posture did not change.

"Duke Stefan also said good things about Raul." Aron took his time to empty his third glass, then raised his eyebrows, waiting for another acknowledgment.

"What do you intend to do with Jara and her daughters?" Maud asked.

The same things I would do in bed with your daughter. "Instead of waiting for some bad people to attack the ladies, we take them under our protection and move everybody to a place... To a place of your choice." Aron's mouth curled up in a knowing smile.

Maud accepted his proposal with a catlike blink of her black eyes and pondered for a while. "Would you agree to a plan where my men *save* them from your men? Just a show to impress the ladies and make them more amenable; there is no need to spill much blood."

"Yes." Aron nodded and filled his glass again.

"Jara has Cantemir's countenance for the moment, and her daughters are protected by the Circle."

"There is a Black Warrant on Jara's name," Aron said, casually. His smile made it clear he knew exactly what he was saying, the Master Sage before Cantemir had made the warrant.

"It's frozen until her youngest daughter will be tested by the Circle." Maud found a loose lock of hair and tucked it absently away, her eyes still on Aron.

Aron is a brute. It may end badly. We need to keep a tight leash on him, Drusila thought. "We all want the ladies to be safe. That means no physical harm. They are all women who attract a man's eye."

"They will be safe. You have my word on that. I am the Knight of Seged." *But who will blame me if Jara tries to escape and vanishes? I will keep her for a while in my castle. She will provide good entertainment during the cold nights.* "I will bring them to you." *I will bring the girls to you.* "We have always worked well together, and Mohor's army did not join Malin's against Orban in the last battle. To our future collaboration." *We helped Orban, but I did not expect Malin to lose so badly. No one had expected it.* Aron raised his glass, a wry smile lingering on his face.

You are a bastard, not a knight. In all the meanings of that pitiful word. "I would like to talk to your son." Maud's voice was flat and precise, carrying a subtle tone of command, and she raised one delicate eyebrow, ignoring Aron's overture.

"Before or after...?" Aron looked at her, then watched a spot on the wall, his eyes intense, his narrow lips pressed together in a stubborn line.

"As soon as he returns from Peyris."

"He should be in Seged by now," Drusila said, and Aron frowned, surprised by her Vision. She allowed him his delusion; her knowledge came from another Wanderer, who had returned from Peyris.

"I will send Raul to you. If you don't mind, I need to leave today." Without waiting for an answer, Aron stood up. "Maud, Drusila." He nodded and turned away. They did not try to delay him.

"I don't believe Aron is scared about Orban invading Severin," Maud said, when the door closed behind Aron.

"It may happen. Orban wants both Severin and Mehadia."

"Nothing else?" Maud looked thoughtfully at her sister.

"I didn't say that." A trace of smile, and a deep look. Drusila rotated her glass, this way, then that way. "Aron is the second in line to take Severin if Mohor dies without children."

"The first in line is old, without heirs and almost deaf. Don't you find it *strange* that the other three people who were before Aron died in ... accidents?"

"Why should that be *strange,* when Aron wants Severin for himself? Six years ago, Mohor's betrothed died in a riding accident too, and she was an excellent rider. What Aron is worried about now is not Orban, but an eventual marriage between Jara and Mohor."

"Is Mohor blind?"

"Half blind, because of his loyalty to the man who helped him when he was still a child. Aron made him Seigneur of Severin. We know that. You did not plead too hard for Jara's life."

"There is a Black Warrant on her name."

"What did she do to incur a death sentence from the Circle?" Drusila was frowning in thought; she knew that Jara's only crime was that Cernat refused to make her Orban's wife and Candidate Queen. *The severity of the punishment did not match the crime, if it was really a crime.*

"It doesn't matter. A warrant must be fulfilled. I have nothing against the poor woman; I even like her. She is strong and intelligent, but the rules must be respected. We are nothing without rules."

"Rules should not blind us. What do you want to do with Saliné?"

"Marry her to a Knight. As she has passed the test and was marked by the Circle this spring, I am bound to protect her. A marriage would do exactly that, shield her from unwanted dangers." Maud's expressive mouth quirked a little, and her dark eyes glimmered.

"Vio has a strong Light; she belongs to the Wanderers." *Why is this* young *girl so important to the Realm? But are not all people young before they become important?* There was a thing that she could not say if it was a Vision or not, an elusive and slippery premonition. Drusila would be the First Light who will receive Vio as a Wanderer, and the one who will lose her. A Wanderer could only be lost to death, yet death would not be involved in this loss. *What kind of riddle is this?* She shrugged. Sipped some wine. "That would free Marie's path to become the Candidate Queen of Frankis. Of course, we still need to think about Cleyre Peyris. She passed the test too."

"I want to learn more about Raul; I will allow him to kidnap Jara and her daughters later. I am sure that Jara has more pressing things to do now than seduce Mohor into marriage. I will send a courier to Aron in two weeks. Duke Stefan's only capable son died in the last battle against Loxburg. His last son alive is a joke."

"Do you think Stefan will groom Raul to take over the Duchy at his death? The young man has spent his last three years in Peyris."

"We may suggest that to him. After we learn more about Raul. Even if he is chosen by Stefan as his heir, Raul's position will be weak, and he will need our help. Severin may fall to him too, and I will take care of Leyona. Marie has Tolosa behind her. A marriage will bring Tolosa and Peyris together. The Duke of Loxburg can't fight against such a large force and, in a few years, we can put a new King and Queen on the throne. Forty years of lawlessness are enough."

"And you will be the *Master Sage* of the Circle." Drusila lowered her voice for emphasis.

"I hope that you will not object to that." Maud raised her glass. Drusila did the same, before realizing that hers was empty. "Allow me. Damn that savage bastard," Maud said, shaking the bottle. "He emptied it." As so many times in the past, their twin laughter filled the room.

⁓⧲⁓

The swift summer rain ended as fast as it came. Except for the rushing of the wind and faraway thunders, the day remained silent. Stirred by the breeze, the thin patch of mist vanished, and the man was able to see well from the ridge at the fringe of the forest. Careful of not being observed, he stepped back, hiding behind a thick oak. His shift was swift and smooth, the movement of a well-trained man. He could see the four people walking down the road – two girls and two soldiers, one of them carrying a bow. He recognized the eldest girl. He recognized the soldiers too, and moved back again, deeper into the forest. He could still see them, through the dense foliage. The hilt of his sword got stuck into a small branch, and he froze for a long moment, then he smiled, his gaze fixed on the eldest girl. It was hard to say what was the reason of that brief reaction. The more the four walked on the road, coming closer, the more he walked back into the woods. When they reached the place in front of him, he was already hidden behind a large rock, forty paces away from the edge of the forest. It was a peculiar rock, and some old women told stories about the powerful witch who changed a giant bear in a rock, but he was no longer scared by fairy tales. Or so he thought. His horse snorted softly, and he embraced it, his hand pressing on the animal's muzzle. "Shh," he whispered. Leaning against the cold stone, the man peered out carefully, his eyes narrowed to slits. The four were right there, at the edge of the forest. The wind was flat, and the birds were now silent in the branches above.

On the road, the archer was walking three paces behind the girls, scouting the forest. His keen eyes found footprints, behind a thick oak. They looked fresh. Unwilling to scare the girls, he leaned lazily against the tree, trying to figure where the footprints were going. "One man," he whispered to himself. "He was spying on us and went back to the forest. Perhaps behind that weird rock. He must be well trained." Slowly, he freed his bow, unsure if he should follow the traces on the ground.

"The Bear Rock." The younger girl pointed at it – even when half hidden by the forest, the rock still resembled a large animal. "Let's climb." She ran suddenly, with amazing speed, dodged under the lower branches of the old trees and slalomed between the bushes. In front of the rock, she stayed motionless for a moment, then started to climb, a large smile spread on her face.

Behind the rock, the man gripped the hilt of his sword intermittently, his fingers tightening and lessening on the cold steel, in a strange cadence. But they never relaxed. *I should run. The plan was to go after her tomorrow. I will have two more men with me.* He put a carnival mask on his face, and moved closer to his horse, ready to mount.

Losing the start, the archer ran after the girl as fast as he could. He was tall and heavy. After a few steps, he had to drop his bow. That helped him, but not well enough, a thick branch grazed his skull, then a another one. *You are both a pest and a nice girl.* With all that pain, he managed to smile and arrived at the rock, massaging the skin on the top of his head. "Not now, Vio," he said, and hurried to surround her waist with one arm — she was already at the level of his bruised head. "I promised Lady Jara that we will not leave the road. Sir Mohor warned us about a band of robbers. They were skilled fighters, too skilled for some simple robbers. His patrol killed most of them, but two scoundrels managed to escape."

"One of them was wounded, and you are two hard soldiers." Vio tried her luck, unwilling to release her grip on the rock.

"Wounded men can be dangerous too. Let's go back." A twig snapped behind the rock; it sounded strangely clear and strong. *That was not the step of a man. He must have a horse.* The archer said nothing.

The girl sighed but allowed him to take her in his arms. Their way back was longer, he had to avoid those bloody low branches. Close to the road, he half turned, pretending to throw her in one of the bushes at the edge of the forest, and she laughed with delight. In that moment, he checked the rock again, and made the sign for danger to the other soldier, who unsheathed his sword and, at leisure, started to chop a hardened root going out of the ground. The tension in his eyes contrasted with his careless moves. Saliné felt his strain and freed her dagger slowly, then let her mind feel the Light, and see into the future, but she was too young to feel much. She remained silent, and hid her armed hand behind her back, to conceal it from Vio, who was still laughing. After a minute, the swordsman walked away with the girls. In haste, the archer grabbed his dropped bow and stood behind the old oak, close to the footprints. Watching the girls walking away, he listened to the forest. It was still quiet. *Saliné is a clever girl,* he thought, seeing the dagger in her hand, her arm parallel with her body, concealing the weapon both from Vio and the hidden man in the forest. He counted to thirty, shifted his tongue in his dry mouth, drew a long breath, then peered out from behind the tree. There was no one in sight. An unconscious grin of relief tightened his lips, and he left too, keeping an eye on the rock. He did not hurry.

From his place, the hidden man saw the girls turning, and he caught a glimpse of Saliné's face through a gap in the foliage. *She is even more beautiful now. Tomorrow... Tomorrow will be my day.* He waited patiently until the girls and their soldiers vanished, and mounted his horse, riding it down the road, in the opposite direction. Close to Severin's gate, he met three riders, and they stopped suddenly, none of them expecting the encounter.

"What are you doing here?" Aron frowned at his son; he thought him in Seged, their fiefdom.

"I heard that Saliné Midia is in Cernat's hunting house," Raul said, ignoring his father's displeasure, and hiding that he had seen the girl just minutes ago. "I met her once in Midia, when Duke Stefan sent me with his embassy."

"Do her mother and grandfather know you?"

"No, I met her on the streets and saved her from a horse which was racing like mad. Father, I like her, and I think that she likes me too. Now, that she is no longer a Grand Signora, maybe we can... I plan to visit her tomorrow."

"Tomorrow, you will return to Seged. No, you will return today."

"Why, Father?"

"Because I say so. The Circle set an important mission for us. Saliné and her sister are in danger. In a few weeks, you will take and escort them in a safer place, and no one must know about that, not even Mohor."

"Then we can talk with them tomorrow."

"You will talk nothing. Their mother and grandfather are stubborn people who think themselves above others. They refused the Circle's help. We must take Saliné and her sister against their mother's will because the girls are important. Saliné was marked by the Circle." *And I will take Jara for me. That will keep Mohor safe from her.* Suddenly amused, he almost smiled. It was the cold sort of amusement. "Soon, you will go to Leyona. Some important people from the Circle want to see you. This is a secret too. Understand? Good, in a minute, I want you on the road to Seged."

"Do you want me to attack her family?" Raul asked, without looking at his father.

"You will attack whoever I tell you."

"That's wrong, Father." Raul braced himself for his father's fury. He knew the signs, a lifted head, a narrowed gaze upon him.

To his surprise, Aron only grimaced, his eyes cold and staring. "You are still young. Go now. At home, you will train Bucur."

Raul began to play with the halter, leaning his body forward, biting his lower lip as if thinking of something, then turned his horse abruptly and moved on the road. He was silent, but his eyes were speaking for him. There was not anger in them, it was mostly contempt. *Leyona... Maud is using Father. Again. And he is using me. Nothing good comes from the Circle, especially from Maud. Cantemir serves one of the worst men in*

Frankis, but he is better than Maud. Most people are better than Maud. Tense, he grinded his teeth and pushed his horse to a gallop. *And I have to train Bucur.* He shook his head and, this time, his eyes sparkled with anger; there was not much love between Raul and his younger brother, who was a bad character. Or even worse than a bad character. *I should have stayed in Peyris.*

Motionless, Aron kept his horse in place long after Raul had vanished from sight. *Is he too weak for my plans? It doesn't matter. He will obey.*

Chapter 5 – Codrin

At the edge of the forest, the isolated house looked larger than I expected in such a wild place, an old inn, its name almost erased by rain and neglect. The paint was peeling in many places, and yellow flecks fluttered in the wind. Two cows were visible in the stable and a huge, wounded dog was lying on the stairs, its eyes fixed on me. It tried to move, but gave up, still staring at me.

"Anybody home?" I shouted and moved around the house in a silence that followed me. In the backyard, a fresh grave had been dug, aligned with two old ones.

"Get off our land!" The order was shouted in Silvanian, even though I was now in Litvonia, but I did not have time to wonder.

I turned cautiously, gripping the hilt of the sword. My movement was deliberately slow, swift moves attract swift reactions. I did not feel much danger – you do not shout when you want to kill, it's the other way around; you kill then you shout. Three people were standing in front of me, at a safe distance for all of us: a woman, in her early fifties, looking sturdy and agile, a thin boy of around twelve, and another one about my age, with the same sturdy stock as the old woman. They were armed only with hayforks, but what's the difference to you if you are killed by a fork's spike or a sword? Tense, and filled with wrath, they were glaring at me. *All wounded*, I realized. *Nothing serious.*

"I mean no harm." I raised my arms to calm them. "You were attacked." A short statement, in a gentle tone, telling them that I both realized it and felt sorry.

"Some bastards on horses. Just like you." The woman's voice was bitter, yet my feeling was that somehow, I had passed a first test. A curse may sometimes be just the needed release of tension before dialogue can start.

The grave, I suddenly remembered. *It was fresh.* "There is nothing bad about having a horse. Evil can both ride and walk."

Frightened by something I could not understand, the younger one jumped forward, attacking me. The other two followed just because they had to cover him. I grabbed the hayfork from his hands and parried the attack of the elder one with it, moving behind him, releasing the fork, my knife pressing at his throat. Grabbing a stone, the younger one hid behind the woman.

"I mean no harm. I will release him if you drop the forks. And the stone." Tense, she was gripping the hayfork, and our eyes locked. *She is unsure...* "He could be already dead." I tilted my head toward the immobilized boy who was breathing hard, my knife pressing on his throat, giving her more time to decide.

The moment the hayforks hit the ground, I released him, stepping back, and he jumped forward to reach the other two. The young one still had the stone, his hand ready to throw it. "Drop it," I said, and the old woman forced him to let it fall.

"What do you want?" She glared at me; her narrow lips pressed together in a stern line.

"I am looking for a place to sleep." I gestured to the old painting with the inn's name. *For a night or a winter.* "Payment is not a problem, and if the riders come back, I can help." I looked at her, allowing a smile to cross my lips. How much I wanted to be a grown man, I knew that I looked like a child, and that would play in my favor, at least partially.

"They may come back. They killed … my husband, and we killed two of them. Why would you help us?"

"You help; I help. My companions were killed too, and I need a place to stay over the winter." It looked a good trade to me; my gut trusted the old woman. "I may be young, but I am good with the sword. Or the knife."

"Let's eat first," she said, undecided; her intelligent eyes weighing me.

Two months later, my birthday came with the first serious snow, but I kept it to myself. The only celebration I could mentally afford was to climb a small peak overlooking the valley. In that white, silent beauty, I mourned again, as in every other day until now. At sixteen, you are no longer a child, but not a man either.

I stayed all that long winter with the old woman, Gran, Pintea, the younger boy and Vlad, the older one. We traded housing, safety and skills. I learned Litvonian – at borders, people know two languages – to farm, and to cut wood. The boys learned to fight. Vlad was strong and a promising swordsman and, after five months, I thought him good enough to honorably defend their house against robbers.

My brother's and mentor's death filled my nights, and my twin sister, Ioana, appeared in my dreams too, her lovely face illuminated by a bloody moon, her hands glowing white, and each time she was just staring at me in silence with her large, green eyes. And each time, I woke howling at the red moon still shining in my head, yet my eyes remained dry. I could no longer sleep those nights, memories of better times haunting me: riding with her, climbing trees together, her reading in my arms. There was no one in the whole world closer to me than Ioana, and nothing could replace her.

With the first warm wind from the south, I prepared to leave, but my ring-mail, gathering dust in a corner of the room, no longer fitted me. I always was tall and skinny, a bag of bones and sinews, as my mentor liked to joke. Slender like a rope, my body always made me fear that I would never be strong enough to become a good fighter. Yet, when I probed the mail, my shoulders no longer fit well inside, and that worried me. Speed was my first ally in a battle, and tight armor my enemy. Checking whatever parts of my body I could see – there was no mirror in the inn – I had the impression that my limbs were thicker, and for sure, my shoulders were broader, the unfitting armor proved it. An encouraging sign, but without armor, the road could be deadly. *I need to cut it. Here and here,* I mentally marked some lines from my neck to my elbow. *And under my armpits too…* There were many tools for handling iron in the inn, the remnants of better times; it had a small smithy for horseshoes among other things. In the enlarged cuts, I put some old, hardened leather – not as good as the iron rings, better than nothing – then I did the same for the six-inch-long split on the belly. It looked like an old bag full of patches. The third thing I did was to take down the Royal House of Arenia insignia from my helmet; a vagrant could not use royal signs. The quality and shape of my weapons would still betray a noble Arenian origin, but they were safer for me now.

"Tudor, stay with us," Gran said, using the false name I gave them, when she heard my decision to leave. I don't know why, from all the names in the world, I had chosen my mentor and friend's name; maybe just to keep a link with an old life that had vanished. "You have a safe place to stay, and we like you."

Tempted, I avoided a final answer for a few days, but in the end, I could not see my future in the old inn. There was nothing to help me return to Arenia and take back what was mine by right, and that Vision about the caravan was still fresh in my mind. I left Vlad my brother's sword, and the horse that was not mine; Zor was now completely healed.

I went directly to Muniker, the Litvonian capital, where caravans from many parts were arriving; the Spring Fair was about to start. The roads were generally unsafe everywhere, but a total disaster in the former Frankis Kingdom, and I hoped to be hired as a caravan protector, as Tudor had planned a year ago. It took me four days to get there.

Inside the city's walls, close to the Swest Gate – their name for the south-western gate – The Caravans' Inn was a three-story large building, well placed for merchants from the caravans or the people dealing with them. Around the large door, two large frescoes depicted marching caravans. I entered, moving slowly, marking everyone's place, armed or unarmed, looking at me or not; a vagrant, and even more so one as young as me, had to learn, to observe. The man who seemed to be the innkeeper glanced at me, then continued to clean the glass in his hand. Composing the hardest face I could gather, I rested my hand ostentatiously on the hilt of my sword. It did not work; he picked another glass to clean, ignoring the annoying intruder who looked heavily armed only by mistake.

"I need a room," I said, dryly.

"How do you want to pay?" His left thick brow went up for a moment, but he did not look at me.

"Money," I shrugged. "Isn't that what all innkeepers want? One week, room and food."

"Four galbeni. You pay in advance."

"I did not ask for room service and women."

"Women?" His eyes squinted, slightly amused, trying to guess my age, but it passed fast. "For that, it would be eight galbeni."

At that moment, a large man, well soaked with alcohol from the smell of his breath, hit the counter with his fist. "Damn you, Movil. I want another bottle of wine, and I will get it. You can put it on my slate."

"Your slate is already too long," Movil, the innkeeper, said in a careful tone. "But I can add a half-bottle," he conceded, seeming to fear the disruptive potential of the massive man, and he turned to reach the wine barrel.

"We did not finish." I pointed at Movil, reminding him that we were still in some sort of negotiation.

"I will finish you," the large alcohol sponge growled, turning toward me, his huge fist prepared to smash my head.

My right arm sprang aside, and the lateral, hardened part of my palm hit his throat; a move that Tudor had made me repeat ten thousand times and more until it became instinctual.

"You don't think through fights; consciousness is slow. It's the unconsciousness you need, your primal mind. Touch a hot surface, and your hand reacts before you can even think about it," Tudor told me over and over. Now that the fight had ended, my mind claimed supremacy over instincts again, and his words flowed inside me. For a moment, it felt like he was still alive.

That blow on the neck could kill, maim, or just immobilize the opponent. There was no deadly danger, so I instinctively chose the immobilize style, and the man fell under the counter. The shock of his large body hitting the floor made the windows tremble a little. In that strange moment, when the man was sliding downwards, I recognized that I was a well-trained Assassin. Nine years of training, with one who was legendary among them, had worked for me. *I am better prepared than I thought for this new life.* Movil's eyes widened briefly, but that was all the unusual moment extracted from him. A dozen pairs of eyes gazed at me from the room, in a silence that was eloquent. *What a pity there are not more, to spread word of my exploits. And none is a merchant...* "How much do I need to pay for my room?" I asked, as if nothing had happened, while two workers from the inn were dragging out the unconscious man.

"The dog is heavier than a horse," one of them complained and cursed heavily. "Half of his weight must be alcohol."

"Three galbeni," Movil answered promptly.

"I need a room with a view of the caravans, and something to eat." I pointed to an empty table separated from the rest of the room on three sides, then placed three galbeni on the counter.

"Everything will be ready in half a turn." His voice was slightly amused, leaving me the strange feeling that a part of his deference was pleasure driven – Movil had enjoyed the large man's misfortune.

It was interesting to see how they were using the same measures of time as in Arenia. A turn has sixty minutes, and a minute sixty moments or seconds or heartbeats. The day has, of course, the same length everywhere: twenty-four turns, or hours.

Late in the evening, Movil visited me and placed a bottle of wine on the small table, then had a long look at me before saying, "Five-year-old Tolosa wine from Frankis. The best one I have. I don't know how you did *that*." He imitated my hit against the large man's neck. "But you *know* how to do that. Keep peace at the inn during your stay, and I will give you back one galben." Before I could answer, he left a piece of gold close to the wine bottle and looked at me through narrow eyes. I nodded, protecting an inn should not be much different from protecting a caravan. I knew nothing of both, but I was willing to learn. "Good. In the main room, I will set you at a table where everybody can see you. I suppose that you are tired. Have a good night." He bowed slightly and left me alone. The wine was excellent.

ಲ∽

I woke too early in the morning, and from my window, I could see an empty Protectors' Arena. The name was misleading, it was not for fighting, just a place where the merchants could negotiate with their protectors. There was no customer yet in the main room of the inn, and Movil looked at me, but served the breakfast without a word. He was probably laughing inside. Or he didn't care. My table was indeed in a place that could be seen from everywhere in the large room. Movil was an old fox, and he hammered a nail in the wall, close to my chair, in which I had to hang my sword in plain view. I forced myself to eat slowly, then to walk slowly toward the Arena.

"Looking for a protector?" I asked the owner of a small caravan. The smaller the caravan, the cheaper the protector, and I was ready to sell myself ridiculously cheap, just to enter the trade.

"I don't need more children," he laughed. "I already have two at home."

I shrugged and left the place; it made no sense to argue. As similar things happened with all the other small merchants I contacted, I spent the next day guarding the inn or staring from the window of my room at the caravans. Some of them were already leaving. In the evening, the huge man came again and talked with Movil, who pointed at me. The man coughed to gather my attention, then paid his slate.

The third morning, I walked around the Arena – two of the merchants I talked with were still there. My mentor taught me to observe without being caught, to pick out things that did not fit the context, to keep the mind open without prejudice.

"Just observe," he said to me. "Don't predetermine. Let things come to you."

Three men walked with no apparent aim, back and forth. From time to time, on intersecting paths, they were exchanging signals, but never a word. Posing as innocent bystanders, they could not fool me; they worked together. Their leader, a tall, dark-skinned man entered the Protector's Arena, and I followed, walking at leisure, thirty paces behind him. He stopped in front of two merchants who were Mesters, the heads of the Merchants Guild in their city. Depending on the size of the city, a Guild could have up to five Mesters. Glancing at the Mesters, I recalled the Vision I had after I took my oath, in front of the graves. They were the same people. Lost in that strange memory, I stumbled on my path.

"Where is your wet-nurse?" a bystander, walking along in a group of four, asked me, and laughter filled the place.

I drew a deep breath and cleaned my mind of any thought, the Assassin Cool technique. The guffaw around me diminished in a cloud that seemed farer and farer until it vanished in my inner world, and I forced myself to walk and contact the closest merchant to the Mesters, settling myself between him and the pair from my Vision, at a distance from which I could listen without being obvious.

"I have three men as sturdy as me," said the dark-skinned protector, and he was indeed well clad. "I am sorry to hear that your protectors were killed, but their loss could be my gain. We are qualified soldiers."

"I am not from here," I said to my merchant. "Are we far from Arad?" It was one the few Frankis cities I had heard of, and it was relatively close to Litvonia.

"Yes." Having nothing to do, the merchant looked disposed to talk with a young stranger. "One of the two Mesters behind you is from Arad. They lost their protectors. Mesters have their own permanent protectors."

"I did not know that. They are rich, I suppose."

"Yes. Most of them are crooks," he spat, with evident envy, "not hard-working people like us."

"It's hard be a merchant, for sure. How were they killed?"

"I want to see your men," one Mester said to the dark-skinned protector, behind me.

"Poisoned." My merchant shrugged.

"Terrible death. They would have preferred to die in a battle."

"They would have preferred to be still alive," the merchant said, gruffly.

"No one wants to die. I just wanted to point that it was a cowardly act."

"I will be back in one hour," the dark-skinned protector agreed with the Mesters' request.

"Cowardly indeed," my merchant agreed with me.

The dark-skinned protector went away and met one of the two men still outside – the oldest one, in his early fifties – then came back with three others and, under the old man's intense scrutiny, they entered the Protectors' Arena.

Later in the evening, I contacted the Mesters too. "I am a stranger, esteemed Mesters Panait and Iaru, good with the sword and other weapons. I heard in the inn that your protectors are dead in some weird circumstances, and you may need more security than usual. A great and unfortunate loss." I bowed slightly. "Strangers have the weakness of being *strangers*, and their price is lower."

"How much?" For the first time, the child label did not send me away; there was a faint interest in their reaction.

"Half price." Short, straight answers always give an impression of toughness. A month-long journey to Dorna, passing through Arad, would give a protector seven galbeni. A lot of money for a commoner, yet still less than the ten galbeni needed to hire a soldier for war.

"An interesting proposal coming from such a young … protector to be," Panait said thoughtfully, with just a hint of irony. He was the second Mester of Arad, the other one the third of Dorna, and Arad was a larger and more powerful city. "We need more time to think of your proposal."

I went away with their agreement, but the next day came with another refusal.

The last day of the Muniker Fair ended, leaving me empty-handed. *It did not happen*, I recalled bitterly the Vision I had in front of the graves, in which I was Panait's protector. With fourteen galbeni still filling my purse, things were not desperate, yet I had to decide. Head in hands, I stood on the edge of my bed. *Should I stay here and wait for the next Fair?*

During my stay, I had to interfere only once to keep the peace at the inn. Late in the evening, two men quarreled and stood up abruptly. One of them raised his bottle, ready to smash the other's head. He was half drunk, and his moves slow. The bottle was dangerous though. With my scabbard, I hit the second chair at my table, the one Movil was using when talking to me. It produced a bang that echoed hard in the room, and all the eyes moved on me. I shook my head, and the two men sat slowly, like any drunkard. They continued to drink, and everybody ignored them again.

In the afternoon, Fate decided for me when an embassy from Arenia came to Muniker, passing along the Caravans' Inn. *Fifty-eight*, I counted, and most of them were soldiers from the Royal Guard. *Way too many, and the royal guards do not protect embassies.* Hidden behind my window, I even recognized some of them, and all were my cursed uncle's trusted men.

It was almost dark when eight riders came in front of the inn. Five of them wore Litvonian colors, and two were royal guards from Arenia. They dismounted, and I lost sight of them as they approached the main door. Gripping two daggers in my hands, I ran out of my room and crouched close to the stairs going down to the hall of the inn.

One by one, they entered the inn, the Litvonians, followed by the Arenians. Then I saw the nomad of the eastern steppes. His presence gave me shivers, and I made myself smaller. He was short and sturdy, his arms as thick as my feet, his legs slightly curved because of the long time spent in the saddle. A rider of the steppes with a flat face and thin eyes, like slits. His black hair was half shaved, and half tied in a ponytail. They look all like this, the Toltars. Dangerous savages.

"You will know a man of the steppes when you see one." Father's words. I saw them during the invasion, when they burned more than fifty villages, but at least they couldn't attack fortified cities. Father defeated them in Hotin, close to the Nestro river, two months before he was killed by my cursed uncle.

I shook my head to escape the past and looked again at the nomad. One hand resting on the hilt of his yatagan, a slightly curved forward sword, he stood, with an impassible face, five paces away from the group, looking nowhere. Then I saw the crimson serpent embroidered on his black vest, over his chest. That was strange; they usually have the sun and the black arrow, their symbol of Fate. The civilized world uses the hand and the quill, the goddess's handwriting everyone's fate. For the nomads, she writes with a bloody arrow. The crimson serpent captured my eyes once more, and I shivered again, even stronger. *Why do I fear that serpent?*

"We are looking for a sixteen-year-old boy from Arenia. He may have a few guards with him." It was a harsh voice, accustomed to command. I could not see its owner, but he was from Muniker.

"The only strangers here are from Frankis or Silvania," Movil said.

"The King wants him. Inform the Guard if you learn something."

"Of course, captain Frinz. I am always eager to please the King," Movil said, and I heard the men leaving the inn.

Back in my room, I watched the soldiers mounting and riding away. *It was close...* Eyes closed, I set my brow against the window, and gripped the edge of the sill. The glass was cold, but not cold enough to calm my mind, and I forced my breath to go long and slow, the Assassin Cool.

"Something interesting to look at?" Movil asked behind me, and I started.

I was careless. "Riders," I shrugged. "Some of them seem to be from far away."

"They are from Arenia, and they may come here again." Movil walked toward the wall where my sword and ring-mail were hanging in a peg. He touched the hilt of the sword, then scratched his beard. "Quite a strange sword you have. It seems to be from far away." His intelligent eyes fixed me, as if trying to take my measure again. "The Muniker Fair ended. You should leave tomorrow, before dawn. I will be awake. Join a small caravan toward Frankis and stay on the road. They will be happy for one more good sword to protect them. Free help is always appreciated."

My words stuck in my mouth and, unable to speak, I bowed slightly. *Thank you, Movil.*

Long and uneasy, the night was passed in watching, small strings of whispers to myself and touching the cold steel of my sword just to prove that I still existed behind the locked door. *Why did I fear that serpent?*

Chapter 6 – Jara

"A tree like a forest," I whispered at the large cherry tree, the breeze playing gently on my skin, stirring me. I turned, singing softly, arms outstretched, once, twice... Answering me, the wind played like a hundred violins in countless tones; a music that I did not know or understand. A sudden urge to dance went through me, and I looked around, afraid that someone would laugh at my childish reaction. In the other corner of the garden, Saliné and Vio were playing together.

What if they see me? I shrugged. The wind changed the rhythm and my body wound left and right. Vio turned, and her bell-like laughter filled the garden. Saliné followed her, and there was no way to stop my laughter either. They waved at me then, clasping their hands together, started to rotate in a Hora dance.

A gust of wind passed through the tree, and a myriad of petals left their flowers, floating around. Like small butterflies, they surrounded me in a whirlpool of white wings under the golden-yellow brightness of the spring sun. The warm sunshine gave depth and dimension to everything, and I moved back, to take in the view, then further back, until the gate stopped me – the huge tree still occupied most of my vista.

"Jara," a well-known voice whispered behind me, and I turned, feeling a surge of warmth. His hands grabbed my waist, helping my rotation, and we stared at each other wordlessly.

"Kiss me." I laced my arms around his neck, desire mounting in me.

"Wake up, Jara," Malin said, worried.

"Malin..."

"Wake up. Now!" He urged me and vanished.

Awake and depressed, I found myself breathing hard, half fallen from my bed. Mindlessly, I clung to the pillow, as always after dreaming of Malin. Still warm, it allowed me to linger inside my lost dream, and for a while, I seemed separated from my body, as though split between two worlds. *What's life when dreams are more beautiful to inhabit than reality?*

A neigh pierced the early morning, erasing the last remaining traces of my dream. Swift hooves clopped on the stones, and I went to look outside. Colors were changing in the morning light, red shone out bright and clear and the blues merged into the surrounding dark green of the forest. My mare was galloping toward the forest, and human silhouettes were running through our backyard. *Robbers!* In the stable, a horse neighed in pain, as if it were dying. Then another one. I grabbed my chemise and ran out of my room. Father was already heading down the stairs, and I stopped to dress and close a few buttons. Veres and the girls erupted from their rooms too.

"Follow me," I said, running downstairs.

In the entry hall, Father, Horia and Mugur were already armed, and Meline was shaking in the corner. Even with all that panic, it was hard to stop a smile; armed men dressed in night clothes were not a usual sight. *I don't look much better.* My chemise was too short to reach my knees. I snatched my bow, and the children armed themselves too.

"They want to burn the house," Father said – the attackers' torches were lighting the early dawn. "We must confront them outside."

They are not robbers, I thought, afraid to speak and scare the children even more than they were. *Yes*, I nodded to Father and picked a sword too. Father was the first to exit, his sword up, in Alta Guarda, a stance that I knew so well. Mugur and Horia followed.

"Stay here," I told my children as I crept through the doorway. "Meline, fill whatever buckets we have."

Outside, I released my arrow without thinking, and the first body fell in the grass. Father was already fighting three swordsmen, one of them wearing a mask. Horia and Mugur had their enemies too, more were coming from the stable, and the dawn was full of screams. I counted eight still alive, before releasing another arrow, killing one robber coming from the stable – it was hard to hit the ones fighting Father and our men.

From the forest, an arrow whooshed and pierced Mugur's chest. His hand clutched the shaft. A sword pierced him. He fell in silence, and our whole world turned to chaos. Horia was now fighting three men, and he was not as skilled as Father, who had already killed an enemy. The archer hiding in the forest came halfway out, aiming at Father. Seeing my bow, he changed his mind and aimed at me. His arrow scratched my right inner thigh, burning my flesh. Released a few moments earlier, my arrow pierced his chest. Blood filled my fingers when I touched the wound, yet it was light; I could still move with ease. Father's sword split a skull while I was cleaning my fingers on the shirt.

"Help!" Horia cried when a sword cut deep into his shoulder.

Panicked, I released two arrows in swift succession. One hit and one missed its target, but it was already too late, with a last cry, Horia fell too. *They are winning*... A brief thought of my children steeled me, and I killed one of the three who had slain

Horia, but the remaining two joined Father's opponents. In his struggle, Father stood with his back at me, and I could not hit any of the five robbers attacking him. He turned in a swift half-pirouette, his longsword cutting a large arc, forcing them to step back, then moved out of sight, turning the corner of the house. My arrow put down another robber, before they disappeared, following Father.

Four more men appeared from the forest, sprinting toward me, screaming some inarticulate battle cry. They were already too close, and having no other choice, I grabbed my sword, stuck in the ground behind me. One of the thieves was in front and lateral, and to the side of the other three. I sprinted to confront him, and dodging his blow, my sword raked across his face. When he opened his mouth to scream, only blood came out. I moved back, close to the door, to cover my children, thinking that Veres could help.

Grinning and waving their swords, the remaining three spread out to surround me. Wearing a mail-ring of good quality, one of them was moving slower, but the two in front of me did not attack until he joined them. Barefoot, I slid sideways through the cold dew of the early morning, trying to keep the slow one between me and the other two. They regrouped, and I moved sideways again. At that moment, Vio ran out from the house, and her small spear pierced the back of the one trying to sneak behind me. She did not have enough force to kill, but the man growled and turned toward her. She was already gone – her speed was amazing. I moved further, with odd, dance-like steps, trying to avoid a direct battle and come closer to the man attacking Vio. From a distance, she menaced the stalking man, her spear moving back and forth in nervous gestures. While the wound was not deadly, he could no longer walk well, and Saliné came from behind, her long dagger piercing deeply into him. Howling like a mad wolf, the man turned with a last savage effort, his sword moving in an arc, trying to cut Saliné in two.

She rolled backward in the grass, and the sword passed over her head. Vio pierced his back with her spear again, and he fell to his knees. Saliné slit his throat, ending the fight.

I sprang, dodging the sword of the man in armor, and I moved behind him. In the wrong position, all I could do was to hit the second one, yet he was not close enough, so the cut on his shoulder was just a scratch.

"Bitch!" he growled through his long, fluffy beard.

The man in armor turned, and our swords met for the first time. Under his strong blows, I retreated, step by step. While I was good with the sword, I did not have enough strength to match a man's blow.

"Take the girls," he yelled to the other robber. "I'll take the bitch."

"Veres!" I cried desperately; he was still inside. I glanced at the corner of the house, hoping that Father would appear soon, but I only heard swords clanging faintly.

Reluctantly, Veres moved out from the house to intercept the bearded robber while the girls were retreating slower, shaking their weapons to distract him. My girls were fast, and while at fourteen Saliné already had some combat training, Vio's reaction was a surprise.

I grunted and attacked the armored man, with a series of fast blows, hoping that Veres could hold off the other one until Father came, but he was knocked down fast, losing his sword. The bearded robber caught him by his hair and put the sword to his neck, grinning at me.

"I surrender," I blurted out, struggling to control the tremor in my legs. "You can do whatever you want to me, just let my children go."

"You don't have much choice." The armored man measured me up and down.

"It will be more pleasant if I cooperate." I writhed, pushing my half naked breasts forward.

He grew tense and undecided, snarling like a savage, his eyes filled with lust; in the fight, some of my buttons had been lost. "Drop your sword," he growled, and I dropped my weapon. "You too," he said to Saliné and Vio.

The bearded robber pressed his blade to Veres's neck, who cried from pain, and seeing blood, my will almost crumbled.

"Do it!" I snapped at the girls, staring at Veres: there was just a thin line of blood on his neck along the sword's blade, and he was breathing unevenly, but he was breathing. Saliné whispered something to Vio and they stuck their weapons into the ground, upright. *Good strategy*, I thought involuntarily, and moved toward the armored man diagonally, forcing him to do a half-turn.

"Move away from the weapons, and lay on the ground, face down," he ordered to Saliné and Vio, and they complied. "Take off your shirt," he growled at me – there is nothing more men want after a fight than a woman.

The bearded one pushed Veres to the ground, face down, then half-turned to stare at my body. "Watch and learn to behave like a man," he sneered at my son, keeping the point of the sword at his neck. "There is no one to please you in bed," he snorted at me, showing good knowledge about us. "The bitch is ripe for pleasure." He winked at the armored man, and mimicked intercourse with his free hand.

At leisure, I unbuttoned my shirt, letting it slide down slowly while I stepped back, again a little to the side, forcing the armored man to turn after me. With each new patch of naked skin, his eyes bulged more while his tongue wet his lips. The one immobilizing Veres turned too, and his sword moved a palm's width away from Veres's neck.

"Look into my eyes," the armored man said, and I obeyed. Behind him, I saw Vio and Saliné edging closer to their weapons in silence, and Father coming back. He took a longer route to hide behind the robbers.

I grabbed the armored man's neck with one arm and kissed him. I felt nothing. It was not a woman disgusted by an unwanted man, it was fighting for my children's life, and my body turned into another weapon to overcome the enemy.

"She likes it." The bearded one laughed. Unconsciously, he moved closer to me, away from Veres, and I prayed that my son would not move to distract the men's attention from my body.

Saliné sprinted, grabbed the spear, and pierced the back of the laughing man. He howled like an animal and fell to his knees. The one in front of me said nothing, the knife I had snatched from him cut his throat. He slid down, leaving a trail of blood on my body, his hands trying desperately to cling onto me. Vio attacked the other one too with the dagger Saliné had left behind, but Father arrived, and the robber's bearded head rolled in the grass, eyes wide and white, leaving behind a red line.

Dead and dying men lay all around, some screaming or moaning. Shaking, all I could do was to take my girls in my arms, pressing my hands over their ears. *I was so close to losing you...* Father raised Veres, and after checking his neck, patted him, like a man acknowledging another man. *He must talk with Veres, and I must talk with Vio. She is too young to understand the risks. But she helped...* I could have sworn we had been fighting for hours, but the sun was still hidden over the horizon. His face betraying his sorrow, Father closed Horia's and Mugur's eyelids. Calm again, and poorer, our world was filled with a deep pain that would not pass soon.

In the afternoon, we buried Horia and Mugur at the end of the garden. Crying, my girls covered their graves with flowers from the huge cherry tree. I stared at the graves with the bitter feeling that another part of my life had vanished – I had known Horia and Mugur since my childhood.

When the ceremony ended, Veres went back to the house, followed by Milene and her family. His head lowered, Father remained alone in front of the graves, kneeling on one knee. He had taken Horia and Mugur into his service twenty years ago, when they were just sixteen or seventeen-year-olds, young sons of two captains from our Guard. Father shaped and trained them.

With my girls, I sat under the cherry tree, leaning against the old trunk, my arms wrapped around their shoulders. A gust of wind passed through the tree, and myriad of petals left their flowers, floating around. Like small butterflies, they surrounded us in a whirlpool of white wings under the golden-yellow brightness of the spring sun.

A part of my dream became true. I stared up at the large tree shedding petals, and silent tears ran down my face, mourning everyone we had lost during the last year. *Malin warned me again.* His first warning, which I could not understand, was just the night after he was killed; his death still unknown to me. Dreams come from another world – the other side – and there are hidden, enchanted links between here and there. Mother had a strong Light and taught me the way of the spirit, a world of uncommon knowledge; the world where she lived now. And she taught me to seek the beauty of nature, to love the light of the fireflies in the starry darkness, the song of the nightingale at dawn and the circling ripples in the water born from a finger's play. Still a child, I longed for her touch many years after an arrow took her from us, a bloody arrow that was meant for me. She died in my arms; her gentle eyes staring at me until they could no longer see. For several years, Mother came into my dreams, but I still missed her. In one dream that Father revealed to me much later, she also advised him to refuse Orban's request for my hand. Sometimes, I dream of leaving our wicked world too and join both Mother and Malin in peace. The only thing stopping me are my children. And Father.

By tacit understanding, we did not try to assess the attack that evening; there was too much sadness in our house. The next morning came without relief, but after breakfast, Father and I stood together at the table, each waiting for the other to make the opening.

"You have to talk with Veres," I said reluctantly, deciding to speak first; Father's grief was deeper, and Veres missed his own father.

Father's expression was oddly inward, and he took his time before saying, "Vio is a born fighter. Saliné can be a fighter when needed. Veres will never be one. If I lean too hard on him, his will, as little as it is, will break. We must pray that, maybe, in time he will gather enough wisdom to lead our family. But we must be prepared for some kind of ... adjustments."

"I wish Saliné was a man."

"She is not. We live with what we have."

"The attackers were not here to steal," I moved to another uncomfortable subject. "Orban..." I did not finish, letting him take over. Maybe Orban's spies had learned something about our nascent alliance against him and had tried to solve the issue his way.

"Orban would have sent trained people. These were just robbers," Father said casually, but something in his voice told me that it was just to hide things from me.

"Or maybe he wanted things to look that way. They killed our horses. My mare escaped only because she wasn't in the stable. Robbers don't kill horses; they steal them. Someone wanted us grounded," I suddenly realized. *Why? To stop us running?* "They tried to burn the house. One of them wore a mask."

"Perhaps." Father sighed and withdrew behind his tired pale eyes. "And he was too good with his sword to be a robber."

"Do you know him?"

"I have the feeling that I met him once, but my memory is getting old."

"I know him," Saliné said. She just entered the room, going for a glass of water. "I saw him in Midia. He..." Her voice dropped to a shy whisper.

"The young man who helped you when that horse escaped, racing wild on the streets?" I suddenly remembered and, with all the tension around, I stifled an impulse to smile – that was the first time Saliné had an interest in a young man, other than as a partner for games. *Even dead, he was good looking.*

"I don't know his name, as we did not speak much, but he had come with the embassy from Peyris."

"Thank you, Saliné," I said, struggling to keep my calm. "When will all these complications stop?" I burst when she left us alone. "The last thing we need is the Duke of Peyris as enemy. Or someone from his court," I added after a few moments of silence.

"I don't think that the Duke was involved, and nothing makes sense in this attack. Nothing."

Soon, I need to find a husband for Saliné. It's a pity that we can't afford anymore to look high right now. There are few girls like her in Frankis. Only Cleyre Peyris and Marie Tolosa rival her in beauty and intelligence. But their grandfathers are Dukes. We are ... nothing. Oh, my poor Saliné. "I had the impression... I am not sure, but I think they were here for the girls."

"Saliné is marked and protected by the Circle. The Sages will not allow anyone to harm her."

"Should we contact the Sages?" Our relationship with the Circle was glacial at best; several times the Sages had helped our enemies. They even helped Orban defeat us.

"Maybe we should keep this hidden." Father's voice thickened midway through the words, and he looked away.

"At least tell Mohor about the *robbers*. He might be able to watch the roads."

"That I can do." There was a restraint in Father that worried me. "I'll need to go north soon, to hire two of our old retainers. We are more vulnerable now."

"We might need to run away from Frankis." My children's lives counted for more than my desire to revenge Malin and recover what was ours by right.

"We need even more men if we are to run."

I nodded, feeling that Father did not want to talk further, and he left the table in silence.

"There are three women outside," Meline entered while Father was still out. "Strange women, on horses, dressed like men. Armed, but they could not fool me. One's name is Lena."

Dochia... Lena was her name outside the Wanderers' world, and very few knew their real names. "Let them enter."

"Lena has a peregrine raven on her shoulder."

Umbra? I involuntarily smiled, remembering the bird's name. "I know." *More bad news?* The Wanderers were the most informed people I knew, and Dochia was the fifth leader of the Frankis Wanderers, the Fifth Light as they named her. While Mother had the Wanderer Light too, she rejected them to have family and children. I am happy for that, but she died young, and my two brothers even younger, so I can't say if her choice was the right one, even though I am still alive. Some whispers spread the word about the Circle trying to end our family's male line – Father's genealogy went back to the last Empress. There were not many able to claim such an old, noble line, not even Orban, the Candidate King. Other rumors said Father was not pliable enough for the Circle's liking, but how much should one trust a rumor?

"It seems that I came too late," Dochia said when our eyes met – she was never bothered by formalities. She wore light, sleeveless ring-mail, but there was no way a trained eye would confound her with a man; Dochia had an austere beauty that commanded respect.

"Avae, Jara," Umbra greeted me, using the Wanderer salute and Dochia's voice.

"Avae Umbra." Amused, I raised my arm so he could land on it, and I ruffled the smooth feathers on his chest – he always enjoyed that. "If you came to warn us about the attack on our house, yes, you are late." I could not stop a hint of recrimination, even though it was not her fault. "Have a seat," I gestured to the sofa.

"Any losses?" she asked, even before sitting.

"Horia and Mugur. Orban sent fifteen thugs to attack us," I spat, hoping that she would confirm my guess.

"All your guards are gone," she said thoughtfully, and I just nodded. "And the attackers?"

"All dead," I boasted bitterly, subdued by her brusque way of dealing with my sorrow.

"Good. Both Cernat and you are tough fighters, but you need to find new guards. It's a hard world."

"The Circle and the Wanderers, always competing, under a mask of cooperation. There's no limit to our complications, is there?"

"Cantemir asked me to warn you, and there will be no more attacks. For a while," she added after a brief pause. "Robbers don't really count."

"Cantemir? The Master Sage?"

"Do you know another Cantemir able to find what black mind was planning this in secret? This was not done by Orban. I have the feeling that somebody else from the Circle was involved."

"Their leader wore a mask. Saliné knew him from Midia. He came there with an embassy from Peyris."

"That's strange. I will see what I can learn about him. The Circle doesn't care about you, Jara, but it cares about your daughters."

"That bunch of incompetents working hard to rebuild our kingdom. More than forty years of mistakes, and not even one small step forward to make Frankis a decent place to live in again." Remembering everything we had lost because of that bloody Circle, I could not speak easily even about their sins.

"Power is not always matched by competency. That doesn't make it less dangerous." Her tone was patient and reasonable, but Dochia looked at me with some indefinable amusement, and I could not escape a mounting feeling of childish resentment.

"I suppose so." I shrugged, and it was only with effort that I could answer. "It's just strange; they are so terrifying in their incompetence, sowing even more chaos. How many are placing their hopes in the Sages' hands? I can't even say minds."

"Fate is a harsh mistress, isn't she? Things are not going well for you, right now, but everything could be worse. Even when help is scarce, you are not alone. If handled well, many would join you, just because they fear Orban. Mohor is not strong, but he is a Seigneur. Use him."

"War is coming." Umbra sang this time: Second Life, the song for dead people; then flapped his wings at me. "Fight, fight, fight."

"Maybe we have to leave Frankis," I said abruptly, fear filling my mind.

"You don't have the liberty to leave anymore. Saliné is marked by the Circle," Dochia said, a cold warning in her calm voice: we could leave, but without our daughters. It was a warning from a woman for another woman, and from a friend too. The Wanderers had their own role to play in Frankis, and often they backed the Circle just because there was no other alternative. "I have to leave." She stood up abruptly and went for the door.

When our eyes met, I saw a flicker of genuine concern, but I also knew that nothing could change her mind, making her stay the night. When Mother was still alive, she visited us from time to time; they were friends, even though Dochia was eleven years younger. It didn't happen often after she became a Wanderer, I had to recognize, and she was the Seventeenth Light at that time – they advance in ranks following funerals.

Old memories... Old indeed, resembling a stranger's recollections of events whose familiarity was only coincidental. "Why are you blaming me for Mother's choice to reject the Wanderers?" I asked, unable to control my anger, and I regretted the question even before finishing it.

"Is that what you think?" Dochia turned back to me, and her head tilted to one side, eyebrows arched expectantly in that expression I knew so well.

"You never stay in our house now, so tell me what I should think."

"You look so much like your mother." Her look of inquiry was almost gentle in its sharpness, but for the first time her voice warmed to me, taking me back in time, a mere child in my parents' house. "You and Cernat still have a role to play in Frankis, and Saliné even more. And Vio ... her Light is very strong. Give me your hand."

I executed her command unconsciously, and she gripped my palm between hers, as she had several times in a past almost forgotten. Strong warmth moved through my skin, and Dochia's hands started to shine, a faint white glow – the White Light of the Wanderers. Through a long moment of silence, I just watched: her immobile eyes staring through me as if I weren't there. Then she started to hum a tune that I knew well. On my arm, Umbra closed his large, dark-blue eyes – a peregrine raven's night vision is somewhere in the middle range between a raven and an owl. Her tune ended, and silence reigned the room, in a hard contrast. A minute passed, then another one.

"It is said that help comes from where you least expect it. Watch the road to Arad for a young man." Dochia's voice was grave and strange in inflection, her words slow and deliberate. Breathing hard, she let my hand free with the same brusque gesture and moved away from me with a distraught air. Something was bothering her, the part of her Vision that could not be shared with me. Umbra's eyes remained closed. She reached up and stroked the bird. I could feel their disquiet too, the mirror of events that could change the world. Or at least my world.

Umbra knows what she saw. There is a bond between a Light of the Wanderers and her peregrine raven, and they are able to read each into other's mind. The Wanderers receive their companion bird, always a male raven, during the Rite of Passage.

What did they see? "Something wrong?" I asked, a little too eager.

"La naiba!" Dochia threw an archaic mild curse still used in some isolated places in the mountains. It meant deuce or damnation, depending on content, but I was never sure what she really meant; it was a cryptic collocation that she used frequently. "I can't hide it from you." She frowned briefly, walking away. "Change is coming."

"One young man dies. One young man lives. The wheel is turning." Turning his head from side to side as his wings slowly flapped, Umbra interjected – the solemn voice of an old oracle man. His movements slowed; the noise he made becoming stretched out, attenuated.

"Shut-up, Umbra," Dochia snapped at him, a slight amused tone lingering in her voice.

"Shut-up, Umbra." He mimicked Dochia, using her voice, then puffed his feathers briefly before flying back to her shoulder.

Their words were so general and cryptic that I could not base my children's future on them. I didn't have much Light, and that made me feel awkward; I was my mother's daughter in everything bar the Light.

Two days later, Mohor and Aron came to visit us; it was more an assessment after the attack than a social visit. Father decided to let me deal with them; they did not enter the house, and we walked through the backyard while the attack was dissected in all its aspects.

"Any hints where they came from?" Mohor asked when we arrived at the place where the fifteen thugs were buried, at the edge of the forest. I did not know why they wanted to see the grave, but Aron had insisted on it.

"They wore no colors, and we did not find any particular object of value on them. Robbers." There was no reason to let Mohor know that they were more than some simple thieves – their young leader, who Father had killed in the last duel, was a well-trained swordsman.

We stood in front of the large, unmarked grave, and I saw Aron staring intently at it, mouth twisted, eyes buried in dark pits, his body rigid with anger. His hand flexed intermittently on the hilt of his sword.

"He lost his eldest son, Raul, just the day before you were attacked," Mohor whispered when I threw a questioning glance at him. "He was coming from Seged to Severin and vanished without a trace. It may be that the men buried here are his assassins."

We did not know the young man, who was said to be intelligent and strong, but I knew what it meant to lose someone close to you and, despite Aron's arrogance, I could sympathize with him. "I am sorry to hear that. It's just one more reason for them to be in that grave, and one more reason for you to guard the roads better."

Before I could finish, Aron turned abruptly and walked away. His stare was full of hate, and I understood his rage; we felt the same against the thugs in the grave. "One day, I will make you pay," he whispered to himself, his voice filled with venom.

"Do you know something about the robbers?" I asked without thinking, but there was a sudden surge of Light in my mind. Aron ignored me and walked away.

"Please excuse him," Mohor said, and after I nodded, he left me too.

Raul's death was quite a strange coincidence. I looked at the two men as they mounted their horses. Mohor saluted, and they went away. Aron rode hunched over, big and silent beside Mohor.

Chapter 7 – Codrin

Before dawn, I left Movil's inn through the backyard. The city was still sleeping under darkness; the streets were silent. Two hundred paces from the Swest Gate, I hid behind a large fountain, unwilling to be the first one leaving the city. Ten minutes later, two small groups went to the gate, ghostly figures against a dark-grey background. Gripping the hilt of my sword, I followed them in the low light of the nascent dawn.

In front of the gate, a guard intercepted me with the irritation of a man not yet fully awake. "Boy, where are you going?"

"Arad," I said dryly while two other guards surrounded me. "I have an errand there." I added a sense of urgency, the growing light was my enemy – my Arenian horse and gear would raise unwanted questions.

"You have a funny accent. You are not from here." There was tightness in his voice, and he walked around me on slow feet, a deliberate kind of slowness, as if he could move faster but didn't see the point. I forced myself to stay still, as another guard was frowning down at me.

"I come from Baia." That was the region where I spent the winter in Gran's house. "We don't speak as well as people in Muniker."

"How old are you?"

"Eighteen."

"Liar." He shoved me from behind, and I crushed into Zor, who snorted softly. I patted his neck, then stood straight again, turning slowly to face the guard. "How long did you stay in Muniker?" the man barked into my ear, and I felt his hot breath on my skin. That and the rotten stink of his mouth.

"One week. I stayed at Caravan's Inn." I tried to anticipate his next question just to shorten the interrogatory.

"It's damn expensive." He found another annoying thing about me, and I tightened, expecting another blow in my back. It did not come.

"I know Movil."

"Come here," a tall knight, who seemed to be the captain of the gate, ordered. He looked at me under the soft torches' light. "Yes, I saw you there." We recognized each other at the same time, he was a habitual customer – Movil's inn was not far from the gate. Behind him, through the open door of the Gate Room, I saw two royal guards from Arenia, and a man who looked more like a scholar than a soldier. He looked indefinite and olive tanned, like the southern people, but I could not figure his origin. They stopped talking and glanced at me. The light was brighter inside, and one of them came closer to the doorway, for a better look. "He is Litvonian," the captain said, still leaning against the wall of the doorway, and the scholar translated into Arenian. The royal guard returned to his comrade, and they resumed talking. Slowly, I half turned. "You tamed the beast," the captain laughed. "You are good for an eighteen-year-old man."

"I trained hard."

"Did you see any people from Arenia on the road to Muniker? A sixteen-year-old boy and an escort?" Both roads from Silvania to Muniker passed through Baia.

The Arenian embassy worked fast. If I can't escape now…. "How can I recognize an Arenian?"

"There is a wealthy reward for capturing or giving information about the boy, so you will *want* to find a way."

"How much?"

"Two hundred galbeni for information. Two thousand for capturing him dead or alive."

"That's a lot of money," I said, filling my voice with greed. *Two thousand galbeni for the head of a vagrant.* "Anyone can kill a nameless child and pretend he captured the right one. I will come to you if I hear something."

"Gold makes people think." He laughed and patted my shoulder. "Ask for Knight Altmayer, the commander of the Swest Gate. Manfrid, open the postern."

I left the city at leisure, without looking back, like any man having nothing to hide, and took the road going to Frankis. After the first curve, the gate vanished from sight, and I pushed Zor into a gallop like there was no tomorrow. We did not slow until I could evict that paralyzing fear in a far corner of my mind. A day later, in front of the mountains bordering Litvonia and Frankis, we left the road, going in parallel through the forest, keeping pace with the caravans. Sometimes, deep ravines forced me back to the road, but the caravans were moving slowly, and my spyglass – another Assassin's gift from Tudor – helped me track things from far away, without being discovered. Close to the top of the first small mountain, I watched the road back to Muniker. The sky was clear, and the view was going far away. In the afternoon, a column of fifteen riders from the Royal Guard of Arenia appeared on the road. They went north, toward Loxburg, the city of Duke Manuc, but another column could come on my road too. It took three days for the caravans to pass the Frankis border, slow days yet safer than the ones ahead; the law was better enforced in Litvonia. From the moment I entered the high mountains, the land had grown steadily darker and more foreboding, and I rode with a sense of danger that had hounded me from the first steps inside the forest.

"Be careful," Movil told me in our last morning together, "the Cursed Forest doesn't like strangers, and there are ghosts feeding on men's souls. The Black Prince is leading them. Join a small caravan and stay on the road."

I knew about the Black Prince. The story was told in Arenia too, without the ghosts. He was an ignoble man, like my uncle, and started their first civil war, trying to kill his sister, the legitimate Queen of Frankis. But that almost two-hundred-year-old story ended well – the Queen prevailed against the usurper. The Black Prince was killed in the Cursed Forest while running toward Litvonia. For the first time, I realized that returning to claim my throne, I would start a civil war, an event with an unpredictable end. Frankis was a good example; they had three civil wars, in the past two hundred years, and a ravaged former kingdom.

The forest was savage, with trees as massive as the towers of a small palisade, thicker around than could be embraced by three men clasping hands. No axe had ever touched the Cursed Forest, and every moment I felt many eyes staring down at me from the tall oaks. From place to place, smoke and steam went out from the underground, enhancing an already dark mood. Everything was strange, like a dream, but this was not my land, and who knew what menaces could hide in the darkness. The most dangerous thing is the one you don't know. Not yet ready to join a caravan until farther inside the Frankis lands, I feared more the Assassins and the Arenian guards than legends that might or might not be true, but my fear felt tighter in the forest.

At noon, a group of five riders arrived at a point where I could see their faces through my spyglass. *The old man from the Protector's Arena...* Intrigued, I tried to keep pace with them through the forest, but after a while, I lost sight of them. To feel safe, I went up, keeping a longer distance from the road, and my pace slowed as the path was more rugged, though I had a better overview in both directions. The rest of the day was quiet, and I stopped above a large fork. Late in the evening, four caravans of different sizes and richness camped in the small meadow between the forking roads. There was a swarm of people moving around the campfires, and involuntarily I caught the smell of roasted meat. *Just an illusion,* I shook my head; they were too far, and my own loneliness struck at me. I watched them just for the pleasure of seeing people caught up in normal activities. A small comfort.

In the morning, I woke up staring at the face of my dead brother, contracted and cut in two by a stream of blood that was almost dried. Gasping, I pressed my fists to my temples and fought hard not to scream. It was hurting, yet I had no control over my tormented memories; they were coming to me by their own evil will. Perhaps it would have been easier if I could cry, but no tears left my eyes from the day we had learned that our parents and sister were killed. *The caravans are splitting*, I realized, when my mind recovered, and pushed Zor forward, to the west; it made no sense to wait and be drowned in that pain again. Looking back, I saw the two largest caravans going toward Arad, too.

Distant, angry shouts pierced the forest when the dawn broke through the trees. *I should have been awake.* The thought mildly surprised me; it was never an issue to wake up early. *Tired?* In haste, I mounted Zor. The trees were muffling the sounds, and that could explain my longer sleep. I laughed at my lame excuse and galloped down. Betrayed by most of the protectors they had hired in Muniker, the caravans were under attack. The merchants were up, gathered in one place around a large fireplace, armed with clubs and three spears. Five people were already dead in the grass. By the time of my arrival, the dead had already gone up to eight, but only two were robbers. The old man heard trotting hoofs behind him and turned, to face me.

"A boy with a sword," he sneered, pushing his horse with a savage kick. "A rare thing." He laughed, and our swords met for the first time. In a strange coincidence, both of us underestimated our adversaries. A second clash of swords, and we turned the horses to face each other again. "You are good, but I will still have your head and sword at the end," the old man bragged. He was wrong, but it took me more than three minutes to put him down, and in a fight against many, even a minute may be too long.

Four dead robbers, I glanced around me. *Five still alive.* The real protectors were dead too. Everything was on me and the merchants armed with clubs and spears. Another robber died before realizing it; my sword killed him silently from behind. Alarmed by a neighing horse carrying a body with one leg jammed in the stirrup, the next one turned to engage me. Caught between my sword and three clubs, he died when I pierced his throat, and things were almost settled. I rushed Zor to the left, where the last three robbers were still fighting, and I put down the closest one. From the right, a club came at full speed toward me.

I woke moving in a slow rhythm, shaken slowly, with a hard thumping in my head. *A wagon... I am alive.* The realization took longer than one might have thought. I opened my eyes to the face of a woman smiling shyly at me. *Am I really alive?* She was in her mid-twenties. *Attractive...* Her hand was on my head, pressing a cold, wet cloth against my skull. *The club hit my helmet*; I realized why I was still alive and tried to stand. It was the wrong thing to do, and I lay back with a groan. "What happened?" I asked when my pain had subsided.

"You were wounded," she stated as if I could not know.

"Obviously." I pointed to my head. "Who wounded me? There was no robber on my right side."

"He was scared."

"Who?"

"My cousin. You had a horse, and he mistook you for one of the robbers. He was scared," she repeated, struggling to find her words. "I apologize and thank you for saving us. I am Delia. You know my husband, Panait."

Panait remembered me. Staying in a wagon leaves you much time for thought, and I fell asleep. When I could stand, I saw my things packed close to me, and a new sword in its sheath.

"Winner's Right." Delia smiled, holding out a purse that felt heavy in my hand. "From the old man who led the robbers."

By habit, I was about to reject the purse – it was not kingly to rob the dead. *Vagrants don't care about kingly things.*

After a while, Delia wet the cloth again. "Keep it tight." She took my hand and pressed it against the cloth. "Let me have a look at your cut. I am a good healer." She smiled, and I realized that the pain in my jaw was not from the club's hit.

I slid my finger over the wound. "It's nothing."

"It will not hurt you more if I have a look," she said gently. Once satisfied, she kept me entertained with many stories about Arad and the northern part of the former Frankis Kingdom.

Ten galbeni, I checked the content of the purse when Delia left me alone; it would have been rude to do it in front of her. A rich one, but the old man was not the usual robber. *I now have twenty-four galbeni. With twenty, I can buy a hectare of land.* During the winter, Gran taught me not only how to farm, but the value of land, too. Five hectares of good land could provide a decent peasant family life.

At noon, I was able to ride again, and the caravan continued to Arad with its only protector, hired at full price, after I signed the contract with my new name, Tudor. I still did not know why

I chose his name; maybe because I yearned to be like my mentor.

Panait stared at my name in the contract, then cursed loudly in two languages, leaving me baffled and understanding only the Litvonian ones – the merchants were some living dictionaries of colorful words. Delia moved behind him and gently covered his mouth with her palm, whispering something to him.

"I did not curse Tudor," Panait protested. "I apologize," he added in haste, looking at me. "Did you stay in the Caravans' Inn?" he asked, just to confirm something I was not aware of, and I nodded. "And you cuffed that..." His hand moved up to describe the height of the drunken man. *Yes*, I nodded again, and Panait took his time to stare at my body, comparing me to the other man, unable to understand how it happened. "Movil recommended you, but I thought I had enough protectors."

My mind recalled the Vision I had at the graves, telling me that I will lead this caravan. *Only women can have Visions*. It was a known thing. Not yet fully recovered from the blow on my head, and afraid of the implications, I forced myself to ignore that weird Vision.

We stopped for the night earlier than usual – people were tired and frightened – and arranged the large wagons in an easy to defend square resembling a fortified camp, on a plateau with steep ridges on two sides. For me, it was strange that nobody had thought of that, but their lack of military knowledge suited me. I evaluated Panait's men, setting defensive places behind the wagons for each of them, just in case. The fires were lit, and food prepared. The wind stirred the land. It brought a touch of coldness form the mountains, and distant noise of hoofs clopping on the ground. In moments, the sound became stronger. Fifteen riders, wearing the colors of the Royal Guard of Arenia appeared on the road coming from Muniker.

Not enough time to run… I measured the distance to the riders and their speed – there was no way to take my horse and leave in time.

"Don't panic!" I shouted to be heard by everybody. "They are soldiers, not robbers." *The only one who should fear is me.*

"They might attack us," Panait whispered through gritted teeth, fighting to control his fear. "It's happened in the past."

In silence, the people from the caravan gathered around us, staring at me with wide eyes of fear.

"Everybody, take your weapons and occupy your positions. Now!" I said in a stern voice, and they obeyed, running to their designated places.

I sprinted toward Panait's main wagon and exchanged my Arenian sword and helmet for the old man's helmet and sword. Then I bandaged my wounded jaw to conceal my face as much as I could. Leaving the wagon, I grabbed my bow too and ran back.

"Take it," I pushed the bow to a small man who could not harm even a cat with his club.

"I've never used…" he said meekly.

"They don't know that." I pointed to the riders. "They will see a dangerous bow. Panait, let me speak with the soldiers." *If the riders are going to recognize me, it should happen before they enter our camp.*

Panait stared at me, moistening his lips, then bit his moustache. He nodded reluctantly, not very convinced.

Captain Iulian, I recognized the first rider. *He knows me.* I pushed the helmet down until it half covered my eyes, hoping that the bandage, the large blue bruise and the swelling covering the right side of my face would do the rest. I glanced up in the dusk, to estimate how fast the darkness would fall. Taking a step forward between the wagons in the middle of our defensive barrier, I took care to remain half hidden.

The Royal Guard column stopped at a safe distance, their horses trotting nervously, a sign that the men were nervous too. Two riders came closer, dismounting not far from me. Captain Iulian was one of them, and he took his time to check our defenses.

"Knight Gaspar from Arenia," the unknown man introduced himself in an approximation of Litvonian. His voice was deep, his tone unexpectedly tart. He was tall and muscled with a brutish face but, from the way he dismounted, he was agile too. A hard fighter from head to toes. "Who Lead Protector?"

He still might know me... "Me." I forced my voice to sound tough and adult. "What do you want?"

"Peace," he claimed, his voice cold. "We stay there," he gestured to the free half of the plateau.

"Go on," I nodded. "Our archers are skilled, and we are more than enough to defend ourselves if attacked."

"Attack?" He lifted his voice, unsure of the meaning of my words.

"Do you speak Silvanian?" I asked, knowing that the language was more used in Arenia – our conversation could go in the wrong direction because of some linguistic misinterpretations from two people having only loose knowledge of Litvonian.

"Yes," Captain Iulian said before Gaspar could answer. He came closer, but he was a shorter man, and looking down at him concealed me even better under my helmet. Short as he was, Iulian was a sword master, and many had paid the price for not taking him seriously. "We are going to Arad and mean no harm to you. Allow us to join you." He gestured toward our fires, taking a different course, even though Gaspar was the leader of the riders.

The evening was warm, but his searching gaze made me shiver, and I leaned back, against the cart. "We were attacked this morning," I said, neutrally. "The robbers are all dead now."

I glanced at him, then at his soldiers, then finally at our men spread between the wagons, all armed. Both Iulian and Gaspar followed my eyes. If they thought something, when I pointed to our armed men, they did not say. *If I refuse, we look both unfriendly and weak.* "You can eat with us but make camp outside our perimeter."

Iulian nodded, his immobile face showing nothing, yet I feared that he had recognized me. I went back to Panait, and he reluctantly agreed with my solution.

"Spilt your men in two," I told him. "Half should eat now with the soldiers, the other half after they leave our camp."

The light was fading when the soldiers came, and my fear of being recognized subsided. Poised to eat with the first batch, I settled the Arenian soldiers at a separate fireplace, and everybody ate in silence. Joining Panait's fire, I scented the sharp lingering sweetness of incense, stirring vague emotions stripped of memory. *Tamaie from Putna*, I recognized the substance that only Arenia produced and was used to open your mind to Fate. For trained people, at least. Eyes closed, I tried to feel whatever the elusive scent was trying to tell me. I failed, and that left behind the bad feeling of something important avoiding me.

"Tamaie from Arenia," Delia smiled, misunderstanding my reaction, "for our good luck."

After I got seated on a small barrel, Delia made a fuss of me – she knew well what would have happened to her, waiting for a ransom to be paid. Capturing a Mester's caravan was always a robbers' dream, both for the rich merchandise, and for the money the Merchants Guild would pay for its detained Mesters. Like a spoiled child, I received the best pieces of food from her, and the moment I finished my steak, some unknown cakes filled my plate. The men around the fire grinned but said nothing.

"Piss on them." Panait patted my shoulder. "They are worth less than the food they are eating." There was some anemic laughter, and I had to smile too, although I was still unfamiliar with the merchants' humor. As I learned later, Panait was a subtle man, able to talk and amuse everybody from stable-boys to Seigneurs, and that evening he looked in good form, telling many stories and jokes – sometimes he spoke Litvonian to keep me entertained too.

Feeling my uneasiness, Delia took me aside. "We lost nine people," she said sorrowfully. "And in caravans, we all are more or less relatives. My husband is hiding his grief to keep up the morale."

One by one, the soldiers left our camp, and I watched them discreetly until they were gone. In the end, only Gaspar and Iulian remained, expecting a bit of entertainment from us, which meant from me, Panait knew a few words in Silvanian.

"So, you are going to Arad," I said, sitting as far as I could from the fire without risking being considered impolite. *Looking for a young fugitive...* Talking to them was a risk. It was also a good chance to learn more about their mission, and the place I still called home. We were facing each other, the embers of the campfire glowing between us, casting a faint brightness through the shadows of the night. A gust of wind stirred some dried leaves into the flames, and they and burned with colored sparks, raising into the darkness of the calm night. "That's a long way from Arenia."

"We are soldiers," Iulian shrugged. "We go where our orders say, which for us is Arad and Peyris. There are two other groups, one going south to Leyona and Tolosa, one north to Loxburg."

"An important errand."

"Yes." He took some time to stir the fire, and I turned a little away from him. "We are looking for a sixteen-year-old a young man, and a small escort. Have you seen any Arenians recently? There is a two hundred galbeni reward for valuable information."

"Quite a good reward. We saw no strangers after we left Muniker, but he's more of a boy than a man."

"More a boy," he conceded. "But more than that too."

"He is a snake." Gaspar spat his words, his body stiff with anger. "The sooner we find him, the better. I can't wait to crush his head." His large fist moved up and down, hitting his knee in a show of force. It was a different kind of force than the one I had met in the drunken man at the inn. Trained. Lethal. He laughed suddenly, like the snarling of dogs before a fight, a vulgar delight of anticipation.

Human animals follow their nature with savage enthusiasm; I could not stop a string of futile philosophy. My cursed uncle was a fine thinker, able to extract the most from his men. "It should not be difficult," I said with studied indifference.

One side of Gaspar's mouth stopped smiling, the other extended his snarl. His face resembled a Scarvish dog. The dog's skull is too thick to grow large enough and presses on the brain. They are the best hunting dogs, but they are killed before getting five years old, before they are going mad. Gaspar was older, and he was not mad, just a fighting beast. At the corner of my eye, I saw Captain Iulian touching Gaspar.

"Do you know what happened in Arenia?" Iulian asked.

"Vague rumors about some internal disorders." My phrase seemed to be coming from someone else, a long way off, even when Iulian's words went through me like a knife, stirring memories I wanted to forget. "I mean no offense; it's a long way from here."

"None taken. Everything is under control now in our lands," Iulian said in a low voice, "but a new king can never be careful enough, and the Arenian King is a wise man."

"Who could blame him after what happened?" I asked with dim irony, then I coughed, feeling that I was losing control of my voice. "We also have a wise King in Litvonia, but look what is happening now in Frankis."

"Yes, who could blame our King? Yet, some people are not content with the new order, but they are a few and weak. Our King is strong." Iulian's voice was strangely flat and distant, and I sensed tension mounting in Gaspar.

"In time, they might grow in numbers," I said, tentatively. *Does he hope to stir me, and lure me with hope, to reveal myself?*

"In time," Iulian agreed. He dragged a fingertip slowly across his knee, drawing invisible circles. "If they are not all dead by then. The King's second son will marry the Silvanian King's elder daughter, and this new alliance will calm things even more."

She was supposed to be my bride... "A good political option." I shrugged, and both of us remained silent for a while. "Our King's wife is Silvanian too."

"You speak Silvanian well." For the first time, captain Iulian moved to question me. In the firelight, the scar on his cheek showed white. There was another one on the hand resting on his knee.

"Large caravans travel everywhere, and few hire a Lead Protector just for one country."

The silence lasted longer this time, and Iulian stirred the fire again, tension visible in his gestures, then stared intensely at me, the flames playing games in his eyes. Discreetly, I released the band tying the hilt of my sword to the scabbard and gripped it tightly.

"There are corrupt people waiting for the return of the traitor we are chasing, but as I said they are just a few." His words stirred me even more, and I was unable to react in any way. "Despicable men, like Duke Anghel could still make some trouble at home." Anghel was my second uncle, and I thought even more that Iulian's peculiar story was not meant to entertain a stranger; it was a trap to catch me. "And some relatives from the fugitive's mother's side. His mother's cousin, Strajer, is wiser and plays with the King now. But the best thing is that Sir Baraki has recovered." Iulian looked around at the barely visible camp, then up into the void, but I felt watched.

I stretched my body, struggling to keep an appearance of a stranger hearing interesting news – Baraki was supposed to be dead. But I learned that Strajer betrayed us in Silvania, and my brother's and my mentor's blood was on his hands. *Be cursed.* I breathed deeply, and gripped harder the hilt of my sword, ready to fight.

"Baraki is the strongest man in the Kingdom," Gaspar interjected, his voice slightly annoyed. It suited me. "The King and his son are strong too," he added hastily, yet it sounded like an afterthought. "They killed that weak man on the throne, his witch wife and the daughter. Oh, how that little bitch cried and begged when the princes took her maidenhood. It was a pleasure to hear her moaning."

They raped Ioana. Suddenly strained, I felt taut, like a bow string. In a split second, my training took over. Ready to bounce, my right boot touched a log, which rolled out of the fire, spreading sparks into the night. That was my luck. Instead of jumping on Gaspar, I leaned forward and picked the wood. I tried to force myself to move slowly. It didn't really work, embers and ash spread when I placed it back into the fire, then I retreated to my place, and covered my face, pretending to defend it from the flying sparks. My breath was ragged, but now I could control myself. *Gaspar is just a tool. It makes no sense to die, punishing the tool. I killed Jan. I will kill the other three. I took the Sacred Oath. I will have no peace until I kill them.* I breathed once more. A long one, the Assassin Cool. Then I stretched myself, yawning.

"You are fast," Gaspar said, and I realized that his hand was gripping the hilt of his sword too. "But that log is not a snake. It can't bite." His voice was half amused, half inquiring. His eyes were even more inquisitive.

"Once, I saw a caravan burning from a log rolling like that. In half an hour, everything was gone. Beautiful sparks may start ugly fires."

"Ah, that." Gaspar relaxed and took his hand from the hilt.

"An important man, that Baraki, I suppose."

"The Chief of the Royal Guard. He can barely speak now from a wound on his neck, but he is a strong man," Iulian said.

The strong man waited until the end of the fight, to attack Tudor from behind.

"Sir Baraki is my relative," Gaspar interjected curtly, "and his daughter was married with the King's son. Fate blessed her with a son just before we left Arenia, so the kingdom's future is assured. And the Assassins Order is helping our King."

Jan sired a child before I killed him. "What is this order?" I asked, wondering if the Assassins were involved in the attack against my family. "It sounds like a bad name." Gaspar appeared a nervous and ignoble man, easy to stir, having a much better opinion of himself than his qualities warranted, but he was a trusted relative of Baraki.

"The best warriors in the world. They helped our King to take the throne. No one should speak bad of them," he snapped.

The Assassins bastards helped the Usurper. The realization made my return to Arenia harder than I thought. Not that I planned to return soon; I was barely able to lead a caravan. "I apologize. I know nothing of them, just that the name seems peculiar."

Silent, Iulian touched Gaspar again.

"Maybe we can learn some things about Frankis?" Gaspar asked.

"The road in front of you is more dangerous than anything you have encountered up to here, but you are fifteen soldiers. Trained swords with no precious merchandise. I doubt that you will be attacked. On your road, the first town belonging to S'Arad is Nancyer. It's not a large one."

In the former Frankis Kingdom, usually, a Seigneur's name was derived from his main city, so Orban S'Arad was the Seigneur of Arad, and the name of his house was S'Arad House. The prefix S was just an acronym for Seigneur, or Signora for ladies. There were exceptions too; when the name of the city ended with the letter 'a' the S was left off and the suffix 'n' was added, for a reason that was long lost. The Seigneur of Leyona was Leyonan.

"You should contact the governor of Nancyer, present your papers, and ask for protection before going to Arad. If you are lucky, you will find an envoy from the Duke of Peyris in Arad. He is a powerful man, and Arenia is far away from here."

"Thank you," Iulian said, in a bland tone. "We are to stay in Litvonia and Frankis for a month or two to find the traitor, and we will need political protection. It's now time to join our soldiers. We leave tomorrow at first light."

Leisurely, they stood up and walked away in silence toward the wagons fencing our night camp, and I followed them. Captain Iulian was the last one to pass. He stumbled over something on the ground, fell onto his hands, and cursed the invisible obstacle.

"You are getting old," Gaspar guffawed, without looking back, and disappeared in the low light of the moon.

It took a few long moments for Iulian to stand again, and his hand gripped mine. "Two Triangles of Assassins are after you, and they are not travelling dressed in black," he whispered, showing good knowledge – very few knew that an Assassin group of three was named a Triangle. "They want you alive; the Usurper wants you dead. If it helps, your family died with dignity. They did not beg for mercy."

"Thank you, Captain. I saw a strange nomad in Muniker. A Toltar."

"The Serpentist. The nomads in Nerval worship a new god, the Serpent. They may have some strange powers. Rumors. I don't know if it's really true. Ten of them arrived in Alba, the day ... the day after... They stayed hidden. Our people don't like the nomads, but Baraki seems to be their friend. Two nomads came with us in Muniker, then went to Tolosa with another squad of the Royal Guard. This is not the right time to return, but we will wait for you. Good luck, Sire." He gripped my hand stronger, then disengaged, and hastened away.

Left alone with my own thoughts, I cursed Baraki and the Silvanian King; the path back to my throne was now closed with the new political marriage in sight. *If only Strajer had not betrayed us...* I hated that despicable man as much as I hated my other uncle – Radu and my mentor died because of his treason. I cursed Fate too, for letting my sister being raped and killed. She was only fourteen years old. I could not sleep that night, and kept myself busy, patrolling inside the perimeter until Delia came to stop me.

"I can't sleep," I said before she could speak, my voice raw.

"You have to. The sentries took over this watch. Whatever those soldiers said to you, we need you in good shape tomorrow," she said gently, and took my arm, leading me to the cart where my bed was prepared. Delia stayed with me, singing softly, until I fell asleep. Strangely, it happened faster than I was expecting it.

The next morning was unhurried, even serene. Iulian kept his word and left even earlier, without trying to reach me again. From a nearby hill, I watched them until they disappeared. *Thank you, Captain. I hope to meet you again. In different circumstances.*

The caravan was in a better spirit; I was still haunted by Ioana's memory. *She did not cry;* I shook my head. *She fought. She was a fighter.* During the following days, I rode through the hills, in parallel with the road and the slow caravan, ready to catch any movement back and front with my spyglass – our best defense was to see what was coming and prevent. It was also a way to avoid any Assassins band coming after me in disguise, a proof that they wanted me as badly as my uncle. A lonely protector has a dangerous life, and having lost a third of its men, the caravan was moving slower than usual – without coachmen, some wagons were tied to the still manned ones. Small bands of robbers attacked us twice. I ambushed them from the forest with my bow, and the caravan went on safely with no more casualties. After a while, we went out of the mountains and passed Rhiun River over the only bridge not destroyed by the passing of time. With the demise of the Alban Empire, knowledge about building long bridges vanished too.

"That's Arad and its main gate." Panait swept his hand toward the valley and the thriving city, his voice filled with pride – built of orange stones with thick black veins, the southern gate was indeed spectacular.

Arad had been a royal residence when the kingdom still had a king; an old and large city, named Orleane in the past, famous for its architecture and beautiful women. It was ruled now by Orban, a Grand Seigneur, and a man of bad temper and character. I did not know if I could offer my services to such a bad ruler, and I needed a powerful player, yet Panait represented a good start. That allowed me to postpone a tough decision. I spent two days in Panait's house until Iaru's smaller caravan left for Dorna, with two new protectors hired under my command. On the road, nothing happened, and in three weeks, I returned to Arad.

On my last day in their house, Delia filled my backpack with food, and she was now trying to add a small box that intrigued me – a faint smell of cakes making me smile.

"Let him go, Delia," Panait said, amused. "Tudor is not a child. Well, not in the sense that you are spoiling him." He laughed this time, and she menaced him with the small box in her hand. "I have not yet the guts to lead another caravan in mid-year. Our next one moves in autumn, and I will not leave Arad without you." He patted my shoulder, then stopped, trying to remember something. "One week ago, the Arenian riders we met on the road left our city for Peyris."

One menace less, but there was no one to warn about the Assassin Triangles hunting for me. They would try to recover the curved swords from an impostor, and from their point of view, I was a fraud. Being trained by an Assassin made me a target, and that was their only reason to capture me alive, but I did not want to become one of them, even if I was able to perform the inhumane Assassins' rite of passage. I wasn't a cold-blooded killer, ready to murder innocent people when ordered. Neither was my mentor, but he was kidnapped by the Assassins in his childhood and had no choice until my father's protection allowed him to run away from them. Great swords, Flame and Shadow were forged for my mentor, Tudor, the Assassin Grand Master, and they should have been cleansed and destroyed with the proper ritual at his death; an Assassin's sword is his twin soul. There were only seven Grand Masters in that bloody sect. I would have delivered the swords to them, if I could, but there was no safe manner for doing that.

After a while, Delia found a way to arrange the box in my backpack, and I was free to head south to find Tolosa, the place my mentor had told me about.

Chapter 8 – Codrin

At noon, the forest is usually quiet. A bird may sing here or there, and the landscape's beauty invites daydreaming. For a lone traveler, it could be the last dream. Sinuous, the road passed through the small mountains, and I gave the horse its head. A clap of thunder frightened Zor, and scattered birds left the trees around. A horse neighed not far in front, and I rose in the saddle to see better. Occasional droplets hit the road, leaving small craters in the dust, but the rain did not come. The air was humid and rusty. Another curve revealed movement between the trees in a small clearing inside the forest. Dismounted, I left the road, approaching cautiously, hidden by some thick bushes.

Six soldiers... Well-armed and trained. From their horses and weapons, they were elite fighters, nothing like the caravan raiders I had met before, but none of them had any heraldic insignia. There are always ways to estimate the value of a fighter from his gear and stance.

A hundred paces from me, half-hidden, one of them was holding a bunch of horses; the other five gathered around a woman wrestling on the ground. Ogling at her half naked body, the sentry wiped some sweat from his forehead.

There was no way the woman could escape, yet she was not crying, just trying in vain to free herself. *She fights well though...*

The men were laughing and playing by letting her free for a moment, just to put her down the next; they could have immobilized her in a moment for all her effort and fighting skills. *Six hardened soldiers... Too many.* In that moment, she let out a cry of despair, and the image of my twin sister resurfaced. *Six men... One mistake and...* Around me, the ground under the trees was patched with shadow and slashed with sunlight from a bruise in the clouds, shifting as the branches danced in the wind. *Too much light.*

Two horses moved between the watching man and the group of five. Annoyed that he was being left out, and now losing sight of the show too, he stepped forward. My arrow pierced his neck, and he fell with almost no sound. The horses trotted away. *Don't neigh...* I froze behind the bush hiding me. The trees creaked and rustled. Some birds tweeted and warbled. A ripple of laughter came from the five thugs. It sounded like one long vile noise. I could see one pair of eyes bulging at her. Uneasy, and ruled by their herd instinct, the horses moved closer to the group, hiding the fallen man. *Five men...* The Assassin swords were better suited to fighting alone against many, and I gripped the hilt to unsheathe the long sword.

"Shadow..." a whisper came to me, inside my mind.

I pressed my lips tight, to stifle a cry. The sword felt alive, and there was an undercurrent passing, back and forth, between the cold steel and my hand. It did not feel dangerous. It felt strange, though, as if the sword was now glued to my skin. I swung the sword twice. It whistled softly as it cut through the air. Tense, I took one step, then another one, Shadow in my right arm, Flame and the bow in my left. Silent, I followed the horses, some forty paces away from the group. *Five men... Just five men.*

Dressed in elegant blue clothes over his ring-mail, the leader kneeled in front of the woman, who was held tightly by the other four. Even at this distance, I could hear his ragged breath. *The leader... You kill the leader; you are halfway to victory.* Tudor's words. I stuck the swords into the ground. Eyes closed, I tipped my face back to feel the cool breeze on my skin. I forced myself to breathe long and slow. In and out. The Assassins Cool. An unknown bird called, high above the trees. *A sign from Fate.* The main thug had just taken down his pants and raised the lower part of his ring-mail, his neck and head hidden behind the man restraining the woman's right leg. My arrow pierced his buttocks, the only visible, naked part of his body from where I stood. The mind has a morbid penchant for details in dangerous times, maybe just because even the smallest element can be lifesaving. The arrow passed from one side to another, and his lower back looked like an impaled apricot. Wailing, he fell, pushing away the man on his left. Stunned for some moments, they allowed me to release three arrows, in swift succession, into their legs. For the face or neck, you need quality aim. I did not have that time. The one still unharmed, jumped toward me, unsheathing his sword. I threw my bow and grabbed the swords. Shadow vibrated in my hand. He tried to split me in two with one strong, vertical cut, a raw move I did not expect from an elite fighter, maybe just because he underestimated the youngster he faced.

Tudor taught me that the easiest way to overcome an enemy is to let him defeat himself, so I ducked, and he went down on all four from his own inertia. Shadow fell on his neck like in a mundane execution. My thumb swiped over its blade. It felt cold and comforting. It felt like an extension of my own arm, part of me. The remaining thugs moved in an almost normal succession of steps, trying to encircle me – hardened fighters, the wounds on their legs were not incapacitating them. The woman sprang up suddenly, hitting one's leg with her own, and he tumbled to the ground. There was an elegant efficiency in her movement, and she was now crouched, ready to fight, a dagger balanced in her hand.

"Bitch!" the soldier growled and stood up fast, turning to her, then changed his mind coming toward me. "I'll deal with you later. Stay warm for me," he said to the woman over his shoulder.

I threw Flame into the face of the closest thug, and Shadow finished him a moment later. *Only three left. She really helped.*

At that moment, the woman chose to run toward the edge of the clearing. Kneeling again, now for a quite different reason, the one with the arrow in his buttocks finally broke its triangular iron point and was now trying to take the wooden shaft out of his body. I ignored him; he was too busy to be a threat.

Stepping back fast, I forced the two thugs still able to fight to follow me, then I disengaged, running around, counting on their wounded legs, until one of them was blocking the other, and I cut his face with a swift cross, on the run. The last standing one ran toward the horses, trying to escape. Scared by his erratic movement, the horses moved away from him. Before I could catch him from behind, an arrow pierced his neck. I forced myself to turn slowly. Half-kneeled on the ground, the woman had a bow in her hands, and seemed accustomed to using it. With the leader, I played the same game they had played with the woman, allowing him for a moment the impression that he could escape. He did not.

I half-kneeled beside the woman, who was breathing hard, her eyes fixed on me. I had a habit of leaning my sword on the knee that was not on the ground, and accidentally Shadow's blade touched her body. She stared at me, her eyes wide.

"No fear," I said one of the few phrases I knew in Frankis. "No fear," I repeated after a while, as my first words did not calm her.

Her nostrils were flaring, and she pushed my blade away with a stiff hand.

"Sorry," I suddenly realized, and stuck Shadow into the ground, raising my empty hands in front of her. That improved the situation, and I gently pulled her until she was finally standing. In the silence that followed, I stared at her, unable to speak; her beauty erased any trace of Frankis from my mind. She was like a dream.

"Thank you." She stepped back, measuring me with inquisitive eyes, her face already composed, as if she had the strength to erase every bad memory from her mind. There was a fleeting hint of warmth in her stare, before her stance turned back into that of a cautious warrior woman.

The most beautiful woman I ever saw. She will not bite if I speak wrongly. "Codrin," I patted my chest. *Very impressive speech.* "You?" I pointed with two fingers toward her. Her eyes widened; her face stiffened. *You must be surprised by my fluency.*

She slapped me with surprising force, pushing my body into Zor, already staying behind me – a habit from his training. He moved unsteadily, trotting on the ground. *Stupid woman! I just want to know your name. If I wanted something else...* I had never hit a woman, but there was also a look in her eyes telling me that she was genuinely angry, frightened and determined for I did not know what, and all those feelings enhanced in a strange way the gracious contours of her face.

Easy... She must be in shock. Let's try again. "I am Codrin," I finally found the right Frankis words. *The slap worked well...* "Who are you?" I pointed again at her with my fingers. Realizing too late that twice I had given her my real name, I cursed loudly at my own stupidity. Spoken in Arenian, the curse had no influence on her.

A flurry of feelings reflected on her face, then she smiled coyly, and touched gently the same part that she had slapped before. I was totally aghast, my experience with women was close to zero, and anyway, there was nothing usual in her behavior or mine. She grabbed my hand, arranging my fingers until I was pointing at her with one of them.

What's wrong with two?

"I am Jara. Sorry. You are so young. Never…" A mumble of unintelligible words followed.

"I don't understand."

"Never … two fingers … woman." She spoke slowly this time, and the four words I understood made me guess that it was more than rude to point with two fingers at a woman.

If you say so. "All right," I shrugged. "Horse," I pointed with two fingers, and she burst into laughter. *It must be wrong with the horse too.*

Annoyed, I ignored her and went to the thugs' dead leader, a young man in his early twenties. She grabbed her bow from the grass and followed me while I watched her feline movement. Catching my eyes, she just shrugged. The man had no colors, but even dead, he had that cockiness suggesting someone important. I did not know him – nothing unusual for a stranger like me. There was no reaction on Jara's face either, just a deep gaze, trying to anchor his hated face in her memory. *He is dead…* I shook my head and looked again at his body. *The armor…* My ring-mail was now too small, and the cuts were endangering me. He was almost as tall as me, with a larger frame. *I will fill it well in a year or two.* It was not easy to take off his ring-mail, but it was worth the effort. A heavy purse followed, his heraldic ring that could help to identify him later, then I saw the necklace with a small medallion. *Tomis,* I instantly recognized the place where it was made. *Really far from here.* Tomis was east of Arenia, but there is no other place in the world able to beat them in crafting gold and gems.

Jara reacted strangely. She bit her lip, and her eyes widened, yet I did not see greed in their sparking eyeballs, just sadness and grief. Uncontrolled, her hand moved, stopping just before grabbing the necklace from my hand. She froze instantly, then her hand recoiled, her lips moving with no sound.

It must be a sad story... "Jara," I said gently and offered the necklace.

There were tears in her eyes when she took it from my hand. "Thank you," she said. I understood nothing from the torrent of words that followed.

In silence, I pointed to the bodies, and she nodded. One by one, we carried them toward a deep ravine, fifty paces inside the forest and threw them there. His people could come and follow us, and I supposed that Jara was living nearby. I looked for their horses, but they were all gone; the smell of blood had frightened them off. There was nothing left to show that death had visited the place, apart from some dark spots of blood on the ground, which would vanish with the first rain. Hidden hoof-beats came to us through the forest, and I could not know to whom those horses belonged. I grabbed Jara and raised her onto my horse's back. She stiffened, but I escaped unharmed, and I jumped in the saddle, passing the halter over her head. "Where?" I asked.

"That way." She pointed toward a small path into the forest, then another rain of unintelligible words followed. There was no need for more, and I pushed Zor into a gallop. After a while, she realized that I could not understand and fell silent. The rain started and, a minute later, another horse appeared, riding in parallel with us. Jara stopped me. The mare came to her, and she mounted fast.

The rain was gone when we entered the house through a sculpted door made of dark brown wood – a hunting scenery, rich in details: an archer on horse following a deer through the forest. Our boots left two small trails of water through the hall. In a corner of the next room, a servant was cooking dinner.

Known and unknown flavors stirred my hunger, and I swallowed hard. Jara said something to the servant, pointing to an adjacent room. I understood nothing. The servant left and came back with a bathrobe and hushed me out from the kitchen. Inside the small room, I took all my wet clothes off. The bathrobe was too large, but dry, and that was good enough. Back in the large kitchen, Jara was gone and the servant had tied a rope close to the fire, to dry my clothes.

"Thank you," I said to her. Then I dared to ask, pointing with the correct one finger. "I am Codrin. You are?"

"Milene." She smiled before returning to her pots.

I sat in a chair, close to the fire, waiting for Jara to come back. Feeling no danger, I fell asleep until a man's voice woke me up – Jara was still away. Women need a little bit more time to change their clothes than men. The tall and well-built Knight frowned at me, then at Milene, who answered him. I understood only Jara.

"Good evening," I practiced my Frankis skills, standing up. "I am Codrin." He nodded to me and left the room with the moves of a skilled fighter. *At least I understood the nod.*

The man came back, then two girls erupted in the room. They stopped, looking startled at me. The man shook his head, making the girls ignore me, and I avoided interacting with them – misunderstandings may be dangerous. The oldest girl resembled my twin sister, and I struggled not to gape at her. Jumping on one foot around the table, the youngest one started to pick things from the plates, and I swallowed again. Smiling, Milene menaced her with a long spoon.

Back in the room, Jara placed me at the table in front of the youngest girl. *Eleven years*, I guessed while she was staring at me with undisguised curiosity. *I am not an ogre.* On my left, a boy close to my age ignored me. There was a moment of silence until Jara presented me.

"Codrin," she said in a warm tone, and I nodded toward them before sitting. "... forest he ... life..."

She spoke for a few minutes, her voice calm as if she were telling an old story. The girls' eyes widened, upgrading me from ogre to something better. I used the moment to smile at the girl in front. She smiled back. I caught the eyes of the man; he was studying me with a strange intensity.

We ate with foreign words flowing slowly around me, leaving a faint impression of restraint caused by the stranger arriving from nowhere. At the end of the meal, I took the ornate box Delia gave me when I left Arad and opened it on my knee, so they could not see it. I took out a small cake, and keeping it well hidden in my palm, I placed it slowly in front of the younger girl, Vio. There was sudden silence, their eyes fixed on me, but no other reaction around the table. I pulled back my hand, leaving the cake in front of her. Her eyes wide open, she glanced at Jara, who nodded with a smile, and the cake vanished from the table, a moment later, filling her mouth.

"Vio," Jara reproached her, half-amused. "Is it good?" *Yes*, Vio nodded, unable to speak. "What do you say?"

"Mmmmmh," Vio mumbled, to everybody's laughter.

I pushed the second cake to Saliné, the eldest daughter, around fourteen years old, and she acted with natural elegance.

"Thank you," she said, staring at me with her green eyes.

There was an enigmatic deepness in them that did not match her age, and I realized that she had inherited her mother's eyes, while Vio's were blue. Then she smiled, just barely, a brief, flitting thing. *Beautiful.* Short as it was, that smile was warm and endearing, enhancing even more Saliné's fair face. Unable to avoid another glance at her, I gave cakes to all of them.

"Mefilene from Muniker." Jara recognized the cake made of almonds, and I had the strange feeling that the famous cake enhanced my status as much as the quality of my curved swords.

The dinner ended in a serenity that I wanted to feel again, and Jara took me to the room I was to sleep – a large one, and there was a bathtub made from a barrel, filled with hot water. *How long would they allow me to stay? Maybe they need a protector...* Late in the night, unable to sleep, I sat down in a recessed window seat and leaned against the cold glass. Shadow was leaning against the wall, close to me. Slowly, I gripped the hilt, breathing fast in anticipation. Nothing happened. I clenched and unclenched my fingers. *Still nothing. Perhaps it behaves differently before a battle. Or perhaps it was my imagination. I was scared.* I relaxed, feeling the quiet of the house, and reached over to unlatch the window. The breeze came in, and the unfiltered light of the trembling stars too; there was no moon yet. I could hear the wind running below in the darkness, making a soft, continuous murmur through the forest. With the passing of time, the stars turned with the sky, and far in front, the moon crept over the mountains.

In the morning, after breakfast, the children and Milene left the room, and Jara asked me to stay. She started with small questions that I handled well, then everything moved to more complicated things until I was no longer able to understand or answer.

"Litvonian, Silvanian, Arenian?" I asked, frustrated that our conversation was going nowhere, and the risk of misunderstandings was too high. I had enjoyed the evening and hoped to stay a few days more, just to rest and feel normal again.

"Litvonian." Jara smiled, and everything became much easier.

I could not tell them everything, but I did not lie to them, just avoided strange things like being the legitimate King of

Arenia. My tale became the story of a young nobleman, who had lost his family and found refuge in Frankis. The names of the merchants I worked for and their cities were kept hidden, too – they belonged to the other me, Tudor. Cernat, the tough man who spoke little, asked once about my castle and city, but I ignored his question, and he no longer insisted.

When I finished, Jara told me that she was hunting in the forest, and hid behind some bushes, dismounted, when the men appeared on the road. Her mare was scared by the thunder – the neigh I heard – and ran away. On horses, the men surrounded her fast.

Slowly, she took out the necklace with the medallion I had given her. "This necklace was my wedding gift to my husband. It was stolen when … when he was killed a year ago. I am grateful for recovering it, and please forgive my reaction in the forest." She stopped, looking at me with her large green eyes. "Thank you."

"The necklace found its legitimate owner." I shrugged and glanced at Cernat.

"Cernat is my father. And a second story." This time, there was a glimmer in her eyes. "Pointing two fingers is reserved for asking sexual favors from whores or if you want to force a woman. Arenia seems to be different in this aspect, and he used it for me, with some … unpleasant consequences," she explained to Cernat, who looked at me with a brief glimmer in his eyes.

"Well, I understand now why you laughed when I pointed in the same way to my horse," I said, amused, and she burst into laughter.

"May I see the ring?" Cernat asked when the laughter subsided, and it looked to me that his question followed naturally after the necklace story. "Just to see the heraldic insignia."

I kept it for the same thing, I thought, pushing the ring to him. *I bet you have a much better chance of finding something.*

"S'Arad house," both whispered with a sudden anger, without touching the ring, and a flurry of unknown words followed.

"From Arad," I said, just to remind them that I was still there.

"Sorry," Jara went back to Litvonian. "Just some bad, old memories. Hide the ring; it belonged to Bernd, Orban's eldest son from his first marriage. Orban S'Arad is the Grand Seigneur of Arad."

Yes, I nodded, suddenly trying to understand the consequences of killing the son of the most powerful man in the region. *Did Orban kill her husband?* I glanced at Jara's necklace.

"I will keep it hidden, too," she misjudged my glance. "Why did he ride incognito?"

"I have to train Veres." Cernat stood up. It looked again natural, but my impression was that he was trying to avoid further discussion about the men in the forest and their stealth ride. "Codrin, would you like to join us?"

"Yes, my last training was a long time ago." *If I don't count my fighting to survive.* Taking my curved swords, I followed him into a Weapons Room, and that made me wonder about their status. The house was large, but not a castle – it was missing any defensive walls, and I saw no other armed man apart from Cernat. Jara had a bow, but two-armed people were not enough to guard such large property. It looked like a hunting house belonging to a Seigneur, but having no knowledge about the Frankis architecture, I was not sure.

"May I see your swords"? Cernat asked.

I knew of no one outside the Assassins Order fighting with curved swords, and I watched him closely, but he seemed unaware. There was an explanation for his lack of knowledge:

after the first kingdoms emerged from the remnants of the old Alban Empire, the Order settled in a lawless area south-east of Arenia – it did not suit the Assassins to stay inside a zone where authority backed by superior force could endanger them. They had business, but not settlements in the kingdoms; the liaison people Tudor knew in Tolosa were not Assassins.

Because of the blunder of giving Jara my real name, I decided that 'Codrin' would always use curved swords while 'Tudor' the straight Arenian one, to keep my identities separate. *Maybe it was a lucky blunder... Tudor, who is Panait's Lead Protector, has nothing to do with the man who killed a powerful S'Arad.*

Cernat touched Shadow's blade, then knocked it with his knife. "Good steel," he reacted to the high pitch sound. Veres came closer too but did not touch my swords.

"Shadow," I bragged involuntarily. "Its name," I added quickly, pointing at the dark hues playing on the blue blade.

"You are naming them, interesting. And the other one?" He pointed to the short sword.

"Flame," I said only because I had to answer; it came too late to me that revealing the names was another blunder, linking me even more to the Assassins.

"Elegant and well-crafted. You have good smiths in Arenia." If Cernat had some peculiar thoughts about the number of swords I carried with me, he did not show it. The Assassins' swords were better than the Arenian ones, which anyway were better than the ones used here; Arenia was a more developed place.

"Our swords are made of iron from a large meteorite, and its place is known only by a few," Tudor told me once. "The blade is folded back on itself a thousand times in the forging, to gain strength and springiness. But these are the only things I can reveal to you." His voice was still fresh in my mind and the memories overwhelmed me. Busy checking the sword, Cernat ignored my lapse.

"Take a leather armor and a wooden sword." Cernat pointed to a wall where several of them were hanging. "I need to make an assessment before training. Veres, watch us."

We performed some warm-up steps, studying each other, then he moved fast with a series of cross-hits that I parried. He was not Tudor, yet he was better than most of our sword masters in Arenia – of course, it's difficult to be equal to an Assassin Grand Master. He tried a second series, with stronger hits. I answered by dancing around to avoid the full blows, parrying when they were already half-consumed, and set several traps of my own, too. He avoided them easily, but I had used no Assassins' tricks yet. After another series of blows, I found a split-second and let his sword come down unanswered. He leaned forward from his own inertia. I slid aside, and my blade touched his neck.

"Clever move," Cernat said, stepping back, and I enjoyed my moment, trying not to look too obvious. In his corner, Veres was frowning, irritated by my small victory. "You are fast and have very good body coordination, but I told you this is not a duel or training, just a trial to understand your aptitudes."

"What do I have to do?"

"It seems that we have a different understanding of the same thing. We come from distinctive fighting schools, so no offense. Don't attack, just defend yourself."

Cernat threw everything at me for a long time, pressing me forcefully. Twice he scratched my leather armor, and once I had to roll on my back, after letting his sword pass without a parry. Trying to meet it would have altered the equilibrium of my body, pushing me onto the wrong foot. You can roll back only when the enemy is slightly destabilized, like when his hard blow goes unanswered and the body is following it by inertia. Then tiredness started to take a toll on me. *It's not fair*, I mumbled, usually I could counteract fast and stop the fight. When I thought that there was nothing else to come, a swift suite of very strong strokes followed; up, down, down, up again, down, and each time I recovered slightly slower for the next hit until the last one caught me in full. His blade hit my chest, yet the impact was not hard; he had already anticipated and slowed his hand. In his corner, Veres was jubilant.

"Interesting," Cernat said thoughtfully, as if speaking to himself. "I never met anyone faster than you. In a two or three, your force will match your speed. I would not want to meet you in battle. Wrong," he said, after a short pause. "I don't want to meet you even now in battle."

It felt good, yet I saw again a bad spark in Veres's eyes, and this time I was annoyed. *You will make problems for me...* I left the Weapons Room and went out of the house to see Zor in the large stable that could host twenty horses. The girls were in the garden, and I watched them playing, without getting too close. *I would like to join them...* The next days passed intensely slowly, in a wait and see feel that no one tried to resolve – they never mentioned anything about my stay, and I did not have the nerve to ask, trying passively to prolong the good moments as much as I could.

⋙⋘

"Higher!" Vio said, sitting comfortably in my raised arms, trying to reach a bunch of cherries, and I turned a bit to give her a better position. "I want the big ones there," she pointed to a branch that was not far from her hand.

It was my third week in their house, and we were in full cherry season. At the edge of the garden, Jara and Cernat were caught in a discussion that, if not an argument, was at least contradictory. *They are pointing at me...* I watched them out of the corner of my eye, pretending to be unaware. When Vio finally reached her treasure, I let her down, and walked quickly to the garden's edge. Saliné was waiting for the same thing, but something was obviously wrong in my behavior. The *two fingers* misunderstanding resurfaced in my mind.

"I apologize for my behavior with your daughters." I tried to pre-empt any negative reaction. "From now on, I will stay away from them." Jara and Cernat stared at me in silence, with a weird expression on their faces. *What was so bad? Just helping them to pick cherries, nothing inappropriate.* "I can leave tomorrow," I said hesitantly, with a calm that was only apparent, leaving place for a longer stay if things were forgiven.

"What are you talking about?" Jara asked, finally.

"You were worried when I raised Vio in my arms to pick cherries. I assure you that there was nothing inappropriate."

"Codrin, we are planning to leave for a day soon and let you guard the house and the girls."

"Then why were you angry?"

"I was not angry." She smiled, placing her hand on my shoulder. "It's just that we have only one horse, and … and we did not know if you would agree to lend Zor to my father."

"Of course," I said at once, even though it meant letting someone else ride my horse for the first time, and I wondered if my desire for a longer stay was not slowing my survival reflexes. *What is done, is done.*

"Thank you," Jara smiled again. "I think that Saliné feels mistreated right now; she did not receive the inappropriate cherry-picking session from you." Her laughter filled the garden and, involuntarily, I caressed her hand, still on my shoulder, before turning back to the girls.

That evening, Saliné pulled a lyre from a large chest made of polished acajou wood, dark red color like her hair. Her elegance and charm struck at me, and having once seen this, I could not forget it, just as we cannot forget a revelation. Gently, like a mother caressing her child, she plucked a string with delicate fingers, and the note filled the room, warm and vibrant. When her fingers moved to play, all my thoughts vanished. The music became a lonely spirit in the room, creating space for even more beauty in the candles' light. With a clear, rich treble, her voice joined the crystalline vibrato of the strings. Unknown, her song swarmed through me with the warmth of sunshine and the softness of silk. My mind recessed and sailed in the faraway – inside the Music Chamber of the Arenian Royal Castle, where my sister, Ioana, used to sing for us – and stayed there until the last note vanished. When Saliné finished, my chest felt strangely hollowed, from losing again even the shadow of my family. It took me a while to recover and observe that I was alone in the room. That night, for the first time, my brother's bloody face did not haunt my dreams.

Chapter 9 – Jara

"You are enjoying it." Father was testing Codrin's horse, on the road to Severin. *Zor*, I remembered his name, meaning haste in Arenian. It was a short ride; down in the valley, the castle and city were visible from our house.

"Damned to be if I don't. I never rode such a horse. Codrin told me it comes from the dry steppes south-east of Arenia. Never heard of them until now."

Listening, a curious thought resurfaced in my mind. "I just remembered... The King of Arenia was slain two years ago. It matches Codrin's story. Maybe he is..." There was something mysterious in the air, making me part of an old story.

"When kings are killed, other people of high rank lose too. Codrin told us little of his past, understandable from what happened to him, and he could be a Seigneur by birth, but there is nothing to tell if he really is a King's son. Disappointed?"

"Well, yes. The princess is usually saved by a prince," I laughed. "He is good with the sword and with the bow."

"He maybe even better than Marcus, the famous duelist who found refuge at my father's court and put the first sword in my hand. And Codrin is not even seventeen years old." Father shook his head in wonder. "Arenia has a level of training that is hard to imagine. It's almost like dancing. And Codrin is one with his sword when fighting, something that I could never achieve. You are thinking of Codrin to replace...?" Father wanted to bring some of our guards from the past, but I doubted we could trust them again – allegiances change fast, and we no longer had the power to renew old bonds.

"Another team of assassins may attack us." *Orban's men in the forest had no colors. Were they here for us? None of them knew me though, that's why they tried to...*

"We should be more careful before letting a stranger settle in our house," Father said after a while, as if he did not want to touch the subject.

"A stranger from far away has no links to the S'Arads, and there is bad blood between Codrin and Orban. He saved my life, fighting alone against six men. Codrin is longing for a new home. I feel it. And he is too young for a double game or treachery. How many would give me back a necklace worth five hundred galbeni just for some tears in my green eyes?" I waited for an answer that did not come; Father was a caution man. "We are always paying our debts, aren't we? He works well with the girls." *And he likes me*, I almost smiled, remembering his discreet gallant gestures that were not at all impolite; there was a certain subtlety in Codrin.

"If Orban finds out who killed his son..."

"There are only two survivors, and Dochia may be right..." I recalled her Vision that could apply to Codrin, or to somebody else, but a tingle of instinct rippled through me. *Codrin came from Arad. And what did Umbra say? 'One young man dies. One young man lives.' Bernd was twenty-three.*

"Did she speak Codrin's name?" Father asked, a hint of aloofness filling his voice. He had a grudge against the Wanderers because they had tried to stop his marriage with Mother, and that made me hide from him that Vio had the Light.

"No." I shrugged, but we both knew how difficult was to decrypt a Wanderer's message – it was never clear to me if their words were obscure by intention or because their Visions were limited. "We have already left him alone with the girls." Father did not answer, and we continued the ride in silence, yet I was sure that Codrin was occupying his mind, too. "He will be a good match to Saliné." *He is intelligent and … handsome.* There was also a surprising sensitivity in him. People who suffer his kind of fate in their childhood, choose to harden themselves, raising barriers, suppressing their feelings. Stones that walk, think and eat. There are a few, however, who develop a new understanding of events' consequences on people. They remain human, tough and kind at the same time.

"You are going too far. Saliné is special, and she was marked by the Circle. Not to mention being too young for marriage right now. Vio will pass the test, too," Father said, thoughtfully. "There are only five more marked girls in Frankis, and three scored far lower than Saliné. Only Cleyre Peyris and Marie Tolosa are equal to her. Strange that they tested Saliné one year earlier than usual."

Yes, but Cleyre and Marie are Dukes' granddaughters... "What can be stranger than the Circle? I don't think Veres will take the test." As much I liked Vio's chances, it would be better for the family if Veres were marked.

"He will not be tested. If everything goes well, we will match Saliné with a Seigneur."

Arriving in front of Severin main gate, we slowed; there were merchants on the road. Flanked by two brick columns each decorated with a single letter, S, the gate was open, and Vlaicu, the Chief of the Guard, stood under the portcullis, waiting for us. The walls were not tall; Severin was a hard to defend city. Mohor's residence was small, but it had a terrace and a garden in the backyard. The terrace was filled with people that I had known for a long time already, and our greetings did not lack warmth, even when we were ready to stir a war.

Before anything would start, Father made a brief summary of our ingrate condition. "Once the armistice between the Dukes in the north ends, Orban will attack us to expand his lands further. We all know that." He gestured around the terrace. "Cantemir, the Master Sage of the Circle, is Orban's Secretary, and Bernd, is a good army commander." He avoided the rumors about Bernd's disappearance, but Arpan, the Spatar of Arad was a fine commander too. "If Orban wins, we will lose our lands, and our lives. We must stop him." He stared at each of us, one by one. "For our alliance!" Father raised his goblet, and everybody drank the wine in silence.

"How strong is the Circle?" Knight Konrad asked. The Circle was a secretive order, working at a certain level, and many Knights and even some Seigneurs had not much knowledge about it.

"The Circle has no army, if you talk about that kind of power, but it influences many things through its net of Sages. We know some from their council and the Itinerant Sages, but no outsider knows the Hidden Sages among us."

"You were once part of the Circle. Any chance to open some negotiations?" Mohor asked, looking at me.

"Sage for one month," I said with bitter humor, "as Secretary of Midia until they decided that I can't be part of the Circle."

"It may be a cause for that," Aron said slightly derisively, implying that women are inferior stock.

"Of course, there is, just not the ignorant people think of. Dukes, Seigneurs and Knights, are not allowed to be Sages." There were exceptions though. I heard rumors that a few Knights were accepted, but never a Seigneur or a Duke; the Circle did not allow people of great power in its ranks.

Our talk moved in waiting mode, so only general things were touched on, just to create an ambiance for the more serious things to come later, and everything went well until Aron began to act erratically. With no visible logic, he injected things that usually come after the main points are agreed. We were far from there, but he started a quarrel, asking three important fortresses for Mohor.

You need only one of those fortresses, I glanced at Mohor; he was calm. *What strategy is this? It's just poisoning the atmosphere.*

Irritated, our would-be partners in the alliance refused to debate the spoils of war in such an early phase, and Aron acted even more strangely, raising his voice, and making rude comments. The others answered in kind.

"If you don't mind a break." I smiled icily, and stepped down from the terrace, to walk in the garden. With a calculated delay, Mohor came after me.

"Can we take a few steps together?" He lent me his arm, the first familiarity of this kind from him.

I turned my head, and together with his face, I saw all the guests staring at us; the terrace was in a higher position. "You are pressing them too much, and for some theoretical land gains you may weaken the alliance. From all those three fortresses, only Magura is of strategic importance for you, it guards the northern route to Dorna. The other two are liabilities; there are no easy access roads for you, and the costs of keeping them will be too high." It was an oblique insinuation to his low revenues – Mohor's lands were mostly average or under the average quality.

"Good evaluation. I wanted to discuss two things with you and Cernat, but it would have been difficult to extract him from the terrace right now. Their position is weaker than mine," he gestured at the nervous people still seated at the table. "Two of them are Orban's vassals. If I remember well your opinion, it's as bad to be his vassal as it's to be his enemy. Any negotiation is just an art to extract the most possible in a given situation."

"I hardly see any art in Aron's growls and brutal maneuvering."

"Art may sometimes depict a brutal world. You live on my land, even though there are no hierarchic links between us. In many ways, both of you," he included Father, "are still a *Grand*."

You are trying to sweeten the pill. We are Grands *on your lands.* I smiled at my involuntary rhyme, and he glanced curiously at me. "So, you want to say that our particular geographical situation should be reflected in negotiations."

"Can I rather say that it's in our common interest," his hand gestured fast between us, "to have a better-coordinated approach?"

"We all have a common interest. Orban. And some private ones that may compete here or there."

"I would like a more explicit answer to my question." We were no longer walking, and our bodies stopped in a position that let our eyes meet. There was a moderate expectation in his eyes and a smile on his lips. Mohor had some charm, and he knew it. "Any alliance needs a leader, and there are now two candidates for it. The ones who will tip the balance are you and Cernat. My feeling is that the geography will work to our advantage."

"You want an alliance inside an alliance," I advanced prudently. *Are you proposing marriage, too?* There were already some subtle signs from him regarding some interest a man can have for a woman. I remembered things from the last month's encounters, disparate words, he touching my shoulder when inviting me inside today, some glances during the negotiation, and I was still hanging on his arm.

"Yes. I don't need an answer right now, but I will appreciate some help: to stop any discussion about land and castles. I know," he laughed. "Aron started it at my request. Let's say that I needed it to happen, but now we have to move on."

It took a while to calm the spirits back on the terrace but, guessing that something had happened, Father helped me stop the quarrel, and things advanced fast afterward.

"Mohor expressed some interest in you." Father raised a brow at me after we left the castle. "Maybe you should encourage him." This time, he smiled.

"There were some signals." *Thirty-four... I am still young. Mohor is not Malin, but not a bad choice either. I am three years older than Mohor. No, that is not the right choice of words. He is three years younger.* For some time now, Malin had morphed from my beloved husband into a dream coming from another life that had nothing in common with the new one. *Only the children... Mohor can help them.* For a few moments, Codrin's image overshadowed Mohor's, and I shook my head in disbelief. *He could be my son...* "Mohor proposed an alliance, based on our ... geographic proximity. He considers us the ones who decide the leader of the alliance."

"So, your walk in the garden was more than an agreement to stop the fight for land. Why did he start it?"

"He needs only Magura but wants to keep some pressure on them. And we need to keep some pressure on him." Both of us started to laugh, pushing the horses to a gallop.

We arrived home just in time for dinner, and afterward, in a succession of things that had already become routine, Father and Veres went to sleep, and I stayed, taking turns in reading a book with Saliné and Vio. Codrin stayed with us, hoping to improve his skills in Frankis, or perhaps he was enjoying the calm of evening too. There was longing still burning in him; the desire to feel the warmth of a family. Unaware, this tough young man was, in some ways, still a child in his heart and mind, and his untimely interactions with the adult world would provoke and test him further. I had the feeling that his toughness, great fighting skills and titled past would be, at times, his weakness. Through my Light, I foresaw that Aron will be a threat for both Codrin and my family. I tried to evaluate him again: how the tenderness in his hazel eyes suppressed the hardness of the slight scar along his chin, how his self-confidence balanced the boyishness which made him seem naive.

"Tell me a story," Vio asked Codrin in Litvonian and moved on the sofa close to him, raising her legs on to it, in parallel with the backrest, leaning back on Codrin.

Surprised, he put one arm around Vio's shoulders, then glanced at me, a touch of panic in his eyes, and I could not but smile, both to calm him, and in reaction to her outgoingness toward him. *She needs support... Father is too old and busy. Veres too young and... Insensitive*? I wished Veres were like Saliné; she was more mature, even when she was two years younger. Visibly pleased, Vio stretched a bit more, making herself comfortable in his arms. *Can Codrin...?*

Gently, his hand covered Vio's head with spread fingers, turning it slowly until she faced him. "What kind of story do you have in mind?"

Like Malin was doing it. Even the question was the same. The corner of my eye caught Saliné gripping the chair with her right hand. There were both a spirit and a young man filling her mind. *She likes Codrin...*

"One about Arenia," Vio answered, a large smile spread on her face – she was in the middle of the action.

"Arenia." Codrin sighed, struggling to control his emotions; Vio was so good at stirring everyone's ghosts.

"Do you want to be my father?" Vio asked when he finished the story. It was just a spontaneous question from a young girl who missed her father, yet we looked started.

"What?" Vio asked again, not understanding the silence.

"Perhaps Codrin is too young to be a father," I said softly. "Would you consider a brother?"

"Yes," Vio smiled. "Can I have another story, brother?"

After a month, Malin appeared again in my dreams. He was warm, gentle and merry. He was Malin, and Fate seemed to grant me sometimes in my dreams what was seized from me in the real life.

Is Codrin the sign of better times to come?

Home

Chapter 10 – Codrin

"What are you doing?" Vio asked, her voice tight and worried, and she extended her hand, ready to help me. Behind her, all the family and Milene, staring at me with various facial expressions. Vio had alerted everybody that something strange was happening to me in the garden.

Trouble... I was standing on one foot, the other one raised almost vertically, half flexed. My hands spread wide, at different angles to my body, all my parts contorted in strange ways – the Assassins Dance in its full splendor. For the uninitiated, everything seems bizarre or wicked. It's not really a dance, not in the generally accepted sense of dancing, yet some steps look that way, fluidity and grace. Others make you look like a deranged crane, which is how I looked now. In the end, everything is training, hard and strenuous.

"Training." I forced myself to keep moving like a deranged crane, just to enforce an impression of normality. "The ... hmm

... Warriors Dance." I moved with fluid and elegant dancing-like steps, hoping to convince them.

"Tumbler," Veres sneered, and his eyes glittered with derision.

"Veres!" Jara snapped, but her nervousness did not disappear when she turned to watch me again.

They think I am crazy. Mostly Veres. He never liked me. Why? I am not competing with him. I checked them all; only Cernat retained a studied calm. Vio and Saliné were worried. Jara was undecided. *I need something...* "Can a tumbler do this?" I jumped to a height of a normal man, almost horizontally. Twisting my body, I hit an imaginary enemy with my right boot and landed on both feet. *Eh?* I proudly looked around.

"Tumbler!" Veres shouted and clapped ironically.

I failed. And there is no way to put Veres in his place without escalating things. In silence, I continued my training, hoping that at least they would ignore me.

"You are wrong," Vio scoffed at Veres, moving between us.

"That was not nice, Veres," Saliné said, gentle and firm at the same time, stepping closer to Vio. "Codrin is our friend. And it doesn't look to me like tumbling at all. It's just a ... different type of training. Some steps were indeed like dancing."

Veres looked suddenly uncomfortable, and his face reddened. "Girls," he snapped derisively, and kicked a pebble toward Vio that slightly missed her left foot, and I laid a hand on her tense shoulder to calm her. Jara looked at me, nodding slightly, and Veres stepped back, his eyes moving fast from one girl to another.

Veres is afraid of them. It can't be.

"You are wrong, Veres," Cernat said thoughtfully, trying to anchor my moves to his fighting knowledge. "That kick would have put a man down."

"Put down or killed. It depends on the speed, force and my foot's position against his neck vertebrae. I can do the same with my hands. Look." I demonstrated another set of moves, hitting my imaginary enemy with the edge of my palm, as I had with the huge, drunken man in the Caravans' Inn in Muniker.

"What's a *vertebrae*?" Vio asked.

It must have another name in Frankis... The name was similar in Litvonian, Silvanian and Arenian, all four main languages were derived from some colloquial dialects spoken in the old Alban Empire that vanished six hundred years ago. "Did you see Milene taking the meat from a rabbit? There are some small bones in the spine, linked together by cartilage: vertebrae. You have them too. Where the marrow is."

"Aha!" Vio exclaimed, the marrow finally told her something that she could understand, and moreover taste.

At that moment, Veres chose to leave, and Jara tried to say something to him. She stopped for a moment, then addressed me: "Codrin, lunch is ready in one hour." A neutral remark that said nothing about her real feelings.

"Mother, I will stay with Codrin," Saliné said, and again, I observed that depth in her green eyes, unusual for a child.

"Me too," Vio added quickly, grabbing my hand, yet something was bothering her a little.

"Just don't be late," Jara agreed, leaving us, and this time there was a slight amusement in her tone.

"Thank you," I whispered to both girls.

"Are our vertebrae like the rabbit's?" Vio let out her worries, and I nodded, winking at her. "I am not a rabbit!" she exclaimed, half-amused.

"Yes, you are," I laughed, catching her in my arms. "A little rabbit. See?" I moved my fingers on her ribs, like playing a flute, and she started laughing in outbursts while my fingers moved faster and faster. Her laughter got louder, and she tried to fight back.

"Saliné, help!" she cried through her laughter, and both attacked me until I surrendered and begged for mercy.

When they were finally satisfied with my torture, we lay down on the grass, my arms spread wide, their heads leaning on them, close to my shoulders. Jara turned back to the house, laughing. *Life is all about moments.* Somewhere in a tree, unknown birds were singing a melodious trill. Another group answered, farther away. There was humming in the air and a blue sky. *It's good. It's so good.* And after so many years, tears filled my eyes, and I forgot everything.

A finger moved slowly over my face, tracing the tears. The touch was light, as if Saliné was afraid to hurt me, and I said nothing; I could not explain in words, neither to me nor to them, and I could not look weak either.

"I liked some parts of your dance." Saliné moved things away from my weakness. "I would like to learn it. We were attacked a month ago."

"I will teach you. And I will always protect you."

"Always," Saliné agreed and placed her small hand over mine.

The next day, I trained Jara and the girls, and it was soon clear that Jara was well trained, and that Saliné had learned some things too while Vio moved with puzzling speed and body coordination. Veres refused categorically to be a tumbler, not even Cernat could convince him. A week later, Cernat came with Senal, the Secretary of Severin, and with Vlaicu, the Chief of the Guard. I was able to fight both Vlaicu and Cernat at the same time, and no one said anything about my training anymore. At least, nothing bad. I did not cross any sword with Senal, an old man with long white hair, tied in a ponytail, yet I felt instantly close to him – by some strange circumstances he reminded me of Tudor, and we talked many things about Arenia and Silvania before he left.

"Some fifty years ago, I traveled to Arenia. I was still young," Senal said with a sigh. We were sitting in a corner of the dining room, all other adults absorbed in some political conversations. "I arrived in your capital, Alba, at the coronation of the new king. A lot of glamour; I still remember the festivities." He stared at me, and I forced myself to look away; he was talking about Grandfather, and everyone in Arenia knew that I resembled him.

"Alba is a large and rich city. I never saw a coronation, but we liked to celebrate."

"Yes, yes, Alba is a large city. And you have good wine." Senal seemed almost asleep, his eyes squinted, and he asked me nothing more.

Did he recognize Grandfather in me? It was almost fifty years ago.

The winter was almost gone, and the snow vanished from the land. Only the peaks of the small mountains were still white. Day by day, I felt myself becoming part of the family, and they accepted me too, except Veres. With all my efforts, something didn't work between us. I grew closer to Saliné, but we remained *siblings*, because I was afraid of losing my place. It was strange how swiftly love could re-enter one's world. So, staying at home throughout the winter was in various ways, for some of us, just about different degrees of avoiding each other. There was also the announcement that Jara will marry Mohor at the end of spring.

Twice a month, Mohor was coming to visit Jara and Cernat and, usually, she was sending her children and me to Milene's house on those days, so we never met. That was until the day Mohor came earlier than usual, catching me in front of the house.

"Boy, take the horses," Aron, the strong, tall man I knew was Mohor's Spatar and his most trusted Knight, ordered in a baritone voice that I suspected was not all that natural. He took both horses by their halters and pushed them toward me.

"Take them yourself." As a fugitive I usually did not react that way, with men of power, but I was still a king's son in my heart, not a stable boy, and I could not accept such humiliation.

"Take them or I'll smash your head until you obey," Aron yelled, and this made his voice turn to tenor. Under two bulging eyes, his face reddened, and his right hand shook the halters as if he were thinking to hang me with them. "I will split you into pieces," he growled, almost chewing his words. "Raise your sword." That was the usual Frankis way to provoke a duel, and he unsheathed his sword.

"What kind of duel do you prefer, Big Mouth? First hit, five hits, or to the death?" Prepared for a ride in the forest, I was also armed, and I edged a finger along Shadow's hilt. It answered me with a strange vibration, and I felt danger.

"Codrin! Stop it," Jara said, breathing hard after running out of the house, attracted by the shouts. "Mohor, you are expected in the house."

"Aron will just give a small lesson to your stable boy." Mohor winked at her, amused by the way things had turned. "He deserves it."

"He is not a stable boy. He is part of my family, and I expect him to be treated accordingly," Jara reacted coldly.

"Death duel," Aron said.

"Don't worry, Jara, there will be no death," Mohor whispered to her as if in secret, but loud enough to be heard by everyone. "The boy should be thankful for the lesson." He laughed, lending her his arm, and she had to accept it, but I read in her the confidence that the lesson would go the other way.

Aron was an average swordsman, a pack of trained muscles, a brute. He was using the sword almost like a club, but he was very strong, and that's why he was somehow equal to Vlaicu in duels. As I realized later, neither Vlaicu nor Cernat had told them much about my sword skills, and that explained their confidence. Tudor taught me that the easiest way to fight a brute is to let his force work for you. After several moves countering his sword when the strength of its hit was already half-spent, I dodged, and he lost his balance, his sword hitting just air. Haunted by the *stable boy* slur, I hit his hand with the edge of my blade, making him drop the sword. Then my boot went for the back of his knee, making him lose his footing, and I pushed him to the ground – some basic moves from the Assassin's Dance.

I pressed the tip of my sword to his neck. "Do you prefer a swift death? I don't hear you." His mouth was moving spasmodically, but when you press on a certain point on the neck, the words just refuse to come out.

"Leave him." Mohor's voice was tight and angry, his eyes narrowed to slits, and his soldiers unsheathed their swords, moving closer.

"Codrin, let him go." Jara found her voice. "Mohor, remember that I asked you to stop this."

"Go back," Mohor ordered the soldiers. "Now, young man, let him go."

"Should I understand that the lesson you talked about has been taught?" I asked.

"Codrin!" Jara snapped. "We agreed to end this. Now behave."

"Yes, all of us had something to learn today. Though it may be that some will realize it later," Mohor said, his eyes cold and hard.

I pushed things too much... Need something to give him. "By the Winner's Right, your sword is mine." I picked up Aron's weapon from the ground. "You are not dead yet. I will allow you to buy it back. I trust Seigneur Mohor to price the ransom fairly."

"That's a family sword," Mohor said, after a while. "Passed through generations from father to son. Such things are not for sale."

I hope I placated you well enough. With a brief gesture, I presented the sword to Aron.

"And you have won the right to take our horses to the stable." Mohor's voice was bland, and his face unreadable, but his right gloved hand was opening and closing at his side.

"Codrin," Jara interjected, "help our guests and give the horses to Jeon to take care of them. Mohor, Aron, please come with me."

"As you wish, milady," I said sourly, frowning at her. *I am a stable boy...*

"Thank you, Codrin." She ignored my irritation and went inside with her guests.

Aron's back was covered in mud from his fall, and I caught the soldiers smiling discreetly. *You are not very popular.* One of the soldiers winked at me and, mechanically, I returned the wink, then went away with the horses. In the stable, I mounted Zor and rode up the hill, just to cool my mind. *I am not a stable boy.*

I returned with the darkness and tried to skip the dinner – they were already at the table. In their gentle way, Saliné and Vio forced me to join. Everybody was almost silent; the girls knew what had happened, and I was sure that many things were discussed during lunch. *I would give a finger to know what they said.* Then we read together, without Jara, and during the night, the duel and the *stable boy* taunt haunted me.

Despite the early spring, the next day stayed cold between Jara, Cernat and me. Retrospectively, I conceded that I could have done some things differently with Aron, but it was not my fault. I waited all day to have at least a formal talk, but it never happened; an unpredictable lack of reaction that troubled me.

In the evening, I grasped that my duel had affected their relationship with Mohor and the marriage plans. It was time to leave before being shown the door.

"I will leave tomorrow." Speaking, I turned slowly a glass of wine that looked like an unwanted extension of my hand, and closed my eyes for a moment, hearing my own words like a distorted echo in the room. Jara, Cernat and I, all three of us gathered over a bottle of wine that was not able to stir any conversation. There was a remarkable meaning in the silence that followed, and the short glances exchanged between them.

Cernat reached for his wine and drank. The motion itself seemed strange and unnaturally slow, then he stood up, and walked away. "Codrin," he said, from the door. "We must know what we want from life; if not, we just struggle to survive. Ask yourself where you want to be in five years from now. As I see it, your future is here, with us."

Jara stayed with me, her fingers moving nervously around her own glass, imitating mine. It looked like a magic mirror reflecting a different person. She moved abruptly and sat in the chair next to me, her hand sliding slowly over mine.

"How long do you want to stay away?"

"I won't come back."

She was obviously expecting my answer, as there was no reaction in her fingers. "The girls will miss you, and I like that you are so close to them, especially to Saliné."

Saliné... You are afraid that we would become too close, I suddenly understood. "I have to leave."

"Shh," she pressed a finger to my lips. "Let's talk about yesterday. It seemed that both of us waited for the other one to make the first step."

"I don't know what they told you, but it was not me who started it. The first rule before judging is to hear both sides." I shrugged, knowing that she would have no answer to that. "But

I am just a stable boy," I added, after a while, and tried to pull my hand away from her.

Her grip tightened, stopping me. Not that I could not escape. "Codrin, you are not a stable boy. You are a just young man unable to find his place in the hierarchy," Jara sighed. "You are a noble by birth, and raised in that spirit, but you can't act as an equal to a Seigneur or Knight now. I know how it feels. I was once a Grand Signora. Now I am just a Knight. Isn't that funny? There is no feminine equivalent for Knight," she joked, and her eyes warmed to me. "You made a fool of Mohor's most trusted man. I had to be harsh with you, to placate him for what happened to Aron."

"Big Mouth threatened to smash my head if I didn't take the horses. Did they tell you that?"

"Stop with this Big Mouth thing. Aron is a Knight and Spatar of Severin, a man of power." Her tone was now slightly colder. "You set a trap, pushing him to ask for a duel – don't protest, you knew your skills and assessed Aron's. Aron is Mohor's top dog; you humiliated his dog and put Mohor in a bad position. Not that Aron did not deserve it." She smiled, and her fingers tightened their grip on my hand. "Please understand, sometimes a pinch of humility is needed to survive; that's why I asked you to take the horses. At any time, Mohor or Aron could send ten or more soldiers to kill you."

"Then I need to find my own place." *It will not be easy, and for sure nothing like here.*

"This is your place," she gestured around. "Your home. Some doors will open for you after my wedding. Mohor..."

"Mohor is your future, not mine. During that last stay, I will be more careful with Saliné," I said, with unwanted sadness in my voice, and pulled my hand from hers.

"I don't understand."

"You are working hard to find the highest possible place for your daughters," I repeated her own words. By marriage, Jara would become a Signora, reflecting her status onto her children, and there was not much place for people like me in their new ranks. I knew it from my previous life. Things happen.

Alone in my room, I forced myself to recall every pleasant memory I could remember. Some flowed freely. Others drifted in and out of my brain, half-forgotten fragments of life. Nothing worked; the bitterness of the fugitive was in me again; there might always be that bitterness. *Maybe she is right; we can restart this later, and I can have my place back. And Saliné...* I retraced everything in my thoughts, and it was almost morning when I fell asleep.

Chapter 11 – Codrin

Delia and Panait welcomed me, but it was not the right season for caravans, and I left a few days later, knowing all that moved in Arad and around it. There was an intricate layer of interactions between the Dukes and Seigneurs, more complex than at a royal court. Under normal circumstances, a kingdom has one source of power. Here, the central authority went away after the civil war, and there were many rival centers of influence, a mosaic of competing interests. After the two Dukes in the north, Orban was the strongest Seigneur in the northern half of the former kingdom, and he wanted to extend his power further, becoming a Duke too. The easiest place for him to conquer was south, Mehadia or Severin, or both, and by extension, Jara.

Panait considered me trustworthy, and all other merchants accepted his judgment. It's how I learned about the strange entanglement between Jara and Orban – he both wanted, or even loved, and hated her for reasons that were still unknown to me. One merchant mentioned the Circle, something so powerful, obscure and tenebrous that I considered it just a merchant's story, something like the Flying Mester, another old and famous legend.

The Merchant Guilds were the money veins of the society, and they were linked, in complex ways, with functionaries working in high positions for Seigneurs and Dukes. After the kingdom's dissolution, the merchants were the back channels for communications, arranging peace treaties and marriages. Delia was the daughter of Balan, the First Mester of Deva, and her sister was married to Dan, the Chief of the Guard of Deva, a city smaller than Arad, but two times larger than Severin. We met in Panait's house, and we trained together. Teaching him a few Assassins' tricks helped to make us friends.

Unable to return to the place that I still wanted to call home, I tried my luck guarding the roads out of Arad – it could be a source of friends and money. I was not lucky; the poor family I saved from some petty robbers was, and that came with a hot meal and an evening's talk around the fire. It was a large family – man and wife, with four small children, joined by a strange woman, whose eyes were like burning amber through the flames – moving out from Arad, after Knight Arpan, Orban's Spatar, grabbed his land. Still alive after being chased by a powerful man, the family was not entirely unlucky.

"Cursed be all those thieves, and Knights and soldiers. They burned my house and killed my father." The man burst his anger, after getting accustomed to me. As many other commoners, he believed that Knights were nothing more than thugs who lived for the reckless massacre of innocents.

How often are they right? I did not speak much, just listened; even the humblest peasant could be a good source of information.

"A soldier like Tudor." The strange woman's harsh voice interrupted him. The first words I heard from her. In her early forties, she was tall, dressed as a man, and armed with a knife and a dagger, the length of an arm.

"I apologize," the man added in haste. "Punish me for my weak mind but spare my family."

"Cursed be all the robbers." I smiled to calm him, but his fear lingered. "Quench the fire," I said when the silence went on too long. *Strangers are clear to me*, I involuntarily thought. *Those closer blur my sight.*

"Wait." The old woman spoke for the second time, in a commanding tone, and the man froze, slightly bent. The odor in the air was earthy and damp after the evening rain, and she was rubbing some leaves between her fingers to release an exotic scent.

"Witch! I should not have taken you with us," the man growled, his frightened eyes fixed on her. "She is not part of my family."

"Oh, that is so obvious," the woman laughed. "What a pity that I saved you from that bastard Spatar. Give me your hand," she continued when the man moved his family away, at a safe distance from which they could no longer hear us. "Are you afraid of one woman?" She grabbed my left hand, and I felt her thick tendons pressing on my skin. Then I felt warmth when her palms sandwiched mine. I could not afford to look weak, so I let her play her game. "You are the son of a king," she whispered after a while, and the warmth got even stronger, "but you are not a king." She was forcing herself to breathe hard, trying to impress me.

"Or the son of a shepherd." I barked a brief laugh at her choice of words. Making someone feel important was a known trick for any beggar trying to get money by reading your future.

"Beware of beggars wielding swift swords."

Beware of wolves. It was another known trick, to make you feel a nebulous danger. Fear pays well. "Other than beggars, is there anything else I should worry about?"

"Sickness. Bad weather. Women talking too much." She smiled — a small thing, but it marked her face's muscles even after it was gone. "The *beggars* will cross your way in … two days." She started to hum a slow song and continued like this for a minute that seemed longer. It was a wicked lullaby, taking over me, and I fought hard against a sudden need to yawn. Her palms were glowing white, and I blinked. The light did not vanish, and an inner feeling told me that it was genuine, and known to me, yet I could not remember; my mind was almost paralyzed. With surprising speed, she grabbed her knife and sliced my palm – a small cut. I did not pull my hand from her; she could have cut my throat already.

Are you a Wanderer? Her swift, trained move recalled some almost forgotten words from my mentor:

"The Wanderers sect is even more reclusive than the Assassins. They are the best archers and knife throwers I know, yet they will not shy away from using a sword too. They can see through the future with their White Light. Rumors say that they are witches, who can change a man into a pig, but I'll believe that when I see it. Sometimes they help us, sometimes they don't. The Assassins play with lives; the Wanderers play with information in the same game of power, but don't be fooled; all will play both ways when the necessity arrives. You can recognize the Wanderers by their tattoo: two pairs of wings on their left forearm."

My mentor was not eager to reveal much about them, even when I tried several times to extract more from him – warrior women are both interesting and mysterious. Witches even more. Perhaps I was too young. My short political education ended abruptly at fourteen. In my previous life in Arenia, I was trained to be the Pillar of the Kingdom, the power behind my brother's throne.

The Light. The White Light... Where did I see it? I shook my head in anger, unable to remember. The mind does strange things sometimes. My mind does, at least. Mostly when I am not expecting it.

"Are you trying to remember something?"

"The White Light."

"Did you see it before?" She looked at me with frank curiosity, the first feeling I could see reflected on her face.

"Yes, but I don't remember. Maybe it was just a dream."

"Don't try now. You are under the spell of the trance. The first one is always hard."

With my free hand, I raised her sleeve. Slowly. The Wanderer tattoo appeared, flickered with the flames, and the wings flapped, or so I thought. I blinked, and they became motionless again. *The Wanderers can see into the future. Shall I tell her my Vision about Panait's caravan?*

"La naiba!" She used an archaic vernacular form of damn that was long gone from the standard language. "You've started to think," she snorted before I could decide about my Vision. Leisurely, her thumb rubbed a small circle with my blood. "You will have an interesting life, full of danger and rewards. Hard to say which would be more." Her voice was now remote, almost careless. She let my hand free and became silent for a while. "Tell me about the White Light."

I thought suddenly of a faraway garden, bathed in the scent of oranges, and a girl trailing behind me in the green grass. I turned to face her, and she smiled at me. A fourteen-year-old girl. Her eyes green, she placed her hands on my shoulders. *Ioana.* "My sister had it," I breathed. "The night she died. My twin sister. Ioana."

"That was interesting. We will talk about it later," the woman said gently, and the memory of the White Light became remote and volatile, like a dream. There was more unknown than known behind her calm face, and some softness too, and expectation. I had nothing to say, and we went to sleep.

Is she a witch? Or she knows me from Arenia. Or she saw my royal sword. If asked, I would have preferred that she was a witch from a legend, able to help me regain my throne, but she could be just an intelligent and observant Wanderer. There was something else I wanted to remember, I did not know what, but I fell asleep before it happened.

In the morning, the woman walked for a while beside me; the man and his family were gone. "They are looking for you." Inclined, her palms touched each other at the tips of her fingers, improvising the letter A, the Assassins' salute. "Did you use your mentor's swords in a battle?"

She knows about Tudor.... "Shadow felt strange in my hand, as if being alive. The long sword."

"An Assassin's long sword has a mind of its own and only one master." She frowned, throwing a hard stare at me. "Shadow accepted you." It was both a statement and a question.

"I suppose so, but how can I be sure?"

"It did not let you die. The sword felt both strength and kindness in you." She shrugged and pressed a small badge into my hand. "You don't know our way, but this is something that few people have. Show it to any Wanderer, and she will help you. The letter proves that it was made for you."

Swiftly, I checked the badge, convinced that I would see a T for Tudor, the name I had told her. It was a C.

"A cautious young man," she smirked without looking at me. "Events are taking place these years that are going to define the future for all of us, one way or another. In the big game that you've just started to grasp, the Wanderers recognize you, Codrin of the Arenian House, as the legitimate King of Arenia, but your time may or may not come." Her voice was now tentative and grave, and she turned to face me with a questioning look of skepticism.

With some effort, I ignored it, moistening my lips without thinking. Whatever she thought of my reaction, she kept to herself. There was no way to quantify her statement, but I could not doubt it. For whatever reason, I trusted this woman that I had met only the day before.

"I am Dochia, and we will meet again. And we will talk more about your sister." She gave me her Wanderer name; until that moment I had known her as Lena. "That means that you will live until you see me next time." She laughed and went away. There was much of a warrior in her build, the crisply defined muscles and stance, and everything else.

Was Ioana a Wanderer? It can't be. I should have known it. Staring at the badge – two pairs of wings and the letter C in the middle, crafted from polished bronze – I realized that I did not even thank her, and she was now far away. Two riders appeared from the forest and followed her. Two women, one carrying a third horse. Under the impression that Dochia was looking at me, I bowed in her direction. She waved her right hand. Unconsciously, my fingers rubbed the badge: there was an intricate pattern of curved lines on its back. A hidden certification message, I supposed. It had no meaning for me. *This is a Wing Talisman*, the thought came to me from nowhere, and there was a surge of tension in my body that I could not understand. It passed after a few moments.

Fate... I continued to rub the talisman, thinking that my journey to Frankis had not been just an escape from the desolation at home in Arenia; it had been a journey toward destiny. Or so I hoped.

Three hundred paces east and down from my hidden place, five men were watching the road, and they did not look like the usual robbers. Silent and showing no trace of tension, they were just waiting for the prey to come. It was not dark enough to be sinister, but the surrounding forest was dense and the low clouds even denser. A boring hour passed until five more men appeared on the road, riding fast. *An embassy,* I recognized Orban's banner through my spyglass. Taking Zor by the halter, I sneaked down behind some dense bushes from where it was easier to control the battle, although the hunters were now out of my sight. Feeling the fight, Zor tossed his head, nostrils flaring with unease, and I shared his trepidation.

On the road, the embassy passed close to my place, and I got the impression of recognizing one man from Arad. A long shrill raised from the forest, and the hidden riders burst onto the road, swords up, screaming some wordless battle cries. Driving their horses, the men circled in pairs, trading blow after blow; their wild shouts echoing back from the tall ridges. Frightened, some birds flew away from the bushes along the road. Three riders died fast. At my arrival, the man I thought I knew, and three hunters were still alive, one of them wounded. I pushed my horse in parallel with their leader, keeping him between me and the other two. He was good, but not that good. Caught between the S'Arad man and me, another one died fast. The wounded tried to run, and I had to use my bow. For a few moments, I listened to the forest; it was peaceful again. When I turned, the surviving man was searching the body of the hunters' leader, who was dressed like a beggar.

The beggar that is not a beggar... Is Dochia a witch, or she had knowledge about the attack? "That's my reward," I said, touching the man's neck with my sword, and he stood up, slow and calm, raising his arms in a pacifying gesture.

"Winner's Right," he agreed, and while he looked uncomfortable, he did not look scared; there was a good restraint in his manner – a man of power able to handle all sort of troubles.

The dead leader had a sword of surprising quality, but the most interesting thing was a letter, a contract to kill the man in front of me. There was a lot of money in that contract, for a good reason: the man they wanted dead was Cantemir, the Secretary of Grand Seigneur Orban.

"So, Cantemir," I looked at him, "what now?"

Unimpressed, he took my measure, before his gaze moved from one dead body to another, and back at me. "First, I have to thank you for saving my life, then... How old are you?"

"Old enough for this game." I pointed to the bodies around.

"Are you for hire?" He frowned, as though speaking to a child who could not be trusted with important tasks.

"It depends on the price." I shrugged to show a small trace of interest, and he made a careless movement with one hand. "Where are you going?"

"Dorna."

"Seven galbeni to go there, and five if you want me for the return, too. And you pay for my lodging in the city."

"You are not cheap." He looked suspiciously at me, not because the price was too high; he was too rich for that.

"You are alone in the forest." *And you have an urgent errand.* I knew from the Panait that war was ready to erupt in the west, and from my evaluation, while not a weak man, Cantemir was not a real swordsman – owning a sword does not necessarily make you a warrior. The road back to Arad was as long as the one in front, not leaving him too many choices. "Protecting you seems to be dangerous."

"Who are you working for in Arad?"

"Panait."

"Are you the protector that saved his caravan in the Cursed Forest?" Cantemir's eyebrows raised abruptly, and he measured me again.

After I nodded that *yes*, I am that man, believe it or not, he paid me four galbeni in advance, and the day continued in silence; perhaps he considered me too young and unimportant to deserve his attention. Before sunset, we left the road to find a hidden place, easier to defend, and we took watches through the night.

"Do you know what?" I asked, in the morning, when we moved again. "The road is shorter when people are talking."

"What do you want to talk about?" Cantemir looked uninterested.

"I spend most of my time protecting caravans and traveling people. The last thing I want is to bump into an army or a battle. Soldiers don't have a reputation for being kind. Will war start between Lenard and Konrad?"

"Perhaps." He shrugged, and from that moment, we moved slowly into a new game: trading information.

In Dorna, Cantemir rented an apartment in White Spring Inn, the best one there, and dinner was served in our living room. When the wine warmed us well enough, I took out the letter captured from the hunter and handed it to him. "You may have an interest in this."

He read it slowly, me watching him, but Cantemir was not in a high position for nothing, his face kept his thoughts hidden. "Why now?" he asked after a while.

"Such news is more digestible in a safe room, after a good wine, than in the forest, between bodies."

In Dorna, I realized even more how important information was; it could give me some relevance in the game the Seigneurs were playing. *And having a double identity helps my game. Nobody knows that the man here, Tudor, is the same as Codrin from Severin, at least for a while.* Protecting caravans represented a stable source of income; it was just that I need twenty lucky years to buy enough land to become a Knight – the first step to claiming what was mine by right in Arenia. Twenty years is almost a full life, and I did not intend to spend it on the road. If properly handled, Cantemir could give me some insights into Orban's plans, and the merchants news from everywhere. *And Jara... I must stay close to her and help both of us.* My thoughts flew back to their house: the peaceful reading evenings, carrying the girls in my arms, riding in the forest, training, a world that was mine too, and I wanted it back. *And Saliné...* I knew that Orban was their worst enemy, and my game would be dangerous. *And that means getting close to Mohor too. And his big mouthed Spatar…*

"Just the two of us?" I asked Cantemir when we left Dorna.

"From your self-described qualities, it should be enough." He smiled for the first time.

On the road, I pushed Cantemir into more interesting exchanges, but he avoided them elegantly. *I have to make the first step.* "One week ago, there was an embassy from Duke Stefan in Dorna."

"Valuable information. It would have had even more value in Dorna."

"It came to me just yesterday, and I don't really know what has and does not have value for you." Keeping an eye on him, I shrugged, to emphasize my innocence.

"There will be no war," he replied with a pensive look. "You can drive your caravans safely in the west."

"Was this war the reason for killing you?"

"I don't know. This is a long-term game. The war in the west was meant to cut off some lines from our defense. There is a subtle reassessment of power around us."

Was Mohor involved in all this? Even in the killing? "Speaking about reassessments. There are rumors of a wedding in Severin." I bet that Orban would anyway know about it soon, if he was not already aware. "S'Severin and Lady Midian." Midian was Jara's Seigniorial name, and Midia her former city that she had lost to Orban.

"Yes, some negotiations were taking place." Cantemir valued my information just for being fresher. He was a subtle Secretary, and I did not feel like a traitor. He reminded me of Sandor, the Arenian Chancellor, who was killed in that bloody night, too. "Jara is an intelligent woman, but I am curious if she and Aron will be able to work together at the same court. He is upset by the marriage and wants her out of Severin," Cantemir said, and I did not react, waiting for him to speak again.

"Who?" I asked when the silence became too long.

"Nobody," he said distraught, his expression oddly inward, as if just realizing that I was still there.

Back in Arad, I visited Panait to inform him that the roads would be safe in the west, and I learned that both Orban and Mohor had sent embassies to Leyona a month before – Panait's sister was married in Leyona. And now came the hardest step: going back to Jara.

❧

There was no one in the courtyard, just silence dancing around. There was no sound from the house either, and I pushed the door slowly, entering the hall. The second door betrayed me, and Jara turned from the window. She stayed silent while I advanced hesitantly.

"Jara," I said finally, coming face to face with her.

"What took you so long?" Before I could answer, she embraced me warmly. "Welcome home."

"Thank you, Jara. You have a well-known reputation for being tough."

"I should chain you. Just to confirm my reputation." She ruffled my hair, and I felt home indeed.

At that moment, Vio entered the room, and she stayed still, stunned for a moment. It took her the blink of an eye to jump into my arms, and I twirled around twice, her legs flying around. "I know you from somewhere. A cherry tree?" I asked, and she nodded, raising her arms, mimicking how to pick fruits. "What can we find in the orchard now?"

"Cherries!" She laughed, and the sound was like magic.

"Codrin." Unseen, Saliné came up behind me, and I turned to face her with the sudden feeling that she was no longer a child; her journey to womanhood had started some time ago, but I was not consciously aware of it. Being away for more than a month, gives you new perspectives on old perceptions. "What took you so long?" she asked the same question, embracing me, her voice nuanced, joyful and bitter.

"It was long for me too, maybe even longer." I stroked her hair, trying to put the child back into her, yet the womanly part remained anchored to me in a way that I was just starting to understand. She stared at me, and my hand slid down her face, lingering on her chin. "I am glad to be home. What's new with my girls?"

"I lost my last old tooth," Vio answered at once. "I buried it in the garden. We finished a new book." She extended a finger with each item of news. "Three days ago, I cut my skin training with a dagger. Look." She opened her palm to show me a pink mark. "Saliné has a new green dress for the wedding. Mother promised me one, too. Blue." She pointed to her blue eyes with a large smile. "Milene is pregnant..."

"Vio," Jara interrupted her torrent of words; Vio was able to speak as fast as she moved. "You should leave us something to tell him." She smiled, and there was a moment of silence, Vio pondering if she could really leave somebody else the important task of feeding me with the local news.

"Cakes?" Vio broke the silence, her eyebrows raised in expectation.

"Cakes? What cakes?"

"You promised," both girls lamented, their smiles vanishing.

"Well, if I promised." There was a box of Mefilene in my bag – a gift from Delia.

Later in the evening, I sat with Jara and Cernat around a bottle of wine. The conversation flowed, but not like in the past; a thin, invisible barrier was still raised between us.

"Tell Mohor that Orban's embassy went to Leyona just after his own. He is moving many pieces around, as you are."

"What pieces?" Cernat asked, neutrally.

"The small war between Lenard and Konrad was prevented. Orban's diplomacy," I said, and they looked at me in a way that confirmed my assumption about them trying to weaken Lenard's position. "And ... a certain plan to kill Orban's Secretary failed." This time, they looked surprised, even worried, so it may have been done by Mohor alone, or by an unknown party. "It may trigger some kind of tit-for-tat reaction." The conversation turned back to more mundane things.

"Do you want to talk?" Jara asked when Cernat went away. "We left some things open."

"Do you think it will help?

"The truth is that I don't know how I can help, apart from chaining you here where you belong, but I am willing to try."

"I am fine, Jara, and working to find my place," I said, assured by her words. "The first steps are to understand where you stand, but I am noble-born, and I will not remain a stable boy for the rest of my life."

"So, after all those words about understanding your place..." There was no mockery in her voice, just worry that I was unable to adapt to my new life.

"Stable boy, protector, swordsman..." I shrugged. "There is not much social difference between them. A commoner like me is just a tool, used and discarded when no longer needed. I need to become a Knight." *And get fame... Only then men will enroll under my banner to help me take Arenia back. Wars... Am I suited to command an army?* Father was a brilliant military strategist, who never lost a battle, but I was not my father.

"You will become Knight, Codrin. Maybe not so soon as you hope, as the road to Knighthood is not easy, but you will be.

Some doors will open for you after my marriage," she repeated her offer I received before leaving.

"We'll see," I said, unconvinced. "One more thing, I am not sure how to tell you... Aron sees a rival at the Severin's court in you, and he will try to marginalize you." I was not entirely sure, but it was the most logical conclusion from Cantemir's information. "I know, coming from me, it might sound..."

"Codrin," Jara said softly, and her fingers gripped mine. "You are like a son to me, and I trust you, but I need to know more."

"By luck, I heard a conversation about this subject," I said carefully, hoping she would not ask for more – I wanted to keep hidden my links to Cantemir.

"It may be true," she said thoughtfully, biting her lip for a few moments. "In many aspects, a court is like a war zone." She tapped my hand to reassure me, and I left the room with the feeling that their home was still my home.

The next day we picked cherries in the garden, and everything seemed to be back in place, with one difference, though: Saliné and me. In the evening, she wanted to walk out; the full moon was shining over the land. I took her hand in mine, and in silence, we walked through the grass, the pleasant warmth of her palm going through me. Far away, a wolf howled, making her shiver, and we stopped.

"I will always protect you." I remembered the words I had said a year before in the same place, and I smiled in the dusk, gently gripping her hand.

"Always," she whispered, and it struck me that she meant a different thing than I initially thought. She raised her head until our eyes met. We had stared many times at each other, but there was something different in her gaze now, an intensity I did not know. The green of her eyes filled mine, and my pulse quickened.

Feelings came to me, and it was almost like tears. I had known contentment before, when I still had a family, but this was different and indefinite. "Always," I whispered too, and leaning against the tree behind me, for the first time, I took her in my arms in the way you embrace the girl you love. Silent, I pressed my face into her hair, and I stayed motionless, afraid to break the spell. Alert, my mind registered that she was still too. Closer, the wolf made his presence felt again, his long howl echoing around in cascades. It sounded strangely melodious.

In the large hall hosting the wedding, many candles flickered in the crystal chandeliers, a thousand points of light, like the stars in a dark night sky. Piled up with plates of suckling pigs, fish, chicken, turkey and countless wine bottles, long tables were lined up, draped in white to suggest happiness. The air was warm with fresh bread, fruit, spices and merriment. In the dim light, people blended into a blur of unknown eyes, faces, and hands already stained by grease from the meat they were devouring. Jewelry was sparkling, here and there, with no discernible patterns. Mohor was a Seigneur who liked to entertain and had many political links to keep alive, so he opened his pockets wide.

Settled at a different table than agreed, I had a bad feeling and slipped a hand under my shirt to touch the Wing Talisman. It vibrated in my hand, and cold fingers crawled up my spin. I did not want to come, but Jara had insisted, and there was no way to refuse her. Yet instead of being placed between Saliné and Vio at the main table, I was sent to a different one, and my back was toward the main access road. Catching her eyes, I saluted Jara, and she answered back with a surprised look. There was a flurry of words between her and Mohor, too far for me to hear. He patted her hand, smiling at her, but she did not smile back.

The second bad feeling came when I saw Aron speaking in a corner with a troop of fools. A brief Vision flashed in my mind: the fools coming close to me. *One more fool*, I looked at Big Mouth. For the next hour, I tried to exchange some polite words with the people around me, but they were too busy eating, comfortably seated on the oak-wood benches.

"We are merchants," one of them finally said, with a gesture that involved more than half of the people around the table. "We serve the castle," he added, in a proud voice.

"A very important job." *Mohor has a strong sense of hierarchy. I am where I belong.*

"There will be a big fight tonight," a strident voice shouted, unfortunately not far behind me.

Laughter burst out in the hall. I ignored it until I heard Aron shouting and laughing, pointing at me. I turned: the fools were faking an attack against me. One of them hit me with a kind of spear having feathers as a blade. Attached to his spear, a little bag suddenly opened, and a cloud of small feathers covered my head and shoulders, white against the dark colors of my hair and clothes, and the laughter became louder. I saw Jara and the girls laughing, trying to hide behind their palms. In all that noise, the only thing I could hear was Saliné's laughter, inside my head, as every other sound vanished around me, and all sense of time disappeared. I caught Jara's eyes and she stopped laughing, from the savagery of my look; my mind was boiling, and my right hand moved unconsciously for the sword's hilt. I was unarmed, and that was the fools' luck and mine. There was little chance that Mohor and Aron would have let me leave alive after spilling blood at the wedding. My senses came back, and the laughter continued unabated, yet the girls looked now serious and upset. Eyes closed, I inhaled deeply, one slow measured breath, repeated it for a few times, the Assassin Cool, and I forced my mind to stop thinking. When I opened them again, Jara was trying to leave her chair, but Mohor held her shoulders, keeping her seated, whispering in her ear while Cernat was advancing fast in my direction, behind the tables.

"Fight or we will beat you to death," the strident voice shouted, and more things were thrown at my head, to general laughter.

Calm again, I stood up and caught one piece of wood flying toward me. "Let's play with this," I said, and the laughter stopped abruptly. "You and me," I gestured to the one who seemed to be the troupe's leader. He was barely taller than my waist.

"Yes," he said, jumping onto his hands and back on his feet, all the other fools making a lot of noise with trumpets.

"You stand at the wall, and I will try to hit you with the wood. Then you do the same."

He had no idea what I wanted, but the game was there for the crowd, and they started to clap, shouting: "Fight! Fight! Fight!"

"Stand with your back to the wall," I said, hafting the piece of wood in my left hand; it was something small that could not harm anyone. Faster than their eyes could see, I took a knife from my boot and threw it at him. The knife pinned his bonnet to the wood decorating the wall, just a finger or two from his skull. There was a thump in the wood. Then silence. The dwarf's body slid down until it hanged on the string tying the bonnet to his neck. His mouth moved without sound. The remaining fools grabbed the mute dwarf from the wall and left the room, their short feet moving faster than I thought possible. After recovering my knife, I returned to my table, surrounded by a heavy silence. Cernat was already there, and he gripped my shoulder in acknowledgment, before going back to his place. A team of musicians entered the hall, and the servants hurried by with more platters of food and barrels of wine.

"I apologize," Jara whispered in my ear a few minutes later.

"Why? I am always glad to make you laugh." There was a glacial sarcasm in every nuance of my voice and words, and it came to me as a surprise that I could still talk to her without shouting, or even that I could talk at all.

"Please come with me."

"I have not finished my steak," I refused dryly, not even turning to look at her.

"Please," she insisted, seizing my shoulders from behind, trying to make me turn to face her. There was a terrible desperation in her voice that went through me, and I reluctantly followed her outside the hall, into a small, empty room. "I apologize," she said again, grabbing my hands. "That miserable Aron. I knew nothing about it. Mohor told me just as you arrived that he had to give your place to one of his cousins."

"You laughed," I growled. "All your family laughed." *Even Saliné…*

"Yes, I am sorry. It was involuntary. Maybe this will erase what I did," she said, embracing me. "Stay with me. Like a son with his mother." Her gentleness, and the warm tone of her voice finally calmed me. "Better?" she asked, stroking my hair, and I nodded — we were face-to-face again. "Please," she said nervously, as if forcing herself to say something unkind. "Please don't try anything, Codrin. Let me find out what happened."

"I don't want to give them any satisfaction."

"You managed it well. Big Mouth was unhappy that his stupid ploy had unraveled." There was a sudden involuntary gesture of relief in her body as she looked at me. "Please forgive my girls. It was just a spontaneous reaction. They are still children. Even Saliné."

"I leave now, and tomorrow I will be gone from Severin." I ignored her words; their laughter was still burning in me.

"Yes," she agreed at once. "I will tell Saliné." There was a slight hint in her voice that I should not try to talk with Saliné right now, perhaps because I was too upset to have a calm conversation.

After Jara left me alone, I went to take Shadow from the Weapons Room. *I am Free... Free to run again.* Out of Mohor's residence, a swift draft of cool air almost blew out the torches. It passed with a long wail through the narrow space between the walls. *Bad omen.* At the stables, two unknown men asked the reason for my presence there. There was a deliberate slow and mean reaction from them, another harassment coming from Mohor or Big Mouth. After I stated my name, seven soldiers with halberds surrounded me, six of them having Big Mouth's colors.

"You are under arrest," the only one representing Mohor said, coldly. "Give up your sword."

I stepped back, looking for an escape path, gripping Shadow's hilt. "No..." the sword whispered in my mind.

"Vagrant, try to obey, for your own safety," a familiar voice mocked, and behind the soldiers, I recognized Veres in the torches' light – there was a malicious smile on his lips.

Chapter 12 – Jara

Midnight passed slowly, and apathy took over. There was the fire, a few people still dancing, the smell of food and burnt wax, and the wine inside me. *I drank more at my first wedding, terrified of what would happen next. I was only eighteen. A wonderful age.* Unseen, I sneaked out through a small door leading into the garden, where the air sang with roses and honeysuckle. A spider's web hung between the bush on my left and the wall, glittering with droplets of water in the moonlight. The cold was refreshing, and stirred by the breeze, gray stripes of mist surrounded my feet. Slowly, they changed into red, then orange and purple before a white path opened through the mist. It forked after a while, where a man was waiting. The spider's web spread and morphed into shimmering silver wire, singing in the wind around us. The castle's bell struck the quarter.

"Malin," I whispered and walked fast toward him.

"Two paths were open for you," he said, and the world around us became wrapped in mist, like a creation of dream inside a dream. "One vanished today."

"Malin, are you upset because of my wedding?" I breathed, grabbing his hands. He answered gently to my grip and that calmed me. *There was no other way, Malin.*

"It was your right to choose, and our children need protection." His lips formed a gentle smile that I knew so well. "There is only one path left and no more choices. Make good use of it."

"What should I do?"

"Make good use of it," he repeated. "After a while, everyone's fate will move into Saliné's hands. You must prepare her to lead a court. And that young man."

"Codrin? He had to run."

"No, he is still here, and you have to help him. He is part of the Prophecy. So are our daughters. Prophecies may be exalting and, perhaps, filled with glory, but they are not kind. Prepare them."

I woke up, breathing hard, trying to gather my thoughts. *What was the other path? What Prophecy? Why couldn't he tell me more?*

A hum persisted in my mind from the wedding party, coupled with the almost forgotten feeling of sharing the night with a man, and that roused more feelings of nostalgia. The castle was silent in the early morning, and I stretched, wondering if I should go back to sleep. *I can't.* Disturbed by my movement, Mohor mumbled something in his sleep as I got out of bed. On the opposite wall, there was a large mirror, reflecting my naked body in the gentle light of the dawn. *I am still young...* With all the horrors of the last two years, physically at least, time had not been unkind to me. *I need to think. Is Codrin hiding around here? Father must find him before things turn even worse. I have to sort out what happened last night with Mohor. At our wedding. It's a loss of face for me. It will not be easy... Aron could not do it without his approval. Everything is because of that stupid duel. Men...* I shook my head, but that stupidity had chased Codrin away and put me in an awkward position; many knew that he lived in my house. Touching him touched me, too. *Codrin...* Thinking of him, I caught sight of myself again in the mirror, the reflection of an expression that I did not expect.

Lunch was brief, nobody felt hungry; the girls were unhappy, and Saliné let me see that she was upset – she was good at hiding her feelings. Only Veres seemed to be pleased and tried to stir a feeble conversation with some bad jokes about what happened to Codrin. Everybody ignored him, even Mohor.

Both girls left the wedding party shortly after Codrin, a way to punish themselves for laughing at him and me because I was not able to preempt the awful show. And they knew that Mohor planned many things for a memorable wedding. *It was memorable in more than one way,* I sighed, still remembering the pain and fury in Codrin's eyes. Mohor tried to stop Saliné – he liked her – but she refused even to talk to him.

Mohor and I dined late, as the remaining day was short, and many things were to be settled – like the rooms for my daughters. They went home with Father and would come back a week later, leaving us to arrange their accommodation, and they would no longer sleep together – at fifteen, Saliné needed to be alone from time to time.

"Knight Grama was convinced to join our cause. "You brought a lot of people from the north. We now have half the soldiers we need to attack Orban." Mohor shook Grama's letter in front of me. "They are slowly accepting our lead, and we are now strong enough to go harder for the Devans. With them..."

The Devans were Grand Seigneurs, yet Mohor felt confident, because our alliance against Orban was now large enough, that they would accept our lead, too. Three years ago, when we still were Grand Seigneurs of Midia, we also negotiated with the Devans, and in some ways, it was a continuation of that when Father went a month ago in Deva, their city.

Saliné was included in the negotiation, I suddenly remembered. She was supposed to marry the Devans' first born. *There was no Codrin at that time. We need the Devans. In all the noble families, marriages are a political thing. Saliné will not be happy. And Codrin... How will Codrin react? He also comes from a noble family. But he is different...* Losing his family and social position changed him in a way that I could not fully understand, as if he was no longer ruled only by the strict rules of the nobility. "Yes, with the Devans our chances against Orban will grow," I continued his words just to stop my inner rumbling. *We are no longer what we were at that time. There will be no marriage.* "Things went too far last night with the fools," I said after all the political subjects were exhausted.

"Codrin handled it well."

"That is not an excuse."

"I understand you, but I have to understand our Spatar and main Knight too. Aron was badly humiliated in that duel."

Last night I was humiliated, too. "Nobody pushed Aron to act so poorly, nor with the duel," *apart from Codrin...* "or with the fools. Codrin is not even eighteen years old, and he could have reacted in a violent way, and ruin the night, by killing a fool. Did our wedding matter less than Aron's pride to you?" I let another dose of disappointment pass through my voice.

"Jara, we need Aron, and I had to tolerate his revenge. A childish one, I recognize, but nothing harmful in the end, and it went less well than he expected, anyway."

"At our wedding," I insisted.

"It will not happen again," he said in his most serious voice, but his eyes were humorous, and I had to fight hard to stop a smile; of course, that we could not marry again. "Everything was … settled last night." There was a brief hesitation in his voice, and a search for the proper words to convince me. "Codrin means a lot to you, and I respect that, but he must learn his place in the hierarchy and the rules." Mohor looked at me and tried to smile, but it didn't come out well, and I remained silent. "He has qualities, and his time will come. It may be sooner than everyone is expecting, and I count on you to keep him close to us."

❧

I went to collect my girls, five days later than planned – their rooms were still not completely ready, but at least they were habitable. Things were moving slowly in Mohor's castle, because of an old inertia, because they were still not accustomed to a woman giving orders in the house, and generally, there was a careless attitude about everything.

Well, now they have to handle three women...

"I could not find Codrin," Father whispered while I was leaving the house. Sometimes, even my special dreams were misleading.

As he had done in the morning, Vlaicu opened the gate to let us pass. The Chief of the Guard was the man I was the most accustomed to after Mohor and Senal, as he had visited our house several times before. "Did our guests come?" It was probably too early for the embassies from the northern territories to arrive, but I wanted to be sure.

"No, only Mohor and Big Mouth." Vlaicu winked, and the girls chuckled, while I could not stop a worried smile – the pejorative nickname was spreading fast.

I left the girls in their rooms, promising them a tour of the castle the next day, and went to the council room.

"They will come tomorrow," Mohor said when I entered. "How are the girls?"

"Ready to explore," I smiled, and sat down.

Mohor pushed a letter across the table, with an intense look at me. It was not a long letter, so I finished it fast. *Tardin... That traitor. How is he daring to propose an alliance with us?* He had left our army just before the battle with Orban started, and that disorganized our left wing. "Tardin is a traitor," I said, struggling to control my voice.

"We need him," Aron answered. "We need as many people as possible."

"Tardin betrayed once; he will betray again."

"He betrayed *you*, not us. He is in a difficult position now, afraid of Orban. I know what I am *saying*." Aron's voice became rude and heated, and his last words rolled barely understandable.

I waited for Mohor to react, yet he said nothing, his eyes fixing a point on the wall, and I remembered Codrin's warning that Aron would try to marginalize me. "Your job is what we tell you to do. Tardin is a known traitor, and we may lose some of our allies." In contrast with his voice, mine was now chilly.

"Mohor, we can't continue like this, it will impact any further development," Aron snapped. "You have to decide if I lead the negotiations, or Jara." He pointed toward me, and his mouth twitched insolently, as if I were just another councilor.

"Lady Jara. I am the Signora of this house." I frowned at Mohor; his intervention should already have happened.

"Aron, leave us. I have to talk with Jara."

"Finally." Aron puffed out his chest with a deep breath, seeming to filter it through his unruly moustache, and moved out with deliberate slowness, just to annoy me even more. I gripped the table with my fingers to stop a curse.

"It seems difficult for you two to work together," Mohor said calmly when we remained alone.

"So, after his insolence, you just philosophize about some vague difficulties."

"Ignore his words; it was an ill-tempered reaction. It's nothing serious. Sometimes, he is rude to me, too," Mohor shrugged. "I don't feel the need to react."

"I can see that. Aron seems accustomed to ordering you around."

"You are going too far. This is Aron. He exaggerates sometimes, his temper might fly, but he works well for us. You need to know him better and see the full picture. It will take a while, though," he said thoughtfully. "And that brings us to the negotiations again. I know it will upset you, but Aron started this a long time ago, and we have a better chance to win if he continues to lead our negotiations. He is capable to deal for us, and he can travel." Mohor took my hand over the table, but I swiftly retracted it, to evade his touch, and he smiled gently before saying, "I was right about you being upset."

"Yes, you were right," I said, bitterly. "But you did nothing to prevent it. And he is not that capable, but you think I am biased, so I will not push it. Time will tell which of us was right. And what kind of *good man* he is, I saw at our wedding."

"I thought we have left that behind."

"What we leave behind doesn't change that he is a wicked man. And I can leave one thing behind, but they are accumulating quite fast, and I don't know where this will lead in the end. You see me in a place lower than your main councilors."

"Jara, my decision is hard for you, and I apologize, but it's the right one. Many times, we think the same, sometimes we differ."

"You don't even realize that a Signora, your wife, cannot be treated like that. My authority was already low from the wedding night – everybody knew what Codrin is to me, and that Aron had your approval to play against me. Day by day, my authority went lower, and Aron is speculating this." Codrin's words about Aron seeing me as a rival came to me again, raising my anger. "Tomorrow, Aron will brag how I was kicked out of any political negotiations. He is not called Big Mouth for nothing. This may have long-term consequences that you don't seem to see. Now, I will take the good part, having more time for my daughters." I stood up, trying to leave the room.

He moved swiftly in front of the door, blocking my path. "You have been part of the council for two months already." There was a slight underlining that I was favored by receiving a place in the council, even before the wedding, but he never said it directly. And it was true, there were very few Signoras in the councils of their courts. Our brutal world was a man's world.

"You don't even consider that I need a certain authority to play my part in our house."

"Jara," he said softly, pulling me closer to him, but I disengaged, trying to move past him. He stopped me again, his hand moving around my waist, pulling me with my back against him. "Your rank is granted by marriage and your place in the council, but I will be more careful from now on. This house has functioned in a certain way for many years. Things started to change with your arrival, and I am sure you will find ways to improve many things." He pulled me even tighter, and I realized that the tone of his voice stayed calm and gentle all the time.

"Well," I said, unsure how to react. "I tried with the Secretariat, you stopped me. It looks like I am not suited for diplomacy, either. I may be the right thing for my girls, though."

"The Secretariat," he said slowly, turning me in his arms. "I talked with Senal about how everything was structured at your previous court. He agreed with you, so ... you will have less time for the girls than you think. And even if Aron leads the negotiations, it doesn't mean that we are here for nothing."

"Well, if I've received Senal's approval..."

"Don't you think that I should have talked to him about that?" he asked, slightly irritated for the first time.

"No. I think that we should have both talked to him and let me explain. I know better how my previous court worked."

"Right," he agreed, with a sigh, and smiled. "At least I learned something today. Can we make peace now?"

I nodded, not very enthusiastically, and left the room. I heard him draw breath to speak an instant before I left but did not wait for the words to come.

❧

Things advanced slowly, both in the Secretariat and in the castle – some people were almost ignoring me. *It took me two years to become a real Signora in Malin's house*, I remembered. *But I was so young and inexperienced. Three weeks and a few days here*, I complained to myself, then burst into laughter because of my childish eagerness. Three weeks means nothing when you move into a new castle. I entered the dining room still smiling, ready to give Mohor the news that I had kept hidden for a few days just to be sure. He and Veres were already at the table, and I suppressed my smile to avoid unwanted questions. A few minutes later, the door opened again.

"Sorry for being late," Saliné said, panting and, joined by Vio, she took her place at the table. "We trained later today." Even with Codrin missing, the girls were training almost every day; the exile and the attack on our house had altered their childhoods too much.

"That's not training," Veres sneered. "You are moving like a drunken crane. Like this." He stood up and moved his hands in a hilarious way. He was both malicious and wrong, yet I bit my lip not to laugh. And even worse, he used Aron's pejorative way of describing the Warriors Dance.

"Veres, we are eating right now. Sit down and stop playing the fool."

"Codrin is the fool, not me. Fight!" Veres mimicked the fool that attacked Codrin at my wedding. "Why are you playing at being outraged now? You all laughed at him. It was a good show." His finger pointed to all of us, and he was right, we had laughed.

"It was just a stupid game set by Aron. He was upset for losing the duel with Codrin and couldn't find another way to get revenge. The big fool paid the small ones to fight for him." The influence Aron had on Veres was unnerving me, and despite all my efforts, it was not possible to cut the links between them. Veres did not like Codrin and found a natural ally in Aron.

"There was indeed an exaggeration that night," Mohor interjected, "but Aron is not a fool. Let's have a..."

"Yes, we can agree about exaggerations. Big Mouth is not a fool. Codrin is."

"Neither is Codrin," Mohor shrugged. "But he does not have a position I need to consider."

"It was an accident," Veres jumped in before I could talk. His strange reaction came late; something had boiled within him and was bursting out only now. "Aron's foot slipped, and he lost his sword when he fell. Codrin will never win against him."

"You missed the duel. Codrin took away Aron's sword with a maneuver that you never tried to learn." *You never try to learn.*

"You always take Codrin's part," Veres snapped. "Mohor said the same thing to me as Aron, so you are wrong."

"We should stop now," Mohor interjected, a slight urgency in his voice. "The steak is going cold."

"Mohor, it looks like my son thinks I am *wrong.*" I avoided the word lie, but my tone was harsh, and I had to leave the part about me always taking Codrin's part for later.

"It doesn't matter who won or not, that is something we should pass over, the same as that unnecessary event at our wedding. It's a family dinner." Mohor smiled irritably and started to eat.

"As Mohor has finally agreed that our troublemaker Aron lost the duel, we can eat," Saliné interjected subtly, in a charming voice. "I am hungry too."

Mohor was both annoyed and amused that she had ruined his strategy, but he continued eating in a silence.

"Shut up!" Veres shouted, disappointed that Mohor had not put Saliné in what he considered her place. "You have no idea. Aron is a great Knight. Codrin is the troublemaker. That's why he is in jail now. Downstairs." He pointed with his hand, a wicked smile spreading across his lips.

"Veres!" Mohor growled, and our family dinner became a total disaster.

Vio ran out in tears, and Saliné followed, when I nodded to her.

Malin was right about Codrin being here... I was too lenient. "Mohor, we have some things to settle, but they may burst out if we talk now," I said in a glacial tone. "Enjoy your steak."

In her room, Vio was settled in Saliné's arms. "Why did he do this?" Vio asked. "It's not fair. Big Mouth should be in jail. And Veres."

"Vio, it's not nice to say such a bad thing about your brother."

"Codrin is our brother too. Didn't you say so? And Veres..." She did not finish, pointing out that Veres enjoyed Codrin's misfortune.

"Yes, Codrin is like a brother to you, too," I sighed.

"Sorry, I did not really mean it about Veres," Vio whispered, only half convinced. "Why does Veres hate Codrin?"

"He doesn't hate Codrin. Veres is under Aron's influence," I said feebly, and Vio did not insist and did not believe. Father told me that Veres envied Codrin's fighting skills, and I thought it only a boyish reaction. His behavior at the table convinced me that Veres saw a rival in Codrin. *He is wrong, but he is young, and I should have been more careful.*

"Because Codrin saved mother," Saliné answered softly to Vio, after a long pause.

"And Veres did not even try to save me when we were attacked in our house," I whispered, and Saliné nodded. *My son is not a fighter,* I shook my head. *Codrin will not stay in the castle with us. Maybe this will calm Veres.*

During the night, we slept together, all three, a thing that had not happened for a long time. *The first days here after we escaped from Orban... It's not that bad now, but it's still bad.*

That morning came earlier than I wanted and, in a room suddenly too small, I walked restlessly in a confused state of mind – any acceptable strategy was eluding me. The girls were still sleeping, their calm breaths contrasting with my agitated thoughts. All marriages are challenged at a certain point, but things do not go well when it happens so early. We were both adults, and not without certain qualities and logical minds, but there were many other things to consider. My position was stronger than a Signora would have at a court, in general, not to mention after a three-weeks-old marriage, but Mohor was the Seigneur, and the authority was on his side – he could keep Codrin jailed as long as he wanted, and I could do nothing. Where a man exercises inherited power, a woman can use only persuasion, or risk being exiled at her own court.

"All night I tried to find a way to talk," I said to Mohor, meeting him after breakfast – we ate separately. "I came to the disappointing conclusion that it makes no sense to talk at all. Aron's stupid desire for revenge counted more than our wedding. No wonder that no one respects me in *our* house." My voice was unexpectedly calm, and with the last word I went for the door, but Mohor was already there.

"Codrin is alive, Jara, and I could not negotiate his fate with you, just before our wedding. A Seigneur must balance things, and Knights are his instrument of power."

"And I was just another instrument, paraded at your wedding for some political reasons. One of a lesser value though."

"Is this what you really think?" he asked, coldly.

"Everything was on the brink of a disaster when Codrin's hand went for the knife. You saw it. The fools could have been dead before our next blink, and our wedding famous and subject of many bad songs. Don't tell me that you did not see it, but feel free to tell me what I should *really* think about that."

"You are too emotional about that..."

"What an ungrateful wife you have. The man who saved my life and is like my own child was wonderfully treated, and I can't rejoice. No wonder why you have kept the best part hidden from me."

"I wanted to tell you everything myself, just before freeing Codrin, and took precaution to keep everything hidden. But Veres is..." He shrugged as if to say that Veres was not the cleverest man in the world, and I could not contradict him.

"You will not free him now?" I asked, struggling to keep calm.

"I am sorry, but Codrin will be free in three days, when his month's sentence expires. Jara, Aron saved my life too, and I am Seigneur because he and Senal wanted it to happen. When I was fifteen, my uncle poisoned my father, and I relied on them to save me. Senal convinced some Knights to stay on my side, and Aron killed my uncle in battle. I am not trying to imply that my life is more valuable than yours. I am glad and have my own debt to Codrin for saving you as you are now my wife. The only difference is that Aron means something in the hierarchy keeping us in power while Codrin might mean something in the future. Codrin must learn this," he said, in a tone implying the same need for me. "Codrin has no social rank, and until he gains one, he remains a minor swordsman, protector or whatever. Talented, but no different from many hired here or there. He must understand *this*. The most stupid Knight or Seigneur represents much more than a peasant, merchant, or swordsman many times smarter than him. This is how our world works. As a Knight, Aron had the right to kill Codrin for that humiliation, but I don't kill easily, at last that you know about me. Codrin should have stopped after winning the duel, but he is … young." He smiled, tentatively, and it was true; Mohor was a kind and intelligent man, reminding me of Malin.

There was more spark in Malin. And he was … more a leader… "We both agreed that Codrin is as my son, and I am expecting you to keep your word."

"Codrin has been well treated, having a separate room, outside my prison. And I already told you that everything was settled. I don't want Aron to try something else behind our backs later. Three days pass fast."

For you… It made no sense to argue, as there was some truth in his words. Things were somehow settled between us, in a manner that was both convenient and inconvenient for both. I knew that nothing could erase what had happened, but I also believed Mohor that Codrin was no longer in danger. "I just wished you were more open with me earlier," I said, trying to end things in an amiable way.

"How are things working in the Secretariat?" His wide mouth curved up, in a tentative smile.

"Senal is still in bed, and I have to deal alone with the main secretaries. Jorn refuses to take orders from me. He told me very plainly. Just to avoid using the word rude." I looked at Mohor, and his smile vanished.

"Why did you not tell me?"

"Do I really need to come and complain to you? What am I? A child?" *Why can't you understand this?* There were so many small things done against me. A little push here, an impolite word there. On purpose laziness. The only exceptions were Vlaicu's men. Mohor stated several times that I had full authority, but what happened at the wedding, Codrin's arrest, my exclusion from negotiations, and mostly Aron and his men's subversive work convinced many people that it was just a facade: Mohor had to say it, but he did not mean it. One morning, I heard Jorn, through the door, saying that he would push me out from the Secretariat as Aron pushed me out from negotiations. I had to let things accumulate and serve everything to Mohor in one large package. "Don't worry, I know, you can't reign over Aron and his brother and his cousin, and in everything related to him. They rule here and force you to keep an inept man like Jorn in the Secretariat." When you have little or no chance in a game, you should not play by the rules, you must turn the tables.

"Jorn is indeed average, but trustworthy," Mohor said, avoiding to look at me.

"Average?" I snorted. "He is a halfwit, and you depend too much on Aron. Secretariat, army, even the money in the Visterie. His men are everywhere. You have other competent people..."

"The truth is that I don't have, but things are under control. Among the guards, no one is Aron's man, and Vlaicu is not exactly his friend. What about Aron's cousin?" Mohor remembered the other relative in my list of complaints – he was the Vistier of the castle, taking care of all domestic affairs, including finance.

"I needed some money for my daughters' room, and he refused me. It seems that I need your or Aron's approval first. I preferred to use my own purse."

"There is a rule when large amounts are requested," Mohor said awkwardly. "I will change it so that you can approve them too."

"I did not know that ten galbeni means so much to you."

"Ten?"

"Don't worry; I know you can't do anything about him. He is Aron's cousin, after all."

"Demin can replace him, so I will..." he said in the morose tone that I was starting to know so well.

"No. I will fire the Vistier." I pointed to my chest to underline it. "In the council."

He stared at me for a while, then nodded in silence. "We should wait until Codrin is free."

"If you say so... I wanted to tell you something yesterday," I continued in a flat tone, and he nodded again, a slight irritation visible on his face, warning me not to push things too much. "I am pregnant."

With some confidence restored, I thought it a good time to reach Veres. It was a peculiar situation as after our marriage, Mohor became his tutor, and Veres training for Knighthood was left in Aron's hands. And mind. A wicked mind that perverted my son. I was the last one to hear that he had left Severin the day before, to stay in Aron's castle for a while. There was nothing I could do for the moment, and bitterness swelled inside me – his own mother counted less than Aron. At a certain age, sons settle away from their mothers, slipping inside a man's world, but not like this.

The day came, and I have never felt more ill-prepared for a talk. Escorted by two soldiers, Codrin entered the room, pale, like anyone who had not seen the sun for a month, a bit thinner, but he looked to me in an acceptable physical form. *He may disagree.* He looked calm, expressionless.

"Sit down, Codrin," Mohor said in that special tone fathers use to speak to children when hard issues are at stake, and I waited for some small effects. There were none – Codrin sat in his chair in complete silence.

The effect may be delayed, I still hoped.

"You are angry, you may feel persecuted, and you want to know what happened. I will let Jara explain everything to you. For various reasons, a ruler is not always able to take a just decision. He must take the right one, and sometimes they are not the same. Don't think of this being a kind of apology, as there is none, just a lesson of life. Once I told you a thing about learning," Mohor recalled what happened after the duel. "Now it has come to pass. Your future is here, in Severin, but after all that happened, I can understand your necessity for some reflection. It's all yours." He gestured to me and left the room.

Your part was easy; I glanced after him disappearing behind the door. Codrin's expression was still void of feelings; he was staring at nothing. "Codrin, I know you are angry." I copied Mohor, but all my strategies vanished because of his unexpected calmness. *It's just appearance. It must be.* "I knew nothing that night, about your arrest. I learned about it just four days ago. It was not easy..."

"Am I free?"

"Yes."

"Then I am leaving." He stood up in silence.

"You are free but not that free." I smiled, trying to sweeten my words.

"Veres was with the soldiers who jailed me. Say what you have to say." He pressed himself against the chair, his eyes fixed again on a point somewhere in the room.

Mohor! What have you done? One month thinking that I jailed him. "Look at me!" I yelled. "I did not know that Veres... I know how stupid it sounds, but I did not know. Please believe me. Look at me," I said, moving to his side of the table and leaning on it, in front of him. "I did not know."

He finally seemed to notice that I was there and looked at me.

"I did not know," I repeated, touching his face. Cornered, my mind entered a repetitive cycle, but that seemed to raise his interest in what I was saying. "I learned that you were jailed while having an argument about you with Veres. My family is split, with Veres against you, and you are my family, too." I continued caressing his face, like a mother, and his body revealed tension for the first time, an inner struggle that I could only guess. "Veres is Aron's friend now," I said bitterly. "And Aron forced Mohor to jail you."

"Poor Mohor."

"You know that my first husband was killed, and that I lost almost everything. Does it matter if it was wrong or right?"

"I guess not. Can we stop now?" His voice was again normal.

"Codrin, I know this is a difficult time, but your place is here, with me, with Saliné, with Vio, with us. Promise me that you will stay."

"I can't."

"Don't make any decision now; there are too many bad feelings. And … I have something for you. I filled these papers before … before my wedding. I wanted to give them to you, the day after, but it all went wrong. I bestowed you the small house where the hunters used to gather in the past, before the chase, and five hectares of land."

"Thank you, Jara, but there is no need," he said dryly, turning to leave.

Unable to find another solution, I pulled Codrin back to me and embraced him tightly. He straightened a little, then embraced me too. Our tension became strangely pleasant, and we stayed like that for a minute or two, then separated in a tacit understanding that a message was both delivered and understood.

Going back to the table, I took the papers and pressed them into his hand. "Please."

There was a subtle change on his face, and still silent, he nodded, then kissed my hand.

"May I see Saliné?"

"She is not here. Father went with her and Vio to visit Knight Marin, who has a daughter her age. It was planned two weeks ago, and I could not stop it. The visit will also help our alliance against Orban."

I sensed a hidden approval in his reactions, like he knew something about the danger coming to us, yet he just nodded in farewell and went out without a word, but at least he was holding the bloody documents. *Come back, Codrin. Please.*

194

Chapter 13 – Jara

One long month passed with no news from Codrin. Saliné never complained, but there are other subtle signals telling you when someone is suffering, and I hoped that I was hiding them better. Sometimes, we rode along the road in front of his house, but his house was always empty. Two days later after our last ride, Saliné entered my room and closed the door behind her, leaning back on it. She was happy, happy in a way that I had almost forgotten.

"I met Codrin," she said, without leaving the door. "In our house."

"Everything went well," I smiled.

"Yes," she smiled back.

"How was he?"

"Afraid and upset." Saliné was in a state of mind that allowed only short phrases.

"And now?"

"Afraid and less upset. We ... clarified the fools' episode," she sighed. "It was ... easier than I expected, like he wanted to forget too, and we talked like before. It feels so good to be with him, mother. But he is not happy," she said abruptly. "And he is afraid," she repeated.

"What is he afraid of?" I had no doubt about the reason, but she wanted to talk, and with all that regained happiness, his troubles were marking her.

"Mohor and Aron. Codrin said nothing about them, but he always stays just one night here; that's why we've never found him. I want to see him more, Mother, but I am afraid that he will be harmed."

"Saliné." I went to the door that she was not able to leave, and led her to the sofa, taking her in my arms. "There is nothing to fear. I agreed on this with Mohor. I know what you want to say: that I knew nothing about his jailing on my wedding night. It will never happen again. I promise you."

After a while, she calmed herself and went to the door more confident.

"Did he kiss you?" I asked spontaneously, before she could open the door.

"No," she said, her face suddenly red, and left the room.

❧

"Codrin came back today," Father said, with no other introduction. It was the evening of a rainy and cold autumn day. It looked more like the beginning of winter.

"Is he hurt?" I whispered, unable to fully use my voice.

"No, no. There is some important news for you."

"I will send him an invitation for lunch tomorrow," Mohor said, after a short silence.

"I doubt that it will work, and I can't blame him, Mohor. Neither should you." Father always had a direct style in dealing with Mohor, and in most cases, it worked well. There was a bond between them that I envied and appreciated at the same time.

"Any hints?" Mohor asked hesitantly, rubbing his chin.

"No. He asked me to invite you two and old Senal to my house. It's inappropriate, I know."

I knew that Mohor would not go, and he was right. "I will go to see Codrin tomorrow," I sighed, and Mohor nodded in agreement.

In the morning, it was sunny again, and Father came with me. We found Codrin enjoying sunshine on the small terrace that I knew so well. Close to him, his bow was leaning on a pole. Tense, Codrin came down, and I could see the shadow in his eyes. They were as cold as a winter's morning. I decided to wait for him to speak first, or perhaps I did not know how to react to his strange behavior.

He stopped in front of me, hesitantly, and the shadow in his eyes seemed to recess. "Jara," he said coldly, looking surprised at my body, which was showing some small signs of pregnancy. He was quite observant; few women were able to guess my state.

"Three months." I smiled, embracing him before he could speak again, and some of his tension vanished. "I am glad to see you again, Codrin."

"Sometimes, I dream that we are as we were before the wedding when things were *different*. How is Saliné?" he asked with unusual bitterness, then looked away, beyond me, toward Severin. "And Vio?" he swiftly added, as if trying to hide something, his voice still bitter. "I miss them."

"The girls are fine. They are missing you, too," I gently reproached him for his lack of communication. "Would you join us for dinner?"

"One month feasting in your jail was more than enough," Codrin said resentfully, and he frowned, that dark shadow filling his eyes again. "Sorry," he added swiftly. "You can't understand what kind of... Anyway, I have some important news that Mohor and you need to hear. And old Senal too if his health allows it. No Big Mouth. Please find a way that is acceptable for all of us. I am probably not the best diplomat in this situation."

Probably?

"Codrin," Father interjected. "Mohor is a Seigneur who keeps his word. You are…"

"Mohor is a Seigneur who doesn't respect even his wedding guests," Codrin snapped, in a way that was not really him.

"We will go together." Father was still calm, but under that layer of coolness, I read his frustration. Something of a great importance had happened, and however strange Codrin's reaction, I could not entirely blame him for it.

"Can you at least tell us what is at stake?" I tried to move things away from his safety until he had accepted what Father had said. Sometimes, the mind cannot immediately grasp the situation when too much fear is involved.

"Your lives."

"Please, Codrin. We will be there, Senal too. We want to keep our heads safe, mine, the girls', yours. I hope that you think the same."

"Yes, you are doing many things to keep them safe," Codrin said gruffly, climbing the stairs, and I tried to go after him.

Father stopped me, whispering, "Let him be. You have chosen the right words. Wait for them to have an effect."

"I will come, but I put all the blame on you, if something happens," Codrin pointed at me, "not on Mohor." He came back, after a while, fully armed and in his ring-mail.

Not a confidence building thing, I sighed, and we rode in silence until Codrin said in a morose tone, "I have an important letter that was addressed to Mohor. The messenger was killed on the road."

So many dead. "Codrin, we are glad that the letter did not fall in the wrong hands."

At the entry in the residence, Codrin took my horse instinctively, as in our old, good times. From the stairs, I turned my head and, caught in the net of my memories, I watched them go to the stable with the horses.

"Codrin is downstairs," I said to Mohor; he was alone in his office. "We've lost some important letters. Call Senal. *Only Senal.*"

Mohor looked at me, tried to speak, but chose not to, and sent his secretary after Senal. The old man entered the room together with Father and Codrin, who handed the letter to us, grimaced and passed a hand over his scalp, saying, "It came to me in a rather unorthodox way."

Like children around an interesting book, we read it together, all four of us gathered at a corner of the table, Codrin watching us intensely from his side. Reading, a shiver racked along my spine. Knight Konrad wrote to us about the latest developments in our alliance, in the north. Names, numbers for the army, finance, everything was there. In Orban's hands, the letter would have meant our end. *Codrin knows all this.* It was even more quiet in the room now and, through the open window, I could hear the lingering calls of the merchants in the market, one of them praising the weapons he was selling. *Swords and death and more death.* The outside noise vanished from my mind, as we settled back in our places, in a silence that was difficult to define, each trying to evaluate the consequences, preparing arguments for a decision that could be hard to make. *Codrin will never betray us… Who else has read the letter?* The paper on the table was more dangerous than any sword a merchant could sell.

Mohor cleared his throat. It sounded harsh in the lingering silence. He had picked up a half empty glass from the table and held it now in one hand, rotating it one way, then in reverse. "Was the letter open when you found it?"

"No," Codrin answered simply, and it was a palpable relief on our side, visible in small gestures that Codrin was absorbing with a tight concentration. "I learned that it was addressed to you only after I opened it."

"No one else saw the letter," Mohor whispered as if talking to himself, and Codrin shook his head. "How did you find it?" Mohor's next logical question, a most dangerous one.

"Some robbers attacked us. I found the letter in the pocket of their leader."

"Robbers," Mohor repeated, confused, none of us expected some petty robbers to be involved in such important things. "What kind of robbers?"

"Rich men dressed in poor clothes. Very skilled with the sword."

"I think we have everything we needed to know." Under the table, I signaled Mohor that he should keep things on a safe path. It could be, indeed, that Codrin had interfered with one of our paid mercenaries, but he did not act to harm us. It was a coincidental event. Even if he was hired to guard our enemies, it was still accidental. He was hired by many people in power.

"Yes," Mohor said thoughtfully, and I glanced at him, frowning slightly, trying to enforce on him that we had nothing to fear. He caught my stare, and I felt reassured. "Whatever the reasons, we were in great danger from the moment the document was lost. Thank you for giving it back to us." He took the letter in his hand and stared intently at it. "A valuable service. You will receive ten hectares of land." It was a good reward, but Orban's larger fortune would have paid much more for that damned letter, all of us knew this.

"Thank you, Mohor," Codrin said softly. "Without being disrespectful, would it be possible to request a different thing?"

His newly acquired diplomacy surprised me more than his unusual request. Others could have a different point of view, but they did not know Codrin as I did. Trying to avoid an answer that would be harsher than needed, Mohor gestured to him to continue.

"You are in negotiation with the Devans for Saliné." His stare moved back and forth between us, and I was sure that we reacted in a bad way; the negotiations were a secret that was no longer secret. Codrin moistened his lips before saying, "I ... I would like to ask for my own chance with Saliné, instead of receiving the land." Speaking Saliné's name, his voice became normal again. I realized that only as an afterthought; the previous tension in his voice matched well the one still lingering in the room.

"A girl like Saliné needs certain rank. At least a Knight." Mohor did not set a higher rank or add a castle as a precondition, convinced that Codrin had no chance of being a Knight anytime soon.

"I understand," Codrin answered calmly, "and I agree. Saliné is fifteen right now. May I have the first choice and three years to fulfill our agreement?" In a subtle move, he both accepted Mohor's conditions and transformed the discussion into an agreement that would carry consequences.

"Yes," I said before Mohor could react. We planned to have Saliné married in two years, and she was not aware yet, but one year more, while adding some more complexity to our negotiations was not something unattainable. *And it will be better for Saliné too; she will be more mature.* I knew that Mohor was upset, and I touched his knee to calm him. For a moment, I pondered how Codrin learned about our negotiations with Devan. It was not the right moment to ask.

"Codrin deserves his request," Senal said, looking nowhere, as if speaking to himself, but he knew how to handle Mohor better than me. There were some links developed between him and Codrin. The snippets of news Codrin was bringing went mainly to me and Senal, and once I found them talking alone before my wedding.

"And as your gain is hypothetical, you should keep the land," I added, knowing now that Mohor was, if not fully convinced, at least not opposing the agreement. *Saliné will be Grand Signora, but she will not be happy,* I thought bitterly. My marriage was also arranged, as for any noble family, and it went well for me until Orban destroyed almost everything, but Malin became for me what Codrin already was for her.

"Thank you," Codrin said.

There was nothing more to say at that moment, and Codrin left, followed by Father, and I joined them too, as we had agreed. Not that there was really nothing else to say, just nothing while Codrin was still there.

"Codrin, please understand, we are in a bad position and have no other choice than getting closer to the Devans," I said, avoiding the word marriage.

"You are working hard to find the highest possible place for your daughters," he served me my own words that I wished to have never told him, without even looking at me. "Please follow me out of the castle." It was more an order than request, yet I followed, even though I found his caution ridiculous, but at least it stopped the recriminations about Saliné.

Outside, he eyed me aggressively while saying in a flat voice, "Your men tried to kill me."

"I suppose that you were protecting their target..."

"No, they were sent to kill me." That intense pressure never left his eyes; there was a strange contrast between his bland tone and his stare.

"That's not true," I whispered. *It can't be true...*

"What is true is that you did not know." His eyes were light again, like I had passed a test, making me angry that he could think of me being involved. "I am not sure about Mohor, so it's up to you to tell him or not, but I don't want Big Mouth to hear that I know. Things will escalate. None of us want this." Codrin's finger moved in a circle to include all three of us in his statement, and he mounted his horse without waiting for my answer that anyway did not come; I was too confused.

Aron tried to kill Codrin, I realized, but in a strange way I was relieved that Codrin did not work for Orban, and he captured that damned letter just because Aron had used our links in the north to attack him. "How could he think that I...?"

Before mounting too, Father said in a low voice, "He didn't. Codrin had a hard time these months. Let it pass. Aron started his own game, which doesn't suit our interests. Codrin is more than a skilled swordsman and protector. He was born to lead, and we need him."

I found Mohor alone in his office, still playing with the letter, without reading it. "What happened?" he sensed my turmoil.

"More bad things," I whispered, and he gestured me to continue when my silence went on too long. "I need more time to assimilate everything." *Mohor was not involved. I am sure.*

"Is Codrin working for Orban?"

"He is hired by many high-ranking people," I said evasively, because I could not be entirely sure. "But in this thing, Codrin was involved just by coincidence. Don't ask me more," I stopped another question. "It was stupid to send the letter with the assassins," I blurted, taken by a strange thought coming to me from nowhere. Sometimes, the Light was speaking to me, and while, in general, I did not desire it, now I wished to inherit my mother's strong Light, and see through the future. *"That could be in dangerous hands by now if it weren't for Codrin."* I pointed to the letter, still lodged between his fingers. "And it's time to stop this killing game." I had never agreed with such course of action, but Aron convinced Mohor that we should forget about honorable things when dealing with Orban and hired a team of assassins to kill Cantemir. Aron did not hire the assassins directly, but even with such precautions, I feared that Cantemir would learn about, and he was not only Orban's Secretary; he was also the Master Sage of the Circle.

Mohor glanced at the piece of paper in his hand as if just seeing it, then nodded. "We owe this to Codrin, and I am ready to hear whatever bad news you received from him, whenever you are ready to tell me." He stood up and surrounded my shoulders with one arm, the other one still holding the letter.

Chapter 14 – Codrin

I left Jara speechless, and headed for home, thinking that the main judgment and reactions would come later. *One day, I will show them the letter where Big Mouth paid for my head.* The irony of his attack was that together with my life, I saved Cantemir, for the second time, and that brought from Orban's Secretary a level of trust that I needed for my plans. Perhaps they could guess about my links with Cantemir and indirectly with their main enemy, Orban, even when I mentioned only the assassins' attack on me. *I don't work only for Cantemir,* I shook my head. Now, I worked for many powerful people: Mesters, Knights, Secretaries and Spatars in the most important cities of the former Frankis Kingdom. Delia's brother-in-law and Devan's Chief of the Guard told me about an important embassy to Severin, and I thought it was just about their alliance with Mohor. Soon, I heard that Devan had ordered an engagement ring from Tomis: a small one, for a fifteen-year-old girl, and I found that Saliné was their choice.

I don't work only for Cantemir, I came back to my double identity, *yet I work mainly for Cantemir.* Everything became so interlaced, until he considered me more than his eyes and ears, and slowly immersed me in the political game, talking of many things over a bottle of wine. Saving his life played a role, and the information game too, but I learned what was important for him. The only city missing from my briefs was Severin. Each time Cantemir asked about Severin, I just shrugged that such a small city did not attract my attention as protector. Tudor was an unknown entity in Severin, and even more, a Mester from Arad had seen me twice in Tolosa and spread the news that I am from there. I took care of not contradicting him.

After a last journey to Leyona and Tolosa, the winter finally came, and kept me stuck at home along with a loneliness that was almost physical – nothing like this had touched me before. I was a happy child or a fugitive, but I was never alone. Only Cernat and Milene kept me afloat from time to time. *And the spring predicted a perfect end of the year...* My solitude ended when I met Saliné again in Cernat's house – he had sent a message to me.

"You must come, Codrin," Saliné said gently, caressing my face, and I reacted by taking her in my arms, trying to avoid answering. "It's the main party of the year, and we can stay together at the table again. I am helping Mother to organize it, and I will be your Court Host. This year we gather three days after the winter's solstice, in two weeks from now."

"I wish you came here more often," I whispered. There were too many ghosts in my mind, but I had no real chance of escaping both Saliné's charm, and my own desire to be with her again.

"You are the man, so you have to chase the lady, and I take your answer as a yes." She smiled, yet there was a trace of sadness in both her voice and smile, and I understood that for whatever reason she was not allowed to come.

At the party, there were far fewer people than at the wedding, and stealthily, I moved between the valets swarming the room until I arrived at the main table, just behind Saliné and Vio. Mohor was the first to see me, and nodded, well disposed.

"Mohor," I saluted; Jara was missing, probably caught in her duty as host.

"Welcome, Codrin." Mohor's voice was casual. "This time you are at the main table." There was a touch of amusement in his voice, not enough to alarm me, yet uncomfortable, but nothing could be read on his face.

"Codrin!" Vio shouted, rising from her chair. She jumped into my arms, and all the people were now gazing at me with various expressions, from contempt to amazement. I was a strange appendage, one moving arcanely between parties, fools and jail.

"Vio." I raised her up; the show was already here. "Saliné," I said, when free again, stepping toward her.

"Codrin." She nodded graciously, without leaving her chair, and I stopped abruptly, my body ending in a slightly contorted position from the sudden stop, and that brought some more smiles.

Etiquette... Under the impression that my place would be next to her – she was supposed to be my Court Host – I stumbled, seeing it occupied by Bucur, Big Mouth's son. I stared around uncertainly until I saw the only free seat, at the other end of the table.

"I suppose that's my place," I asked Saliné, trying to be casual.

"He's finally realized his place," Big Mouth interjected, drowning out Saliné's attempt to reply, and he guffawed loudly, followed by several others. Her words got lost in the noise.

"I am sure Saliné reserved for me the place I deserve," I said, ignoring that she had tried to speak too, and I understood that my answer hurt her, but I was angry and went slowly to occupy *my place*. In another distressing repetition of the wedding night, it was impossible to have any conversation with my neighbors. They ignored me in stony silence, sometimes staring at me in a cold way which seemed calculated to make me even more uncomfortable – my rank was not high enough to merit their attention. For no reason, one of them shot an angry glare across the table. I ignored him and sat in a dreamlike silence, startling from time to time, at some noise behind me, like a distressed rabbit.

Saliné is upset, I realized after a while. *So am I.* The music finally provided some diversion; it was a dancing party, and I went back to her, deciding to make the first step.

"May I have this dance?" I asked Saliné, thinking that she would explain what had happened, and I had that strange feeling of breathless anticipation, of fear and excitement, that I had used to have when I warmed myself for a fight.

"The vagrant wants to dance," Veres derided me, and I noticed a short glance between him and Big Mouth. "With a Signora. I can't allow this to happen. She deserves better dancers." He stood up, just a few paces from me, ready to interfere physically, with the unintended consequence of extracting some smiles from the people around – with all his massive frame, his fighting weakness was well known, and all that unwanted attention left me alone for a while.

You want to provoke me. Not you, Big Mouth. You are just a tool.

Saliné's face looked troubled, and it took her a while to answer. "I am sorry, Codrin, but I promised to dance with Bucur."

"Bad luck," I shrugged, struggling to remain calm. "I'll come for the next one."

"I promised him all the dances," she said in a weak voice, her eyes pleading at me to understand something that I could not. "I will explain everything to you later."

Bucur interrupted us, asking for his dance, and I had to step back, making room for him. "You can dance with the little girl; she is *precocious*," he said, in that tone adults used when they meant insufferable, and pointed maliciously at Vio, lending his hand to Saliné, who followed him, speechless. I was much taller than Vio and the effect would have been strikingly odd. The laughter around us proved it.

"May I have the dance, Vio?" I asked promptly, before she could burst out.

"Show us the drunken crane steps that you name dancing," Veres mocked, and the laughter became louder, led by Big Mouth. It was hard, but I ignored him again, gripping Vio's hand to calm her.

"Don't worry, Veres." Vio grinned, her fingers answering to my grip at the same time. "They will sing The Snail for you later, so you can *dance* too."

Dancing was the last thing Veres could do, with his clumsy gait, and his smile froze on a red face. There was no such thing as The Snail song, but from that evening on, Veres was called Snail. He mouthed a silent bad word, swept us with a baleful glare, turned on his heels and walked away from the table.

For different reasons, neither Vio nor I knew the local dances, and we learned by trial and failure, raising some more smiles. *A stranger and a child.* The second dance was acceptable; the Assassins Dance lessons, and having innate good coordination, saved both of us. By the third dance, Vio was smiling again. After seating her, I tried to slip out while people were still walking around. No one saw me. Almost.

"Codrin," Jara stopped me. "I am sorry, but Aron asked for Saliné to be Bucur's Court Host at the party. We could not refuse him and found it prudent to settle you away from them."

"I understand; vagrants are dangerous people. I suppose Bucur will obtain the favor again; Big Mouth is good at exploiting your weakness." I realized that behind my anger, my words could be in fact true, and he was planning something related to Saliné. *Are you involved in this, Jara?*

"It might be," she said wittily, trying to make my irritation look unnecessary and excessive. "Let's go back, the show starts now."

"The last one did not end well for me. This looks the same. I am played again by my hosts and the fools are waiting." I had seen them preparing their show in the opposite room. They were unknown to me; the last team was unlikely to visit Severin again.

"You don't believe that." She smiled and landed her hand on my arm. "I know you are upset, but Saliné did not know the rules about dancing and fell into Bucur's trap. She had to keep her word. It's her first party, and important to her. A court is similar to a war zone, only the weapons are not the same. You need to find your way here too, Codrin. You will not protect caravans all your life."

"Oh, that so important etiquette. For some, it counts more than people. No one bothered to warn me that I'd lost my Court Host. But who am I to ask you to keep your word?" With a calm that was not real, I tried to move away from her.

"Codrin, please stay. Aron's request came just before the party started. Saliné will explain everything to you. We have a family dinner after the party, and you are invited. Just one more hour to wait," Jara said gently, pushing me back by the arm.

As it was usual in Severin, the Winter Solstice Party finished at sunset, and Jara came to me with Vio.

"Vio and I will be your hosts." She smiled, a little trifled, a subtle message that Bucur was invited too, and Saliné would continue to host him.

"Big Mouth forced you to invite Bucur," I mocked her.

"No, I invited Bucur before knowing about Aron's request for the main party."

"You planned for them to stay together. Bucur is your second choice for Saliné, if the arrangement with the Devans fails."

"That's not true, but let's not discuss it now." She nodded briefly toward Vio – who, standing a half-pace in front of Jara, missed the sign – telling me to keep their negotiations secret.

"Please stay, Codrin." Vio interjected before I could snap again at Jara, and she grabbed my right hand. "Saliné wants to talk with you. I don't know why all this happened," she glanced disapprovingly at Jara, "but Saliné is upset too, she wanted to be your Court Host at her first party. And I want you to stay too."

Slowly, Jara took my left hand, squeezing it gently, and they dragged me further.

In front of the door, Jara stopped, looking at me. "This is a court, Codrin," she said in an even voice. "A small one, but still a court with its rules, and the need to survive. You may not be given the right position at times. Sometimes you will not have a place at all. But here," she touched her chest, "you have the same place as my children." Before I could answer, she opened the door and stepped inside.

Everybody else was seated when we entered; there was a square table, able to seat two people on each side, and the cast was already set. There were free chairs only next to Mohor, and on one side, so everything was clear. Saliné smiled at me, and just by habit, I briefly smiled back. The smile was bitter. Vio at first had the impulse to sit on my lap, as usual. She stopped herself, and I noticed Jara nodding approvingly at her.

"Sorry," Vio said after she sat down. "There are new rules, but I can still do this for my brother." Her hand found mine over the table, and she smiled at me.

"Brother!" Veres sneered.

"More than you will ever be," Vio said, her voice sweet.

"When you grow up and become more intelligent, you will learn to stay away from vagrants."

"It's true you two don't have the same level of intelligence." I gestured between him and Vio, and Veres grinned, satisfied, until Vio could no longer stop her chuckles. He reddened but kept his mouth shut. "Don't worry, Vio, your mother is just using me to make you and Saliné fit for high society."

"That's why she invited you?" Vio asked, starting a chain of tiny physical reactions that died fast around the table. She pouted in a mix of innocence and amusement.

"And I thought we were having dinner, not a training session," Mohor said in his casual tone, so difficult to read sometimes; there was a veiled subtlety in his words.

"I was taught to be *reserved*," Vio stubbornly turned everything back. In another situation, she would have extracted smiles; now it was different. "What about Saliné?" She looked at me as if I was the one to know.

"Ask Jara. Perhaps she planned something new today." Unable to control myself, I glanced at Bucur, and everybody became aware of it – they were staring at me. *So what?*

"The steak," the chef announced in a proud voice, and in tacit approval, things moved instantly in a more benign direction.

Now and then, sporadic strings of conversations sparked, in a peculiar way, involving mostly the two persons on the same side of the table, which for me meant Vio. Saliné was at a diagonal, the farthest person from me, and I did not feel compelled to enter in a conversation that took a more general turn until Jara addressed me.

"Codrin, would you stay here overnight?" she asked. "The girls would be happy to read some stories again. We have a larger library here."

"Sometimes, we read together. A real pleasure," Bucur interjected before I could answer, and he looked at Saliné, who let a trace of a smile appear on her lips.

Her reactions had a new degree of social maturity; I could not tell if she smiled because of remembered pleasure, in approval, or just for acknowledgment; it was so neutral, so far from her usual expressive reactions. *They are reading together...* "As I see, Jara, you've organized their literary activities very well," I said coldly.

Anticipating the end, I planned to go out onto the terrace in the break before the dessert, just to be left alone; it was relatively warm for winter, which is to say that it was not frozen.

"Codrin, would you join me on the terrace?" Saliné whispered behind me, and I started; lost in my inner world, I did not feel her coming.

Outside, we leaned against the wall, which leaked some warmth from the room, her shoulder touching mine.

"What does Mother want to teach me through you?" she asked, amused.

"Ask her," I said, not at all amused.

"I am asking you."

"What different places we have in society?"

A sudden cold blast from the mountains hit the terrace, and Saliné shivered, crossing her arms over her chest. Instinctively, I acted as many times before, passing a hand over her shoulder, taking her in my arms. She leaned back on my body, and after a while, she shivered no more.

"Then she is doing what any other mother would do."

Stubborn... "Yes."

"What is bothering you?"

Bucur. "Nothing." *Are they preparing Bucur for her if the marriage with Devan fails? I made that agreement for nothing... And I can't tell Saliné why I am upset. They are betraying me, and she thinks I am acting childishly.*

"Would you stay overnight? We have a lot of books."

"It appears there are plenty of people to read with, too."

"Ah, that *nothing*," she chuckled, then turned, embracing me. "You are right; Mother is preparing me and Vio to survive the court. It was not needed in our house, but now... I made some wrong steps, not knowing the rules, and ended up hurting you."

"Ah, those rules..."

"They are important. For women, even more than for men; we are more vulnerable, but I understand what you mean, some things are more important than rules. A girl's first party is like sparkling wine; it takes her mind away. You can't have a second first party, can you? Aron and Bucur played us against each other. It was my fault that I let it happen, and a hard day for you. That sparkling wine was too strong," she sighed. "I am sorry."

It may be my fault too. Aron's reactions stopped Saliné from answering me. In a retrospective way, things no longer looked spontaneous, and a tightness I had not realized eased a little.

"Codrin," she said gently, as I was lost in my inner world. "We have the places we have, and ... there might be some plans for me. Nothing clear yet, so I still hope for us..." Her voice became barely audible, and I held her tighter in my arms. "But we are what we are to each other, and this will never change; it doesn't matter who I must entertain at the table or where I spend the rest of my life. Always." Her last word was just a whisper.

"Always," I answered like a mirror that reflected sounds too. *She doesn't really know, but they can't trick her; she is already guessing.*

"And Mother... Mother is trying in her way to help both of us to cope with a future that may come even though none of us wanted it. Don't think wrong of her, she is very fond of you. Please stay tonight," she pleaded, leaning her head on my shoulder.

"I will." *And I will fight for you, Saliné. I am weak, but I will fight. Our chance is so small ... I cannot even tell you.* "If you play for me." An image from the past flashed in my mind: the curve of her gracious neck bent over a lyre, and dark red hair gleaming in the firelight. Her fingers were carved in my memory too: slender and delicate like flower petals. *How I wish to have our moments again.*

After dinner, the evening was as before at their hunting house; Jara left me alone with Saliné and Vio. We finished reading, and Saliné went to take her lyre. Her fingers touched the strings gently, and her song imitated the waves lingering on the shore in a day without wind. Through the large window, the full moon was hovering over the land, and we were happy.

And for a second time, I slept in the castle, in different conditions though. However, I did not sleep well that night, because of all the tension bustling around. A few strange dreams haunted me, but one of them was stranger than anything else I had ever dreamt. Tudor came to me in that dream, emotionless and severe, staring at me as only he could do when I was failing in my training. The only missing thing was the scar on his face, but dreams are like that.

"Tudor!" I cried, my mind filled with joy.

"I have not much time," he said coldly. "When a large fire burns the land, you run for your life, or you fight fire with fire. Time is running out. For both Jara and you. And for Saliné too." He stared at me for a few moments, his thick dark red brows drawing together. "Be careful when and where you start your own fire. It may save you. It may burn you."

"What should I do?"

"That choice is your own burden," he said and vanished.

"Things are taking a toll on me," I whispered, suddenly awoke, then I forced myself to forget the dream and sleep again.

The longing that followed me in the days after was much less pleasant, and I still could not figure what was in Jara's mind.

Chapter 15 – Jara

From the light passing through the thick curtain, it was midday. I tried to change my position in bed. *It hurts.* My lower part of my body was aching. *This time it was harder.* On my right, Mark was doing what all the newborns do: sleeping. *Really hard*, I remembered the tough labor that took so many hours and left me worn-out – sweet and acrid, my own blood's smell was still filling the room. *Four children... Five, if I add Codrin.*

"Finally awake." Mohor entered the room and moved the curtain away, then opened the window, before sitting on the edge of my bed, taking my frail hand. Strong light pierced my eyes, but it felt good, and the cold air was refreshing. Spring was coming. "How do you feel?"

"Like I've been gored by a bull. Help me stand. All my bones are aching." I slowly raised my upper body, and Mohor arranged a pillow behind me.

"A courier just arrived from Devan. His embassy will be here in two weeks. I need you in good form to negotiate the contract."

I sighed without answering and closed my eyes. A bird started to sing close to the window. *Yes, spring is coming.* I tried to avoid any thoughts about Devans and marriage arrangements.

"We need the marriage contract," Mohor said, gently. "And young Devan is a decent character. Like his father."

"Yes, we need the contract." *I know it as much as you...* Behind my closed eyes, Saliné's image surfaced. She was crying. Shaking my head, I opened my eyes to Mohor's worried face, but I ignored him. *What can I do? Poor Saliné will accept. She will cry alone in her room and never complain. Codrin... I will keep my promise to wait until Saliné is eighteen. Then... I hope he will understand and not hate me, after all... It's necessary to separate them, now. They are still too close. Harder now, easier later. He thinks of having a chance with Saliné. As much as I want his chance, it will not happen. We are too weak. I am sorry, Codrin. Fate...*

"Jara," Mohor stopped my swirling thoughts.

"Saliné and Codrin must not know until the negotiation ends."

"Codrin is not here, but Saliné... She is a clever girl."

"Yes, she is."

Mark woke in that moment, crying aloud for my breast, and stopped a discussion that I hated.

I received many visits, some of them just to pay homage to the Signora, some of which I enjoyed and raised my morale. Codrin surprised me with a box of mefilene, and I caressed his face; for my own pleasure, and to maintain a bond that was fading, because of the wall I was slowly raising between him and Saliné. He did not avoid my touch, but he seemed colder and did not stay long. I could not blame him.

It took me two long days to get out of my bed and a week to start working in the Secretariat again.

"We need to talk." Unannounced, Codrin entered my office, pushing the door in the angry face of the guard behind him, who did not dare to interfere. Codrin had open access to me, but this was too much.

"Wait outside until I finish," I said coldly. Father was helping me arrange Saliné's dowry for the Devans, and I was struggling to keep my head cool. Your daughter's marriage should be an exciting thing. I begged to differ; the last name that could be given to our circumstances was exciting. I hated it. And the Devans were pressuring us because everything we could put on the table was just a hypothetical gain. We could never recover all our lands; there were too many political complications, so I had to reduce Veres's inheritance, and most of all Vio's. I was sure that Veres would react badly. For him, it did not matter that we were in a bad position. *Vio will accept… Why was Saliné not my firstborn?*

"Now!" Codrin retorted, killing my thoughts.

"I hope you have a good excuse."

"Jorn, his son and a soldier raped Meline and killed her father. Is this excuse good enough for you?"

Jorn was Aron's brother and a perfect match of *character* for his sibling. Codrin's deliberate coldness reminded me of things that he wanted me to remember, and things he did not know I would remember. My own experiences and the story of his sister, raped by their cousin before being killed, together with his parents.

"Are you sure?" I asked, without thinking. Jorn was a pitiful man, and I supposed he raped and killed, as many men in power do, just because they believe they have the right to do it, but molesting a woman working in my house was unexpected. I breathed deeply, unable to reconcile the *normality* of behavior forced on commoners and my own miserable experiences. *It should not be* normal. As many times in similar terrible situations, my hand unconsciously moved to sketch Malin's face on the paper in front of me. A small comfort. Codrin stared at the paper with a curiosity that I could not understand – he did not know Malin. Yet he looked startled, giving me the impression that he was hiding something. Nervously, I turned the paper face down.

"You may think that I am crazy, but I will describe to you a man. A man a bit taller than me. Dark red hair. Blue eyes. Straight-edged nose. High forehead and unruly eyebrows that often gave him the appearance of frowning when he was not. Delicate mouth for a man. A thin scar on the left side of his face: eye to earlobe."

"Quite a general description, but without the scar, it matches my first husband, Malin."

"I can add a small, light brown spot on his skin. Here," Codrin said after a moment of silence, touching the left side of his neck.

"The shape and size of a wolf's fang," I added quickly, and Codrin just nodded. "Who told you about that? There was no mark on my drawing of Malin."

"I had a dream," he said reluctantly, drumming the table with his fingers.

"Codrin," I whispered, grabbing his hand. "Tell me the dream. Please. It's important." *Malin did not come to me. Why did he choose Codrin?* After my wedding, there were no more dreams with him, pleasant or not.

"I don't believe in dreams," Codrin said sheepishly. "But..." he shook his head. "That man said something about fighting a large fire with fire in a dry land."

"What does that mean?"

"I don't know," he shrugged. "I was hoping you could tell me."

"Codrin, are you hiding something?"

"Your Malin with the scar on his face was my mentor, Tudor," he said, irritated, and there was pain in his voice.

"Malin had a twin brother," Father said thoughtfully. "And his name was Tudor."

"Tudor died a long time ago," I interjected.

"No, Jara. Thirty-seven years ago, four-year-old Tudor was kidnapped in Tolosa. The year I married your mother – Malin's father was there to negotiate our wedding in my name," Father said in a nostalgic voice that stirred me, and for a moment, Mother's fair face filled my mind. "The kidnapping was kept secret, for political reasons. Tudor was the firstborn, and without his disappearance, he would have been your husband."

"How did you tell Malin from Tudor?" I asked, bothered, unable to explain why such a hypothetical situation could unnerve me.

"Tudor had another spot," Father said gently.

"Light brown again, under his left armpit. The size of a thumbnail, no regular shape," Codrin said edgily, and his spellbound stare made it clear that from now on he would not disregard his dreams again.

"Yes," Father said in a low voice, then shook his head in disbelief. "Wild rumors spread about three men in black attacking the ten soldiers strong escort, killing everybody apart from the boys and taking only one of them, leaving Malin behind. Just rumors. We never knew what really happened, or if Tudor was really taken alive – there were no survivors apart from Malin, and we found him unconscious." There was a long silence, the old memories were consuming him. He frowned, eyes fixed on Codrin, who was dressed all in black, as usual when riding. "Each of them had two curved swords," he whispered, stepping forward uneasily, grabbing Codrin's shoulder.

"They could be from the Assassins Order. They kidnap children with high potential to fill their ranks. Their training is inhumane, and half the children die before their rite of passage. Tudor was the best of them."

"Are you an Assassin?" Father asked, sharply.

Codrin just shook his head, and I touched Father's hand, urging to release him.

"Tudor was a renegade Assassin. He abandoned the order to train my brother and me. He died fighting to save me." Codrin preempted any other question and left the room in silence. Watching him, I could not help but observe the sadness in his eyes: he loved the man who died for him. Twin brothers are alike, and knowing Malin, I understood that Tudor was a wonderful man too.

"The bloody Circle wanted Tudor dead," Father growled when the door closed behind Codrin. "They triggered…"

I rarely saw Father angered to the point of wobbling, but I wanted to know more. "Why?"

"Your mother had a Vision about a Prophecy. Tudor was starting a chain of events that would destroy the Circle. How I wish it were true."

"It may be," I said gently, just to appease him. I did not believe much in prophecies; mostly, they tell what you want to hear. "The saying was about Tudor starting the Circle's demise, not destroying it himself."

"Codrin might play a more important role than I thought," he agreed, thoughtfully. "And his father had a powerful position. A Duke, maybe. A lesser man would not have been able to shelter Tudor from those black beasts. In some ways, Codrin is Tudor's heir. Nine years of mentoring, starting when Codrin was just seven years old, leave deep marks."

I'd always had the feeling that Codrin was more than we thought. I even believed that he had royal blood, and Father's words vindicated my thoughts. When I first touched on Codrin's origin; he laughed at me. *Could we use the Assassins against the Circle? Is this what Malin meant by fighting fire with fire?*

I waited for the evening to talk with Mohor – after dinner people are more inclined to make good decisions. Yet all the strategies I'd prepared had weak points: the normality of a noble's behavior toward a commoner; and Jorn's high position at our court.

"Jara, I understand you, but if I have to punish my Knights for such things, how long do you think I will remain a Seigneur after that? I know it's wrong, but this is a frequent occurrence. I did not create this world. I was just born here, like you."

In a way, he was right, and rape and violence themselves could not be used as arguments to push my case further. "They attacked a woman working for me, killed her father, and bragged about it. They put me in a bad position."

"A minor servant. And partially it's her fault too. That young hothead tried to kiss her in the market. She slapped him in public and was able to run and escape. He is a Knight. A commoner cannot be allowed to slap a Knight. She should just have run. For Jorn it was justice. I will ask him to pay her damages. Fifty galbeni," Mohor said, then gently covered my mouth with his fingers. "Jara, I know you are upset, but don't ask me impossible things. Please."

Unable to speak, I breathed deeply, for self-control.

Broken Promises

Chapter 16 – Codrin

It was strange how my fate was intertwined in such unexpected ways with the Frankis Kingdom, in general, and with Jara's family in particular. Tudor told me about a strange attraction for Frankis that had developed in the few weeks of his stay in Tolosa, now the most southern Dukedom. *Why did the Assassins kidnap him?* They kidnapped children, true, but Frankis was so far from their Nests. *How could they know Tudor's value?* There was a deep mystery hidden in that old, sad story, and Fate, in her peculiar way, immersed me in something that just started to unravel. Knowledge about Assassins was spread more than I thought, and there was also the issue of the Circle, that ghost thing I learned about from merchants' whispers, but never witnessed myself. *Could the*

Assassins be that Circle in Frankis? It was just a matter of time until news about my curved swords would be passed to people in high positions linked in subterranean ways to the Assassins Order. There was no way to change my habit – it suited me to separate Codrin from the other me, Tudor, the Wraith of Tolosa as people started to call me after I saved the life of Joffroy, the son of the Spatar of Tolosa. The most successful Lead Protectors were called Wraiths, and there were only four of them in Frankis.

Returning from the south, I went to visit Jara again, more than three weeks after Meline's misfortune, when Mark had made his two months. "Would you mind if we go together?" Cernat asked, a request I thought was coincidental.

During the ride, he asked more questions about Tudor, and I had to be careful not to reveal too much about my family. I felt an uneasiness in him that I could not explain, and with all my eagerness to learn more, I decided to ask my questions later, on the way back. At the gate, Vlaicu announced that Saliné was waiting for me in the library.

Alone in the large library, we sat at the table, close to each other out of habit. "Codrin," she said, gripping my hand, her voice trembling. "There are some political dealings... They are not good for us. I learned about them only yesterday, and I wanted to tell you myself. You deserve at least this from me."

We love each other. We don't deserve what they forced on us. At that moment, I understood why she had chosen the library for our talk – it was the place we most enjoyed being together; that, and the cherry tree. "I suppose that negotiations have started for your marriage."

"The marriage contract has been signed, and I am now engaged. The contract will be sent to Deva with Jorn, in three days from now. It's a political thing, against my will, but it's needed for our survival. My family is in great danger. In a year or two, Orban will attack us again. I need you to understand that. My wedding with a Devan is planned in two years."

I forced myself to stay silent, she was distressed enough to deserve another push from me. *They signed it. Jara has betrayed me.* Then I saw the engagement ring on her finger, a delicate one with an emerald stone. *Like your eyes,* I could not stop thinking. *Tomis craft...*

"I have to wear it. I am sorry." She caught my involuntary reaction, and with an uncontrolled gesture, hid her hand under the table.

"There is no way I can offer you such things," I said, bitterly.

"You offered much more to me, Codrin." Her voice was now barely audible.

"Run away with me," I whispered, staring intently at her for the smallest sign of approval.

"Last night, I dreamt that we ran away and lived together. There were even children in my dream, our children." Unable to continue, she stopped for a while and bit her lip, her hand gripping mine stronger than before. "But I would not be able to live knowing that I'd ruined my family. We need this alliance with the Devans; if not, Orban will destroy us. I am at least gratified that I can help my family, which is also yours." She leaned her head on our hands, clasped together over the table, and with my free hand, I stroked her beautiful auburn hair. Warm tears were running down my fingers, and I tried to raise her head. She refused to move, and we stayed like statues until she could control herself. Her eyes were dry now, the traces of her tears running down her face the only witness of the sad moment. That, and the moisture on my hand. "As I am engaged, a certain behavior is expected from me. We can no longer ... act like before. Forgive me."

"There is nothing to forgive you for," I said, trying to take her in my arms, but she slipped away.

"Please leave now, Codrin." Hesitantly, I still tried to close the distance between us, and she stepped back. "Please Codrin," she whispered, and I understood that I was hurting her, just by staying there. She was fighting to keep her composure and wanted to be alone.

I left the room without a word. *I have to settle this with Jara.*

When I entered her office, Jara was looking through the window, and she seemed healthier. *Maybe she just needs some more sun.* With all the bad news Saliné had given to me, I still cared for Jara. Cernat was already there. The room became suddenly silent, and I tried to speak the anger that was boiling in me. The words did not come.

"Codrin," Jara said gently. "Saliné thought that you deserved to hear about the contract from her. Don't think that it was easy for her."

"We had an agreement..."

"It was respected. We negotiated, and the marriage date was postponed with one year, as you requested for your plans."

"No. You signed it, and Saliné is engaged now. You will never cancel their marriage, even if I fulfill my part, and I had the first choice. You broke our agreement." In temper, I raised my voice at her.

"We had no choice but to sign it. You are upset, and I understand. None of us is happy right now." She came closer, trying to touch my face, but I left the room, slamming the door behind me.

"Codrin," Saliné said softly; she was just outside Jara's room. "I thought that you ... understood. Please don't argue with Mother on this subject. It's not her fault." Red and tired, her eyes were almost begging; it seemed that she had done nothing but cry from the moment I left her alone in the room.

"It's a different thing," I whispered, unable to control my voice. "We had an agreement for ... something. It was not respected."

She touched my face with her hand, her glimmering eyes reflecting the same sadness as mine, then she entered the room in haste before her composed face could fail. I leaned with my back on the door, my mind a blank. Eyes closed, I focused on my inner self, breathing the Assassins Cool, trying to overcome my turmoil. Unnoticed, time passed through me without a trace until the door pushed me forward, and from the strong thrust, I guessed it was Cernat.

"Sorry," he said, looking at me, but I controlled my reactions. "Let's walk together. Jara and Saliné are in despair right now, and I guess that you are not much better. They both love you and wanted everything to be different. I asked you something some time ago. Where do you see yourself in five years? Do you have an answer, now?"

"I don't know."

"Time runs fast," he said gently. "I still remember the day when Jara was born. In two years, you will not be a Knight and Saliné goes to the Devans. How does this affect your decision? I am not asking about feelings; that I understand. But here marriages are political. Is Arenia any different?"

"No, it isn't, but we had an agreement that was broken when the marriage contract was signed."

"We appreciated what you tried, but the family's future counts more than our feelings. My grandchildren's fates depend on the alliance we are building. And your fate too. Our whole alliance and survival depend on this marriage."

"It will not happen," I breathed angrily.

"You will stop it," Cernat said, a trace of sarcasm and disappointment in his voice; I appeared too obstinate and lacking any natural or political understanding.

"I wish to have such power... But it will be Orban."

"You may be right, but then another agreement may be signed and another one, or Fate wants yours to be fulfilled. We can't foresee."

Coming to where my horse stood, I kept myself busy with the halter. What could I say? He was right about the alliance, and whatever small hope I had had in the past, had become even smaller with the marriage contract.

"Mohor has big plans," I broke the silence after we passed the gate. "But he has no army. There is no discipline, no good equipment, and his Spatar is a joke. I saw soldiers in Arad, in Tolosa, in Peyris, in Leyona. Here, I see a rag-tag army. On papers and treaties, things may look good for you, but Mohor needs a small war just to understand his capabilities, before making a big step that could destroy everything. And Mohor needs to reanalyze the alliance with the Devans. It may end badly."

"You may be right," Cernat said, thoughtfully. To my disappointment, he became silent, as if wrestling with his own thoughts.

I could not go straight back to my house on the hill. I could not. I went in the old garden, where the giant cherry tree witnessed our most happy moments, and sat against the rough bark while the wind blew the old leaves around me. They were dead and rusted, like my soul. Cernat acknowledged me, but he was a tactful man, and let me alone – sometimes only solitude can heal you.

From that day, I was rarely invited to the castle and then for official reasons only. In the rare moments when we still met, Saliné never embraced me again; the *correct* behavior for someone engaged and ready to be married. Fate had played its dice against us – the marriage contract eliminated us from each other's lives, but not from our feelings and thoughts.

❦

I left my home the next morning, and for two days, I rode east, polishing my plan – the only hope to obtain a status that could bring Saliné back to me, and further to give me a chance to regain Arenia. Nothing happened on the road until Panait and his caravan came my way, late in the afternoon.

"Tudor!" he shouted, pushing his horse closer to me. "I had to move on short notice and couldn't find you in time." Usually, I knew well in advance when his caravans were leaving Arad, as there was no way for him to send a courier after me. "Are you free? You are my Lead Protector."

"Where are you going?"

"Mehadia and then Leyona."

"I can travel with you for the next three days." For a while, we were going in the same direction, and I was eager to hear what had pushed him on the road. "How is Delia?"

"Still pregnant," he said, his voice filled with joy – their marriage was four years old and without children.

"Just for two more months," I joked back. "Or even less. This is what set you on the road?"

"This and more." His voice went instinctively lower. "Trouble may come and keep us at home."

"War?" *I was in Arad less than two months ago. What changed so fast?*

"There were rumors about troops gathering in a month or two. Embassies came from Mehadia and Dorna. Duke Stefan sent an army to our northern border. And Cantemir was nervous when I left, something must be wrong. He wanted to go to Mehadia but sent me when he learned about my caravan leaving."

Merchants were also diplomats, but the stakes of his mission were low; if not, someone from the court would have been sent. *Then why was Cantemir supposed to go? What changed at the last moment?* "Mehadin can be a hothead."

"I know him," Panait sighed. "There are some moves against Severin. Low level. At least for now. Next year will be hard for us, Orban is preparing to invade the south; he still hopes to become a Duke."

Is Orban moving against Mohor now? Using Mehadin? That may be both bad and good for my plan.

I left the caravan in the morning, taking the southern road to the east. After a while, I climbed a hill towering over the large junction of roads, and with my spyglass, I checked a group of four riders that had followed us the previous evening. They took the same south road as me, and we entered the high mountains. Down in the valley, the riders were still following me. In the afternoon, I reached the gorge of Sera. A place of a striking beauty, with tall cliffs almost meeting high in the sky. Here and there, small tributaries fell from the ridges, raising fine curtains of water. Several places could fit into my plan, and I advanced cautiously, searching every nook and cranny. The third one I found was good enough. After a steep curve, the road ran straight toward me, running between the high cliffs. On my right, it bent again. From the small hillock, twenty feet higher than the road, I had the best possible view of anyone coming from any direction, yet the luxuriant bushes would hide me well. For diversion, I arranged arrows of different sorts in the arrow pocket on the saddle. Well trained for such occasions, Zor was as still as a stone. It did not take long for the riders to appear where the curve of the road went on my side. They were in a hurry, and the galloping hoofs stirred many sparks and echoes along the gorge. A few birds scattered from the trees above and vanished from sight. Slowly, I nocked my bow and aimed.

With a soft hiss, my first arrow pierced Jelin's neck. He clutched the arrow and fell silently. The soldiers behind him cried their fear. Jorn stopped abruptly, and turned just in time to see his son falling from the horse. I planned everything in detail after Saliné had told me who will lead Mohor's embassy, but I could not anticipate that my justice would be so complete; the soldier who attacked Meline and her father along with Jorn was there too. The next arrow followed, and the next one, then I pushed my horse down onto the road until I faced Jorn, now alone. I wanted him to know why it happened.

"Traitor! You killed my son! You will be hanged. I will tell Mohor."

"How do you plan to tell him?" I unsheathed my sword. The realization came to Jorn later than I expected, his wide eyes moving around nervously, looking for an escape path – there were just walls, and he drew his sword, too. "You don't know why this is happening."

"You want to stop the marriage. Even if you do, she will marry Bucur, not a vagrant like you."

So, there is a plan for Bucur and Saliné. "Don't worry; there will be another embassy to carry the contract. This is for Meline."

"I paid the bitch fifty galbeni, more than she ever deserved. I can pay more," he added swiftly.

"Yes, you *will*."

The fight ended fast; Jorn was a diminutive copy of his brother. *Justice was served*, I stared at the four bodies, lying on the road in unnatural positions. I owed it to Meline, her dead father and to a long row of unknown victims – Jorn and his son were serial offenders. *I started the fire. Let's hope that is not the wrong one.*

Guessing that the most important things would be there, I took a large backpack from the back of Jelin's horse, trying to retrieve the documents. I wanted to know Mohor's plans, and it was not good for him if somebody else found them. The backpack was heavy, and I found a bag with four hundred galbeni. *Twenty hectares of land,* I counted mechanically. *Or twenty mercenaries for two months. A small army...* Unfortunately, the alliance document between the S'Severins and Devans was not sent with Jorn, only the marriage contract, so my political knowledge did not improve. Before leaving, I made a lot of tracks back and forth with Zor and left some more arrows between the bodies.

I arrived in Arad four days later and spent the night in an inn close to the city. In that evening, I was finally able to open and read the marriage contract that was nagging at me. *I will never be able to match a Grand Seigneur like Devan.* The contractual clauses were at a level that I the vagrant could only dream of, and I threw the document on the floor.

The next day, I went to see Delia and Cantemir. I always started my visits to Arad with Delia and Panait, to take the pulse of the region, and to collect some mefilene from Muniker for Vio and Saliné. Delia always had some for me. She was one of those few people who never forgot the help they received.

Detained by some duties in the palace, Cantemir came home late, at sunset. We were alone in his small office, as usual. Through the ajar window, filtered light and music entered the room. Somewhere on the street, a man was singing his love. It was too far to hear his words, but I knew the song. It did not match my mood.

"Sometimes, I want to quit," Cantemir complained, in a tired voice, his attention split between music and his own thoughts. "Everything has become so unstable."

"Make a King. That will restore order," I half-joked. From the rumors I heard, Orban wanted to become the next King, and the Circle had approved his nomination, whatever that meant.

"Do you think Orban can be the next King?" His brows drew down, as though a hundred thoughts gathered behind his eyes.

"Orban is too old for a long game, and he has already bitten off a little more than he can chew right now."

"It's not that we bit off too much, is more that we lost our main tooth. Bernd, Orban's eldest son, was killed some time ago. He was our army commander." Cantemir stopped talking and went to the window in a show of sudden irritation, opening it fully. The sun was almost gone, a small red arc still hanging over the hills. The words of the song became clearer.

Yes, I nodded. *I know it quite well. But he won the battle against Malin by treachery, not because he was a better commander.* "What is bothering you?"

"Many things." Cantemir shrugged, without turning. "I needed you two weeks ago. We have to establish a reliable way to reach you when needed." He turned away from the window, and smiled briefly, his eyebrows still arched in a deep frown.

"My house is far to the south, and I don't stay there much." My statement was ambiguous but correct. In fact, I never gave false information to Cantemir. The game was there, subtle and dangerous, and the devil was always hidden in the details: what information you give and in what form, what you keep, when to give it. Even though he worked for Orban, Cantemir was not an unfair man, and sometimes I suspected that he did not like his master, for an obvious reason: no one liked Orban.

"Why did you come?"

To spread some rumors. "S'Severin's embassy to Deva was attacked. The rumors say that it happened in Mehadian land."

"The Mehadins?" Cantemir asked, surprise reflecting on his face.

"If not them, then who? Your embassy was in Mehadia." I avoided using the main reason people would think that he attacked the embassy: the two attempts on his life, of which one was planned by Aron, even when Cantemir was not sure about that.

"We were not involved. There are problems on our northern border. Duke Stefan has made some moves, and you never know with him. We may need a diversion to keep the Duke busy until spring. A rift between him and Mohor would be good," Cantemir said, looking absently through the window, smoothing down the front of his shirt. The voice singing on the street became warmer. Perhaps the woman of the singer's desire opened her window.

A rift would free Orban's hands to take Severin. "South would be the best diversion. Mohor is forced to react." *It may fit both of us.*

"Mohor is a prudent man." Undecided, Cantemir massaged his chin, and I could not understand his feeble reaction.

"I can't say the same about Mehadin." Mehadin was not Orban's vassal, but a kind of dependence existed; there were some bonds or debts that were not yet clear to me. *I must start the war before Orban is ready to take Severin. To fight fire with fire...*

For a moment, I thought to ask Cantemir if the Circle was real; he was the most informed man I knew. I let it pass, hiding a weakness in what was my best card in the dangerous political playground, the information game. I could not afford such weakness in general, and even more with Cantemir.

I left Arad in no hurry. Bad news spread fast, but it would take a while for Jorn's tale to reach Severin. I spent the night in an inn again, close to the border, a thing that I would have avoided in the past, because time and money were always in short supply. I was a bit richer now, but I had to think more about those mercenaries; during the war, they could help me conquer a small castle, a power base. In the morning, there was the appealing realization that travels are more agreeable when you sleep in a bed, and my ride south started in a good mood.

When the road was about to pass to the other side of the mountains, a vague intuition warned me of fight and danger. Touching the Wing Talisman only accentuated the bad feeling, yet no Vision came to me. There was also the feeling of being watched. I slowed Zor and left the road. Oddly, there were some scattered flying birds that I noticed first; the land was peaceful, but I still felt watched, and I nocked my bow. After a while, sounds began to filter through the forest: the distant clash of metal and faint cries. A horse neighed, his fear echoing loud between the mountains. *Still in Orban's land,* I thought instinctively; the place was near the border between Arad and Severin. I pushed Zor faster through the forest, and stopped at its edge, close to the battlefield, met by an uproar of men voices. A meadow lay between me and a tall ridge bordering the field some hundred paces away. Pinned with their back against the ridge, six men on foot were fighting twelve riders.

Good for defense, hard to escape...

Five riders and three foot-soldiers were already lying dead in the grass. *S'Arads,* I recognized the riders' colors. The footmen were Mountain Men, or Mountes as they were commonly known, settlers in the White Salt Mountains; the volcanic chain spreading north-west of Arad County, a wild area that no Seigneur was able to subdue.

One of the Mountes on my right stumbled and leaned briefly against the rock, then tensed his body, waiting for the next attack. A large man even by their standards – the Mountes were the largest people I ever saw, both in height and frame. He was wounded; a diagonal cut pierced his leather armor, from his left shoulder to his abdomen. Living in hostile places, the Mountes were too poor to afford ring-mail, and they were peaceful people. Two S'Arads followed him closely. Weakened by the wound, he parried one sword at the last possible moment, but left his other side uncovered. My arrow struck the rider, just before his sword descended on the Mounte's head. With a last effort, the Mounte pierced the other rider, then fell to his knee, exhausted and breathing heavily, his eyes fixed on me. I pressed a finger to my lips.

In any fight, the soldiers mostly have eyes for the enemy in front. Three more S'Arads fell to my arrows until my attack was discovered, and they were now seven against five Mountes.

Abruptly, one rider turned his horse, which trotted for a few moments and neighed before charging. In front of me was Arpan, Orban's Spatar, the commander of his army.

"You!" he recognized me from an accidental encounter when I was with Cantemir. We crossed paths for a few moments and a salute, yet he was able to remember. "Traitor!" Filled with hate, he attacked me, with a strong sidekick, aimed to topple me from my horse. It went a little too high, and instead of countering it, I leaned aside on my horse. Caught in its inertia, his blade rasped on my ring-mail and passed alongside me. His body twisted, opening an ample space for my sword. It pierced his neck a moment later, and there was now even more high blood between Orban and me.

The last S'Arad rider ran in haste, and he was already two hundred paces away when I went after him. Moments later, an arrow coming from the forest stopped him. The archer stayed hidden. It was the work of a master: the arrow entered precisely under the rider's chin, the iron point going out through his neck. I stopped Zor abruptly, nothing could help me if I was the next target.

The best archers I know, I remembered my mentor's words. "Avae, sister," I saluted like a Wanderer, thinking that if I turned out to be wrong, nobody would understand my words.

A burst of laughter came from the forest, and Dochia stepped out from behind a large tree. "Avae, Codrin." She walked fast and turned the soldier's body over with her foot. "One bastard less." She broke the point of the arrow, then took the shaft out from the man's neck, and cleaned the fresh blood from the polished wood on his mantle. Cursorily, she threw both pieces in her quiver. "Family secrets," she mused, and turned toward me, something indefinite in her posture accentuating the hardness of her frame, but she was not an unattractive woman.

I did not have enough time to check the arrow, but I supposed that the craft of its making was different. Fighting skill depend as much on training and weapons as on native abilities.

"You are still alive," she laughed again.

"Thank you for your help," I said, dismounting.

"Cantemir's man killing Orban's Spatar. La naiba! Who could believe this?"

"It happened." I shrugged, and if Dochia was not pleased with my answer, she did not show it. "Let's go back. Some of the Mountes are wounded."

"I have news from Arenia." She raised her eyebrows at me, and I was not able to mask my surprise. "Your beloved uncle is sick. Poisoned."

"Poor him. I hope his sufferance will end soon." The malice in my voice came as no shock to her.

"I don't think so. Baraki is using just enough poison to keep him in bed but alive."

"Baraki?" I asked before I thought, and struggled to keep from lowering my eyes when she looked at me, though there was no special meaning in her stare; it was just my overreaction at being caught unguarded.

"You really think that Baraki risked his life just to keep your uncle on the throne? Your uncle thought the same, so it must be some family trait. Baraki is even grateful to you for killing his son-in-law, Jan − one less obstacle for him. Your cousin if I remember well."

"It happened. Do you think that I should return?"

No, she shook her head, and I was relieved; apart from having no army, it would have been difficult to choose between Arenia and Saliné right now. "The Assassins are still searching for you. A time might come when you should meet them."

"I would prefer to decide that myself."

"Sometimes you make the decision; at times, the decision makes you. Do you remember the story of the poor Arenian

Knight, Gurand? His daughter was raped by Jan, and that started a long chain of strange events which pushed you to see the dangerous beauty of Frankis. What you don't know is that the matter was settled between Jan and Gurand; a large piece of land covered his daughter's honor and lost virginity, and everybody was content. The girl least of all, I suppose, but nobody asked her. That was until Baraki played the honorable man and convinced Gurand to reject the deal and complain to the King, luring him with promises of justice, more land and money. When the occasion arrived, Jan impaled Gurand. How much land does a corpse need? You know the rest of the story. So, who decided what?"

"Baraki is not yet fully in control, but ... he has plans, and my bastard uncle will die in his bed. One usurper less. Baraki will become regent for his grandson. The time when I should return." *If I have an army...* That moment, I remembered one of those mythical dancers from a book about a distant past when trained men leaped over the horns of the bulls for the pleasure of their spectators. Dancing on a slippery path as dangerous as the bulls' horns. This is how I felt.

"Maybe."

"My twin sister had the White Light. That night... That night, she returned to the castle because of it. Was she a Wanderer?"

"She was too young for that, and princesses don't become Wanderers, but she had a strong Light. Like your mother. I know it from my sisters in Arenia. She might have seen something through her Light. Something important. We will never know what. Codrin," she said gently when I tried to speak. "Let her rest in peace."

"She will always live inside me." Recalling her memory, made my mouth go dry, even as a known anger began rising in me. *Fate be cursed*, I shook my head, then swallowed hard. "Where did you see me for the first time?"

"In Pades, from the hill behind the village, the day you left, chased by Baraki. We wanted to talk with your mentor about a certain prophecy, related to him. He was born in Frankis."

"One more unfulfilled prophecy," I shrugged.

"I doubt it." There was some amusement in her voice, and her stare made me feel uncomfortable, as if linking that prophecy to me.

A new death may follow the old one. "Where can I find you?" The Wanderers were more important than I had previously thought in the great political game. They had no army, but their strength was not measured in steel.

"Don't try to find me." Her voice seemed far away. I could detect nothing in it, yet I felt a hidden warning, and we walked back in silence.

Dochia... I suddenly remembered. It was the name of the last Empress, who reigned six hundred years ago, and the proof that the woman walking along me was one of the Wanderers' leaders in Frankis, Lights as they are known. *The Maiden Empress.* Her Imperial Guard had only warrior women, and the Wanderers were born from it, while the Assassins were born from the Imperial Legion. It was a rebellion that destroyed an empire already on a steep decadent slope. Nabal, the Empress's cousin and the commander of the Imperial Legion, dethroned her, but he was not able to rule over the whole Alban Empire. It was split in two, then in more parts when army generals took over the lands they had pledged to protect. Dochia ruled one of them as Queen, and she married at a certain point, but the Maiden Empress name remained with her, and her guard followed her from one city to another, until she settled in Muniker, now the Litvonian capital. They renamed themselves Wanderers, in the honor of the Empress's long march through the crumbling empire. *I am her descendant...* In a way, it was the highest recognition of nobility, but other royal houses were born from her too. Some historians mark Nabal as the last emperor, but how much truth is there?

"The Wanderers see favorably that you helped the Mountes."

"Can you speak for the Wanderers?"

"I am the Fifth Light of the Frankis Wanderers." There was no boast in her tone, just the normal voice inflection of someone giving information, and I bowed slightly, to acknowledge my mistake. "Strange," she whispered and gripped my hand suddenly. I stopped, looking at her, but she released me and walked further, without a word, her eyes steady and unreadable.

All the surviving Mountes were wounded, but only one seriously: the one that I had saved first. "Lena," he addressed Dochia with her common name, "you should have returned faster."

"You are still alive."

They know each other well. "Take all the horses you can capture," I said to the four Mountes that could still move easily – the fifth had a cut on his thigh. "The Spatar's horse and gear are mine. That one," I pointed, as they seemed not aware who the Spatar was. "And that mare," I pointed again, thinking that she would be a good match for Zor. There were no horses of his quality in the former Frankis Kingdom, and I was thinking to maintain the race.

"Let me see your wound," I said to the one with the cut on his chest. He nodded, and I removed his leather armor and shirt. "It could be worse, but I have to stitch it." The Assassins are not only fighters, they are healers too; the best I knew, and Tudor taught me not only to fight. The wounded man suffered in silence until I finished the four stitches on his chest.

Having gathered all the horses they could find, the other five Mountes grouped around me, and only when I finished, I realized how tense they were; their hands were gripped on their sword hilts. "He will survive. Take their mail-armor," I pointed to the dead soldiers.

"They are too small," one Mounte complained.

"You can cut the mail-coats to enlarge them and put leather in the open parts. They will still be better than the leather armor you have now." *I did this for myself too.*

"Do it," the one with the cut on his chest said curtly, and I realized that he was their leader. "And bury our dead. Thank you," he addressed me. "Without you, I didn't have much chance. I am Boldur."

"I am ... Codrin. You are good fighters."

"You too," he said thoughtfully, looking intrigued at me. "Why did you enter into an unequal fight to help some strangers?" The Mountes are cautious people, a side effect of the harsh climate in the high mountains, and the many wars that their noble neighbors had started to conquer them.

Very good fighters... With proper weapons... "Orban is not my friend," I said, casually.

It took a while until he was fully dressed, and in the meantime, the pain silenced him. "You killed his Spatar. This was unfriendly, indeed." Boldur stopped, as his men came back with the mail-armors packed on three horses. The fallen Mountes were already buried in a deep ravine, now covered with large boulders. "Time to go," he said and slowly stood up, a grimace stretching his lips, but no sound left his mouth.

"The road to your home is long, and the wound will not heal properly. Take another man with you and come with me. I have a small place not far from here. In one week, you can go back."

"He is right, Boldur," Dochia said. "We move faster now, and riding, you will be back in *time*." I had no idea what she was talking about, but it was a useful spur.

Boldur scratched his head for a while, then he nodded. Until he was able to overcome his pain and mount, I watched Dochia and the other Mountes galloping away. After a while, a peregrine raven left the forest, and I had the strange feeling that it was following them.

Chapter 17 – Jara

The merchant was nervous. He was a small fish in Severin's Merchants Guild, which was anyway smaller than all the others around us, except for Mehadia. Over the table, he entwined his fingers, twisting them as his emotion battled inside. "I came two days ago from Mehadia. On the road back, we found some bodies. A large force had attacked them. There were many arrows and traces of horses. They were *robbed*." Inadvertently, a dose of regret moved through his voice. "It happened maybe three, four days before we found them, and I recognized Sir Jorn."

My fingers clutched the chair under the table, but I was sure that nothing else was visible. I did not even turn my head to see Mohor's or Father's reactions.

"When did you find them?" Mohor asked with a studied calm.

"Six days ago." Expecting a different reaction from us, the merchant feared that his reward would be smaller than his expectations.

"Thank you for your information." Mohor gave him some hope, and it was interesting to see so many feelings reflected in swift succession on the merchant's face. "My secretary will take you to the Visterie, to reward your loyalty." Mohor wrote ten galbeni on a paper and called his secretary. "We might need to talk to you again."

"Thank you, Sir," the merchant said, visibly pleased, and left the room.

"Some know now about the marriage between Saliné and Devan's son," Mohor said, thoughtfully.

"It depends on the robbers," I shrugged. *Were they only robbers?*

We spent the afternoon remaking our plans to deliver the alliance contract between us and the Devans. Having lost a whole embassy, time was pressing and security even more. In the end, we found no better solution than asking Codrin to be the Lead Protector.

"I am counting on you." With some effort, Mohor cranked a smile, looking at me. "I will send a courier to him. It's still early." He glanced through the window, and his face stretched tight. "But too late for leaving today. Everything is prepared; we just need Codrin." He called his secretary and asked a rider to be ready, then he looked at Father, a frown on his face.

"You think Codrin may not come." Father guessed, and Mohor nodded awkwardly; he was one reason for a refuse, but there were other walls raised between Codrin and us, by me. "I will go after him."

Codrin came, but he was not pleased by our sudden request.

"We have some bad news," I said once he was seated, struggling to calm my nerves. "Jorn and all the people from our embassy to Deva were killed." I looked at Codrin: there was no visible reaction on his face, just his fingers drumming the table, as if playing music, yet he avoided my eyes. *He is still upset because of the marriage contract...*

"From your reactions, this happened before it arrived in Deva, and the alliance contract with the Devans is now in foreign hands," Codrin said thoughtfully, after a while. "And the marriage contract, but that..." He shrugged as if to say that losing it would not affect us too much, another one would be sent.

The marriage contract was secret, and some may guess that we have an alliance too. "People were killed," I pressed him further, without really knowing why, but his behavior alerted my instinct.

"Don't ask me to mourn a murderer and rapist." His voice was now harsh, yet he still did not look at me.

"Jorn worked for us," I snapped, nervously.

"So did Meline and her father," Codrin snapped back.

"Codrin," Mohor interfered calmly, leaving me enough time to recover. "What was done was done, and Jorn had to pay for his behavior. I know you found his punishment rather lenient, but this is how our world works." He glanced at me, to see if I recovered, and I nodded.

"I apologize," Codrin said, looking at me, and I recognized the young man who settled in my house, two years ago.

How fast time passes. "It may be that I deserved it." Slowly, I slid my hand over his, which was resting on the table close to mine. Unconsciously, his thumb glided over my fingers. His hand lifted mine briefly, and I knew that were we alone, he would have kissed my hand to make peace. "The alliance contract was not sent with Jorn, but we need to have it back, signed by the Devans, in two weeks. We need someone we trust, able to protect our embassy. Another attack and... I know you only came back just a few days ago, but it should leave tomorrow." It was a five-day journey to Deva, so it was doable.

He took his time, probably calculating the days on the road too, or grinding over some negative feelings about us. "Yes," he said curtly, a small degree of displeasure in his voice.

"Would it bother you, if we send the marriage contract, too?" I asked as gently I could.

His fingers rasped the table, and he withdrew behind his angry eyes, in need to calm himself and provide a composed answer.

"Codrin, I thought we had already agreed on this. Nobody knows now which agreement will succeed in the future," Father said, "but the immediate situation needs dealing with now. We are ready to consider whatever immediate concerns you have right now."

"My concerns will be always irrelevant for you, and I am damned if I do it, and damned if I don't. I will accept, just to avoid being your scapegoat." Codrin glared at me, his narrow lips pressed together in a stubborn line.

"Thank you, Codrin," Mohor reacted quickly. "Cernat told me about your intuition that things would not work well with the Devans, because of foreign interference. Is the attack on our embassy a proof?"

"You don't know that," Codrin answered in haste.

"Who could have done it?"

"Robbers, Orban, Mehadin... It could be something premeditated, or just bad luck." Codrin shrugged, and there was again something uncomfortable that I was not able to grasp in his gestures. "In the improbable case that Mehadin has knowledge of your possible alliance with Devan, he may feel threatened, but he is not an independent player."

"Mehadin is not an independent player," Mohor repeated thoughtfully, and I suddenly understood what Codrin meant: Mehadin's attack on our embassy could not happen without Orban's approval, or even worse, Orban was behind the attack. "I heard that you have two Mountes as guests in your house." Mohor moved to another thing that was worrying us when I would have liked to continue with the hidden links between Orban and the Mehadins.

"It's my house."

"I never doubted that." Mohor's eyes squinted, but he remained calm. "They were wounded."

"Codrin," I interjected, feeling that their irritation was ready to move into a quarrel. "There is no fault in helping wounded people, but we are living hard times, and it's normal to ask what happened. We are the Seigneurs of this land."

"I saved them from Orban's soldiers," Codrin finally answered, then looked away, his jaw hard. "In S'Arad's land."

"The war horse you gave me came from this fight. Who was the owner?" Father asked.

Codrin glanced at us in irritation, mostly at Mohor, and I saw his fingers drumming the table again. "Arpan, Orban's Spatar," he said, visibly annoyed. "I would appreciate some discretion." He gestured to us just to enhance his words, and I looked at Mohor, to make him understand that Codrin needed an assurance from him, not from me.

"Well," Mohor said, both favorably and worried. "That is news. Don't worry, it will remain among us. Time to convene the council and plan our embassy." He stopped any other discussion about Orban's Spatar; there were indeed too many political implications to deal with it right now.

Our council had only two more members: Senal and Aron, but Senal was ill again, and I was leading the Secretariat. Mohor lacked resources for our great game, an issue that I raised often, but we were generally able to cope with it. *Codrin would be a good choice to help me in the Secretariat. I just need to persuade him and Mohor. Who will be the hardest to convince?*

"Could we continue as we are now?" Codrin asked, knowing well who was missing. "We might finish faster." Mohor pondered for a while, then nodded. "Orban and Mehadin may try to block the roads. Give me Vlaicu and three more men. We need to ride fast and stealthily, through Mehadia."

"Mehadia?" My voice thickened midway through the word, and I coughed to get some control back.

"Nobody will expect that. The southern road through Leyona is too long, and the northern road through S'Arad's land is better watched; Orban has more soldiers. An embassy is not a caravan, the risks are different, and I set the course."

"You have experience with embassies." Mohor looked at Codrin, his lip curled just slightly in amusement.

"Yes," Codrin said, looking straight into his eyes.

I kicked Mohor under the table, and he nodded, almost imperceptibly, then stood up and went to the window, giving me a free hand. "You set the course," I said to Codrin. "What about the Lead Protector's fee?"

"I don't work for money with you," Codrin said sharply, and his aggressive posture convinced us not to insist.

"Thank you, Codrin," I said, not knowing what else I could tell him.

"May I speak to Saliné?"

"I am sorry, but Saliné is indisposed." It was not true, and that made me feel ungrateful, but they needed to stay apart, just to make their lives easier in the long run. *Sorry, Codrin*, I apologized inside, and I almost tried to grasp his hand again. I stopped in time; it was not the right moment. *How I wish everything be like before.* I sighed involuntarily, stirring some small reactions in the room.

"I should have asked before accepting. Or be lucky and come ten minutes earlier at the stable," he subtly told me that I was lying; Saliné had come back from a ride just before Codrin's arrival.

"You would have received the same answer. What's bothering you?"

"I want to tell her what happened today, and that your embassy will carry the marriage contract."

"I will explain it myself," I said softly, trying to calm him.

"That's exactly what I am afraid of, what you and others will tell her." Codrin could no longer restrain himself, yet his voice was apparently cool, and I did not react, letting him enough time to recover.

"Vlaicu is waiting for you," Mohor interjected when the silence went too long.

"Codrin, please stay," I said, when he tried to leave. When Mohor left the room, I went to him and touched his face. "There is too much anger in you right now. It will subside. You are an intelligent man who knows what is possible and what is not. Come back safe. We are your family."

He moved away from me, slowly – a deliberate reaction. "You don't really want me back." His tone was icy, and he left the room in haste.

"That's not true," I whispered bitterly, but it was too late.

"Jara, you are pushing Codrin too hard," Father said. "It's not your style, and he doesn't deserve this."

"Codrin is like a son to me. I am walking a tight rope, to keep him away from Saliné and close to us at the same time. Saliné will marry the young Devan. That cannot be changed. Like Saliné, I wish Codrin could be her husband, but we need the Devans to survive. Now that was stupid. I am telling you about the necessity of all this. It was a hard evening, Father. Both Saliné and Codrin accepted their separation in theory, but mind and heart are not the same. Separated, they have a chance to forget each other and start a new life. And if for Codrin it would mean Vio, I will fight for them."

"You can let them meet from time to time."

"Their bonds will become stronger; Saliné's wedding a nightmare, her life a nightmare. I want Saliné to have a chance with her husband – arranged marriages are more difficult for women – they have a whole life to stay together."

"I am not convinced, but you are the mother. At least take care of Bucur. He is becoming too close to Saliné, and that is poisoning Codrin. He fears that you plan to marry Saliné to Bucur if things fail with the Devans. Aron is pushing slowly in that direction, and it would be a bad idea, Bucur is not what he appears."

"Bucur has some charm, and he is the only one with decent manners close to her age here. She needs some training in how to play at court, and he might help to distance her and Codrin. But to marry him? No. It's Devan or Codrin."

"Bucur is a well-known seducer. He has had many women; even now he is *entertaining* two of them at the same time."

"Bucur?"

"Jara, I could understand that you knew nothing when Codrin was arrested; you were new here. But you did not know what happened to Meline and to her father. Don't take me wrong; you are working hard as Secretary because Mohor has none other to take over when old Senal is sick, and you do a lot for our alliances, but you need to keep an eye open here too. Aron is a cunning man and has many plans."

"Codrin told me the same about Aron's plans, but I thought it only jealousy," I said, suddenly worried.

"Then you should be more careful, and Saliné too. She is more mature than her age, but still a sixteen-year-old child. And Codrin is not much older. Just one wrong step, and everything might fail in a way that cannot be foreseen."

I went to the library, bitter and nervous; it was a long time since Father last time castigated me like this, yet he was right. Saliné and Bucur were there, reading a book at the table, seated on opposite sides. It was her turn to read aloud, and I stopped for a while, just to hear her pleasant voice and intonation. That calmed me.

"Saliné, I need to talk with you," I interrupted her. "It will take a while." I gestured to Bucur that she would not return.

Back in my room, I decided to tell her directly. "Saliné, keeping into account your actual status, it would be better to spend your time with Bucur only during the day."

"Why, mother? It's pleasant to read like this in the evening. And Bucur would be upset. He is a nice companion."

"Don't worry, Bucur always finds some consolation overnight, with *two women* in the city."

"Bucur?" she asked incredulously, the same question I had asked before, just that she was so young, while I was not, and there was no excuse for my lack of knowledge.

"It's a well-known thing. I thought you were aware of it." *I cheated... It was necessary.*

"We don't discuss such things, mother, and I never thought..."

Did he kiss you?" I asked, without thinking, hoping it to be untrue.

"Mother, I am engaged. Bucur is just a companion, nothing else."

I took her in my arms, feeling that she needed it – despite all my efforts, Codrin never left her mind alone.

❦

Despite the freshness of the morning, a strange smell emanated in the room, the rotting odor of a decaying body, a thing I had almost forgotten. Old Senal lay in the small bed, his body slightly contorted, his face bluish. Death had caught him in his sleep. We were now alone, Senal and me, if I could say that – Mohor had gone out to gather the right people for the burial, and the quiet room made me feel as if there was no one in the whole castle. *The only friend I had here.* I stared through the window, trying to avoid the cold numbness of his once intelligent face.

"Jara?" a familiar voice asked, and I whirled to face Codrin, finding the comfort I needed in his arms. "Mohor told me. I've just arrived for the embassy." His voice was distorted too, and I fought hard to stop a sob.

It took me a while to leave his arms, and I watched him approaching the bed; Senal was his friend too. There was something morbid in my stare, observing Codrin's reactions. He was calm until his body stiffened. He touched Senal's immobile face, then studied his fingers and nails.

"What are you doing?"

Codrin did not answer. He leaned over the body and grabbed the second pillow, which was resting close to the wall. His fingers traced something on the pillow. "Senal was murdered," he muttered in a bland voice, without looking at me.

"No."

"I know how to read death. I am a trained Assassin. His face is bluish; there are slight lacerations on his cheeks and neck, blood and traces of tissue under his nails. And look at the pillow, there are faint parallel scratches on the cover, nails scratching through the fibers."

"Orban," I breathed.

"I doubt it. Orban is a rabid dog, but he finds pleasure in overcoming his victims and bragging about his exploits, not in paying hidden assassins." Codrin shrugged, then searched the room, calculated and professional. On the table, there were some papers, and he took all of them to the window. They were white and unused, yet he checked each sheet against the strong light. One of them grabbed his attention, and he went to the stove, where he rubbed some ash between his fingers. Carefully, he laid the paper on the floor, then moved his dirty fingers over it until some faint writing appeared. In haste, I kneeled behind him, working to decipher the message which was only partially visible. It was not much:

'Jara,

I feel close to the end of a long life that was both rewarding and spent in vain. As any young and ambitious man with some traces of intelligence, I had higher expectations in the beginning, yet life makes you bend when circumstances outside your control come along. I think you know that awful feeling as much as I do. When you find this paper in my safe box, all my past and remaining expectations will be well buried, together with me. Forgive me that I used this way instead of talking to you, but it is easier for me, as among other things, I will tell you why we have left you to fight alone against Orban, and that Codrin is more important than you think.

I have good reasons – everything will be explained at the end – to believe that Orban or the Circle, or both, placed a spy in a good position at our court, yet I am not fully confident of my judgment, and it will be on you to carry my worries further. If I am right, Mohor is not the right one to tackle...'

The writing ended abruptly, with a long line heading off diagonally, down the page.

"Someone killed him and took the letter," Codrin whispered.

There was the sudden noise of people coming along the corridor, and we stood up, staring at each other in silence, unsure how to proceed further.

"Give me the paper." *Is Codrin a king's son?* He complied without a word, and I rolled it carefully, then hid it in my dress. "It's too early to discuss such things, but you can..." At a loss for words, I just gestured toward Senal. Mohor entered a moment later; behind him, three women to take charge of Senal's body. "Wait a moment," I told the women, offering no other explanation, convinced that the emotion in my voice would hide the real reason behind my order. Mohor just glanced at me, in silence.

"Codrin." I nodded, and he explained everything again, except for the stolen letter that left a writing trace on the paper under it, while I watched Mohor's ashen face.

"We should keep this hidden and play the unaware game," Mohor said in a way that was questioning too, and I nodded. "At least for a while."

There was nothing more to do; the women could now take over and prepare Senal for his last journey. We went out followed by our own silence; Mohor alone in his need for solitude; me with Codrin, in my need for comfort that I could not get from my husband right now, and for getting closer again to the young man, who was like my own son.

In the courtyard, he stopped, his eyes fixed on me, that strange, troubled stare he had in distressed times. I had no idea what would happen next. He moistened his lips.

"Where is Veres?"

"Somewhere in the castle," I said, surprised by his unexpected question. *Most probably with that young servant...* I considered Veres too young to know a woman, but our bonds were strained enough to preclude a formal interdiction that could not solve anything. My first guess was that Aron had arranged the thing, though I was now thinking of Bucur too. After talking to the girl to confirm that she was not coerced, I let it pass. She wanted money, and Veres was the only one who didn't realize it.

"He left early in the morning – we met at the gate when I was coming here. Big Mouth sent him away." Codrin sounded almost apologetic, and that did not make me feel better. "There were some deep scratches on his face and neck that he tried to hide from me. He joked that his girl went wild last night."

Unprepared, I stepped back in shock. "Codrin," I stopped him, struggling to overcome my anger. "Veres has committed some sins and has a bad entourage, but he is still mostly a child. Come back well," I said and embraced him coldly. *Codrin is wrong, it cannot be Veres who killed...*

After the funeral, we had another moment of astonishment when opening Senal's will: he left everything to Codrin. There was not much; Senal was so devoted that he never took a wage from us, yet he had inherited twenty hectares of land and passed them to Codrin.

Chapter 18 – Dochia / Maud

The road climbed up through forest and came to a crossroads. Looking back, Dochia saw the meadow and the ridge where the fight had happened. Codrin was no longer in sight, but she did not expect him to be. *One part of my White Trance was properly addressed*; she thought. *We are at the Wind Crossroads. I am at a junction too. There are so many roads into the future. Why did Fate choose me for the White Trance?* It was a rare thing. Only one or two Wanderers in a generation were blessed with it, though many considered it more a burden than a blessing; the trance carried so much responsibility. Of the living Wanderers, only Ada, the Second Light of Arenia, had experienced a White Trance, and a Prophecy, more than fifteen years ago. One outcome of it was Tudor's defection from the Assassins Order and Codrin's training as an Assassin. Only four people knew what had really happened: Ada, Eisha, the First Light of Arenia, Tudor and Primus, the Assassin King. A paper of understanding was signed by all three and left to Primus as keeper. At his death, he passed it to the next Primus, and Ada went to explain why the defection was needed, even when Tudor was supposed to be their next Primus. It was related to the new Serpent God, who was plotting to replace Fate, and the coming Fracture menacing the whole continent. What no one could explain, not even the last survivor of the initial pact, was why Tudor had to die so early. Fate.

"We split up now," Dochia said to the Mountes, who bowed to her, asking no question. In general, you don't ask about a Wanderer's next step. Alone at the edge of the forest, she waited, leaning against an old tree. Umbra, her peregrine raven, was the first one to arrive, and landed on her shoulder.

"The young man has played his first card," Umbra said, using Codrin's voice.

Absently, Dochia ruffled his feathers. "If you consider what we know from our White Trance, yes, but he played many cards before. Some more successfully than others."

"We are ruled by the White Trance."

"But he is not, and that gives him more liberty. Soon, we will forget most of what we learned during the trance, and we will reclaim some liberty too."

"Do you see it as some kind of shackle that Fate has put on us?" Umbra was part of the Trance too.

"I have no words to describe the White Trance, and I have no memories of what was already erased from our minds. I have only my duty to the Realm."

During the trance, many things were revealed; things that were; things that were happening now, and things that might happen. One of them was the attack on the Mountes, and Codrin riding toward the battlefield. During her trance, Dochia did not see him intervening, and she had to make it happen. She followed him along the road from Arad. Not exactly following him, as she rode ahead of him, Umbra spying for her. When she was sure that Codrin would arrive in time, she felt relieved. Dochia knew that Codrin would not let the Mountes die. The battle set a new course, not only for Codrin, but for Frankis too. One of many. And there was personal relief too. Dochia was only half-Mounte, and she had grown up in their mountains, in Long Valley; not in Boldur's clan, but close enough. They were second cousins. Apart from that, the Mountes would have to play their role in making Frankis a kingdom again. A new King would stop the greedy Dukes' invasions of their lands in the White Salt Mountains.

What should I do next? She felt overwhelmed; there were so many things that she saw in the future. There was another strange thing with a White Trance. If she was unable or chose not to change the course of an event that she observed, it would vanish from her memory. One by one, she forced herself to recall the events she could still remember: battles, wounds, death. Arrows, swords, spears, poison. All in the course of just a few months. And most of the events were bonded like the links of a bloody chain. Hoping for a clue, she attached figures to the events: Jara, Saliné, Codrin, Mohor, Bucur, Aron, Cleyre, Cantemir, Orban, Mehadin and his sons, Mara, Calin. People she knew for a long time. People she cared for. People she despised. Her mind moved to Arad and further on, to Peyris. *The links.* She suddenly understood how the White Trance worked. *If I am not able to solve the first link in time, then all its chain of events will vanish from my memory.* Dochia closed her eyes and felt the wind and the flutter of leaves in her ears and heart. There were birds above too. *I need to decide. The longer I wait, the more I lose. We lose. I feel so weak.* She shook her head, unable to extract herself from her inner rumblings.

There had been mornings in the last two years when she had awakened feeling ancient in the bones, but not in knowledge, wondering if the six-hundred-year-old Order of the Wanderers had not outlived its time, before the world began to change around them. Change was coming, she was at least sure about that; the world was now at the precession of the equinoxes. Change and transience were built into the way Fate had remade the world in the last four thousand years. It was slow by necessity, or at least that was what Valera, the First Light of Frankis and her mentor, had told her during the novitiate phase. The White Salt War almost destroyed their world, and Fate was the chosen goddess to rebuild it. Dochia had accepted that all her life as a Wanderer; it would be improper to complain now.

I feel so weak. She opened her eyes and found that Mira and Irina had arrived. The two young women were her Wanderer sisters and her guards. "We are going to Peyris." *I am sorry, Jara, the longer chains are the ones that really count. You will be tested during the war, and Saliné too, and you may lose everything again, but I have no choice. I leave you in Codrin's hands, and even though I will forget my awful Vision about you, I will come to Severin too.* Her face went stiff, her eyes glassy with moisture that did not fall. *I feel like a traitor...* Being a Wanderer forced Dochia to hide her feelings, but Jara was almost like a daughter to her, and she took a long breath to calm herself. She had to pretend to be composed and sure when all she wanted was to curse Fate for the hard choices the capricious goddess had imposed on her. *One long chain started today with Codrin and the Mountes. Cleyre Peyris is the next one. She must become Duke Stefan's right hand, and then Duchess. She will help Frankis. She will help Codrin. These are the most important chains in my Visions. Let's hope that I am right. Let's hope that I can help Cleyre. I've never felt so lost.*

"You look calm," Mira said. For some time, she had watched Dochia's inner struggle reflected on her face.

Dochia wondered if her understanding was deep enough, in the way she interpreted the White Trance, to reach back to the roots and chose the right path. "Some of my burdens have vanished." Once she had made her decision, everything else started to leave her mind, all the horrors of the war which was ready to start in Severin and around it, and which will hit Jara like a hammer. The only remaining things from her White Trance were Cleyre, Codrin, the Mountes and the three questions she was allowed to ask at the end of the trance. She swallowed with difficulty; her mouth was dry. "We will leave in a few minutes." Before standing up, she felt the need to recall what was still left in her memory, and she closed her eyes again. The image of Dochia, the last Empress, came to her.

"I feel strange calling somebody else Dochia," the Empress said in an amused tone. "The White Trance was fulfilled. You are allowed to ask three questions. You can skip them. The choice is yours."

More bad news? Dochia stayed silent for a while, pondering if she could handle even more trouble. "Will Vio arrive at her full potential?" She had sensed the girl's strong Light and her intuition was that Vio's power would be a pivotal factor in the future of Frankis. There was something different in the little girl, something more than in a Wanderer, a power that she could not explain. She looked at the Empress, who remained silent.

"Will Codrin become King?" There was something different in Codrin too, very few men had the Light, and Dochia cheated by not naming his kingdom, but the Empress denied her an answer again.

"Why did you choose me for the trance?" She knew that apart from receiving new burdens, she would also receive new powers.

"Soon, you will be tested by Fate. The nomads of the east have found Talant artifacts, which can control one's mind. They will try to subvert you and the Wanderers. It will not be easy, but we hope that you will be able to overcome the attack on your mind and set a new course of events. You will not tell anyone about the trance until you return from the Sanctuary in Nerval. Ada, the Second Light of Arenia, will tell you more." The Empress raised her hand to prevent any further questions and hid from Dochia the resurgence of the Serpent Sect, and the menace of the new God, a deity of war and destruction. Most of the eastern nomads were Serpentists now, and the

Sanctuary was their most important temple. "The signs of the trance will stay hidden until then. In the Sanctuary, you will meet a woman named Ai. She will help you." Each Wanderer who had a White Trance was marked by Fate: her eyes were receiving some specks of gold. When Dochia recovered from the trance, her eyes were still unaffected. It was her secret. And her burden.

✌৩

"You've returned early." There was no reproach in Maud's voice, and her eyes, in one of those rare moments when they were not guarded, revealed a hint of contentment. The third Secretary of Leyona in plain view, and Hidden Sage of the Circle's Council in secret, Maud was a powerful woman, more than most knew, but she was rarely happy. Losing a husband and two children comes with consequences. She stood up to greet her visitor. Only three people could stir such a reaction in her. Her daughter, her granddaughter and the man who had just entered her office.

"What punishment lies in front of me?" he asked, embracing her.

"More days here. Perhaps." She disengaged and tried to walk toward the door.

"I told your secretary that we aren't to be interrupted." He placed an arm around her shoulders and walked her toward the sofa.

"Tell me." She didn't want to deal with matters of politics right now. She wanted music and what warmth the sun could offer in the middle of Frankis, during the summer. Many times, she dreamt of the even warmer south, and her happy childhood. She craved the warmth of her memories, yet she had to deal with the coldness of her own machinations. It was like drinking poison but, in small amount, poison can be so sweet.

"Chaos. We are entering a phase of foreseen and unforeseen chaos. Your sister, Drusila, told me that war will start this year. She did not know why and when, or who will start it. Her Vision of the future was scant. She will write to you if she learns more." *Or she hid some parts of her Vision from me. It wouldn't be for the first time.*

"We have had forty years of chaos, but this is a different sort of chaos; it's planned. Most of it. If our plans bear fruit, Frankis will have a new King, and order will be restored. Are we poised to gain or lose from this new course of events?"

"Both. Mohor's embassy was destroyed on the road to Deva."

"Cantemir?" Maud asked, lifting one eyebrow. "I don't think so."

"I don't think so either, yet the rumor mill has already found him guilty."

"Let the rumors spread."

"Aron's brother led the embassy."

"Jorn... A pitiful man. Nobody will cry for him, but I can't see any reason for this killing. Who will lead the new embassy?"

"That young man who grew up in Jara's house. The Arenian refugee."

"A man with some qualities, I am told."

"It depends on whom you ask," he laughed. "Aron swears that he is a nobody; Jara thinks him an Arenian noble, and some people call him the young wolf. There are rumors that he bites hard."

"Ah, Aron still hasn't gotten over that issue with the duel. Something doesn't match," she said, thoughtfully. "From Severin we know that... I forget his name. Codrin. They know that Codrin is a successful Lead Protector. Mohor wouldn't ask him to protect a dangerous embassy if that weren't true. But," she raised a forefinger, "nobody outside Severin knows anything about him. We need to discern the value of each man around Jara and Cernat."

"I am working on that, but Codrin is too young to cause real problems. At least for now."

"Does he really fight with two curved swords, or it's just a rumor?"

"Yes, but he can't be an Assassin. Their novices must be twenty years old to have the Rite of Passage. Codrin is nineteen. Some Arenians are using curved swords."

Maud leaned forward, hands on her knees, her eyes looking inward, a passion, a want, and a powerful will fixed upon that want. "Raul, who was our first choice for the next Candidate King, failed to place Jara's girls under my protection. Jara and Cernat were stronger than we realized and killed him. They are not aware that the young man they've killed was Aron's son. Aron *is* aware. It's a pity that we have a Black Warrant on their names. We must keep Aron in check. Sometimes, he may be really stupid."

"He again insisted to avenge his son, but I let him know that Jara is outside his reach. For a while. The Black Warrant is dormant until Cantemir decides otherwise, but I will keep an eye on Aron. There are some political movements around Cleyre Peyris. Duke Stefan is trying to make use that she is marked by the Circle."

"Yes, I know. Saliné is still the first on the Circle's list, but she would be easier to solve. Bucur will take care of that, at least he is good at seducing women." Maud remained quiet for a while, her eyes fixed on him, her mind searching through his words. "There is more on this."

"Cantemir is mediating between Duke Stefan and Devan. I heard something about Orban being given a free hand to take Severin, but I am not sure if this is the whole thing. Too many embassies went north and south."

"A grand bargain, I suppose. Stefan's granddaughter, Cleyre, for Devan's son, who will become the Candidate King. A Duchy for Orban. Cantemir will stay Master Sage for another ten years. It will set Tolosa and Peyris on a collision course. That's dangerous. Devan's son..." Maud thought for a moment. "He has some qualities, but being a commander is not one of them. Not yet. He is too young. Devan or Nicolas, the Spatar of Peyris, will lead their army."

"What would Leyonan do if...?"

"By that old treaty between Dukes Leon and Stefan, Leyona, Severin, Valeni and Mehadia were created as a buffer between Tolosa and Peyris. With an all-out war, they will lose their reason for existence. Severin and Mehadia were ready to fall next year in any case. I will have to leave Leyona and return to Grenbla. Sometimes, I miss my castle." She shook her head and stayed silent for a moment. "If we want to have a new King, Tolosa and Peyris must work together. We need to preempt this new alliance Cantemir is planning. I am afraid that nothing can be done through diplomacy."

"Who would be an easier target?"

"Cleyre, I think."

"I am thinking the same." His face formed a smile, but his black eyes did not. "Young Devan is better guarded; he is the heir to Deva, after all. Cleyre is just one of Duke Stefan's granddaughters. She *still* is. I will leave tomorrow to hire ten mercenaries," he sighed. "Sometimes, I wish I could resign as Primus Itinerant and spend more time with you."

"Aurelian," Maud said gently, "our time will come. If everything goes well, we will be the real rulers of Frankis until my granddaughter grows wise enough. Who do you want to hire?"

"Valer has the best men." He sounded a little apologetically.

"Valer plays too much politics for my liking. And he wrinkles his nose when asked to provide mercenaries for ... such tasks.

Sometimes, he forgets that he is only a Black Dervil and acts above his station." The most successful mercenaries were called Black Dervils, and there were only five of them in Frankis. Dervil was a black snake in the south. Poisonous.

"His Father was a Knight."

"One who lost his castle and lands in some political misadventure." Maud shrugged and raised her brows. It made her eyes look even larger on her delicate face.

"I can't ask Eagle; he is the Black Dervil of Peyris. I will ask Bear. He is almost as good as Valer. One more thing... Senal was close to unmasking Aron as our Hidden Sage in Severin."

"An intelligent old man, too bad that we could not count on him. Was the issue...?"

"Yes. Aron used that young idiot, Jara's son, so he is covered well."

"Under that ... Big Mouth," Maud chuckled, "there is a good mind. A bit too arrogant, though. Now let's have dinner. Come, a full night awaits us." She stood up and clasped his hand.

"Not so quickly," Aurelian whispered, and pulled her into his lap.

Chapter 19 – Codrin

Most of the time we rode in silence on our way to Deva. It did not bother me; there were many things to put together about Senal's death. He did not deserve such an end, but not all of us have an end that we deserve. I was not yet fully sure if Veres had killed Senal, but if true, there was no way to convince Jara or anyone else in the castle without hard proof. They would simply ignore Veres's scars and his running away. And Veres could not be the dangerous spy Senal mentioned in his letter; there was a handler somewhere, using him as a convenient tool. It could be Orban's man, or it could be Big Mouth, but why would Big Mouth betray Mohor? At least I knew now that the Circle was real, and probably not related to the Assassins. And Senal must have seen Grandfather's portrait, hanging in the Throne Hall. He was only twenty, just a few years before his coronation, and many at the Arenian Court were puzzled by our resemblance.

Two days later, we passed the place where Jorn and his men had died. White bones and colored patches of clothes were spread on the ground – Big Mouth did not consider it necessary to send anyone after his brother's remains.

Below, following Sera River as it cut its path through the mountains, a second troop of riders was approaching along the road that we had left at noon. *Mehadians again*, I checked the rider's banner through my spyglass from our place on the top of a small hill that overlooked the road. *If there is a third troop... Ten riders,* I counted. *Should we attack them? That would signal that we are here, but it would be one troop less. And perhaps fewer of us.* Unable to decide, I listened to the stirring of the faint wind in the trees. As the riders came closer, I recognized Mehadin's elder son. *Is this the fire I need to start?* "Another troop is coming. Soon, the ridges become steep, forcing us to move down onto the road again, and they can trap us here for a long time. We have to attack them." In Mehadia, most of the time we rode, hidden, through forests, in parallel with the road.

By a strange coincidence, Ban, the chief of the archers, was with Mohor when I had that stupid duel with Aron. *The soldier that winked at me.* I shook my head to escape the unwanted invasion of memories. The road was curving just below us, getting larger, with a small strip of forest stretching in parallel on a small ridge, ten feet higher than the road. "Ban, go to the left side of the forest. Behind that bush with white flowers," I pointed out a place a hundred paces from us. "Wait until I release my arrow. Killing the first one will slow or even stop them. Then you shoot at will from their rear. None of them must escape and reveal our presence here. When I charge, you do the same. Vlaicu, you go with Ban. You too," I pointed to another soldier. "You stay with me," I said to the last one. Go." The riders were coming.

My first arrow killed Mehadin's son, and his horse stopped abruptly, then half turned, with the body hanging from its left side. A neigh filled the valley with fear, and the rest of the riders unsheathed their swords. Ban killed the rider in the rear. They turned, disoriented, and I sent my second arrow. Another one fell.

"Ride!" I shouted and charged, to block them as they started to spread out.

Vlaicu did the same from the other side. Leaderless and caught between two charging groups, the riders lost some moments more. When they finally organized themselves, another two were down. Whatever fear our soldiers had felt, it vanished. In a minute, there was no enemy still standing, and we dismounted.

"This horse is better than yours," I told Vlaicu, pointing at the young Mehadin's destrier. "Is your sword inherited?"

"If getting it from the one who tried to kill me means inherited, then yes." Vlaicu cocked his head, and a large grin flashed across his mouth.

"You just inherited another one." I took the respectable sword, still gripped in Mehadin's hand, and balanced it in my hand, before giving it to him. "And I think that you fit in his armor too."

Mohor's soldiers were poorly fitted with weapons and horses, and Vlaicu, while better equipped than others as Chief of the Guard, was still in the regular range. He had now a Seigneur's horse, sword and armor. Jara told me that Mohor kept a tight rein on his purse, gathering money for the final war, and he was sometimes tighter than was really needed, unable to realize that a strong army is built over time, and it's not cheap.

"Do you know him?" Vlaicu looked at young Mehadin's body.

"One of the Mehadin's Knights." I shrugged to hide my lie. "A rich one. Split everything else between you. Vlaicu, you decide what goes to whom. I want them well equipped, too." The spoils were always a god way to forge bonds that could be useful later.

When they finished, I stared at Mehadin's body. It looked smaller without the armor. *Mohor will have his war now. A bit sooner than he expected. Or Orban expected...*

We journeyed unchallenged to Deva, and Vlaicu delivered the documents while I sneaked in to meet Balan, the first Mester. This time, I avoided Dan, the Chief of the Guard; he knew Vlaicu and the other me, Tudor. In fact, it was not Codrin going there to see Balan, it was Tudor, and to hide things better, I borrowed a straight sword.

"You will have a wedding soon," I told Balan.

"Me?" he asked, surprised; all his children were already married.

"Not you, Devan." I forced myself to laugh. It felt bitter.

"The fool..." He shrugged, annoyed. "What wedding is that? A naked bride with no lands and castles? I know, she is beautiful, intelligent, even marked by the Circle, but no house can survive in the long term with such poor marriage arrangements."

"Marked?" I asked, a little too eager, though I managed to bite off the word Circle before it left my lips.

Balan did not answer for a while, looking away. "You caught me on the wrong foot."

"I apologize," I said slowly. *Are you a member of the Circle?* "We will assume that no discussion took place." *We can't really assume that. Can we?*

"Cernat has a certain lineage that makes him and his descendants suitable candidates for the throne. There are nine lineages still alive."

"Like Orban's lineage." That was one of the rumors I'd heard before: Orban had the right to become the next king, and the Circle was helping him. After all that had happened with Senal, I was now more inclined to reconsider those rumors, especially when they came from the Mesters I knew.

"Yes."

"And the marking?"

"Each promising child with a proper lineage is tested by the Circle. The ones who pass are marked and, with some luck, they can grasp a better future. Will you go to Arad soon?"

Saliné was marked by the Circle... Jara hid this from me. We never talked about the Circle. Isn't that strange? But we did not talk much about Orban either. I waited for some moments, hoping that Balan would say more, and I coughed, unsure if I could control my voice. *Another obstacle raised between Saliné and me.* "In ten days from now," I finally answered. "Delia?"

"My first grandchild." Balan's voice was now filled with joy, and a large smile spread across his mouth. "But I can't go to see her until mid-autumn."

"If you want to send a letter..."

"And a small gift." Balan looked at me, and I nodded. "They are already prepared; I was just waiting for the proper courier. Will you stay for lunch? Dan has a guest from Severin, their Chief of the Guard, Vlaicu. I know him, a fine man; it would be a nice gathering. They should arrive in a few minutes."

"Thank you, Balan, but my men are waiting outside the city," I said, trying to sound apologetic, and rubbed my brow to hide my surprise. "We must leave in one hour." At leisure, I moved closer to the window – it offered a good view of the street. Dan and Vlaicu were coming. "There are some people in the street that I need to avoid." Five unknown riders, armed to the teeth, were storming along the road, so my words sounded true when Balan came to the window. "Would you mind if I leave by the back door?"

"I'll ask Mona to bring the gift," he said, hesitantly. "She is in the kitchen. Do you really want to leave?"

"I apologize; it would have been my pleasure to stay, but you know how hard a protector's life can be." I left the window and went to the door; Dan and Vlaicu were almost at the front of the house. Balan followed me, and I went to the kitchen without asking for his permission – after so many visits, there were no secrets related to the layout of his house.

"Tudor!" Mona, Balan's wife, exclaimed when I entered. "You came just in time; lunch is ready."

Oh Mona… "I apologize, but there is an emergency, and I have to leave. I just came to collect the package for Delia and Panait. I will…"

"Dan is coming." The large entry door of the house screeched, announcing incoming people. "You can't leave without meeting him. And we have a nice guest."

"Mona, don't kill me, but I must run through your back door. Please bring Dan here," I said to Balan; there was no way to leave now without meeting him.

"Dan," I stopped him before he could start the same story about lunch and having a nice guest, "I have an urgent errand, and there are people in Deva looking for me. They are not from here," I said before he could question me; it was his duty to keep the city peaceful. "There is no need for you to interfere, but I have to leave incognito. You know how we work." For any protector, stealth was more important than the forceful protection Dan could offer. And I needed stealth; Vlaicu was now with Balan in the living room; I could see them talking through the ajar door. I was at least lucky that Vlaicu was with his back at me.

Dan's face reflected a touch of confusion and irritation, and lacking any other idea that could help me, I stayed silent, hoping that he would not insist. "Deva is a peaceful city."

"Yes, you are doing a good job, and no one will attack me here, but my problems will start outside your walls." *My problems start outside your kitchen.* I forced myself not to stare past Dan, inside the other room, where Vlaicu morphed into my biggest concern.

"I hope that I did not disturb you." Vlaicu's voice was cautious, and it sounded remote through the small open space in the doorway. Perhaps he knew what Balan thought about the marriage contract he brought to Devan.

"What nonsense is that? I knew you since when you were a child, and we did not see you for more than a year. A friend from Arad is here to take a present for my daughter, Delia. My first grandchild will knock at the gate of the world in a week or two. Unfortunately, I can't go to see her now." It was strange how Balan's voice could reveal so many contradictory feelings, in such a brief time. Slightly irritated in the beginning, it became proud when mentioning Delia, then sad, at the end, as he could not go to see her.

"Arad is not so far from Deva, but why not bring your friend here? I would like to hear news from Orban's city," Vlaicu said.

"Oh, that I understand, Orban knows how to make news. Mostly bad news," Balan chuckled. "Tudor seems to be in a hurry, but I can ask him..."

Balan! Don't!

"For Delia." Mona came with the package for her daughter.

If I could, I would have kissed her. I grabbed the package and went for the door – I was at least lucky that the back door was in their kitchen. "I hope you will still invite me for another lunch." I smiled awkwardly and left the house in a hurry, haunted by a strange silence, just when Balan's face appeared through the other door.

"Tudor..." Balan said, then clamped his mouth shut while I was running away.

The more people I know, the more dangerous things become for me. Sooner or later, someone will catch me...

The journey back was uneventful, and we arrived in Severin just in time for the gathering of Seigneurs and Knights waiting to receive Devan's answer and signature on the treaty. I avoided the castle, letting Vlaicu tell Mohor and Jara what had happened, and rode to Arad. Before leaving, I found a small medallion from my hoard as a gift for Delia's newborn – it belonged to the assassin paid by Big Mouth to kill me.

ೲ౿౼

By a strange coincidence, I arrived the next day Delia gave birth to a boy. Arad was a large city with a flower market, and a bouquet of yellow freesias joined my medallion. It felt awkward to offer just a gift from my spoils.

"Thank you, Tudor, but it's too much." Delia caressed my face the same way Jara was doing it, or my mother, a long time ago. Crafted in Tomis, the medallion, while not as striking and expensive as the one I returned to Jara, was beautiful and worth a small fortune too.

"Oh," I said, embarrassed by her belief that I bought the jewel. "It was paid for only with a bit of blood." *Just a small cut*, I remembered.

"That makes it even more valuable." Delia embraced me, and I realized that she was in much better shape than Jara was after giving birth to Mark.

Maybe because she is younger, I thought, not having much experience in such matters.

"We have some news," she said, tension filling her voice, and gestured to Panait.

"There are two people searching for you. Normally, I would not bother you and send them away. But," Panait rubbed his chin, "one of them has a sword like yours." He pointed to my Arenian sword. "And they came with a recommendation from Movil, the innkeeper at the Caravans' Inn in Muniker. One of them works as protector. Movil told them that you could be found in Arad and my name, too." There was a hint of displeasure in his voice, and his eyes were grave as a guard's. "But he is an old fox, so it must be safe. I told them nothing," he shrugged. "If you want to … they are lodged at Two Roses."

Arenian sword... Vlad or the Royal Guard of Arenia. "Any names?" I asked calmly, not wanting to disturb Delia.

"I should have started with that. The protector's name is Vlad."

"A good friend." I smiled, and their tension vanished. And mine too. "I will see them tomorrow morning. You were right about bad times coming, Mohor's embassy for Deva was annihilated."

"I heard about that. Nobody expected such things, but Mohor deserved it. When you start attacking embassies..." Balan stopped talking, subdued by some new thoughts. "The strange thing is that Orban and Cantemir were not involved, yet everybody is pointing at them."

"Everybody who?"

"Everybody, both friends and foes," he shrugged.

"It may suit Orban."

"Orban..." Panait gestured in displeasure; his first reaction of that kind. "It may be. But it doesn't suit Cantemir. He opposed any tit-for-tat reaction for the attempt to assassinate him."

I convinced him, I almost smiled. It was not easy, but while Cantemir guessed who was behind the attempt; there was no direct link between Mohor and the assassins, and that helped. "Any dissension between Orban and Cantemir?"

"They don't like each other too much, but they are able to work well together."

"Why is Cantemir working for Orban?" Panait seemed to be in a strange mood. *Because of his son...* Split between my loyalty for Jara's family and my friendship with Delia and Panait, I felt uneasy. *This will be my last question for today.*

"Because he could not work for Malin. Lady S'Severin's former husband," Panait clarified, thinking that my involuntary reaction came from not knowing who Malin was. "Very old story. Would you stay for lunch?" He stopped our discussion, and I nodded with guilty relief.

In the evening, I went to see Cantemir, and started with the rumors related to Saliné's wedding.

"Yes, yes, I know. A great wedding. The son of a Grand Seigneur, and a bride with no dowry. The girl has some qualities, like her mother. Unlike her father." Cantemir's voice went gradually quieter until his last words became whispers, so low that I had to lean forward to catch them. "What makes you think there is a chance for the wedding?"

Who informed Cantemir? "Whatever the chance, you will not let it happen. Their plan doesn't suit you."

"Oh, no," Cantemir smiled. "The planning of that wedding suits us well. But the wedding, I agree with you, it doesn't suit us, and it will not happen." He stared at me, amused, as if my appearance was not very intelligent at that moment.

"It suits, and it doesn't suit you," I repeated mechanically, just to gain some time. "If the marriage contract is signed, the wedding's cancellation is a good opportunity to weaken S'Severin," I said hesitantly, unsure that I grasped his logic. "Before attacking him. Next spring."

"The link between the cancellation and the attack is of secondary importance." Cantemir shrugged, his eyes having a withdrawn and distracted appearance, and again I could not perceive his plans.

"The second rumor I heard might be even more interesting to you." I stirred his attention and moved to the window just to create an open space of silence. When I turned back, his eyes were staring at me in anticipation, yet I kept quiet.

"Plenty of rumors today." The fine lines of Cantemir's face deepened with his frown, and he let some impatience to flow in his voice.

"Mehadin's elder son was killed."

"Mehadin's son is dead," Cantemir repeated in a bland voice, his face immobile, but his eyes went a little wide. "Who did it?"

"We can only guess."

"Mohor?" he asked again, and I just shrugged, deciding to keep hidden the *rumors* related to Mohor's second embassy – there was no way to justify how could I get the news in such short time, when all Mehadin's people were killed in the fight. "Isn't that strange? Death opens the way for the small diversion in the south that you mentioned a month ago. It seems that you have premonitions." Cantemir's head tilted to one side, eyebrows arched, and he glanced curiously at me.

"I am not a Wanderer." I forced myself to smile and turned my palms up. "Orban needs that diversion to take the south if he wants to become a Duke or a King. The Circle is helping him, but..." I thought it was about time to learn more about his links with the Circle.

"The Circle is helping Orban," Cantemir said in a strange tone. "What makes you think about that?"

"This is what I heard, but the Secretary of Arad should know better."

"Well, if you heard that." Something flickered in his eyes, as if he was amused by my words, or maybe I imagined that it did. "Going south now could prove unsafe." He moved away from what I wanted, and, followed by the unpleasant thought that Cantemir was laughing at me because of my statement about the Circle, I almost cursed him.

Is the Circle less powerful than I thought? "Most times you stir the main course of action, but sometimes you have to follow or risk to be left behind. Mehadin lost a son and needs revenge, if not, he will lose face. How can a Seigneur keep his vassals after losing face? He is forced to react now, and you must take the lead. Mehadin can't be left to act alone." *If Mohor wins, Orban will have one less ally to attack Severin next year. And I might be able to get a good position too. Wing commander?*

"You are pushing me," he reacted coldly, making me fear that my intentions became too transparent, and there was some quietness between us.

"It's not me, Cantemir, it's Fate." I shrugged, and in a way, it was true: one's action could be somebody's else fate.

"Fate." He shrugged too, mirroring my reaction. "Any other rumor I should know?"

"Will you survive to hear another one?" I laughed as his raised eyebrows. "Don't look at me like this; I have nothing more."

"I feel relieved. Our embassy will leave for Mehadia in two days." Cantemir looked at me, a touch of expectation in his eyes.

"Are you going?" I struggled to hide my concern; there was no way to escape if he would go, and I wanted to return to Severin.

"No." He shook his head and asked nothing more, allowing me to leave.

◈

"What are these strangers doing here?" I winked at Pintea to ignore me, forcing my voice to become grave. There were not many people in the Two Roses Inn, so I did not care too much. "Maybe I should arrest them."

Revealing good control, Vlad turned slowly. "It may not be so easy to arrest a protector, but why would want you that, anyway? Tudor! You've got a weird sense of humor in Frankis." He stood up, and when we embraced, I felt as if being squeezed by a bear.

"When I first met you, I barely escaped alive from your hayforks. And you Pintea, you are almost a man." He was almost fifteen years old now, and where Vlad was sturdy and average in height, Pintea was tall and skinny. *Like I was.* "Why are you here?"

"Looking for you. Gran died last winter." Vlad's voice became sad, and his eyes narrowed – she raised them after their parents had been killed.

"I am sorry. Gran was a fine woman, and I learned many things from her."

"There was no reason to stay in the old inn anymore," he sighed. "We sold everything and went west after you. I thought myself good enough with the sword to be a protector, and Pintea will soon be, too. A more interesting life," he said eagerly, making me feel guilty – in the long winter nights, my stories about protectors, Knights and wars instilled in them the desire for adventure.

A more dangerous life. "You are a protector."

"I was lucky. In Muniker, we stayed at the Caravans' Inn, and the owner showed some interest in the sword you had given me. He knew you well and was happy to hear that I had trained with you. He even shouted that we were from the same fighting school. It was not true, but why contradict him?" Vlad's eyes crinkled with mirth. "And anyway, I did not know what was in his mind."

"Well, I do," I laughed, remembering the huge man I put under the table.

"I learned later, too, after Movil took care to parade me each evening to your unfortunate victim there. After one week, he managed to find a caravan for me. Ah, and Panait, I got his name from Movil too, but he was not happy seeing me."

"Merchants are cautious people. Panait is a fine man and a friend. He sent me here. What are you doing now?"

"Waiting for you. I have no other caravan yet."

"Come with me. I have a house; you can stay there, too. Sometimes, I might have work for you, and you can find your own caravans. Pintea has a safe place when you are on the road."

"I am big enough to come with you," Pintea protested.

"You are tall, but far from big enough. Don't worry, your time will come sooner than you expect." I knew well what means fighting for your life at fifteen. Pintea did not deserve that.

We left the next day, and the road back was safer than I ever remembered. Before arriving home, I told them that my name in Severin was Codrin.

"Which is the real one?" Vlad asked, intrigued.

"Both," I said, trying to avoid a long discussion and bad feelings from giving them a false name. "I have two names." Then I explained the links between the many swords I had and my names, and that nobody else knew about them.

War

Chapter 20 – Codrin

Up on the path from Cernat's house, four riders were approaching, and I pushed Zor faster, to arrive there before them – I rarely had visitors. Hidden in the forest, I rejoiced when I recognized Saliné, the first rider. The second one was Bucur, followed by two soldiers from the Guard. I went onto the road again and stopped in a visible place, ready to meet her.

Saliné turned her horse abruptly, and we circled around each other, moving away from her escort, her eyes staring wide, as they were mine, trying to absorb every trait of her face.

"Last night, I dreamt holding you in my arms," I said, pushing Zor closer.

"You never left my mind, Codrin, but dreams are the only thing we can afford." She smiled bitterly, her eyes in mine. "Always," she whispered.

"It should not be."

"It's the only way."

I dropped the halter and caught her hand. Like in a past almost forgotten, her fingers answered me, then she shook her head. "It's the only way, Codrin," Saliné repeated in a weak voice, breathing unevenly. With a sad smile, she pushed my hand away and her horse to a gallop.

Forcing myself not to stare after her, I rode on to Cernat's house – he had requested my presence, and I was expecting Jara too, but she was not there.

"Make yourself at home." He gestured toward an armchair close to the large window.

"Nothing urgent, I suppose." My voice was bitter and rough, as I felt offended that they wanted to see me only when they needed me – war was coming. *Apart from Vio...* She was the only one not caught in the game at court, and she was still coming to see me and Pintea, who was now her partner for games. *Saliné is forced to avoid me... But she is not forced to ride with Bucur.* The last thought made me even more bitter, and I struggled to stop a curse that was pressuring my lips.

"Mehadin is raising his army to attack us, and Mohor will have the small war you wished for him. It happened faster than anyone could foresee."

Yes, I hastened it... "You will raise an army too." Our eyes locked briefly, but he could not know that in my plans the small war was a necessity for both Mohor and me. *I don't want to be involved yet.* Spatar Big Mouth would lead the army, and there is no better place to eliminate an inconvenient man than in battle. "How is Vio?"

"She is well. Saliné too." Surprised by a question having nothing to do with his opening, Cernat tried to preempt another predictable question.

Jara too, and Mohor... "Saliné just crossed my path, so to speak. She was riding with Bucur."

"Bucur doesn't really count." Cernat shook his head. "Codrin, all of us know what is at stake." His finger gestured back and forth to include me in the circle of the people that knew. "Saliné is as unhappy as you are. Just that you are free while she is in a cage, as large as the castle, but still a cage. Allow her some relief from time to time, like riding."

"Big Mouth started a new game, pushing Bucur closer to Saliné."

"Everybody is playing, Mohor, Jara, you. Aron has a certain position in Severin, and some liberty to move pieces in the game."

"Unlike me," I involuntarily snapped, yet I should have pushed more for the consequences derived from Big Mouth's game.

"For Mohor, your position is politically marginal. You have helped us several times, but it's mostly Jara's influence that keeps you close. Severin is in no way different to other courts, here or in Arenia." What he did not know was that I had no intention to join Mohor's court – it would have killed my political game. "Don't be offended, the same thing looks different to Mohor and you. Aron brings soldiers and contacts with other Knights. Allegiances are slippery these days. If he deserts, Mohor would lose almost half of his power. If you leave…"

"Why are you afraid of things that Big Mouth may do in the future, but not about things he and Bucur are doing right now?"

"Any loyalty has limits. Self-interest is stronger in troubled times. We are living troubled times. Friends, relatives, it doesn't matter. Power is all about foresight, control and balance. Rulers must ignore minor things just to preempt what may become dangerous. As before, the same thing may look different to Mohor and you." With a shrug, Cernat underlined that everybody was seeing my problem in a different way, suddenly degraded to a minor thing with the unintended consequence of making me feel insignificant and annoyed. "You must learn to see through the eyes of others. What happens next might change your place. Would you join our army?" he asked before I could speak.

"I can't. Don't worry, it has nothing to do with some *minor things*," I preempted his argument with a hint of bitter mockery. *What do you see through my eyes?* "You plan to unseat Orban, a powerful Grand Seigneur. Test your army. Test your commanders, before Orban tests them." *If they fail, I might be able to gain my Knighthood and Saliné. If they win...* But I did not see Big Mouth being able to win a war. *The other side may lose it.*

"We want to give you command of the left wing of the army," Cernat insisted, and taken by surprise, my mind split between my strategy and the feeling that I should answer in an appropriate way to their overture. "Jara convinced Mohor."

"Give it to Bucur," I said still haunted by Saliné's ride with him. Jara's name brought back their outing to me, with a peculiar effect that I could not explain, as I already knew about them riding or reading together in the past, a thing I considered just social interaction. Perhaps there is a difference between hearing about it, and actually seeing them riding together.

"Bucur is on the list too," Cernat said calmly, and I almost bit my lip; he was the better player in our game. "There was quite a strong competition for that position; it gives good status. Sometimes, one man can change the course of a battle. A battle may change one's course, too." He was correct, but he did not realize that Big Mouth would try to kill me again. Trying to look *through my eyes*, he thought I was too confident in my abilities and ready to extort a higher price from them, like getting Saliné – a sort of blackmail.

"Battles can be dangerous," I said, and he looked at me, his brows drawn together in a surprised frown. "I am not afraid of the enemy in front, but of the *friend* behind."

"You think that Aron...?"

"He has already tried to kill me, and you know it."

"I don't really know," Cernat said, his voice flat.

Slowly, I pushed Big Mouth's letter, paying a hundred galbeni for my head, across the table. *I have a certain value*; the amount provoked some pride in me. "Read it only if you will keep its content to yourself. Not even Jara should know."

"Why are you afraid of Jara?" Cernat asked, his eyes narrowed in confusion, but I only shrugged, and it took him a while to decide what to do with the letter. "I still don't know why you are afraid of Jara," he said once he had finished reading. "But a deal is a deal." He played with the letter and frowned thoughtfully. "I don't think that Aron will try again, but it's your life in the game." He pushed the decision back to me. This time he did not think again of blackmail, and I shook my head, ready to leave.

"We need as many allies we can gather against Orban. The Circle is helping him." Cernat's eyes questioned me, and I nodded that I know about that. "We don't know much about the Assassins," he said, hesitantly. "Maybe they can help us."

"There are no Assassins Nests in Frankis, or in any other kingdom I know. An Assassins' fortress is called a Nest," I added, seeing his confusion. *Of vipers...* "Four Nests they have, all in the deserted mountains southeast of Arenia: Crown, Sword, Knife and Arrow." For sure there was a logic in those strange names, but my mentor did not tell me. I just knew that with each promotion, an Assassin moves up from Arrow to Crown. "They travel where their interest requires it." *I am their interest here.* "I don't see them acting against the Circle. They rarely oppose the main source of power, and their gain should be considerable. You have nothing to offer to them." *What did my cursed uncle promise to them?*

Nothing transpired on Cernat's face, but I knew that he was disappointed, and I decided to leave without asking more about my mentor.

"Jara will still ask you to lead the left wing. She is well-intentioned," he said before I could close the door, both a warning and push to make me reevaluate her.

I left Severin with the first pink glow of dawn creeping across the tops of the hills, trying to avoid more pressure from Jara, and went directly toward Mehadia, by the northern road, the shortest way to attack Severin.

When I returned, Mohor was in his office with Jara and Cernat. They asked nothing, and Mohor nodded toward a chair across the table. "You've returned early."

"Aron lost the battle," I said bluntly, then told them the whole story, trying not to be too obvious about Big Mouth's failure, and I kept hidden that he attacked against a hill, without resting his soldiers, and the will of the army broke when he turned and ran. *You must learn that by yourself...* "A fifty-strong contingent of riders from Arad joined the battle, and they exchanged their banners for Mehadin's."

"Orban interfered directly." Mohor left the table abruptly, going to the window in rare a display of tension. "In plain view."

"His soldiers used Mehadin's banners in the battle. I saw them when they joined Mehadin's army in his land."

"You were there so early?" Mohor closed his eyes for a moment, as if his own words were giving him a headache. Opening his eyes again, he half-turned toward the window, slowly and silent.

"I tried to warn Vlaicu, but a squad of Mehadin scouts intercepted me. Your army had no scouts." No one spoke for a while, and I understood that I was no longer needed. "May I leave now?"

Mohor did not answer, and the silence that followed was cold. There was something deadly in it, like in the battle that was just lost, and I did not know what to do. He was still at the window, looking out with a kind of detachment that I knew was not real. Jara was white, her face composed. Our eyes met for a moment, and I sensed the ghosts rising from another defeat where she lost almost everything. Her eyes were a curious aquamarine color, nearly green, in the strong light coming from the window.

"You did what Aron should have done, gathering information. I wished for better collaboration, but you two are like oil and water, never able to come together. It appears that my army and commanders were finally tested." There was a subtle touch of weird amusement in Mohor's voice, confirming that Cernat had passed my words to him. "Things are not looking good right now, but how bad they really are we will know only after our army returns. Anything else?"

"Mehadin does not have enough soldiers to siege Severin."

"That much I know," Mohor said, dryly. "But I look weak now, and this will have consequences. I would like Mehadin to come and attack Severin. Would Orban join him?"

"Duke Stefan placed a small army at Orban's northern border too."

"It seems that Orban is your confidant." Mohor looked sternly at me, his lips pressed together in a tense line.

Trying to find an answer, I became suddenly aware that my hands were clenched at my sides. Deliberately I forced them to relax and look away.

"Codrin, there is a lot of tension right now," Jara interjected, "but we are thankful for the facts you provided. We need all the help we can get and a different strategy. Would you join us now? We know your conditions for that."

Big Mouth is out of the game, and Vlaicu will lead the army.
"Yes."

"Thank you, Codrin. Would you stay here overnight?"

Caught by surprise, all that I saw was the possibility to speak with Saliné, but looking at Jara, I hesitated. *She will not allow it.* "Thank you, but it is not necessary. I will return tomorrow morning..."

"Codrin, there are many things to plan, and time is short. I will sleep here too." There was something strange in Cernat's voice, something that I had never heard before and made the room feel cold again. In that moment, I fully recognized the Grand Seigneur, naturally accustomed to being listened to and obeyed.

Jara sent me to the Guard Tower, outside their residence. It was almost deserted; half of the guards were with the army, others on duty at the gate and walls. Several hours later, the first soldiers appeared on the east road, a small number, led by Big Mouth. They arrived in batches, the latest in the afternoon of the next day – no one had tried to gather the army back into one force.

Cernat came to dine with me in the evening. He asked again what happened on the battlefield, and I repeated everything, with suppressed hostility, because I was kept away from Saliné. Then his questions moved more into assessment, what was wrong, what I would have done myself in that case, or I that case. He ignored my barely concealed resentment and did not leave until fully satisfied by my torment.

"Thank you, Codrin," he said, eventually. "With all that anger and pain in you, things went smoothly between us."

The next morning, Jara was the first person I met in their residence. "Some more soldiers came back. Bucur was wounded," she informed me before anything else, as if that was the most important thing in the world. "We considered your advice and made him a wing commander. He justified our confidence. Saliné is with him now."

His appointment had nothing to do with my advice. "People get wounded in battles," I shrugged, annoyed. "And many lost their lives." *You wanted me to know that Bucur justified your confidence, and that Saliné is with him.* "How serious is it?" I tried to show a bit of humanity.

"A cut on his upper arm, not very deep. It will heal soon."

"Then his wound is more a problem for me than for him," I said aloud what I was thinking, realizing that too late from Jara's reaction. *Saliné will spend even more time with him... A hero wounded in battle for her.*

Jara understood me, yet she was not sure how to react, her eyes staring heavily at me, and I was mute, too.

"Codrin." Saliné entered the room and saved us from that long moment of embarrassment. "I did not know you were here. Bucur was wounded." Where Jara used a neutral tone, Saliné was troubled.

"Two angry women that want me wounded in his place," I said, bitterly. "I'll leave now. My own wound is waiting somewhere." I stepped toward the door, but Saliné was there, and she blocked my way.

"Mother, please let me speak with Codrin."

For the first time in months, Jara agreed to leave us alone. "We will meet in a few minutes in the council room," she said from the door, her voice uneasy.

"Codrin, what did I do to deserve that?" Saliné asked, visibly upset.

"And what I did to deserve everything that happened this year?"

"None of us deserved or wanted it, but I thought that we had an agreement."

"Agreement," I shrugged, struggling to contain my anger. "What if we forget about that agreement and live normally?"

"This is *normally*, Codrin. Please understand, I am engaged. There is no other way."

"We can meet from time to time," I pleaded. "You meet only Bucur. Worry only for Bucur."

"Bucur is my companion at the court, and he was wounded fighting for us, but he is not you, and will never be. There is no one else like you, Codrin, and you know it. Please don't make things harder. I want to meet you every day, to read in your arms, to ride with you, to pick cherries together, but... Now, please leave me," Saliné whispered, and I wanted to embrace her, there was so much desperation in her voice. I moved slowly toward her when she stopped me. "Leave me alone." Her voice carried a toughness that I had never heard before.

"I will never leave you alone, Saliné," I whispered, walking toward the door. At the corner of my eye, I caught her tears running down, and I hesitated for a long moment, before closing the door behind me. There was nothing I could do to ease our sadness and pain.

Jara, Mohor and Cernat were already present in the council room when I arrived. *Big Mouth is not here*, I thought, with the hope that he would stay away.

"So, you will join us," Mohor stated formally.

"If Vlaicu leads the army, yes."

"It will not be Vlaicu."

With some effort, I was able to answer calmly. "I apologize, but if Aron leads..."

"It will not be Aron." Mohor eyes did not leave me, and I started to feel more uncomfortable than I was prepared for. Any meeting with Mohor was generally uncomfortable for me, and that gave me a certain degree of preparation.

"It's your army. What do you want from me?"

"To lead the army." There was a sudden trace of amusement in his voice, not matching the seriousness of the situation.

"Mohor, I am honored by your proposal. I am a good fighter, but my battlefield experience is limited. Vlaicu is better..."

"Codrin," Cernat stopped me. "There was a long deliberation until we all agreed, Vlaicu included, with your nomination. It did not happen because you are the best swordsman we know. It happened because you have battlefield experience. You told me of being in war councils before battles when you were still too young to fight, but old enough to understand. They did not keep you there for nothing."

I never fought a war. "That doesn't make me..."

"If you would let me finish," Cernat said, with a fatherly smile on his lips. "We discussed battle situations many times with a bottle of wine between us, including the long one we had yesterday evening. You have the general understanding of an operational plan. Even better, you know how to put it into practice."

I've never put anything into practice, my mind protested, but I kept my mouth shut.

"When you rescued Jara, you took advantage of everything around you. You were just a young man alone against six tough soldiers and needed stealth. The moving horses hid your first kill. Your next hit was the leader, to disorganize them. That's planning, done fast, on the ground, reacting to a specific situation, and you know how to surprise an enemy. Vlaicu described the ambush on the road to Deva when you led our embassy. You explained the tactical reason for your decision. Your orders were brief and clear. The soldiers accepted them without question. It ended with ten dead enemies, and just some minor wounds on our side. You always manage to obtain things with scarce resources, our exact situation. And if you want, not jumping immediately to accept the command is a good recommendation too. So?"

There was no expression on his face when he asked; the other two were also motionless and featureless, as if we were discussing trivial things over a bottle of wine, to use his saying. It was like all my senses were betraying me, unable to feel a tension that was surely there. *If I win, the reward will be greater. If I lose… Saliné, Vio, Jara… Saliné…* I unconsciously repeated her name. *They would lose everything.* The room was still silent, waiting for my answer. "I will try."

"You will do more than that," Mohor said. "Vlaicu will second you in the army, and he will be here in a few minutes."

Unprepared, I wanted a delay to put my disparate ideas in order, but I was ashamed to request more time. The room filled up soon after, and this council was different, its configuration extended for various reasons: Vlaicu as my second in command, Veres and Saliné as future leaders, and Bucur, enjoying their confidence after the last battle, and whatever other confidence they had in him. Big Mouth came too, and he did not look much affected by his defeat. Without any formality, Mohor gestured to me to explain my battle plans.

"The army is not in good shape. Half of it has already deserted. And morale is always low after a lost battle." It was at least a correct assessment, if not the best approach.

"I thought we would hear a plan, not a list of preemptive excuses," Big Mouth snapped.

"Many of the problems come from a weak chain of command that neglected the army for a long time," I paid him back without realizing that Mohor would feel included in the command chain too.

"I know, ragtag army." Irritated, Mohor stopped me with my own words; it seemed that Cernat carried my warning in full, without any diplomatic mediation. "Can we go to the next step?"

"My point exactly," Big Mouth agreed fast, just to say something.

"We cannot engage directly Mehadin's army at the moment. From our last estimations, he still has around two hundred soldiers; his losses were low. We have only one hundred and ten left ready to fight, some of them slightly wounded." Forty soldiers were lost in the battle; some had heavy wounds, and the rest of Mohor's army deserted.

"You forgot Orban's squadron." Big Mouth attacked me again; his usual strategy was to bite fast, not leaving the opponent much time for defense.

"Orban's squadron is already home, and for the moment, he will not be drawn into another conflict. His point was made; he proved to your allies that a small fish like Mehadin can win against you." In the hierarchy of Frankis, Mohor was considered stronger than Mehadin in military terms, a hierarchy that did not consider the total neglect of his army.

"You don't know that," Big Mouth insisted.

"You don't know that, and it was your job to know. His soldiers fought under Mehadin's banner, just to have plausible denial, and no one will believe that he was involved, no matter how many letters you write," I spoke again to Mohor, trying to avoid another conflict with Big Mouth, and Mohor gestured at me to continue. "We have to attack them by surprise, hit and run, no big battles."

"That's not a plan," Big Mouth complained, with a face that looked very concentrated on the issue. "It's just wait and see, maybe something good happens."

"We can't afford a classic battle right now," Cernat said. "Some unorthodox methods, as Codrin mentioned, might work better."

"We need to send scouts to find Mehadin. And we need to check our soldiers. I want to take only one hundred with me. The best prepared. Twenty of them good archers."

"You did not say anything about the left wing," Bucur interjected. "I think I have gained that position."

"The army is too small to have wings. It will act as one. And you are wounded."

"It's not a big deal. I can be your third in command," he insisted, and Saliné's eyes narrowed.

Did you realize that his wound is not a big deal, or do you admire the hero? "Your wound needs attention. I am sure you will receive it." There was no reaction from Saliné this time, but Big Mouth looked satisfied, and that almost made me take my words back. Curiously, there was a slight reaction from Mohor too, he stared briefly at me with a thoughtful look.

"Vlaicu, send more scouts." Mohor ended the council, letting me know that things were already in motion. "You know our soldiers. Codrin, don't leave yet." He asked only for me, but Jara and Cernat stayed too.

The last to leave, Saliné stopped briefly in front of me. "Thank you, Codrin," she breathed and left the room quickly, almost running.

"Orban is gathering his army." Mohor looked at me as if I should already have known about that, and his deep frown proved that my eventual links to Orban still bothered him. Before I could answer, he took a letter from his cabinet and pushed it to me, across the table.

The message was brief and concise – I never saw terrible news written in many words. Orban was raising two armies, one north of Arad ready for Duke Stefan, and one south of Arad, ready for Severin – both five hundred strong. *Vasile*, I read the name of Mohor's spy who signed the letter; it was for the first time I observed such sophistication in collecting information from Severin's Secretariat. *What else am I missing?* I played absently with the paper, my thoughts on Cantemir. *The small diversion I wanted in the south became a large storm. What made him raise the southern army?* "We can only guess Orban's intentions. His southern army may or may not be gathered for an invasion."

"Does it matter?" Jara asked. Her question appeared unintelligent, yet it was not.

"We must act as if Orban wants to take Severin now," I agreed with her, and I almost physically felt the fear behind her composed face.

"Act..." Jara repeated with the resignation of someone who knew that we could not act too much.

"Mehadin should arrive here before Orban's army. We have a chance to take them one by one." I tried to raise their morale, but Jara smiled sadly, touching my hand over the table. "Theoretically," I shrugged.

"Mehadin will pillage and destroy, waiting for Orban to attack too, or just to obtain more favorable conditions. How fast can you rout him from our lands with small attacks?" Cernat asked, his voice showing an optimism that was not there.

"I don't know. There are several places where I can ambush him. It depends on the route he chooses to come here. If he comes here. My main task is to keep him away from Orban's army. You must gather another army here, at least two hundred soldiers."

Mohor had the impulse to interrupt me, then, resigned, he clamped his lips tightly and stayed silent, yet I waited, looking at him. "I sent messengers for more soldiers this morning," he finally said. "Some will come today, some tomorrow. One hundred, if we are lucky. We can't count on the deserters," he sighed.

"Call everybody. Old men, young men. The enemy will not know it. Keep your troops outside, close to the walls and Orban's scouts at a fair distance. Let them learn that an army is waiting here. From far, every pole seems a spear." Severin had weak walls. Most castles were built in the old, good time of the Frankis Kingdom when order prevailed, and there was no need for strong fortifications. Severin's walls were raised just thirty-five years ago by a Seigneur lacking financial resources. A seven-eight hundred strong army had a chance to take it, if not challenged from outside. "You might also call your allies."

"No one will risk helping us now," Jara said annoyed, and she stood up, closing the council before I could answer, trying to shield Mohor, who was not in his best mood.

We went out to the field outside the castle to see the army, and some choices were made, but I was not pleased. And I was even less pleased that I had to sleep in the Guard Tower again – it was now crowded; the guards had returned from battle, and some wounded soldiers were settled there too.

As promised by Mohor, more soldiers came the next morning, and some of them had leather armor.

We are not going training...

"I know what you are thinking," Mohor reacted, seeing the same pathetic picture as me. "Ragtag army." This time his irritation seemed unrelated to me; something was changing in his mind. "The best hundred is not so weak," he said meekly.

"It's not the weakest who lose, but the ones who look back first. If we can't avoid a battle, I want their backs to be against the wall."

"What?" Vlaicu asked, and Mohor stared uncomfortably at me.

"I need them in a position without possibility of retreat. They must know that it is fight or death. It's the only way to forge a winning army."

"We are outnumbered. It will be a fight to death. Do you have another plan?" Vlaicu's hard eyes narrowed almost lost beneath the heavy, drawn-together brows. His nostrils flared in distrust of my abilities to lead an army. Not that I trusted them too much.

"Vlaicu," I laughed, not really naturally. "I don't have suicidal tendencies. We fight like that only if there is a good chance to win. If not, we will just hit and run, until they come here for Mohor. He is good bait."

"I will do my best to charm them," Mohor said for the five Knights gathered with us, and there was some anemic laughter until five riders appeared on the road.

"They are coming," the scouts' leader said, his voice loud and cracked, even before dismounting his horse. "Last time we saw them, they were close to Banya, coming here by the northern road. They are around two hundred fifty now. Mehadin received some reinforcements. That's why they did not come faster."

"We leave today," I said, without hesitation. "I know a good place for an ambush, but we must be there tomorrow evening."

In an hour, we had chosen a hundred soldiers, and our small army left before noon, watched by Mohor, Cernat and Big Mouth. I could not read anything under their apparent calm, hoping that I was keeping my own worries hidden, too. *I wish Saliné and Jara were here...*

Chapter 21 – Codrin

Our army reached the place just in time – a junction with a minor road going into the forest. Vlaicu and I were riding in front, together with Vlad, my personal scout, hired by Mohor as a mercenary, at my recommendation. *The only mercenary in the whole army*, I thought, pondering if it was the right step to involve him in this battle. He insisted to come, even Pintea wanted to join us, but they knew nothing about wars and did not understand the risk. I was feeling guilty because of the stories about Knights and famous battles I told them when I stayed in Gran's house. When the glory glitters, the dead and the wounded are ignored.

We left the main road, going into a valley that soon narrowed to a gorge with high walls of bare rock and crumbling scree. Out of it, we and stopped in a meadow that lay on the right side of the road. There was another gorge in front where the road followed its course through the mountains, along the small stream.

Our war council ended late in the night, brief and with nothing important to say or to plan. They laughed at some of Vlaicu's jokes; the memory of the lost battle was dissipating, but behind that reaction lived their fear. It was not a bad sign, only fools do not feel fear before a battle. I had summoned them just because it was a mandatory step before any fight – I knew that from my long dead past. *Two war councils with the Arenian army... I still remember them.*

The last one had been before the battle against the nomads from the eastern steppes who were invading our lands, as they had many times before. I was almost fifteen years old. *That had been a real battle.* The memory made me feel insignificant; there was no way to compare my hundred men against the fifty thousand Father had commanded in that battle. The Mehadins had two hundred and fifty soldiers, the nomads more than a hundred and fifty thousand. *The ratio is almost the same,* I tried to fill some importance in my first position as commander – indeed, both Father and I faced a stronger enemy. The Arenian army gathered in a tight place that did not allow the nomads to take advantage of their superior strength and speed. *I've copied the same tactic.* Unable to rein in my thoughts, I walked and sat away from our fire. Vlaicu nodded slightly, a discreet way to encourage me. He could not understand. My thoughts were not plagued by the future battle that we could lose, but by a past that I had already lost. With some effort, I forced himself to push the past away, trying to think in present. An image of Saliné under our cherry tree came to me. It seemed blurred and distant.

A strange effervescence stirred my mind. At first, I linked it to the inherent tension before my first battle. It was not cold, yet I shivered. On my chest, the Wing Talisman from Dochia felt warm, and I clutched it. Somewhere in front, the flames played strange reflections in my eyes, resembling some imaginary animals trying to reach me. Like a living thing, the talisman pulsed in my hand. Every sound around me vanished. The fire disappeared too, replaced by the same meadow we had settled in, thriving under the sun. A rider in Mehadin's colors pointed his sword at me. Our eyes met, and I recognized Mehadin's Spatar. The next moment his chest was cut by an invisible blade, and he fell in the grass. Another invisible thing burned into my ribs. I knew that it was not real, but I still gasped. Slowly, my mind recovered, and in the half-darkness of the night I saw my hands glowing faintly, like my sister's hands did before her death. *Is this a Wanderer's Light? A sign of death? Men don't have it.* There was no lingering pain in my ribs, and I fell asleep before answering my own question.

In the morning, I searched my hands for burns from the Light – they were none. *I must have dreamt about it.* Avoiding any thought about the night, I took forty riders, and all S'Severin's banners that we had, rode back through the gorge, and hid at the end of the forest, waiting for Mehadin, who came at noon.

We moved out from the forest, and stopped, face to face with the enemy, as if just now seeing them, five hundred paces away, then turned the horses abruptly, making them neigh, and mimed running away from a stronger army that had appeared from nowhere. Our banners were raised high, just to add more flavor to the bait. A column moved out from their army, following us. I was the last one to enter the forest, and looking back, I saw their entire army chasing us, disorganized, in stretched columns.

In the gorge, a myriad of horseshoes played on the stones, in different cadences, and echoes answered in muffled tones, multiplied by the rocks, tempering the stridency with a weird musicality. Here and there, metal stirred sparks from the stones. Just before the exit, another echo reached us from behind; the Mehadins had entered the gorge too. We moved into the meadow, turning right, and joined the rest of the army that was waiting for us.

"They are coming," I said to Vlaicu, in a thrilled tone that had nothing in common with death coming to chase us, then I signaled for Ban's archers to be ready; they were hidden on the ridges above the gorge. Slowly, I gripped Shadow's hilt, and unsheathed it. The sword answered to me. This time, it did not use words. It felt like a living thing, glued to my hand, an extension if my own arm. It felt deadly.

The Mehadins came into the meadow and slowed their horses, then turned abruptly, to meet the cavalry charge coming from their right. That slowed them further. Caught by inertia, their rearguard was still trying to enter the meadow from the gorge, and their horses ploughed into the ones in front of them. Rocks and arrows fell from above, and the first men died before our swords met. At full speed, we crashed into them, and the melee became even tighter. Some horses fell, crushing the riders. I do not know who my first adversary was, I just met his sword with my small one, then Shadow went for his neck. The Assassin swords were perfect for tight battles, and I pushed on further, guiding Zor with my knees. On my right and left, Vlaicu and Vlad were advancing too, and I knew that I was covered. Two minutes later, there was no way to advance other than killing an enemy; the pack of riders in front of us was now too tight, and everything became static. Now and then, an arrow made room for those still trying to enter the meadow from the gorge. Their horses moved over human and animal bodies, some of them still alive. That put down even more horses, their hooves stumbling on the flesh underneath.

In the fight, your mind and senses are both focused and distributed. The world shrinks to the smallest dimension, the enemy sword rising and falling in front of you.

A clang, another one. A dying cry. Shouts.

"Die!" "Help!" "Move back."

Arrows were coming in waves from above, and our pressure was growing. The first wave of panic touched the enemy – when death comes from everywhere around, your resolve crumbles. Some of the Mehadins were trying to turn, but there was no place to escape. Our force was now a wedge piercing through the enemy lines, and I was in front with Vlaicu and Vlad.

Sometimes the mind loses focus for a split second. A neigh somewhere in front. A rock hitting a helmet. Echoes from the gorge. The horse moving under your body. Another one slips in front of you.

"Die!" "On the left." "Now!" "Nooo!"

A sword moves in front of you. Clang. Metal meets metal, body meets body. Horses clash. You fight to keep equilibrium. You strike at the same time. The one that recovers and strikes faster survives. The other one becomes a falling body. Sometimes there is no cry, sometimes there is. Each has his own way of dying.

I parried the sword of the rider in front of me with Flame and struck with Shadow. He leaned back in slow motion, as if trying to cling on his life. My eyes fixed the next enemy, and I pushed Zor with my knees, turning to the right. Cold iron struck against my ring-mail on the left side, and a pang of pain ran through my body. The spear in my ribs came from behind the soldier I had killed a moment before. He was still on his horse, lying dead on his back – there was no place for him to fall. I leaned back, pushing at the spear with Shadow. His eyes bulging from the effort, the man was focused, pressing hard and trying to rotate the spear for more damage. The sharp pain moved through my ribs up to my head, and I moaned. He was in an awkward position, inclined and stretched forward from behind the dead soldier. That was my chance. He lacked both strength and accuracy for a final strike. I threw Flame. The blade swirled in the air, hitting his face. A curved sword is difficult to channel when throwing it, and he was not wounded badly, yet blood welled from his mouth. His hand, still gripping the spear, recoiled. Vlad put him down a moment later, and he smiled encouragingly at me, raising his red blade. *My brother's blade.* Despite all the pain in my side, I smiled back.

By a strange coincidence, that was the moment when the Mehadians' will broke completely. Terror surged, and they stopped fighting, trying to retreat where there was no place to move. The rest of the battle was a massacre. It is always like this: the fight endures until one army looks back, then everything crashes in a moment. When there was no enemy left alive in the meadow, I rode Zor away from the battlefield.

"Vlaicu, take over, and gather the wounded. Stop any pursuit."

I dismounted awkwardly, and Vlad helped me to take off my ring-mail and clothes, already soaked with red. A line of white bone was visible in the gap, and blood was pouring out slowly from a slit three inches long. Vlad looked at me, panic surging in his eyes. I forced a smile onto my lips, to calm him. It was stiff and cold.

Two wounds, I realized, even though I could not see the one on my back. The point of the spear had pierced my body and gone through. *It did not go between my ribs, just pierced my muscles. A rib may be broken;* I remembered the fierce pain from the stab. I looked for a bulge, the usual sign of a broken rib. When I took a deep breath, the pain did not increase by much, so nothing was broken. "It's not so bad," I said to Vlad, who had little experience with battle wounds. "The spear did not go inside my ribcage." *I would have been dead...* "Look for some tissue in my backpack and a small bottle of alcohol."

Vlaicu appeared a moment later, looked at my wounds, then smiled. "Just a scratch, you are a lucky man. Your sword." He placed Flame alongside Shadow, which was lying close to me. Sunshine flashed from the blade; its blue reflection with strips of golden iridization, holding his eyes. "I understand now why you named it Flame. I am sure that Shadow has its story too. Later..." He turned a palm up to underline both his curiosity and our lack of time. "We have thirty-two wounded. I am not talking about small cuts. And twenty dead. Ban is counting their dead now. Just to keep the score." He grinned, knowing well that the Mehadians had lost many more men in the battle.

I touched Shadow, recalling the strange sensation I had before the battle, feeling the sword like an extension of my own arm. *Even an Assassin sword can't save your live if you are untrained or unlucky.* "Fetch our soldiers with their horses and weapons. The best horse, armor and sword go to Vlad." I knew that both the horse and sword would go to Pintea; Vlad still had the Arenian ones I gave to him, but he needed a good ring-mail; the one he bought before coming to Frankis was average.

Unwillingly, I looked at the battlefield. It seemed to have grown quiet in the valley, but not fully quiet. Some clouds appeared in the west, and I watched them move across the sun. It was warmer now, the midday and the aftermath of so much effort. Below, men were moaning, crying out in pain. *That would go on for a long time.* In front of me, Vlad shivered. The thrill of the battle was slowly leaving him. The stories would come later, in a winter's night, in front of the fire, a glass of red wine in your hand.

When Vlad finished bandaging me, Vlaicu appeared again, leading a horse by the halter. "Mehadin's Spatar died in the battle, and another eighty-six of his men. Mehadin was able to escape," he said with a touch of regret. "Your horse." He pushed the halter to Vlad, measuring him at the same time. "The Spatar's ring-mail and sword are on its back. It will fit you well."

Standing up slowly, I realized that despite the pain, my movement was not impaired much. *In a few hours, I will be able to ride, so long as the blood stops flowing.* I decided to leave the next morning, taking only five men with me. Vlaicu would follow with the rest of the army, a day or two later, when the worst wounded would be in better shape.

Do I have the Light? I involuntarily checked my hands, expecting again to see some burns. My strange night dream became reality during the day: I was wounded on my left side by a spear, and Mehadin's Spatar was dead. *It was a Vision, not a dream. My third one.* I had never heard of men having the Wanderer Light, but never heard doesn't mean never happened. I picked up the Wing Talisman and stared at it in vain; there was nothing new on its smooth surface.

"Take all the remaining horses and weapons," I said to Vlaicu, before leaving for Severin. "Mohor's soldiers need them. And find me a good mare for Zor." It would be the second one. I knew how difficult it would be to get a foal with the same qualities as Zor from a mare of a different race. *He was just six months old,* I remembered when I received him. *I was almost fourteen, and still had a family.*

"I think I saw a prime quality mare," Vlaicu interrupted my thoughts. "If you have a foal from Zor to spare, put me on the waiting list."

How long would Zor stay with me? Fourteen, fifteen more years? If nothing bad happens. Horses live shorter lives than we do, I sighed. *Usually.*

"What?" Vlaicu asked, looking at my wound.

"Just some old memories of a child who no longer exists."

❧

The gates were already open when we reached the city – the watchers in the tower saw us from far away. Vlad took my horse, and I entered the residence, everybody looking at me with various facial expressions, but no one dared to ask what news we brought. Saliné was inside the hall, and she stopped, staring at me in silence, as if seeing a ghost, then suddenly ran toward me. Involuntarily, I tensed my muscles when she jumped into my arms, and I embraced her.

"Codrin. Are you well?" She could barely speak.

"I am fine, Saliné."

"I am sorry that I could not see you when you left. I didn't know when you... Codrin, I was afraid that I would never see you again. Codrin..." Her words vanished in a long cry, and her body was shaking in my arms. Twenty paces behind her a door opened, and Jara came out from the living room. She stayed silent, staring at us.

"Saliné," I said gently.

Still sobbing, she raised her head from my shoulder, and I slowly traced the tears sliding down on her face with my finger. When she wound her hand in my hair, I drew her tighter against me, and we stilled for breath, knowing that we were lost. Any social constraint vanished away from her mind, and I kissed her, forgetting that Jara was there.

"I should have done this before," I said, when we regained our breath, holding her tight and stroking gently her auburn hair.

"Yes, you should have," she whispered, disengaging from my arms, her hands gliding slowly over my palms open up. With all my desire to kiss her again, I had to let her go.

"May I embrace you, too?" Jara asked, her voice edgy.

"Mother!" Saliné exclaimed, and her face reddened.

"I always liked to be embraced by beautiful women," I joked, to give Saliné enough time to recover.

"It appears that you came back well. No wounds," Jara said, a bit maliciously, after embracing me in a formal way, and I answered with a shrug. "Did all go well?" she finally asked, in a tense voice, her eyes intent, fixed on me, as if trying to pierce into my mind.

"We won."

"Thank you, Codrin. Let's give the news to Mohor." Her voice was still edgy, and only now I realized how their eyes were sunk in their orbits from lack of sleep. Inside the room, Mohor looked the same, yet he smiled. Jara made him aware of the news, in a subtle way, or he just read it in the stance of her body.

"Welcome back. You look well. How did it go?" In a peculiar way, all their questions were simple and straightforward, missing the grandiloquence encountered in songs and books about past battles – it was as if I had just come back from a party. All their inner tension surfaced through their eyes, voices and Saliné's outburst.

"They fell into our ambush. We lost twenty people; they lost eighty-seven, including their Spatar, but Mehadin escaped. We have more than thirty wounded. Three are in bad shape. Vlaicu will come with them tomorrow or the day after."

"Thank you, Codrin. From my window, I saw six soldiers coming. I counted several times until I remembered that a good army comes back in one group when defeated, not in small bands. We have to celebrate." Mohor raised his voice, taking out an old bottle of wine that was there in readiness. "And to mourn."

Before I could answer, there was a sudden weakness in my legs. *I have lost too much blood*, I realized, wishing to check under my ring-mail if my clothes were soaked again. "Sorry, Mohor. I am hungry and tired. Tomorrow..."

"Fine, there will be more wine for me," he joked and patted my shoulder with his free hand.

"Ah!" a cry escaped me, and I tensed as my pain surged. It was a friendly blow, but strong, and my elbow went into my wound.

"You are wounded!" all three exclaimed at the same time, and Saliné came closer, taking me by the arm.

"I am fine." I smiled, touching her palm, and our eyes met.

"I will send for the healer," Jara said swiftly.

"Thank you." I pulled my arm from Saliné's gentle grip and swept a finger through the broken rings of my armor for traces of blood. There was not much. "Send him to the Tower."

"You will stay here. Please," Jara stopped my reaction. "From now on, you will stay only here," she said, and I shrugged, letting her seat me at the table. "And I apologize for the bad joke with the wound."

"It seems I will have to share the wine after all," Mohor said, his eyes thoughtful.

The servants came with the food and left, and I had to eat with all three of them staring at me in silence. The pressure from their stare, made me ate fast and without pleasure. Mohor's wine was of excellent quality, and we raised our glasses to salute the victory against Mehadin. Before drinking, we spilled some drops on the floor, a last homage for the people we have lost in battle.

"Orban?" I asked, trying to be casual.

"His army is settled at our northern border but did not try to pass. And we have a hundred fifty soldiers outside. I guess you saw them. We no longer think that he wants to attack us now, so we go for Mehadin." It was a way to tell me that his spy in Arad informed him about Orban's intentions.

Old Felcer, the healer, came to my room and took off the bandages covering my wound – it was not pleasant. Trying to alleviate my pain, Saliné took my right hand, stirring a sensation that I have almost forgotten. Jara, Cernat and Mohor were there, too; my health had suddenly become a political issue.

"That is not a light wound," Jara said, visibly worried, and I felt Saliné's fingers gripping stronger.

"It looks worse than it is," Felcer calmed her.

"The spear just pierced the muscle, and some broken rings from the mail scratched my skin, making it look bad, but my ribs are not affected. In two weeks, I will be ready to fight again." *More or less...* My thumb swept over Saliné's fingers, to calm her.

"I would say three," Felcer cautioned me. "Your wound is worse than the one Bucur received in the other battle," he stated professionally, just to give them a comparison, and in a strange way, I was pleased that my wound was worse than his, and that everybody knew about it. "But not a hard one. You must sleep now," he said after bandaging me again, looking at me, yet his message was for my visitors.

I hoped Saliné will not leave, but Jara stayed until everybody else left the room, and she realized my disappointment, then slowly embraced me.

"Put all the bad thoughts away, Codrin. Some of my past decisions have upset you, and I know it, but we had no choice, and I am trying to protect both of you. You are like a son to me. Please," she whispered, ruffling my hair, then her hand moved down my face. "Good night." She smiled tentatively, a touch of sadness glimmering in her eyes.

Late in the morning, when I entered the council room, everybody was already there, except for Saliné. Vio forget all the etiquette they had forced into her and jumped into my arms. She had come just to greet me – no one could convince her to wait until the meeting was finished.

"I've heard you were wounded." She caressed my face, her way of taking my pain away.

"Nothing to worry about. See, I can easily take you in my arms." I raised her, balancing her body on my right side that was not hurt, after I tensed all my muscles. Convinced, she separated from me, ready to leave the room. I stared at Saliné's empty place, and I caught Jara watching me. *Bucur is not here either...*

"Saliné is indisposed," Jara said, a trace of worry trailing in her voice.

"I am sure she is receiving the best care right now." I could not stop a caustic reaction, despite her concern and everything that had happened between us the evening before, remembering that Saliné was usually *indisposed* only for me.

"There are some sensible people in this castle ready to help her," Big Mouth grinned.

"Yes, Vio will stay with her," Jara added hastily, and I realized that Saliné was sick this time.

"I trust you to take care of her." Surprisingly, Mohor smiled at Vio, who smiled back without really understanding what was happening — not that I could understand anything from his reaction.

"Don't worry. I will not let Bucur with Saliné," Vio whispered, embracing me again. Jara heard her whispering too, and both of us remained baffled by her reaction.

She is thirteen now, I realized that Vio was no longer a small child, she understood my worries, and as always, she was ready to help. "Thank you, Vio," I whispered, low enough to be heard only by her and Jara. I wanted Jara to hear me too. "You are a real friend." I smiled at her before she left, and sat in my chair, ignoring everybody else. *What happened to Saliné?*

"Mehadin lost a third of his soldiers," Mohor interrupted my thoughts. "This presents some opportunities, but we must calculate carefully." Standing, he was studying the large map spread on the wall behind his chair. "Severin, Mehadia." Attracted in equal measure by both places on the map, his head moved several times like a metronome, left and right. "There was no war between us until now. Father and old Mehadin got on well together. Things changed after..." A sudden surge of anger cut his voice. When Mohor was still young and weak, the current Mehadin imposed a new treaty and borders, gaining some land, but there was no fight. "And Arad." In a rare show of tension, his palm hit the map over the city, as if slapping its owner himself. "We must not forget Orban. He will not forget us, either; his soldiers are at our border."

"We attack Mehadin fast, do some pillaging and push for negotiations on our terms," Big Mouth said, excited by the idea, seemingly recovered from losing the first battle and ready to take command again. "He must pay." It was not clear if Mehadin had to pay for defeating him or for the land he had grabbed in the past.

"When you win, some of the past deserters come back," Mohor said, thoughtfully. "But not all. And maybe we can hire some mercenaries. If everything goes well, Mehadin's money pays for them. We need at least three hundred soldiers. How fast can we gather them?" Mohor's question was addressed more to himself, he was not speaking to anyone in particular. In normal times, he would have been able to gather four hundred soldiers, a fourth of them close to the average and the rest low quality but, even after our victory, things remained troubled, and some vassals would avoid answering his call for arms.

"Five days for our army, twelve days for the mercenaries," Big Mouth answered. "We must attack fast, before they recover."

"Our army did not follow Mehadin, and we missed the opportunity to crush him," Veres said with distaste. "I don't know if it was a mistake or..." He left his phrase unfinished, his hand gesturing in a way that pointed to treason.

"Codrin," Cernat interjected quickly. "What was your reason for stopping their pursuit?" There was no complaint in his voice; he was just trying to balance things between Big Mouth and me, and it was now clear that I had been accused in absence for my decision, after the soldiers I came with were questioned by Mohor and Big Mouth.

You bastard, I cursed Big Mouth. "Two reasons," I said when my anger became controllable. "We had many wounded, and the ratio of the dead in the pursuit would not have favored us. If the enemy is two times stronger, you can't afford less than three dead enemies for one of your soldiers, in long battles. The ambush gave us a good ratio; we were too few to attack them again in the open field. A war of attrition is not for small armies. Any real commander knows this."

"A good argument. I am sure Veres learned something today." Cernat stopped any other comment, and Veres threw a poisoned stare at me, but remained silent.

"I agree that we have some opportunities," Mohor repeated. "A fast attack is one of them." He stopped, staring around, keeping his eyes for a few seconds on each of us, like a mute invitation to speak our minds.

Avoiding Mohor's eyes, I surprised Cernat looking at me with some expectation, but it was too early to push my plan forward. Politically, I was still weak, even after the battle, and my presence in the council was just a temporary thing. *Let them talk, and slowly push my ideas when the time is ripe.*

"A fast attack has both strength and weakness," Cernat said, when he realized that I would not answer. "We must gather information before deciding."

"Mehadin is down, and we must surprise Orban," Big Mouth disagreed.

"Orban can surprise us, too," Jara said, cautiously. "He cannot use his full army, but don't forget the five hundred soldiers at our border."

"That's why we must attack fast." Big Mouth pushed again, and no one could say that he was wrong, but his view was limited by the scope he had chosen. "Before Orban gathers information and acts against us again." Briefly, he glanced at me, to leave the impression that I might leak information to Orban.

"Codrin." Mohor looked at me, and I could not say if Big Mouth's glance was the cause of his sudden reaction, but my wait and see strategy failed at that moment.

"What do you want to achieve?" Neither the number Mohor provided for his new army, nor the mercenaries, were needed for a fast attack. Two hundred soldiers gathered in a few days would have been the right approach, but a fast attack did not suit my plans.

"What I want to achieve depends on the means we have, and the means are driven by what I want to achieve." Mohor's finger moved on the map over the land he had lost a long time ago, sliding further east into Mehadin's land, but not by much. Suddenly, his hand passed over Arad again, just to remind us that Orban had a word to say, too. And again, his mute eyes invited us to speak our minds.

"Why not take Mehadia?" I asked.

"Orban will not allow us to take it," Jara said. "The more land we seize, the stronger his reaction."

"Mehadia doesn't suit you." I almost smiled, anticipating their reaction. "But it's possible to turn any situation to one's own advantage, if one approaches it in the proper perspective." In the proper frame of mind would have been even more appropriate, but a proper perspective is built in small steps. "The land north of the mountains is both difficult and expensive to keep in such challenging times, and the trouble will not end soon."

I gave them some hope; with all that optimism derived from building an alliance against Orban, they were weak, and even when not consciously aware, in some corners of their minds there was a different evaluation that they were trying to suppress. As Tudor taught me, hope is a potent tool, habitually used to bend the political landscape to your will. The Assassins were not only the best fighters; they were some of the best masters of minds too. Killing is not a scope by itself, just another way to shape a certain political situation. Born from the remains of the Imperial Legion, the Assassins carried a thousand-year-old culture of fighting and subversion, and I was sure that they were behind many political moves in the four kingdoms, but mostly in Arenia and Silvania which were closer to their hidden sanctuaries. *Were they involved in the coup against my father?* Knight Gaspar told me that they had helped the Usurper, but I was not sure, and many times I recalled all the sparse information about the night attack on our castle. It did not help.

"You are wasting our time," Big Mouth snapped at me, killing my thoughts, and I made a mark to follow that trace more.

"But for Orban…" I ignored Big Mouth.

"For Orban?" Mohor asked, intrigued. "Are you suggesting using Mehadia as bait for his consent?"

"Why not? Everybody gets what is most important for them. You acquire almost two-thirds of Mehadin's land – the richest parts that are better than yours – and Orban gets a strategic fortress that would be a burden for you. You destroy Mehadin; you get fame, the best thing to attract more allies against Orban. The new political situation will work to your advantage."

"Let's convene the council again in the evening," Mohor said abruptly, without answering my proposal, but without dismissing it either. He glanced at Jara and Cernat, and I understood that they would continue without us.

As expected, I was not called to the next council, and no one informed me what happened there, not even Cernat. *I would give a finger to know what Big Mouth said.* I ate alone in my room, both that evening and the next morning, before Vlaicu returned with the wounded, and I went out to greet them.

A new council gathered, and this time I was invited to join. Going to the council room, I saw Saliné in the long corridor, and I moved faster, trying to reach her. She avoided me, entering one of the rooms on her way, yet I was close enough to see that she looked pale and tired, her eyes sunken in their orbits.

In the council, Vlaicu told his part of the story and gave some numbers for the trophies we took in the battle: weapons and horses.

"It seems that you are taking a long-term interest in my army." Mohor looked at me, visibly pleased that his soldiers were now better armed, without spending a coin. "This victory puts us back on the political map. Embassies are on the road to Konrad and Devan to announce the news. Bucur and Antal are leading them." He glanced again at me, and I remembered his reaction when I complained about Bucur receiving too much attention for his wound from Saliné.

Is this genuine interest, or just political calculation? He sent Bucur to Konrad, not to Devan. Just seven days there and back. The road to Deva would have been almost twice as long. If my plan works, I will go to Arad, just when Bucur comes back.

"Three hundred soldiers will be here in twelve days, seventy-five of them mercenaries. In total, we will have almost four hundred. "Mehadia," Mohor's finger touched the place on the map, "is smaller than Severin, but still a good fortress. What makes you think we can take Mehadia with less than four hundred soldiers?"

"We can't take Mehadia by siege," I said, thinking that I understood his question. "Well, we can, if we are lucky, after a long siege, but we will lose too many people."

"Mehadin will gift it to us," Big Mouth snorted.

"His people may do it, if our stars align well, but no one can guarantee that. If we burn a few castles, some vassals will leave him and pay allegiance to you. Fear is a potent tool. Then destroy whatever army Mehadin can still gather, and the road to Mehadia is free. It will take a month or two, as he must be crushed, not just defeated."

"Then we give Mehadia to Orban," Mohor said in a neutral tone, a touch of irritation hidden behind his words; no one likes to take a castle just to give it to his worst enemy.

"If we are able to take it, yes."

"We win the battle, gather the allegiance of some Knights, but we don't take Mehadia." Jara pushed with the second scenario.

"The Seigneury disintegrates, and Orban claims Mehadia. You claim the south, and some negotiations will start, but your position will be weaker."

"We take Mehadia," Mohor switched back. "And give it to Orban, in exchange for the southern area. He will place an army in the fortress, controlling another chunk of the southern road to Deva, and have one more way open to attack us from Mehadia. Another strategic weakness for us, and Devan will not be happy, either. He is our ally."

"An unfortunate proposal that suits Orban and others, but not us. We should think more before upsetting Devan. The marriage and alliance are too important for us." Big Mouth was fast in tackling me, and there was a hidden implication about conflicting interests I had because of Saliné's marriage. "We…"

"No one said anything about giving Orban a functional fortress," I cut in, then stopped talking, leaving them enough time to understand my plan. The room became suddenly silent, and they frowned with varying degrees of surprise, but none tried to react. "If we burn the fortress, it will take years to rebuild it. We leave only the city for him. It has some commercial value but not strategic."

"You are planning a lot of burnings." Mohor was annoyed, for any Seigneur destroying a castle was against everything they stood for.

"If they save soldiers' lives, yes."

"Anything else I should know?" Mohor asked, still annoyed, and I understood that while some things had been clarified, the final decision would not come today. His expression was oddly inward, as if he hadn't been following the last part of our conversation.

"For such a long campaign, we need provisions. We must not rely on pillage."

"Pillage is usual in wars." Big Mouth shrugged, as if my request was illogical. For weak armies, pillage was indeed the usual way to raise the soldiers' morale and fill their pockets without emptying your own too much.

"It will slow us down," I said, dryly. "And keep in mind that you want to seize that land," I pointed to the map.

"Provisions," Mohor agreed. "Anything else?"

"It would be beneficial to test the waters in Arad," I said tentatively, knowing that my proposal was hard to swallow.

"For Orban?" Big Mouth asked, shaking his head to underline the treachery, and the evil that seemed to exist amid honest men.

"Is it really necessary?" Jara interfered, swiftly, to stop me taking a jab at Big Mouth, but there was a real concern in her voice, and that jarred me.

"Not as necessary as trust is these days." My voice was cold, and I fixed a point on the ceiling, avoiding to look at her.

"Testing Arad may be dangerous for everybody," Cernat stopped an exchange of words that could escalate. "Mostly for Codrin."

"Living is a dangerous thing these days. We might be able to extract some benefits from my traveling to Arad; information is important, as you said, but I will not go without your approval."

After Mohor closed the meeting, I asked Jara if she had some time for me, and we stayed alone in the room.

"What happened to Saliné? I saw her and she looked tired." *And she ran from me...*

"Lack of sleep, and too many worries." There was a light reproach in her voice, as if Saliné's state was related to me.

"Maybe we can read together for an evening or two. It's what she likes the most." *And me too...*

"Codrin, you are the cause of her sickness, not the cure. It's time for you to acknowledge this. If you love Saliné, leave her alone." Her voice was gentle, yet there was a veiled firmness in it, and I had the sudden impression that in front of me was

Grand Seigneur Cernat, not Jara – kindness and steel forged together by the vicissitudes of life.

Appalled by her reaction, my first impulse was to scold Jara with an allusion about Bucur being her choice for Saliné's cure. The tone of her voice made me reevaluate, and it took me a while to find a proper answer. "You should know me better. I disagree with you, the more you tighten the leash on Saliné, the harder her life will become. And mine. You are playing us in a way that might haunt you later. For the many things that bond our past, I will pretend that this discussion never happened, and time will tell which of us was right."

Gently, Jara touched my face. Her mouth was set in a straight line that betrayed her emotion. "We love Saliné, and I hope to find a common way to help both of you. Until that time, you must stay separated. Not because I want it, Codrin. She is troubled now and needs time to recover from your … kiss." She gave a slow nod, retracted her hand and went out.

That evening, they finally made the decision to take Mehadia, and allowed me to go to Arad. My mind was filled with a degree of satisfaction that partially blanketed the hard discussion I had with Jara.

At the end of the council, Mohor pushed a paper across the table to me. "Thank you for your good services," he said simply.

I took the paper slowly, trying to read it without being too obvious. *Twenty-five hectares of land…* "Thank you," I said, bowing slightly, and left the room in silence. There was no reaction on their faces – only Mohor, Jara and Cernat were there – and I struggled to hide my disappointment; my Knighthood was nowhere in sight.

My wound was not fully healed, but Vlad came with me, providing a sense of security that had eluded me for a long time in my past journeys. To stop Pintea's complaints that he should come with us, I *charged* him to be Vio's guard; they were comrade in games already. Jara smiled at me, but she agreed; Vio was like a tornado, and Pintea was full of energy too. I entered in Arad alone, thinking that Vlad should remain unknown to Cantemir. I wished that Delia and Panait did not know Vlad's name, but we can't change the past. *The moment someone realizes that Codrin and Tudor are the same person, my game ends. It may be a deadly end.* Delia and Panait were my first stop, then I went to see Cantemir. It was almost dark.

"What's new?" Cantemir was sick, but in a good mood. A summer cold was keeping him in the house.

Your mood will change soon. "Caravans, robbers, Mehadin riding through Severin. Frankis is a dangerous place right now."

"It was like this from before we were born. Why bother now? Let me guess; you had no knowledge of the small war in the south," he said, a flicker of amusement in his eyes.

"My sources let me down. It happens sometimes. But," I raised my forefinger, "when I went south a defeated army was running west. When I came back north another one was running east. I am sure you know who ran west; I saw your fifty soldiers coming back home, but it seems that Mehadin went further and lost."

"Mehadin..." Cantemir took a moment to adjust the drape of the blanket around his shoulders. There was flash of surprise in his eyes that let place to a frown, and the cold calculation happening behind his drawn together brows. "It was not totally unexpected." He moved a hand through his thick brown hair. A slow move. Its shadow swayed and shifted, a ghost sliding across the white walls. There was a shadow of a smile on his lips too before he recited from Farneius, "Fate, show me the path I must walk. The strange thing is..." He paused for a moment and frowned even deeply in thought. "It's quite rare to have only one path in front of you. Dark or not. Do you think Mohor will dare to occupy Mehadia?"

"We both agreed that he is a prudent man, but if the opportunity arrives..."

"Opportunities... That's what I was thinking too." Absently, he glanced out the window, and I involuntarily followed. It was fully dark now, and only a few dim lights shone indistinct through the night.

"You have an army at Severin's border, but from what I saw in the north I doubt that you can attack now. And S'Severin must have sent many letters about your soldiers helping Mehadin."

"I don't think so," Cantemir smiled. "Our soldiers fought under Mehadin's banner."

Of course. "That was clever, but it suits you better if S'Severin destroys Mehadin. You can't get Severin now, but you can get Mehadin's northern territories, including the main fortress, for free."

After a little silence, suddenly stiff and still, Cantemir said, "Soon, the trap will close on Mohor." If his voice could kill, Mohor would be dead right there and then.

"Cantemir, since when are you so sour? It's bad for your health. Bad for or your plans." I forced myself to laugh – his obstinacy did not look good for my strategy.

He shrugged, apparently unimpressed by my words, and went to the map. His finger tapped first over the ducal area, then over Severin, sliding slowly to Mehadia and further to Arad, his reaction eerily similar to Mohor's in the last council. "Mehadin is just a tool, and you are right, we can have Mehadia almost for free. And the Devans." He stared again at the map, unaware of my amusement. "The Devans might see some things differently from now on, a bit earlier than I was planning."

"You need to maintain good relations with the Devans."

"Don't worry, we will cancel their alliance with Mohor."

He knows about the alliance... He knew about Saliné's wedding too. It must be that spy, Senal mentioned in his last letter. "It should not be difficult. Devan's son and Orban's daughter," I suggested, looking uninterested, as if it were the most obvious thing in the world.

"That or Orban's son and Jara's daughter," he said thoughtfully, and I stepped back, struggling to contain my panic. Still looking at the map, he observed nothing. "I want a different marriage for Devan's son. Devan will take Mohor's betrayal hard and fall in our arms. That will bring him closer to Duke Stefan."

Stefan has three marriageable granddaughters... An alliance between Duke Stefan and Devan? Severin will become Orban's reward, and Saliné... "How... How will you convince Mohor?" I asked, fighting to ignore my suddenly dry throat.

"Surprised eh?" Cantemir laughed quietly, not understanding the real reason behind my inner struggle. "The marriage request will come in a package with our army at his borders and the approval for him to take Mehadin's lands. If Mohor fails to win or stays home because he is too weak, we take Severin instead of Mehadia. Our soldiers will fight under Mehadin's banner. If the stars align well, we might be able to take both Mehadia and Severin. We need a disaster to destroy both. It may happen. I planned the war to take Severin for next spring, but Fate wanted it this year."

Fate and me... You are less prepared now, and I have a short window in which to act. "You must be careful of Duke Stefan's reaction."

"For his own interest, the Duke will change his mind until spring," Cantemir said, staring away, as if his mind was split in two, and I knew that my audience had ended. Through the open window, the city murmured inside the silent room. My war was now a wild animal with a life of its own.

Chapter 22 – Jara

I thought that Saliné would recover after Codrin left for Arad. It did not happen; she was still sleepless and cried throughout the night. Her beautiful eyes were now sunken and dark, and smile deserted her lips. She never cried in front of me, but her eyes told many things. Talking solved nothing; I received only short, bland answers each time I tried – it was like reopening a deep wound. From the moment of her engagement, she was no longer the girl she had been, yet she was able to keep her composure. Some mornings, her eyes were red and tired, and I knew that she had dreamt of Codrin. It was her spirit of duty and the sense of self-sacrifice for the family that kept her going. That moment of closeness with Codrin had changed everything. His gentle touch shattered the armor she had built for herself, leaving her naked against a future that we forced on her from lack of better choices, a glimpse of happiness that would never be hers.

The campaign will take two months. If everything goes well, we will make Codrin governor in our new land, to keep him busy until the wedding. He will not be happy... He is already upset by my words. And the land we gave him... The reward for his win against Mehadin was small by necessity, not that we could not afford to give more, just a way to delay his road to Knighthood until after Saliné's marriage.

Stubbornly, I tried each day to reach Saliné until I found her with Bucur in the library, late in the evening; I was already worried for not knowing where she was. It was the fourth day after his arrival from the embassy. She followed me without a word, to her room.

"I thought we had a deal for the evenings," I reminded her that she was no longer allowed to stay alone with him so late.

Staring at her hands, she said, her voice barely more than a whisper, "I need to do something."

"You could at least inform me." I shook my head, but she was too troubled, her eyes sad and unfocused. That unsettled me, as something in my chest grew tight, making me to step back from the interdiction.

"I am sorry."

"Do you think it will help?" I took her in my arms, but she remained unresponsive, and I began to stroke her beautiful hair, feeling that it was softer when she was still a child. There was a father too then, and his death lessened our world, filling it with danger.

"Yes, he keeps me occupied. It feels so bad." She started to cry for the first time in my presence. "Day and night, I am just thinking..." She did not finish, but it was clear that she was thinking of Codrin. "And I have to marry Devan. I wish to be free to..." Her voice broke again, and I caressed her hair, trying to calm her. "Don't worry," she said, after a while. "I know what is at stake, and I will do it."

Her sleep improved; the shadows behind her eyes recessed, and I let them spend the evenings together; in fact, she was splitting her time just between Vio and Bucur. Never all three together, Vio disliked Bucur too much. She was no longer a small child, and she was a more direct and sometimes unpredictable younger version of Saliné. *Vio has a strong Light*, I recalled Dochia's words, and remembering Mother's difficult choice, I forced myself to ignore them again.

I had no time to ponder much about my daughter's misfortune as Mohor entered my room, that subtle troubled look, I knew well, in his eyes. He was a composed man, and many would not even realize his inner struggling. It took me a while to learn how to read him.

"Aron has requested to lead the army," Mohor said, as if we did not have enough problems. "He wants to redeem himself for the lost battle. He thinks that it was just an accident."

"And what do *you* think?"

"He may be right," he shrugged. "I am caught in the middle. Codrin proved himself, and Aron deserves a second chance. We need to find a solution until Codrin comes back."

"And *we* means that I have to prepare Codrin for Big Mouth's redemption," I said, acidly.

"It means that we need to find a solution, nothing else."

"I don't see anyone other than Codrin leading the army. Big Mouth can have his chance later. Mohor, we can't afford to lose."

"Yes, we can't afford to lose," he repeated blandly, and I realized that indeed he was caught in a bad position, just that I did not share it with him; for me, things were clear.

During the dinner, we avoided to talk more about Aron, or war, or even about Saliné, and I all wanted that night was to rest, but sleep did not come easily. It never comes easily when you are in great need. *What makes people so different from each other?* I lamented and felt suddenly cold, in front of the open window, under the bright light of the silvery moon. *Accidents of birth? Good fortune? Misfortune? Tragedy can change a woman or a man. But how much?*

Codrin returned a day later, and Mohor was still nervous, unable to decide. He looked tired and older than his age. "Mohor, every soldier out there," I pointed through the window of the council room to the field in front of the castle where our army was settled, "knows that Codrin will lead them. No one wants Aron. They lost once with him, and he ran from the battle like a coward. Some will desert again if you change the commander now." Waiting for Codrin, we decided that the first meeting would be just with us. Father would join us later; a courier was already on the road to bring him here.

"How can we have both of them?" he asked, exasperated by his own indecision.

"We can't. They will reject even a formal subordination."

"The subordination already exists. Aron is our Spatar. Even if Codrin commands the army, he is subordinate to Aron."

"Codrin will not accept, and we need him now. Keep the coward at home," I snapped.

"We need an army, too." Mohor's voice was bitter and rough, and I looked at him without understanding. "Some of our Knights agreed that Aron should lead the army. The soldiers may think differently, but the Knights decide who or what. Aron has more influence than I thought. I trust him," he added, hastily. "We need some changes, but it will take time."

Mohor does not have full control over the Seigneury. We don't have... How could I be so blind?

Father and Codrin entered at that moment, ending a discussion suddenly more important than it looked at the beginning.

"Well?" Mohor asked when everybody was seated, an encouraging smile spread on his lips, as if his worries had just vanished in thin air.

I must learn to read Mohor better.

Not ready to answer, Codrin stayed silent for a while, giving me the impression that his news was not so good, or at least things were more complicated than we thought, and he was trying to deliver them embellished in some diplomatic cover. I looked at him and decided that it was more on the complications side than bad things. *Maybe*... I sighed, and my involuntary reaction finally made him speak.

"Things are moving in Arad," Codrin said in a hesitant voice, his eyes moving distractedly around the room as though searching for something. After a while, his expression started to change, and his voice became flat. "Mehadin's defeat came at the wrong time and changed some plans, but nobody can guarantee the direction right now. Things at their northern border are complicated to a certain extent that can't give us full assurances. As with any tool, Mehadin may be discarded when his usefulness comes to an end. Mehadia's strategic position became a shifting point in their plans."

"They are considering taking Mehadia." Mohor interrupted him with an unexpected degree of impatience.

"Orban needs both Mehadia and Severin to become a Duke. It's just that now he sees an opportunity to take Mehadia faster and without much effort, before attacking Severin. You have only one chance: to destroy Mehadin before Orban makes his mind." Codrin stopped, and there was a sudden silence in the room, everybody trying to assess the consequences. "Orban hopes to obtain a free hand in the south through negotiations with Duke Stefan."

The Circle must be involved in this, Cantemir is the Master Sage, after all.

"How can Orban reciprocate for such a favor?" Father asked thoughtfully; Stefan, the Duke of Peyris, always helped us discreetly.

"I don't know," Codrin shrugged, looking nowhere. "Maybe Orban is now strong enough to play between the two Dukes of the north. Last week, both Peyris and Loxburg sent embassies to Arad. Your only chance is to destroy Mehadin before Orban convinces Duke Stefan," he repeated. "Some negotiations are expected to start soon."

"Would Orban accept a mutual solution over Mehadin's land?" Mohor asked again.

"His northern border is watched, so that would be the most practical way to settle everything now. You never know with Orban." Codrin shrugged again, and looked at me first, then at Father, and lastly, he looked straight at Mohor, his mouth tight shut. There was no reaction from us, but I did not think that he really expected one. "He may help Mehadin again with soldiers but, show the slightest weakness, and he will attack you before having an agreement with Duke Stefan."

"Why would Orban send soldiers to help Mehadin if he wants Mehadia?" Father interjected.

"To weaken you."

"How much does he want to weaken us right now?" Father asked again, of all of us he had the best strategic mind, and it was comforting to know how far he was calculating everything.

I also realized that Codrin was now more than the young protector I knew. There was a new political depth in him, hidden to me until that moment. *I hope Mohor realizes Codrin's value.*

"If you and Mehadin destroy each other..." Codrin did not continue, but everything was now clear, a fast win over two weakened Seigneurs would not allow enough time for Duke Stefan to react. "You must keep those hundred and fifty old soldiers here while we are away."

For the moment, there were no more questions, and I had the impression that Codrin wanted to leave, but his stance told me there was more bad news not yet delivered to us.

"What about our wedding with Devan?" I asked softly, without naming Saliné, knowing that my question would hurt him. "Will Orban still try to stop it?"

"Yes," he said, dryly.

"What will they do?" I forced myself to ask again.

"I don't know."

There was an open hostility in his voice, and something that resembled fear. *Is Saliné in danger? Orban would not dare to kill her, she is marked by the Circle, and Cantemir will not allow it. No, Codrin would react differently... But he is hiding something. I will talk with him later.* "Thank you, Codrin," I said, covering his hand with mine. As in the past, his thumb slid slowly over my fingers, back and forth, underlining a bond that had many ups and downs, but was always there. *Like in any family.* I smiled at him, amused that no one would understand the real meaning of my reaction, not even Codrin.

Three days later, in the morning, I went to see how the preparations were going. Things were improving; Codrin knew what he was doing, and it was not just about his fighting qualities, but about methods and knowledge too. He knew how to manage an army. *Senal wrote that Codrin is more important that we thought.* I left my mind to drift into the Light. There was no way to see the past, but the more I thought, the more I was convinced that Codrin was the son of the Arenian King who was slain a few years ago. The mercenaries arrived that morning, five days later than agreed, but I never saw a war going fully as planned. I went back with Codrin in good mood, thinking that maybe it was the right time to ask about Orban's plans to stop the wedding, and entered the hall while Saliné and Bucur came out of the library. Bucur had a hand on Saliné's shoulder as if to guide her, and I struggled to hide my surprise. They kept walking like this, and we intersected in the narrow corridor.

"Codrin," she said, nodding at him, then passed with no other reaction, and I caught a trace of a malicious smile on Bucur's lips.

Codrin nodded too, silent, and I was unable to react in any way. After a few more steps together, he turned, whispering, "I forgot to say something important to Vlaicu."

He missed lunch, but still had to come to the council. Pale and with a chilly calm, he stayed silent and never glanced toward Saliné or Bucur.

"Codrin," Mohor finally reacted to his lack of presence. "We need your opinion, too. You will go with the army." He avoided the word lead, unsure about who would lead what. "We are discussing the marching plans," he insisted, frowning at Codrin, his fingers rasping the table.

"It's too early to make a decision. I am waiting for some important information."

"It seems that we don't deserve to be informed that it is too early to discuss this," Aron snapped, and I saw that Mohor was angry at Codrin. "We should stop bothering you."

"I didn't know that Tohani castle is so close to the border and to both the northern and southern roads to Mehadia," Codrin said, calmly.

"And why is this so important?" This time Mohor was ironic.

Codrin either did not recognize or ignored it and answered blandly again. "If we burn the castle, their desertion rate will increase. The faster the better." Mohor frowned, but this time he was listening; Codrin had already explained to us that some Knights might prefer to stay home, to defend their lands or enter in an agreement with us. "They already have some desertions. It happens after a lost battle. Continue with the plans." The sudden surge of power in Codrin's voice made Aron shrink in his chair, and he gaped, unable to react. Codrin's reaction surprised everybody — I saw it perfectly in the sudden glances going back and forth around the table. The council continued as if Codrin was not really there.

"Saliné, could you please tell me what happened? You seem to be much closer to Bucur," I said, cautiously.

"It's better like this," she shrugged.

"What's better like this?"

"There is nothing between me and Bucur, but I can't have another period like..." Her voice faded. "Like I had. You don't know how hard is for me. And it is better for Codrin too; he must forget me. We will never be together; you know well why." Her voice was bitter and angry, but I did not react, letting her have that small relief. "Don't think that it was easy for me to let him see..." She stumbled, but I understood that she let Bucur get closer to her in front of Codrin on purpose. "It will be easier to face my fate, even when I did not ask for it. Codrin will leave for two months, and with his anger, it should be enough to forget me. He must forget me, so I can forget him." Again, the bitter recrimination, and again I did not react; everything I could say, she knew already. "At least I have a purpose for everything I am doing, my family, but Codrin did not deserve all this."

There was some truth in her words, yet deep inside me, I knew instantly that everything was wrong, and even worse, I knew that things could not be changed for the moment without harming Saliné even more, and I shivered in the warm room. *She will calm down while Codrin is away. And Bucur will be gone too. Two months... It may be enough to regain her inner balance. I wish to know what is in Codrin's mind. Small as it is, they still have a chance to be together.*

"I am glad that you feel better," I tried to stop her self-recrimination, and my own thoughts. "I hope that Codrin is well, too," I said without thinking, and she wringed her hands nervously.

"Codrin can't be well right now, Mother, because of what I did, but he will not let us down." There was no doubt in her voice, and I realized that she might know him better than me.

"He may choose to leave after the war, at least for a while. Maybe he will come back, and Vio will be luckier than me."

Future and past seemed tangled and twisted badly tonight, and there was sorrow everywhere. Embracing my daughter to offer some soothing, I was the one in tears.

Mohor was already in our bedroom when I entered after leaving Saliné, and he looked at me, worried. "What happened to Codrin?"

"The same old story, Saliné." I shrugged, trying to avoid another hard talk.

"And what is new in the old story?" he stubbornly continued, and I could not blame him.

"Saliné decided to underline that they don't have a future together."

"He already knows that."

"Yes, he already knows that."

"Jara," he said gently.

"She used Bucur to create a rift with Codrin. The next two months away from Severin should do the rest. Don't think that it was easy for her."

"Not the best time," he sighed. "We gave him only twenty-five hectares of land for his victory in the battle, just enough to keep him close. He said nothing, but we all know that he was not impressed by our gratitude. We agreed that it was the best way. Didn't we?" He glanced at me, and I just shrugged, still unconvinced, but Mohor found an unexpected ally in Father. Both wanted to be sure that Codrin would not achieve Knighthood before Saliné's wedding, so he could not claim our promise. "As agreed, we give him a hundred hectares from Mehadin's land and make him a Half-Knight, if everything goes as planned."

"And if it doesn't?"

"Who knows what happens if it doesn't." He turned his palms out, avoiding to look at me. "After Saliné's wedding, we will make him Knight. He deserves it, but only after the wedding. I don't want more complications. Codrin has a strong sense of allegiance. I know, it goes mostly to you and ... Saliné. And just when I made the right step, sending Bucur away with the embassy. Keep Saliné and Bucur separated, or out of Codrin's sight until the army leaves Severin. I have no other embassy to send Bucur on." He stopped, unsure how to continue. "Aron said something vague about strengthening our bonds, if the thing with the Devans fails."

"And Bucur told Saliné that the marriage contract with Devan may be canceled. There is nothing vague in their strategy. Aron and Bucur should not know about that. Codrin insisted on keeping his warning between us. Big Mouth may use that lever at his own convenience. And the best lever he has is that he knows our information came from Codrin. Bucur underlined that to Saliné."

"Yes, that would be the most inopportune thing," Mohor agreed, but it was too late.

A few days later, I decided to finally risk talking with Codrin, and went into his room, late in the evening.

He stared at me with cold eyes. "I thought I could have some privacy in my own room."

"Codrin, we have to talk." I raised my hand to touch his face, but he stepped back from me.

"To talk, we have the council. Everything happened because of your intrigues to make Bucur the second marriage option for Saliné."

Anger filled me, and sadness because it was not true, and I breathed hard to calm myself, but it was not the right moment to answer, nothing could convince him in that spirit of mind, and from that evening, he slept with the soldiers in the field, which allowed him to avoid dinners with us.

I skipped dinner too, walking with no aim in our garden, that was too small to liberate my mind from harmful thoughts until Mohor came after me, and I just yelled at him when he asked what had happened.

☙❧

"They leave in three days." I tried to make Mohor aware that our army was still without an official commander. Formally, it was Codrin, but Aron's request to lead, and Mohor's indecision, had turned everything upside down. We were with Father in our restricted version of the council.

"There is only one solution," Mohor sighed, and I looked at him with expectation. "I have to lead the army." Mohor was not a real commander, and he knew his limitations, so in the end, it was almost the same thing as before, a compromise trying to please both Codrin and Aron, by avoiding a formal subordination between them.

It will not help… "Who will convince Codrin to come with you and Aron?" I asked.

"You?" Mohor frowned. "Vio? We can't use Saliné." He tried to hide his indecision behind her rift with Codrin. "I hope he is mature enough to pass over that obsession with Aron."

"Mohor, the main thing is not who leads whom, even when we should be clear that Codrin leads the army. The main thing is that Aron tried to assassinate Codrin." Father's face was solemn, guarded, a face that gave nothing away.

"That's not true." Mohor reacted quickly, anger and shock filling his voice. "Aron had his revenge, and you should not take everything Codrin says as true."

"It's true," Father said, staring at Mohor. "And I saw the proof," he added before Mohor could protest again.

I was not aware of any proof, and I had the uncomfortable feeling that I had been sidelined by Codrin long before our actual rift. *Codrin did not trust me...*

"I have to talk with Aron." Mohor neither accepted nor rejected Father's version.

"You will not talk with Aron," Father said evenly, in the commanding voice that he used rarely, and Mohor shifted uncomfortably in his chair. "If Aron learns that Codrin is aware of his assassination attempt, everything will blow up. We should be content that Codrin was mature enough not to answer in kind. He took a great risk."

"You should have told me." Mohor spoke slowly, giving me the feeling that Father had not convinced him yet; there was a delaying strategy in his statement.

"Not even Jara knew about the proof. Codrin feared that she would let you know out of loyalty, and then Aron would be informed too. It had happened with some other things, and we have a crisis right now between Saliné and Codrin that was stirred by a clever ploy, using knowledge that Aron should not have had. Aron is playing his own game, with interests that are diverging from our own. He is becoming a liability, and with all that loyalty you keep from the help he provided in the past, you must control him. The faster, the better."

"Are you schooling me?" Mohor retorted coldly, something that had never happened before with Father – there was a good chemistry between them.

"What bothers you more? That I am schooling you, or that I am right?" Father asked, his voice flat.

"I trust Aron."

"Everyone can be trusted up to a point. Aron is at that point now. We see it in his moves. Why are we having this issue with the commander right now, in the middle of a war?" Father asked.

"Because Aron deserves a second chance."

"Not because half of our Knights conspired with Aron against you?"

"That too," Mohor acknowledged dryly, but he looked more upset by Father's words than by the facts themselves. "I proposed a solution."

"Your proposal will become a solution only after you set the rules for the campaign. We already know Codrin's role. What do you plan for Aron? How you assure Codrin's safety?"

"Do you think that Aron should go too?" I asked, worried that Codrin could be harmed.

"We have no choice," Father said, and I saw a glimpse of relief on Mohor's face. "It's too late to confront the Knights now. When the war ends, you must do it, and Codrin will be your best ally."

"Who will persuade Codrin? Things are cold between us right now," I sighed.

"I will do it," Father said, "after Mohor convinces me he is able to cover Codrin's back. We have a strong army commander in our hands, and this war is just the overture."

"I will give Ban and half of the guards to Codrin," Mohor said, after a long pause. "We must keep Aron's men away from Codrin in battle, but this should be the commander's task." He looked at us, but no one reacted; he was avoiding the main threat. "I will warn Aron to stay away from Codrin," he said, his nostrils flaring in a rare display of tension, his voice edgy and harsh, "but I can't guarantee anything more. And I must give something to Aron, too."

"What something?" I put more pressure on Mohor; it was good that he had acknowledged his partial lack of authority over Big Mouth, but it was not good enough.

"After we conquer Mehadia, Aron will take over."

"Aron will take over the city and the land to organize your possessions, but not over the army," Father underlined, and Mohor nodded, visibly annoyed.

Codrin came in the evening, brought by a letter from Mohor, but it was only Father and I in the room waiting for him.

"There are some last moment changes in the army's chain of command," Father said, and Codrin just looked blandly at him. "Mohor will join the army." There was a moment of silence, he was waiting for Codrin's reaction, but nothing came, and that put Father in an awkward situation, as we were expecting a dialogue to smooth the worst part to come. "He needs to understand his capabilities and prepare for the next year. Isn't what you suggested?" Father asked, and Codrin just nodded. "For similar reasons, and the need for rehabilitation, Aron will join too."

"You know the only condition I set," Codrin said, flatly.

"This is a hard and long war, and we need all our forces to win, Codrin. Every Knight and soldier. Aron is our Knight. His soldiers are our soldiers," Father said. "We need them as much as we need you."

"You need me dead or alive?" Codrin reacted, the same blandness in his voice, as it was not his life under discussion. "Of all the people here," he gestured at me, then to the castle, "you are the only one who knows what happened."

"It happened; it may happen again. I understood you last time; you were still a protector, with not much to lose in rejecting the offer of the left wing, apart from some potential gains that no one could guarantee. Now, you are a commander who has proved his worth. The next campaign will enhance your reputation even more. Are you ready to lose your well-deserved reputation?"

"I will think about," Codrin said, his voice bitter and rough, standing up abruptly, in an impolite way that was not his usual manner, and he left the room in haste; but we could finally see some emotions in his reaction.

When the door closed behind Codrin, Father continued to stare at it, and set his teeth on his lower lip.

"He will accept." Codrin's loss of temper convinced me that Father's words had started a realignment of his thoughts.

In the morning, Codrin consented to join our army, as commander under Mohor's lead, so to speak.

"Thank you," Mohor said simply, and I almost smiled. He had understood for some time that simple words worked better with Codrin. In a similar situation, Aron would have received several long phrases to please his insufferable greed for attention. "After this campaign, you will receive a hundred hectares of land and be named Half-Knight." He stopped and glanced at Codrin, who did not react in any way. "There are three regions in Mehadia's southern part. We plan to name you governor of one of them. We will decide together at the right moment which place suits you better."

What Mohor did not say was that the paper for the first fifty hectares of land was already signed, and Codrin would receive it after Mehadin's defeat, even if we were not able to take Mehadia. The land was in Severin; the other half would be granted from the conquered areas, if there were any.

Realizing that Mohor had finished, Codrin bowed briefly, then things moved to the last mundane preparations for an army that would leave a day later. When they had left, I remained alone in the room, my mind filled with a strange effervescence, unrelated to the war preparations.

You have to stay away for a while, Codrin. After Saliné's wedding, we will make you our Secretary and Knight. You will move here again, and maybe you and Vio... This will repair some things, but there is nothing I can do for my poor Saliné. I gripped the edge of the window until my knuckles went white, forcing myself to look far away, unable to see through my tears. *Nothing.*

"We can't fully trust Codrin," Aron said that afternoon. His face, long and solemn in the beginning, changed as he began to speak, a doubtful look crossing his face. He had requested to discuss some important things with Mohor and me, although my feeling was that he asked for me too only because I was in the room. "Orban may attack Severin in our absence. We need to be careful and leave more people here. Not many, but good soldiers, just enough to keep the enemy busy until we return. Cernat has a lot of experience; he knows what to do, and Bucur could stay and help him. We should not worry while we're in battle." The doubt in his stare increased, matched by a worried frown.

"Peace of mind is important in battle, but I have to speak with Cernat first," Mohor gave him an ambiguous answer.

"Bucur can't stay here," I said, thinking of Saliné, when Aron left us alone.

"He will come with us, just to avoid more complications, but I did not want Aron to think that I rejected his proposal without careful examination."

Next morning, he told Aron the army could not go into such an important battle without a good left-wing commander. Aron blinked once, his face as long and solemn as it was the day before, just that this time it was guarded, a face that gave nothing away.

Learning that Codrin had gone home for some last preparations, I took two soldiers with me and rode to his home. When I entered the house, I found only Vlad in the main room.

"Please leave us alone," I said, and undecided, he just stared at me. "I am not that dangerous." I smiled, and reluctant, he left the house. Codrin entered a moment later, finding himself alone with me.

"We need to talk," I said before he could react. "Some things are not what they seem. What happened on that corridor was just a self-preservation façade Saliné thought was necessary for both of you, nothing else. Please believe me and come back safe." I touched his face and went out without waiting for an answer, hoping that the little I had given would allow him to maintain some bond with Saliné.

Chapter 23 – Codrin

There was not much to do on the road to Mehadia, and my mind replayed Saliné's walk on the corridor, with Bucur's hand on her shoulder. It was painful, yet I could not stop myself. That evening, I wanted to quit Severin and leave them alone. I still do not know what changed my mind. Maybe because my fate was too entangled with Jara's family; or maybe in a corner of my mind there still was a trace of hope. It could have been that Saliné was sick and needed help, or it could have been that people distressed in love no longer think normally, and that would apply to both of us. It was that strange talk with Jara, just before I left Severin, that instilled some life in me again, but it was not much. I wanted to believe her, yet I could not.

We stopped at the fork between the northern and southern roads to Mehadia, the place where my plans had taken shape, preparing to deliver justice to Jorn and create the tension I needed between Mohor and Mehadin. The scouts returned in the evening. Two squads, led by Vlad and Ban, had only men from the guards reporting to Vlaicu. I did not trust Big Mouth's men, and he would not complain; scouting was dangerous, and he wanted to keep his soldiers. The third squad was made up of mercenaries. In the war games we played in Severin, they were more disciplined than Mohor's soldiers. Their leader, Valer, was the Black Dervil of Tolosa, and I accepted him into the war council, despite the opposition raised by Big Mouth and some Knights. We also crossed our swords in training several times, and Valer was almost equal to Cernat when we trained in Jara's house. That left me wondering how skilled was Cernat in his prime.

The council was an awkward thing because of a peculiar issue that had nothing to do with the gathering. Mohor had only one tent, a large one, able to assemble twenty people in the main room, if needed. He and Big Mouth were sleeping there, and many things happened outside the council meetings, in my absence.

"We take the northern road," I said in the council, gathered after all our scouts came back, reporting that both roads were free.

"The southern road is easier," Big Mouth said.

"We will take the northern road," I repeated in a flat voice and closed the council.

"Codrin, why could not you be more diplomatic?" Mohor asked when we were alone.

"Do you think it will help? If I say north, Big Mouth will say south. If I say south, he will say north. He doesn't raise issues to be solved in the council; he just creates them for his own purposes. Beware, Mohor, today it's me, tomorrow..."

"He is a Knight, and many soldiers report to him. There is always a hierarchy and there will always be."

"And you are a Seigneur. Keep your Knights under control if you want to keep your place in the hierarchy."

Tohani was a small castle, yet a frontal siege would have made us lose many soldiers. Ban reported that we were being watched; it could have been Mehadin, or it could have been the Knight who owned the castle. I hoped for the latter. Our squads had the order to avoid the enemy's scouts and leave the impression that we were unaware. During the night, we camped close to the junction where the road to the castle separated from the main route, and in the morning, we moved on toward Mehadia, leaving fifty soldiers behind, hidden in the forest. Twenty riders were following us in parallel through the hills, and I sent Ban back with the order for the soldiers left behind to surround the castle and block access to it. After another hour we went back to Tohani, which was almost deserted, and fell to us in less than an hour.

In the evening, we took council in the main room of the castle, our swords sitting on the big table in the middle; things were calm and bright – we had lost only seven soldiers.

"It went well." Mohor looked around, his brows cocked up, a large smile settled across his mouth.

"Tomorrow we set the fire and leave for Mehadia," I said.

"The castle is too important to be destroyed; it watches both roads to Mehadia," Big Mouth interjected, and I glanced at Mohor. He looked surprised too. "Marcel's younger son needs a castle." Marcel was the second Knight in Mohor's hierarchy, and not necessarily Big Mouth's best friend, but not his enemy either. Marcel was as surprised as Mohor, yet the idea pleased him, placing me in an awkward position.

I waited for Mohor to answer, but he stayed silent, leaving me to handle everything. "We have already agreed about the advantage we gain from burning the castle. We should not..."

"I am a Knight," Big Mouth snapped, beating his chest. "A Knight, like them." He rotated his long arm with an ample movement. "And unlike you, we know the value of a castle." He stood up, his long face ugly with rage, and hit the table with his fist.

"Yes, we know the value of the castle," three Knights, Big Mouth' closest allies, echoed him.

"A castle is something built to endure, passed from father to son, the symbol of our power. How can we rule the peasants when they see a burned castle? It doesn't matter if the past owner was our enemy today; he is still one of us." Big Mouth gestured again to the Knights, contrasting them to the vagrant I was, and he became even more agitated, advancing toward me in a menacing way.

I lowered my body, my knees unlocked, my feet forming a T, and my hands held close together in front at navel level – the Assassin Waiting Stance – ready to repel an attack. Like me, Big Mouth was armed with only a dagger. "If you know the value of it, then you know why we must burn it." I tried to show Mohor that I was capable of diplomacy.

"A real commander wins without burning castles," he growled.

"A real commander wins battles."

"You won a small battle and think you are a commander." Big Mouth's voice became even louder, and he was now just two steps away from me, his hand raised, ready to strike.

With his next step, I caught his hand as he tried to push me, and I turned his body over my shoulder. His back hit the floor with a dull sound, and a gasp escaped his mouth.

"Turn!" Mohor shouted and, turning, I saw Bucur attacking me with his sword.

At the last moment, I avoided the sword, jumping aside and, with my hand on the floor, I rotated, hitting Bucur's foot as his body went forward from its own momentum. When he fell, I pressed my dagger to his throat. *I should kill you...* But that could have unforeseen consequences, and I needed time to think. I did not have it.

"Codrin, don't." Mohor came behind me and gripped my shoulder.

"I apologize. I thought that my father was in danger. I did not want to kill you; it was just a son's reaction." Bucur's voice was calm, like nothing had really happened, his body was not tense, and the thought that I was being framed by Big Mouth and Bucur came to me.

Why did they scheme this? "This castle is not among the lands you will keep, Mohor. Aron knew that well when he suggested bestowing Marcel with it. Everything was just a game to give Bucur the opportunity to attack me."

"There was no plan," Bucur stated calmly. "I apologize once more. It will not happen again."

I must reevaluate Bucur. He is more dangerous than I thought. There was reptile coldness in him, and he could keep well his composure in tight situations, something I did not realize in our brief encounters in Severin.

Undecided, Mohor was rubbing his chin, and silence filled the room, waiting for his decision, not an easy one, I conceded.

"A trial should be set for tomorrow, and the traitor should wait in jail," I said.

Reluctantly, Mohor agreed with me and sent Bucur into a cell in the tower. Big Mouth did not interfere at all, letting only Bucur speak, and I was not able to understand their strategy.

I knew that Mohor would not execute Bucur, but I was expecting to see him in jail for a while, and that could change many things. Before going asleep, I explained our strategy for the land to Marcel, and logically he agreed with me, but disappointment still lingered in his eyes. Greed is a potent tool.

In the morning, the soldiers left to guard the door of the cell where Bucur was jailed were no longer there. Screeching, the door opened, revealing an empty cell. *What options do I have now?*

"I freed Bucur," Mohor said behind me, the voice of man announcing that the sun was rising, or the wind was blowing.

It was early morning, so he had asked a guard to wake him up when I went to the tower – an obvious small bone of attention to mollify me. In a curious twist, we were both in a difficult situation that could evolve in many ways.

"Obviously." I slammed the door of the empty cell and turned to face Mohor.

"You may want to know why I did it."

"I would not get the right answer from you."

"You think I would lie to you?" There was a touch of surprise in his voice, yet his face stayed frozen, a calm I guessed was not there.

"No, you will tell me your *truth*. You believe in what you say, but you are lying to yourself."

"It's better if you two stay separated for a while. I sent him back to Severin," Mohor said, without pronouncing his name. "You should appoint another commander of the left wing."

"Why are you so sure I will still lead your army?" I moved away from him and rested my hands on the cold stone in the gap under a large arch. On its external side, that level of the tower had no walls and no windows, just arch after arch, and their thick columns made of stones of different colors, orange and gray – there was an exquisite symmetry in their alternation. In the valley, the road to Mehadia wound through the forest, and the main part of the army occupied a high meadow. There was no visible trace of movement. High on the hill, the castle offered a good view.

"You are fighting for people that are close to both of us, and for yourself. However wrong everything looks to you right now, I appreciate what you are doing, and we need you." There was a moment of silence, then the sound of heavy boots stepping on the stones, coming closer to me.

Ah, how I wish to leave just to prove you wrong, but you are right. Like a mirage, the road to Mehadia was waiting in the valley, pointing to my only future that had a meaning, and a new idea came to me. I did not bother to share it with Mohor. "The proof of your appreciation is there," I gestured back to the door of the empty cell. "I should have killed Bucur yesterday, when I had the chance."

"And what stopped you?"

"Sometimes, I make mistakes." *It will not happen again.*

"No one is without mistakes, but you did the right thing, and you know it. You don't disturb the balance of power during a war." Mohor rested his hands on the stones, in the same position as me, his eyes watching me keenly.

"Tell that to Bucur and Big Mouth."

"I told them."

"They pissed on your words – no wonder that some Knights are no longer listening to you."

Mohor tilted back his head, and stared at me, jaw hard. Then his eyes relaxed. "I will deal with this at the proper time. This is not that time."

"After your wedding, I stayed one month in your jail for nothing. Now, they tried to kill your army commander, and you are just juggling philosophy. I did not expect you to execute Bucur for treason, even though he deserved it, but you should have put him in jail. You freed a traitor because you are afraid. You are afraid to even recognize that Big Mouth provoked all this on purpose, and you have no idea why he did it. Your Knights see your weakness. Why do you want to be a Grand Seigneur if you can't master a Knight?"

"What makes you think I want to be a Grand Seigneur, or that I want an alliance, or this war and the others to come? Our lives are driven by necessity, not wishes. Sometimes they might align. If I look back over the past years, Jara is the only thing that has happened to me fitting both, nothing else. Give the order to burn the castle and prepare the army for marching. It's your army." Mohor leaned against the arch and gestured toward the road in the valley. The mirage was still there.

I went down the stairs, and Mohor did not follow me. Not that I cared. The first person I met downstairs was Vlaicu.

"I am sorry." He apologized for a guilt that was not his, and I just patted his shoulder. "What should we do now?"

"Empty the castle of people and set the fire. We leave in two hours." I glanced east: a thin arc of sun was shining over the hills.

As usual, things took longer, but we still left in the morning. Behind us, the castle was burning, sending thick columns of smoke into the blue sky. Visible from far away, they were telling the story I wanted.

"A wolf's head," a voice shouted behind us, and curiosity made me stop the horse and turn. The whole army did the same. Far above us, the wind was playing, turning the smoke into the ghost of a giant wolf, its large open mouth menacing the land for a few moments, before vanishing in formless patches of white-gray color.

"It pointed to Mehadia." I reacted to whispers of bad omen that could sap the morale of the army – there were many Frankis superstitions I still did not know. "A good sign. We will attack like the wolves. Fast and deadly."

Someone put his hands around his mouth and imitated a wolf's howling – it was quite accurate, and shouts of victory filled the air. All the tension vanishing as fast as it had appeared. The army moved again, and in the afternoon, we came to a small road going right, through the forest. Vlad signaled me – it was the place he had found, a high hill with a bald top, surrounded by forest.

"We go that way," I shouted, pointing to the right, and moved my horse on to the smaller road. It was too early for camping, so my order looked contradictory. Big Mouth protested, but Mohor followed me in silence, and in a short time the army disappeared into the forest, in a long column.

At the end of the forest, there was a small plateau before the hill climbed steeply to its top. Invisible from the main road, the place was a perfect hiding place.

"We camp here," I said to Mohor.

"Isn't it too early?"

"We stay here for a week," I answered, and sensed Big Mouth ready to jump on me. For whatever reason, he just grimaced, saying nothing. "See the smoke?" I pointed back to the castle; the columns of smoke were now even higher in the sky. "It carries a message. I want that message to reach Mehadia and all the Knights between here and there. Not that it will be seen from Mehadia, but news will spread, and fear will work for us." That was the idea that came to me in the morning inside the tower, to wait until the fruits of fear ripened. I looked at Mohor, and he nodded in acknowledgment. "Camp!" I ordered, and the soldiers moved to occupy the plateau.

When everybody had found a place, Valer, the Black Dervil, took me aside. "Any chance I can take over the left wing?" There was no more money for him to get, but his next buyer would see his promotion in a favorable way.

"No, your men will move into the main column." He was not pleased, but no trace of feeling surged on his face. "You will be my third in command." The position was at the same level as a wing commander. There was a peculiar order in Mohor's army that defied the normal ranking. The Seigneur was the commander, but Mohor was not a fighter, just an intelligent man knowing his limits, so he usually did not interfere. The Spatar was the next in rank, but technically I was the commander, and Vlaicu my second in command. Tacitly, Big Mouth's position was established as the third in command, a thing that he would never forget, but there is always a need to have a back-up chain of command, if someone is killed in battle. There is no time for council and nominations in that case. Soon, after Mohor's tent was raised, the council was summoned, and the usual ten people filled the main room.

"You take over the left wing," I said, looking at Big Mouth. "Your men move with you to the left wing. Valer, you return to the main column, and support Vlaicu." It was a way to say that he would become the third in command without saying the word." If Mohor was not happy, I could not tell.

"I am the Spatar of Severin," Big Mouth protested loudly, yet he did not contest my right to make decisions. "What should I do on the left wing?"

"Fight. We need to control both sides of the road. Take your men and occupy that hill," I pointed through the open entrance to the hill over the road. I did not really need the thing strategically, but I needed Big Mouth out from the secret councils in Mohor's tent, of which I was not part.

Undecided, Big Mouth glanced at Mohor, who nodded slightly, and in half an hour, he left the place with seventy-five soldiers, forty his own men.

I have to take care of your men, I thought, staring at the disappearing column. *To clip your power.*

Ten days later, on the road to Mehadia, two squads of scouts returned at the same time: Vlad's and the mercenaries. Two hundred men strong, Mehadin's army was gathered somewhere south of Mehadia, leaving open the road to his capital, inviting us to besiege it while he would attack from behind. The size of his army was larger than expected after a big defeat, and in a veiled way, I pointed out to Mohor that Mehadin had better control over his Knights. A second army, one hundred men strong, was coming from the north: Orban's soldiers.

"We attack Orban's army first," I said in the council. "We have two days to find a battlefield that favors us. They are fewer, but that doesn't mean we should fight them just anywhere. Our scouts must find a good place. We leave in one hour." As usual, the one hour turned into three, but we still left in the early afternoon.

When the council ended, Vlad took me aside. "We met three riders, carrying curved swords like yours. They were dressed in black. The only thing distinguishing one from another were their insignias: one, two and three knives."

"Assassins," I murmured. "Three knives a novice, two knives a trained Assassin, one knife, a Master." The fewer the knives on their insignia the more powerful they were. A Grand Master has no knives; he should be skilled enough to win a fight without weapons.

"Who are they?"

"A warrior order. Extremely dangerous. Most of them are better fighters than me. Did they want something?" I asked, trying to avoid any detail that could reveal my real identity to Vlad.

"They wanted to know the road to Tolosa, nothing else. But one of them saw my sword and asked me where I got it." Vlad pointed to the Arenian sword that once belonged to my brother – the Assassins are trained to observe the most minor detail. "I told them that I won it in a battle. In Litvonia."

"You did well." I patted his shoulder to calm him, and it was true, his answer could be good enough to set my hunters on the wrong course. I left him and walked alone at the edge of the forest, thinking that they might cross my path, by chance or directed by proper information. *For sure one of the Assassins knows me.* There was nothing much I could do.

Chapter 24 – Saliné / Bucur

In Severin, Bucur's return was both unexpected and unwanted. Late in the evening, he delivered a short letter from Mohor. Silent, Jara read it, nodded to him, and he had no other choice left than leaving her office. Looking at him walking away, Jara placed the letter on the table and flattened it with her palm. When the door closed, she hit the paper hard, and the beaten wood filled her office with a resonant sound. It calmed her nerves. It solved nothing.

"Mohor attached Bucur to our garrison. I told him..." She breathed deeply and gave the letter to Cernat. "We've agreed that if something wrong happens, Bucur should stay in Seged. Aron tricked Mohor again." She closed her eyes for a few moments. "Keep Bucur away. Send him out on patrol, to do whatever, but keep him away."

"In four days, we will send the replacement company at the northern border. Bucur has some military qualities. He may..."

"I don't care about his qualities. I care about his defects. Just keep him away," Jara snapped and picked the second letter; it belonged to Vasile, their spy at Orban's court. Opening it, her nervous fingers almost teared the paper in half. "Interesting, no one knows about Codrin in Arad." They had asked about the link between Codrin and Cantemir. Not that they did not trust

Codrin, but it was always useful to have the full picture. Slowly, she pushed the half-torn letter to Cernat, across the table.

"Cantemir is only using his own men from Arad's Guard in his embassies, except for the Wraith of Tolosa, who is Mester Panait's Lead Protector." Cernat read the letter out loud, trying to find something hidden in it – sometimes spies are cryptic when they deliver important information, just to cover themselves. "It makes no sense; a Mester's Lead Protector lives with the Mester and work only for him. He can't be the Wraith of Tolosa." There were only four Wraith in Frankis, the most successful Lead Protectors.

"Is Codrin using a different name in Arad?" Jara asked, frowning in thought – it was just a sudden feeling, but she had some traces of Light, and relied on them from time to time.

"Perhaps. Codrin has his own life outside Severin, and a protector's world is filled with secrets. We should not delve too much on it." Cernat tapped the letter laying on the table with one finger, then continued to read it. "Devan's Secretary visited Arad incognito, to meet a delegation of the Circle's Council. An embassy from Peyris came in Arad two days later. I still trust Devan, but less than before," he said, thoughtfully.

"As you have ordered, we followed her discreetly, day and night," the servant said to Bucur, pulling his boots off. "During the day, she spends most of her time in the garden, walking without aim, or sitting on a bench. Reading. In the evening, she reads in the library. Sometimes, she stays there until morning. Alone. She can't sleep. I've talked to Felcer. Just a little. I did not want to attract his attention. There is something wrong with her; she can't sleep without a potion." Once a week, Felcer was giving Saliné a strong potion of laudanum, the only thing which helped her, but the old man was too experienced a healer to use that potion often on such a young body.

"She did not sleep well even before we went to Mehadia. Something is bothering her. Do you know what?" Bucur looked at the servant, who shook his head. *My stories helped her...* "I wished I knew. Prepare my bathtub and find a bouquet of flowers. Yellow roses. She likes them."

Bucur took his time to bathe and, close to midnight, he went into the library, keeping his bouquet hidden behind him.

"Bucur, you have returned," Saliné greeted him, her voice warm, recalling his stories, which were keeping her mind occupied, helping to forget her despair. And to sleep.

Yes, I've returned for you my dear. Arriving in front of her, Bucur bent and placed the roses in her arms.

"Thank you; they are wonderful."

"It's a pity that we don't have beautiful green roses to match your eyes." Bucur studied her for a while; her eyes were sunken and dark. She looked tired and troubled. *It's true that she is not sleeping well. It suits me.* "We had news that Orban may be ready to attack Severin, and Mohor sent me here to help Cernat."

"Orban..." Saliné grimaced. "How is Codrin?" she asked hesitantly, knowing that thinking of him would make her sleep even worse.

"He is doing very well. Codrin has a mind for strategy, and that's the only thing he would speak now. *Nothing else.*" Bucur paused, looking at her, and caught another little grimace. "Sometimes, too much military chatter becomes boring even for men, but we took Tohani before I left the army." The old horologe of Severin struck twelve times for midnight, and Bucur waited patiently to end. "It's a long story, but I think that we have enough time." Bucur sat next to her on the small sofa. There was a look of a predator finding its prey in his eyes. She could not see it.

Behind them, a white silhouette appeared from nowhere, and Dochia, the Last Empress, looked at Saliné, her eyes thoughtful. She raised her translucent hand, and a sphere, resembling the texture of her skin, materialized in her palm. She blew gently, and the sphere flew slowly toward Saliné. It touched the back of her head and vanished. *Your Light is now awakened. From now on, it will guide you. There are hard times in front, but your sacrifice will pave the way for a new King in Frankis.*

With his persuasive voice, Bucur told an altered version of Tohani story, then other stories and jokes, keeping Saliné entertained. "I think that you are almost ready to sleep," he said when almost two hours had passed. "Let me show you a trick that my mother taught me. I was only fourteen when I've lost her. We have many things in common as we both lost a parent when we were young. It was not easy for me. I am sure it was not easy for you either. Turn with your back to me." His voice was now sad and low, almost a whisper, and he turned her slowly, then started to massage her neck and shoulders. "There was some tension on your back and shoulders. It's gone. You should go to sleep now."

That night, Saliné slept relatively well, and the two next nights too, as Bucur kept her entertained in the library. The fourth evening, he came later than usual, after midnight. He did not know that she was listening each time footsteps were heard on the corridor, hoping to be Bucur, but he counted on her waiting. During his last story, Bucur turned her again, and his hands moved to massage her neck, then her shoulders, fondling them with experienced fingers; he knew how to make a woman feel good. From her shoulders, he went on her upper arms, pulling Saliné gently against him. His voice was now low and hypnotic, close to her ear, sometimes his lips touching it briefly. She felt good in a way that did not happen for a long time and leaned against Bucur.

In the morning, Saliné woke up, looking into her mother's eyes.

"It's late." Jara was smiling, her brows raised a little.

"I slept well." Saliné stretched and recalled her long evening, and Bucur's stories. She also recalled his hands massaging her neck and shoulders. "Breakfast?" she asked and laughed quietly.

"Get dressed, we are waiting for you."

Eyes closed, Saliné clasped her hands under her head. *This night, I still dreamt of Codrin kissing me, four or five times, but I did not wake up crying as before. In the library, Bucur half embraced me. There was nothing bad in that; he was just being friendly.* Then she recalled what happened when she was almost asleep in Bucur's arms, a sort of brief mirage. Two mirages, in fact. *Did I dream?* In one of them, Bucur was standing between her and Codrin. In the second one, an unknown woman was scolding Aron and Bucur. After a while, Aron vanished from the dream, and the woman puled Bucur by his beard. His face livid, Bucur looked frightened, and Saliné laughed quietly recalling that strange fear spread on his face; the woman was small. *They were not dreams; they were Visions,* she suddenly understood, a future that was not far, Codrin and Bucur did not look changed. *My first Visions... Is my Light stronger than I thought? And who is that woman?* Even recalling her presence made Saliné shiver. It was a peculiar thing that she was able to see her own future, even the Wanderers could rarely do this. *Bucur...* she returned to the library. *There is something wrong in him, and it's going worse, but he is not as evil as his father. Bucur was not like this when we've met first. It's not easy to grow with a father like Aron and no mother. And his brother's death affected him, but his stories help me forget that I can't marry the man I love and, perhaps, I might be able to help Bucur too. And I need to know more about my Visions.* "But now, I need to hurry." Saliné jumped up from her bed and dressed quickly.

Two weeks later, Bucur came back from his shift at the border, and reported to Cernat and Jara. It was almost dark outside, and Jara listened to him absently, before sending him away.

The bitch was cold and arrogant. One day all of them will pay, starting with that nomad from Arenia. At his death, I will drink all the night with four naked women in my bed. Bucur almost slammed the door behind him and went to his room. Still swearing, he opened his door with a strong boot kick, stepped inside and unsheathed his dagger.

"Are you afraid of a woman?" There was one standing in front of his window, her back at him, an elegant hood covering her head.

"Maud. I am honored to see you" He bowed slightly, an unconscious gesture acknowledging her power; she could not see him.

"Yes, you should be." Maud turned and threw a cold stare at Bucur as if the man in front did not deserve her attention. "It seems that the plan I've made with Aron worked well. You returned to Severin."

"I worked for it. That man could have killed me."

"Has he a name? That man?"

"Codrin." Bucur shrugged.

"He can kill you at any time, you are not that good with the sword. Seriously, what are you god for? Perhaps for these." She pulled a hand out of her pocket and placed two vials in Bucur's palm.

"I don't need magic potions."

"Ah, you fear my petite vials." She looked at his hands, which were trembling a little, and he clasped them at his back. Stuck to his palms, the vials clacked in the silent room. "All your life, you did nothing but chase women and brag about your exploits, yet you failed to seduce the one who was the most important for our plans." With a strong hand, Maud pulled his head down by his beard until they were eye to eye; Bucur was a tall man. "You," she knocked his head with the forefinger of her free hand, "are now a soldier of the Circle. You will do what you are being told. There is nothing magic there, just old knowledge from the Wanderers. My man in Severin will instruct you on how to use the potions. Listen to him well; these are strong things, and they may create problems if used improperly. Bucur," she stared hard at him, "your brother was stupid enough to get killed by Cernat and wrecked my plans. At least he died fast. Don't fail me, or you would have wished not to be born. See if the corridor is empty, no one should know that I am here." Her words were knives, sharp and precise, an army commander giving orders. Abruptly, she released his beard, and pushed him toward the door.

His face livid and mouth clamped tight, Bucur went out, followed by Maud, who said, "Walk in front of me until we reach the small backdoor opening toward the garden." Before vanishing out into the night, Maud turned toward him, raising two fingers. "You have two weeks." She tightened her cloak around her body and walked away. *It should work this time*, she thought, walking briskly. *The Last Empress promised Drusila that she will interfere through the Light, to help us.*

Back in his room, Bucur hid the vials in a cabinet and stood on the edge of his bed, head in hands. *Potions are dangerous. One little mistake, and they will hang me. I will show Maud that I can solve everything in my way.* He looked outside; it was fully dark. *Saliné must be in the library. She will be ready soon.*

He went to see Saliné close to midnight again, and sat next to her on the sofa, watching her tightly. *She was waiting for me.* Bucur knew well how to read a woman. *She worried that I would not come this evening.* "I think that I saw this before." He pointed at the book in her hand.

"There is nothing new to read in the library."

"Next time, I will bring you some books from Seged."

"Thank you. How was the border?"

"Quiet. Except for the night when the horses got scared by a wolf and ran away. We spent a full day to gather them. You look tired; let's try something else." He took the book from her hand and placed it on the floor. "Did I tell you how my brother, Raul, and I have stolen a purse from Father to help a poor widow, whose house had burned down by half? And how were we punished? I think that I was fourteen; my mother was still alive, just for a few months more." His voice saddened, and he looked at Saliné who shook her head. *You hate Father. I understand you, sometimes I am hating him too, but I have to play your feelings.* "It's a long story, you should be more comfortable." Gently, Bucur lifted Saliné's legs on the sofa, turning her body, and sat behind her. "Last time, I felt a knot here." He placed his hands on her shoulders and pressed his thumbs on a point between her shoulder blades. "I still feel it. The woman was in her early twenties. She was beautiful, and my brother was in love. He was sixteen, and I think that I was in love too, even when, at that time, I did not really know what that meant." Bucur massaged her shoulders until her knot vanished, Saliné could feel that; her spine was now relaxed, and her breath easier. His hands moved on her upper arms, pulling her closer until his lips almost touched her ear. His voice was low and hypnotic, and Saliné found herself leaning against him, his left arm around her shoulders. "The woman was touched when my brother gave her the purse; there were twenty galbeni in it; a fortune for a commoner like her. Father and Mother were at a party somewhere, and we slept in her house." *Each time I speak of Father, her body is stiffening a little.*

"I've met Raul once, in Midia. He saved me from a horse running mad." *He was the first man I liked. Then Codrin came to me, and I lost him because... Because of all the bad things around us.* She struggled to contain her tears.

"My brother was a kind man; you can see that in the story." *And weak. He wasn't able to fulfill the Circle's task. I will.* "In fact, I slept in the barn; there was only one room still habitable in the house. That night, she made my brother a man. He told me in the morning that she was nice and gentle, and he looked tired but happy." Bucur shifted his body a little, and his thumb slid up and down on Saliné's nape. It was slow, gentle move. His thumb went to the back of her ear and down again. He did not stop talking. "... When Father came back, and found that money was missing, he flogged us, but we kept silent. We were afraid that he will burn her house fully down."

"That was brave," Saliné said. *I was right that Bucur was a kind child.*

"My brother visited her for half a year. She resembled you a little. Auburn hair." He stroked Saliné's hair and stayed silent for a while. "Green eyes." His fingers caressed her cheekbone under her right eye. "She was not as beautiful as you are, but her lips..." His fingers went down and touched her lips. "Her lips resembled yours, even this wonderful color. In the end, it was a sad story." Bucur stayed again silent for more than a minute, his fingers paying gently on her neck. *Saliné is now sad too, and a little angry...* "Father found the truth about the purse and chased her away from the village. That night I cried." *Strange, but it's true. I was weak then. My brother was even weaker, but at least he got something from her.*

"It's not your fault."

"In a way, it was my fault too, and I could not sleep well for a few nights. The day she left, I hid in the forest, watching her walking away. I had three galbeni in my pocket, and I ran toward her when no one could see me. She was crying when I placed the coins in her palm."

"You were kind to her." Saliné turned her head toward Bucur until their eyes met.

"Then she kissed me. It was my first kiss. It was wonderful, and I ran back to the forest, pressing my mouth with my fingers, trying to keep her touch alive. I still remember her lips. Warm. Beautiful. Like yours." Bucur lowered his head and pressed his mouth on Saliné's. Her body tensed, but he felt disorientation and surprise, not rejection, and that curiosity, which every girl her age and lack of experience has. His lips played gently until her tension vanished, then he pressed more, building on that curiosity, heightening her senses, making her lips to answer unconsciously. He let her breath a little and kissed her fully. Saliné's arms did not go around his neck, and Bucur knew when to stop. He started another long story. At the end, he only kissed the lifeline of her palm, long and gently. Bucur knew how to behave with a woman; he had seduced more than fifty already. Some of them were in their thirties, married and with children. Some of them were young maidens dreaming of love. He needed only their bodies.

Closing the door of her bedroom, Saliné leaned back on it. Some worries were struggling in her mind, but she felt strangely good. *It's better to think at what happened with a clear mind. I am afraid that it's not the case now.*

In the morning, Saliné woke up with a sense of repetition, looking into her mother's smiling eyes. "I know, breakfast is ready, I will come in ... a few minutes.

"I am glad that you've slept well," Jara said and kissed her brow.

You would not be glad at all to know who made me sleep so well. Or how, Saliné pondered while she was undressing. *Just before Bucur kissed me, I had that Vision with Codrin and Bucur again, and it was longer. I can't understand it;* she shook her head. *It's partially true, but I shall not fool myself that I let him kiss me only because I wanted to learn more about the Vision.*

I've enjoyed his ... attention, and this night, my sleep was even better than after our last evening together. She did not have enough time to choose something else and dressed herself in yesterday's clothes. *Bucur's story was wonderful and sad at the same time. It ... softened me, so he planned everything.* Closing the door behind her, she walked leisurely on the long corridor. *That Vision is important. I feel something bad, and a kind of urgency.* Thoughtfully, she pressed her teeth in her lower lip. *For a few days, I must ignore that I am engaged. Last evening I've already... Something is changing inside me. The world is changing too. I must adapt. It's important.* She shrugged and opened the door.

An hour before midnight, they met again in the library, and Saliné was tense, though Bucur misinterpreted her stiffness. She was trying to use her Light on him, to recall and understand her Vision, and while her Light was stronger than Jara's, Saliné was young and untrained. Bucur made up some stories, sad and sweet, in which he was the savior of women in distress, and Aron played a bad role again. Saliné's tension did not vanish during his first story or the second, and only after the third one Bucur finally kissed her. The Vision came to Saliné abruptly, Bucur standing between Codrin and her, just that there was now a newborn in her arms, its face blurred. Separated from her body, Saliné got lost in her long Vision, and Bucur felt her weakness. When Saliné's mind returned from that inner world, she was straining against his mouth; her arms were tight around his neck, one hand combing through his hair; his hand was inside her chemise, fondling her breast. There was an unfamiliar feeling of warmth and pleasure she found hard to oppose, and she abandoned herself to it.

The next evening, Bucur kept Saliné waiting for him in the library, and arrived half an hour after midnight. Inside, he frowned, looking around the room.

You will not find it, Saliné thought, and passed a hand through her hair to hide her concern; what happened the day before was both wrong and pleasant. She feared to be close to Bucur again, yet she had to continue her search. There was something evil and sad in that Vision, an allegory she was still struggling to understand, and she knew now that it will happen in a month or two. The presence of the child with a blurred face in her arms unsettled her the most. She knew that the child was meant to die, and Saliné wondered who the parents were, and what she could do to save it. There was a sort of unwilling amusement reflected in her eyes too, because of Bucur's badly dissimulated surprise. She waited until his eyes finished to search the room, before saying, "I just spilled some juice on the sofa. They will bring it back in a few days, after cleaning it. I was worrying that you will not come tonight." She gestured at the place across the table; the peculiar thing had two small benches attached to it. Jara had ordered them when they moved in Severin, so Saliné and Vio could read together.

Having no choice, Bucur sat across the table and started the story he had prepared for her. Despite his valiant effort, a girl was killed in that long story, and Saliné felt assailed by a strong wave of emotion; Bucur had a certain talent and the right voice to stir her feelings.

At the end, she took Bucur's right hand in hers, over the table, and their eyes locked. "Bucur, something is bothering you. Would you tell me?" There was a small surge of Light, and Saliné tried to use it, but nothing came to her. *Why do I have Visions only when Bucur is close to me? Is there a price to pay? To pay for what?* Unconsciously, she gripped his hand stronger.

"It's just that in ten days I will leave for the border again."

"You fought well in the first battle against Mehadin, and even got wounded, so I don't think that it's the border. Perhaps I am able to help you."

You can help... Come in my bed tonight, and everything will be perfect. You will make both Maud and me happy. "I am enjoying our evenings together. I will miss them, and I was thinking... If that thing about Devan cancelling the alliance and marriage is right... Do you think... Do you think that we can have a chance together?" He leaned over the table and, turning her hand up, kissed her palm, then interlaced their fingers.

"We need the alliance." Saliné's voice was even and precise, carrying the deliberate tones of a diplomat during a round of complex negotiations, and she pulled her hand back. *If it will fail, then Codrin...* She paused. Looked at Bucur, a different expression in her eyes, and had a sense of having entered dark waters, with complicated currents trying to overcome her. *What do you really want, Bucur? And what link is between you and the way I receive a Vision?*

"Of course, that we need the alliance, I was just thinking... It's a wonderful night, with a full moon. Would you like to walk with me in the garden? It rained this morning, and the air is now intoxicated with the scent of roses." *What can be more romantic than making love in the grass? You are almost ready; it may happen tonight.*

Saliné felt the dark waters swirling around her, and a slight surge of Light, making her recall some moments of guilty pleasure; it warmed her body with a touch of desire. There was nothing clear, and she followed some vague lines of thought, troubled by that desire. *Is the Light trying to push me closer to Bucur? Why? It makes no sense.* "Thank you, Bucur, but I feel tired. I will retire to my room," she said, her warm voice sounding even warmer after the diplomatic lecture before. *What I saw in my Visions will happen after Codrin returns from Mehadia. I still have a month or two to understand them. Perhaps Dochia will visit us; I can't talk with Mother about what happened.*

Staring at Saliné wide-eyed like a lost child, Bucur tried to speak, but his voice seemed lost somewhere deep inside him. His fingers started to drum the table.

He looks ... strange? She glanced at Bucur from beneath elegant level brows, saying nothing. *He will leave in a few days. Perhaps I can try again when he returns from the border.* She wanted to understand her Visions, but she was being separated from her body during the inner trance, and Bucur seemed more than able to take control of it. His skilled lips and fingers could keep that control for a long time. "Goodnight, Bucur. You are a wonderful storyteller; it was a pleasant night again." She looked at his drumming fingers and remembered them playing a different tune on her skin, the night before. *That was pleasant too.* She shrugged and walked away.

"Let me say you good night," Bucur said when they were in front of her door and placed a hand around her waist, pulling her so tight against him that she could not breathe well. His lips played on her neck, stirring her skin. Raw and demanding, his hands played on her body. One sneaked inside her cleavage, the other one went down her navel. It was a show of strength and desire, and she leaned her head on her arms, against the door.

The moment Bucur touched her, the Vision came abruptly to Saliné. It was Codrin again; he was kissing a beautiful brunette. When they ended, Saliné could see the woman's deep black eyes, which moved closer until only the eyes remained in sight, glimmering with pleasure and happiness. The image changed; the brunette now whispered something in Codrin's ear, who was listening to her, a warm touch in his eyes. A sudden surge of sadness and bitterness went through Saliné. It came as a shock. It severed the link with the Vision before its time. Bucur was just turning her, searching for her mouth. The door was already open, and Saliné was in the doorway. Her chemise was open too. Like a dancing pair, they slid inside the room. There were candles alight on the table, and Bucur saw the bed on the left. Inside his mind, he saw her lying there, naked. He turned them slowly, toward the bed, then pressed her against the wall. He did not hurry, and only after a minute or two, his let her breast and stretched his hand to close the door. It was too far, and he moved a little away from her.

Saliné disengaged abruptly, and Bucur's eyes went wide, his body frozen, inclined slightly forward, his mouth open, mimicking a kiss. "Goodnight, Bucur," she said in a raucous voice, and pushed him back, slamming the door, almost to crush his nose. Eyes closed, she leaned against the door. For a minute or two, she forced herself to think at nothing. "I did not know that a man can stir so much pleasure in my body. It made me weak. But why did this Vision come now? Why? It made me bitter and eager to..." She opened her eyes and stared at the half moon visible through the window. It calmed her a little. "I hope that Codrin will find the love he needs, and the life he deserves." A single tear ran down her face. She undressed slowly, fearing another long night without sleep.

In bed, she tried again to think at nothing. Codrin's image from the Vision came to her – people blessed by the Light had an eidetic memory, able to recall many rich details. And that woman. She stared at them for a few moments. Then at the woman's eyes. She fell asleep, caught in their deep darkness.

Saliné slept well that night, and the next ones, even when she avoided the library. Felcer made her a list with all the pregnant women in Severin. It was not a long one; there were only three women, and the first one was supposed to deliver in four months. She started to think that the faceless child she had seen in her warms was just an allegory. A Vision could be like this. She met Bucur only on the corridors. He was distraught and morose, and she asked him once more if he needed help. She received no answer. She had no more Visions.

❧

When the dessert was served, Jara's stomach revolted, and she stood up, then walked quickly away. She threw up in a corner of the corridor, then went to her room on weak feet, keeping a hand on the wall. With a last effort, she crashed down on her bed, breathing in spurts, feeling her heart beating strongly and fast, and there were sharp throbs of pain in her belly. Too weak to leave the bed, she half raised her body, to throw up on the floor. Felcer, the old healer, came a minute later together with Cernat and her girls.

With the tip of his cane, Felcer played on the remnants of her meal spread on the floor, and the stale whiff became even stronger. "Poison. But," he said carefully, tapping with his cane on some spots of blood, "this looks to be the work of an inexperienced poisoner; you ingested too much, and it made you to throw up." He pointed at the mess on the floor again, but Jara had no wish to look at the proof he mentioned. "I will bring you something to drink. Don't leave your bed."

A wry smile spread on Jara's lips, she was barely able to move her feet, let alone leave her bed. Her vision blurred, and a rising heaviness crawled up her throat and clutched at her tongue. *Orban*, she thought. *He poisoned me again.* She thought again and shook her head. *It was not Orban.* A sudden outburst of pain made her curl in bed and moan. Unable to think clearly, Jara bit her lip to stop her moaning, unwilling to scare her daughters. She even tried to smile apologetically at them. It felt rigid and false.

Insipid and odorless, the potion brought by Felcer did its job and whatever was still left in her stomach went into a bucket that he was holding, and bile burned the back of her throat. With all that relief, her pulse kept accelerating, her breath became heavier, and the aching pain in her stomach worsened.

Felcer moved fast on his old legs and opened the window for some fresh air. Sunray warmed her face, a small comfort. "Drink this, too." He pushed another vial into her mouth. "It will slow down your heart."

He seemed to know the poison, but Jara did not have the courage to ask about it. "Now what?" she finally asked, after drinking the bitter potion. *It must be the spy from the Circle,* she thought again. With all their efforts, they were not able to find that bloody spy who had killed Senal.

"Now, you have to sleep. Sleep heals. I will stay with you, but" Felcer gestured to all the others in the room, "you should let her rest."

Eyes closed, Jara tried to slow down her breathing. Codrin had taught her the Assassin Cool, but she never practiced much, yet it helped to recover her mind a little. Inhaling and exhaling at measured times, she remembered Senal's death, and his cold face.

For two days, Jara stayed in her bed, fighting a deep pain that never left her alone, drinking potions, each tasting worse than the previous one. With a strange detachment, she was feeling the poison working through her body, part by part, and she started to doubt Felcer. *I was one year older than Saliné when an arrow took my mother away,* Jara thought. *I would prefer that kind of death. I must live. I must. At least I still had my father. They don't have.* She stared at her daughters as if seeing a talisman crafted against the evil spirits of death, yet a part of her was eager to meet her mother and Malin again.

"In two or three days, you will get out of bed," Felcer said after his last examination.

The next evening, Jara lost consciousness while drinking a bowl of soup. It happened gradually, so she could witness her own misery, following the greasy liquid pouring down on her from the falling bowl. It was hot. She woke up in clean clothes, feeling rivulets of sweat running freely down her face. Her arms and feet were swollen, almost twice their normal size. It was dark outside, and the pinewood fire blazing brightly up the chimney was illuminating the room in a curiously agreeable manner, sending flickering red shafts of light into the dark corners. Unable to speak, Jara just stared at Saliné and Vio, who were stirring the fire with a pensive look, whispering something that she could not hear. Felcer was sitting on the edge of her bed. Cernat was sharing the table with Bucur, who just came with a rare resin that he had at home. It was burning now in a candle, close to her bed.

Eyes closed, Saliné tried to reach the Light and feel Jara's future. It didn't come. *None of my Visions was about Mother, yet I have now the feeling of a link between the Visions, Bucur and Mother. Should I have tried even more with Bucur?* Tears in her eyes, she stirred the fire again only to stop her thoughts, recalling those black waters, which were trying to sink her down. A few sparks flew and landed on the floor. She crushed them quickly.

On his chair, Bucur had the air of a trapped mouse. *It was supposed that Jara would be sick for a few weeks, to let me play Saliné. I hope that Maud' man was right about the dosage.* His eyes guarded, he looked at Felcer. *Each time the old man said that she would go better, it went worse. Jara looks like dying tonight.* His fingers started to tremble, and he forced himself to move slowly and hide them under the table, then squeezed his hands between his knees. *Did Maud's man trick me? If Jara dies, Maud will find me guilty, not him. Why did Saliné refuse me that evening? She was ready. I sneaked my hand under her skirt and felt it. She* was *ready.*

Jara's vision blurred, and one moment she saw her daughters; the next she slipped into a dream that brought Malin back to her. Saliné and Vio were with him too, a six or seven years younger version of them. Out of breath, she gasped loudly, and started to shiver with all that warmth in the room.

"Stay with us, Mother," the real age Saliné said, running fast from the fireplace to her bed.

"Wake up, Jara," Malin whispered in Jara's dream, his face worried. "Wake up," he repeated, and the various strands of voices around her quickened in pace and started to blend into one long whisper without sense.

There was a sudden silence in the room, all of them watching Jara and old Felcer, who was pressing his fingers on her neck. Her mouth dry from breathing too fast, Vio picked up a carafe, to drink some water, only to find it empty.

"I will take care of this," Bucur said, and went out, reaching one of the maids waiting there. After a few minutes, he returned and filled glasses for everybody in the room.

Felcer tried to fetch a potion into Jara's mouth, but her head fell abruptly, her eyes closed.

"Mother," Vio cried, but Jara could no longer hear her.

Moving fast for his age, the old healer placed his ear on Jara's chest and listened carefully. "Don't worry, her heart is beating, she is just unconscious. It will happen from time to time." He caught Cernat's eyes and nodded toward the girls. "Vio, Saliné," Felcer said, "Jara needs more air. You should go to sleep now."

Gently, Cernat made the girls leave, and Bucur went out with them.

"If she survives this night, she will live," Felcer said to Cernat when the girls were out of the room. He forced his voice to sound calm and confident.

Silent, Vio opened the door and vanished in her room, then Bucur led Saliné to hers. Walking on the long corridor, her mind lost to panic, Saliné felt weak, and there was a strange warm sensation in her belly. Soon, she could barely walk, and she said nothing when Bucur surrounded her shoulders with one arm, to help her stand. It felt pleasant, and her worries about Jara's illness recessed, almost vanishing. She leaned against him to walk further until they arrived at her door.

"Bucur, don't," she whispered when he tried to enter, but he only took her in his arms and walked inside. She felt too frail to oppose.

"You need some fresh air," he said, then let her stand in front of the window, and opened it.

I feel strange. Unable to speak, Saliné leaned on her arms against the recess. A little cold, the breeze was refreshing, but she could not understand what was happening to her. *Was I poisoned too?* she pondered. *But I only feel strange, there is no pain, only weakness, and a pleasant tension in my body.*

"This will help." Gently, Bucur started to massage her shoulders and neck. She felt weak and lightheaded, and there was now a strange desire for the man behind her. His skilled fingers were enhancing that pleasure, spreading it in all her body. Bucur's hands moved down her back, then around her waist while she leaned against him. Slowly, his hand sneaked in her cleavage, fondling her breast.

"Bucur," Saliné gasped, but his mouth covered hers. She found herself answering him and tightened her arms around his neck. Button by button, her chemise was slowly being opened, then her belt fell, then her skirts.

Saliné found herself naked, looking at Bucur. *What is happening to me?* "Bucur, please, we should not do this," she pleaded, her voice a faint whisper.

"Shh," he pressed a finger on her lips. "Saliné, this night we will become lovers, and in a few months, we will marry. This is my dream. We were born to be together. You are the woman I love. Have you no feelings for me?" *You have to say the words dear love; Maud's potion is inside your mind. You are ready for me.*

"Yes, Bucur."

"Yes what?"

"You are the man I love."

"Do you accept to be my wife?" Bucur asked and lifted her chin until their eyes locked. *You will bring me Severin and Midia as dowry. And this perfect body in my bed.*

"Yes," she breathed against her will.

"This will be our first night together. Romance and pleasure. Will you take me to your place?" He stepped back and stood still. *You have to do it.* "Please?" *You must act as if it were your choice, the potin will imprint everything in your mind. Pleasure. Feelings.*

Hesitantly, Saliné took his hand, and pulled Bucur toward her bed. In front of the bed, she stopped, tried to speak, to make him leave. The words did not come to her. Under the pressure from her own body and his stare, she lay in bed, on her back, and waited.

Bucur undressed slowly, ogling at her naked body, then half rolled above her, searching for her mouth. Suddenly, he stopped and shook her shoulder. Then shook her again. Stronger. Then he slapped her several times.

"She did not look thirsty, when I gave her that glass of water with potion. I did not think that she will drink the whole glass. I should have been more careful." Bucur shrugged and slapped her once more. "My dear future lover and wife is more aroused than a whore but asleep. It will lower my pleasure, and in the morning, I must leave to the border again. Will the potion still work if she is asleep while we make love? We will restart the game in two weeks. There is enough potion left, but I don't think that we need it again. Isn't it my love?" He leaned over her, his lips moving slowly, down her neck.

Chapter 25 – Codrin

The valley was long and well suited for an ambush. From its southern boundary, we had a commanding view over the road going down in a moderate slope, through a large meadow. To the sides, two great green forests lay, specked with white where the birch trees grew. We were able to capture all their scouts – I had sent five squads, each ten men strong, to clean the road, and leave the enemy with no insight about the valley.

"Aron," I said in the war council, "take fifty more troops, and seize the middle ground between our position and the bottom of the valley. The rest of us will hide in the forest. Our army is larger, and they may want to avoid battle. Vlaicu, choose those fifty, then take a hundred and fifty and go into the forest on the right, three hundred paces down from Aron's position. We must encircle and crush them. If we are lucky, none of them will escape to return to Arad with news. I will take the hundred remaining and hide in the forest on the left."

"I command the wing. Why should I take the middle?" Big Mouth asked.

"They know you well from the last battle." I cocked an eyebrow at him, on the edge of irony. "They will come after you. If they don't attack, you will charge."

After the council, I took Vlaicu aside. "Those fifty... Choose only Knights who are close to Big Mouth and their soldiers." *They would be in the hardest fight.*

"I see." Vlaicu smiled thinly.

Orban's cavalry entered the valley and stopped the moment Big Mouth's soldiers appeared in sight. For a moment, I was afraid the S'Arads would turn back, but they climbed toward the forest on my side, arranging themselves for battle in a position that would force Big Mouth to attack uphill. The strong summer sun twinkled on sharpened blades and polished helmets, glittered on buckles and harness.

More minutes passed with no move from Big Mouth, and I could not send a rider to press him without revealing our position. Even with the coolness of the forest, I was sweltering in my ring-mail and helmet. My curses did not help either. Then it happened; our troops moved, attacking the S'Arads who, at the last moment, charged down the slope, gaining speed, the ground playing to their advantage, the thunder of their hoof-beats echoing round the valley. They clashed. When the last echo of the ride was gone, the valley seemed almost silent.

I led my soldiers forward, some three hundred paces, to fall behind the S'Arads who, absorbed in the fight, did not see us moving through the forest. Their strategy to climb aside, and Big Mouth's indecision, had put us in the wrong position.

"We should charge," Mohor said, worried; things were not going well down in the valley, and the screams of the wounded or dying men were reaching us now.

"Not yet, we need to get to their rear, and surround them."

We charged, two minutes later, when Aron's troop was faltering. The S'Arads saw us, and half of them turned, disciplined, to face the new threat, easing the pressure on our wing. Then Vlaicu left the forest too, and the S'Arads split again, facing Vlaicu too, while a group of ten tried to sneak between our forces. Six of them escaped, and our ten scouts at the end of the valley moved out from the forest to intercept them. The remaining S'Arads gathered in a tight, round pack, like a giant hedgehog. The fight was not going to be swift or easy. Mohor grasped what was happening and glanced at me. I ignored him.

"Archers!" I shouted just before the clash. The first arrows flew over our heads, hitting the enemies a few moments after our swords met. From Vlaicu's side, another shower of arrows flew. After that, there was little chance to lead; the fight was going by its own will. Battles were always like this at their peak, breaking down into islands of savage close combat, just that now it was only one island. I lost sight of Vlaicu. I lost sight of Mohor. Vlad was on my left. That comforted me. The man on my right fell from his horse. Another one took his place. The world shrank around me, reduced to a rising sword, the scream of a dying horse, the impact of my blade on a helmet. I had the curious thought that I knew some of the enemies in front of me. I was most probably wrong. It did not matter. Men always died in battle. Surrounded by a larger force, the S'Arads fought to the last man.

"Vlaicu, see to the wounded," I said, after the last standing S'Arad fell. I was in the middle of the battlefield, among many fallen bodies, and I looked around, as if seeing the ground clearly for the first time.

"We have forty dead," Vlaicu reported in the war council, "and seventeen wounded. I am not talking about small cuts. Four of them are in bad shape. The S'Arads lost ninety-eight soldiers here, and another four were killed by our scouts at the end of the valley. Two of them escaped."

Orban has good soldiers. Maybe Mohor understands now what a good army looks like. The S'Arads were largely outnumbered, yet they still killed forty of our soldiers – I did not expect to lose so many. "It will take them at least three days to arrive in Arad. If Orban wants to send another army, it can't arrive here sooner than two weeks from now. We have enough time to tackle Mehadin, but it will be tight to take Mehadia in such a short time. We leave tomorrow. If the wounded are not able to follow us now, leave ten soldiers with them." I glanced at Vlaicu and closed the council.

Because of Big Mouth, Mohor avoided me after the council, and our relations were colder for the rest of the campaign. I enhanced the security around me using Vlaicu's guards and Valer's mercenaries, and he did not miss it. In a second development, most of the Knights reacted in the same way; they never contradicted me in the council, but my attempts for dialogue hit a wall.

One evening, Vlaicu took me aside. "Big Mouth is stirring the Knights against you."

"Then I shall leave him to lead our brave Knights in the battle."

"No one is contesting your right to command, but the war will end at some point," Vlaicu said, thoughtfully. "That's the moment you should foresee. When the war ends, politics takes over and they don't like it when a young nobody gives the orders. I apologize if... For them, I am nobody too. We don't have a title to snub others with."

It took us three days to reach Mehadin's army, and we stopped in the evening, at a distance that would not allow a battle until the day after. The battlefield was Mehadin's choice, and they were on higher ground, but we could not avoid the fight, time was pressing us, and Mehadin knew it. In the morning, counting on our numbers and better morale, I set the wings to ride first, in large arcs so they could attack from the sides. Our right wing was faring slightly better, and I led the center to meet the enemy closer to it. Already destabilized, and caught in the middle, their left wing cracked in minutes. This time, I stopped the fight and offered them the chance to surrender – Mehadin and his last son were already dead. Their Chief of the Guard kneeled, presenting his sword to Mohor, and all the soldiers from Mehadia kneeled too, in silent surrender. We picked the Chief of the Guard and another Knight to bring home the Mehadins' bodies. They were men strong enough to convince Mehadia to surrender, and both had sons that remained our hostages.

"Big Mouth has just seventeen soldiers left," Vlaicu whispered to me after the council ended. The Spatar was still powerful, but he had lost twenty-three of his men.

We arrived in front of Mehadia two days later, and the negotiators were already waiting for us. Mohor vacated his tent, leaving me to deal with them alone. There was enough space; the team from Mehadia had just two members: Calin, the Secretary, who resembled Cernat, and the Chief of the Guard. Once we agreed that everybody who wanted to leave could leave, and the city would not be sacked, there was not much to negotiate and, for the first time, I signed an official document, on the forty-second day of our campaign. Covering the surrender of Mehadia, it was not a small paper.

Emptied of people, Mehadin's residence was tightly secured, our soldiers guarding the entrance and the Visterie too – the castle's vault stored more than twenty thousand galbeni. There were six guards at the entrance, all chosen by Vlaicu; I did not trust Big Mouth's soldiers, and there was none of his in the city yet, even the mercenaries were more trustworthy. From the main hall, I tried to reach the Secretariat and read the diplomatic exchanges between Mehadin and Orban. On my left, a slight movement caught the corner of my eye, and I turned fast, unsheathing Flame. Someone had tried to enter the hall and stepped back in a split second. I ran, entering the corridor just as a door closed silently, thirty paces away from me. In front of the door, I rotated the doorknob, and hit the wood with my boot. The door opened with a bang. I pushed through it with Shadow in front of me, and Flame over my head. There was no one in front, and I advanced with small steps, looking left and right. A woman was crouched in a corner, embracing her knees in a futile gesture; there was nothing there to hide her.

"What are you doing here?" I snapped. My mind was still in fighting mode, and she was not supposed to be here. All Mehadin's people had left the residence, the day before, and the rest would leave the fortress in another three, allowing Mohor to become the master of the city.

"Don't kill me," she pleaded, her wide eyes fixed on my swords.

"You should not be here. I will escort you outside the residence." In her mid-thirties, she had an austere beauty; there was a deep sadness in her features and eyes. "I don't hurt women. Let's go, now." I sheathed Shadow and stepped back from her.

"Please help us," she pleaded, a tremble in her voice.

"Why should I help you if you don't listen to my orders?" I asked, before realizing that she was not alone in a residence I had supposed empty.

"My father is wounded, and my children are scared. We are in danger. Please," she pleaded again. "I will do whatever you want." She stood up and came closer, offering a good perspective on her body.

How troubled you must be... "Who are you?"

"Mara. Will you accept?" Sitting in front of me, she gently touched the hand that was still holding Flame. "We can go to my room, and I will please you. But you have to promise to help..." Her fingers pressed harder. With all that tension, there was a kind of serenity in her eyes, as if her offer were not touching her; she was sacrificing herself for her family.

Like Saliné... "What do you think I am?" I rumbled, pushing away the hand that was gripping mine. Her proposal and remembering Saliné angered me in an equal way. "Let's get your father and children."

"He is wounded," she whispered, her eyes on me, lines deepening between her brows. "He worked for Mehadin, but he helped you to take the city without a fight. Please do not think wrong of him."

"The Secretary?" *Who would attack Calin?*

"Yes. Do you know him?" she asked, and I involuntarily observed the contradiction – the touch of hope in her eyes, the hard lines around her mouth.

Looking at Mara, I realized she resembled Calin: the shape of her lips and nose, black eyes and hair over a white face. "You look like him. I should have recognized earlier who you are. Don't worry, I will get you out. Let's go, Mara." I touched her shoulder, to encourage her, then I retracted my hand in haste, feeling the tension in her body. "Sorry," I added quickly. "It was just a friendly gesture. You have nothing to worry about. I am Codrin."

"The commander," Mara said after a while, like an afterthought, and turned slowly, walking in silence until we entered Calin's room. He was sitting in bed, his head bandaged with a blue scarf, spotted with scattered red patches.

"What happened?" I asked after a brief evaluation. His breathing and eyes were calm, and his face looked normal. "I thought you left yesterday."

"Someone threw a stone when I was trying to leave."

They considered you a traitor. "It doesn't look so bad," I encouraged him, pointing to his head. "I will escort you out tomorrow."

"It will not be so easy." Calin looked at me, and there was a kind of strain in him; perhaps he was just expecting me to answer, and half a minute of silence filled the room.

"We have an enemy in your army," Mara said when the silence went on too long. "It's better if we tell him, Father."

"Twenty-four years ago, I was a Half-Knight in Severin," Calin sighed. "One day, there was a quarrel between my younger brother and Aron, who was drunk. Aron's elder brother killed mine, and I killed him. I had to run to Leyona. That's why we tried to get away hidden among the people leaving the city. It went wrong." He pointed to his bandaged head.

Mohor told me nothing. "There is bad blood between you and Aron, and Mohor chased you from his lands." By signing the capitulation treaty for Mehadia, covering Calin's fate too, I was responsible for his life. *Mohor did not sign; he may not feel bound by the agreement.*

"Mohor was too young at that time; it was his father who chased me."

A little bit better... "We have a treaty that guarantees your safety. While you are still here... You may not like it, but I want to read the diplomatic correspondence between Mehadin and Orban."

Calin drew a slow breath and shrugged. "Mehadin's Seigneury no longer exists." There was a short exchange of glances between him and Mara, and I pretended not to observe it. "I feel too weak right now, but Mara knows everything, she was my second Secretary."

I opened the door, letting Mara pass, and after a few steps, I decided that she could not be as attached to Mehadin as her father. "I want to know Orban's plans for Severin."

"Orban wanted Mehadin to weaken S'Severin in a prolonged war of attrition and take over his city."

"Mehadin was too weak for such a war," I tested her.

"Orban promised to help and kept his word. Fifty soldiers of his fought under Mehadin's banner in Severin. The war between Mehadin and Mohor was planned for next year. There were negotiations with Duke Stefan for his neutrality in the south. Something changed two months ago – we don't know what – and Orban asked Mehadin to attack this year, with the condition that he stayed away from Severin, but Mehadin felt that it was his time. He wanted to avenge the death of his son. Mohor's men killed him. Someone spread the word that we attacked Mohor's embassy. We did not."

"Maybe the one that killed Mehadin's son spread the word, too."

"Then someone wanted this war now."

Yes, there was someone... "The war would have started anyway. How close were Mehadin and Devan?"

"Mehadin was afraid of Devan. He was afraid of Orban too, but the marriage contract between lady Jara's daughter and Devan's son decided for him."

"Who told you about the marriage?" I asked, unable to hide my surprise.

"We received news from two sources: Aron and Cantemir."

"Mohor's Spatar?"

"Yes, the normal courtesy announcement of a marriage, nothing special. Here," she pointed to a large door. We had arrived at Calin's office, and she was happy to escape my questions.

"I want to see the letter about Saliné's marriage."

"Who is Saliné?"

"Lady Jara's daughter."

She went to a cabinet with many boxes, opened one named Severin, searched for some time among the gathered papers, and came back with an envelope. "Aron's letter." She handed the envelope to me, and I struggled to hide my eagerness.

To Sir Mehadin, I read, *we have the pleasure to announce the marriage of...* Dated a week after my embassy left for Deva, the letter was signed by Big Mouth, yet it had Mohor's seal on it. *Big Mouth wanted to stop the marriage too... To make space for Bucur. But why a letter? It could fall into the wrong hands. It had happened already.* I played nervously with the document attesting Big Mouth's betrayal while Mara was staring at me, unable to understand why an insignificant courtesy letter was getting so much attention. I smiled, a trifle strained. "Do you have a letter from Cantemir, too?"

"No, his embassy told us."

"Who was first? Big Mouth or Cantemir?"

"Who is Big Mouth?"

"Aron," I said, and a brief smile flared on her face; the pejorative nickname obviously pleased her.

"I don't remember. Let me look in the register. The letter came two days after the embassy," she said, after closing the register. "Why is it important to you?"

Because it is... Big Mouth informed Orban first, and Cantemir knew about the alliance, too. "Show me every important letter from Orban."

She came up with five letters, and we spent some time, me reading and she answering my questions. Then I had more questions, and she found more letters; there were so many interconnected things. I let her go, and I did not realize how late it was until the roosters announced the coming of the new day. There was a sofa in the office, and I slept there until Mara woke me up.

"Are there any surviving Mehadins to claim the Seigneury?" I asked, eating what she had brought to me.

"His two sons died, one in battle, the other one..." She shrugged. "There are no grandchildren. His daughter died a long time ago. His two nephews died in the last battle, too. One of them had a son, but he will not claim the succession."

"Why?"

"Because I will never let my son inherit anything from a Mehadin," she said, bitterly.

You are a Mehadin, I suddenly realized, *and you want to claim the inheritance for your son. The bitterness in your voice proves it. Her husband died in battle...* "I am sorry for your loss, Mara, but war is like this."

"I hated my husband," she replied with false indifference; a touch of bitterness in her voice betrayed her again. "I lost two pregnancies because of his beatings."

Another broken family... "You may go, Mara; I can do this alone."

Too tired to continue, I decided to inspect our soldiers, and I was about to leave the building when I realized that I had forgotten my swords. *What is happening to me?* I was tired after a night almost without sleep, but it was not the first time I was tired. Back in the office, I found Mara playing with Flame.

"What are you doing?" My voice was rough and louder than I had intended, and the echo in the large room amplified my angry reaction. *It could have been a man playing with my sword, waiting for me.*

"Sorry, I was curious. They are so different. I came to tell you that lunch is ready." Slowly, she sheathed the sword, and put it back on the table, avoiding to look at me.

"Leave my mother alone!" The voice came from behind me, a seven-year-old child, yet he was able to sneak behind me unobserved.

I am becoming careless. It could have been an armed man. The child had a wooden sword in his hand. *It could have been a real sword, and I have no armor.* A little too long for his height, the blade was pointing at me. If I wasn't so annoyed by my double negligence, I would have laughed.

"Mihail," Mara said swiftly, and tried to move between her son and me. I raised my left arm, and she clutched it, but stopped walking. "Please, Codrin," she whispered. "He is just a child."

"Leave her, or I will attack you," the child threatened me, raising the sword, and I could not pass over the seriousness in his voice and eyes – he believed that I wanted to harm his mother.

"I don't want to fight you," I said, feeling Mara's fingers gripping stronger on me, yet she stayed still and silent.

"Why?" In his mind, everything was already settled for the fight, and he would win against the big ogre, saving his mother. I knew the story – some years ago, I was living in the same kind of fantasy inner world, and like him, I could not save anyone in my desolate reality.

"That's a sharp point." I gestured toward his sword.

"I sharpened it myself."

"May I see it?" I asked, and Mara's fingers lessened gradually their grip on my arm.

"Yes." Mihail moved forward and gave me the wooden sword in the very proper manner: his right hand, turned up, taking the blade close to the hilt, while his left hand handled the point.

I received the toy with the same seriousness he gave it to me and slowly moved my fingers along the wood; it was well polished. "Good work." With a swift move, I balanced the blade. "Well balanced. A little long for you right now, but you will grow, won't you?"

Yes, he nodded in silence, and that unusual for his age seriousness, started to leave his face, making him a child again.

"Why did you believe that I would harm your mother?" I asked, giving the sword back to him, using the same proper manner.

"I ... I don't know. You seemed upset, and I was afraid. Is that bad?"

"It's not a bad thing to be a little afraid; it makes you more careful." *Unlike myself*, I remembered how he sneaked behind me.

"Mihail, go to the kitchen. It's lunchtime." Mara smiled at him, then at me.

"Why did you think I would harm your son?" I asked after Mihail had left.

"I was afraid. Is that bad?" She cocked her brows up, a glimmer in her eyes.

"No," I sighed. "Everybody thinks of me as an ogre; one that scares children and women."

"Even such a terrifying ogre needs to eat." A little smile flashed across her mouth, and she looked younger. Before I could react, she took me by the arm, pushing me out.

After we finished eating, our political game started again.

"I have something more to trade. You may find my request strange, though. I am not a big player, I don't have a castle, in fact, I am not even a Knight, but I need an experienced diplomat to act as some kind of Secretary for me. Just to keep you well informed, I am not rich either. There is no need to write letters for me, nobody exchanges diplomatic messages with someone on my level. I need information. I can provide information too, if you want that kind of trade. I have learned a lot from Mara, and I am sure that your diplomatic letters still have many secrets for me. And of course, there might be interesting things not mentioned in any letters."

"How do you want to play this game?" Calin asked, without accepting or rejecting my offer.

"I would visit you from time to time to talk over a bottle of wine. When needed, I can provide protection, but it will not be easy for you to reach me; I travel a lot."

"We enjoy having guests, so why not?"

How much of your acceptance is because you need me to help you leave the city? The game was that I could not constrain him, such collaboration required goodwill and trust. *Maybe in time, both will come to us.* "Thank you. I have to leave now; if not, Mohor will think I've deserted him." *I can't even tell him what I am doing here...* In my pocket, Big Mouth's betrayal letter was waiting for its time to come. I found Mohor out of the city, in front of his tent, together with Big Mouth.

"What a bright afternoon," Big Mouth said before I could speak. "I can't wait to see Calin rammed on a pole in front of our camp and left there to die and rot in shame. The scoundrel deserves it." His voice was wicked and filled with ghastly expectation. "I have waited twenty-four years for this."

"No one will be executed," I said. "The agreement for surrender included Calin, too. It was Calin I negotiated with."

"Yes, the agreement," Aron mused. "Calin will leave the city, as agreed. There is nothing in that paper to stop me after that."

"Yes, there is. For any decent man, I mean."

"He killed my brother."

"Both of you lost a brother. Things are even. He will leave tomorrow with his daughter and her children."

"The poor daughter... Quite a pretty woman, I understood. Don't worry; I will take care of her after her father's misfortune. I am a kind man. You don't seem pleased by my kindness; perhaps you might want her too," Big Mouth laughed. "We can share the girl, but I must have the first night. I am a Knight. You are..." He shrugged, and his hand moved left and right, the Frankis sign for a leaf in the wind.

"I know, you are strong enough to fight a woman, and these days any thug brags about being a Knight. I will escort Calin out tomorrow."

"Nobody will leave tomorrow," Mohor intervened, and there was a thin smile on Big Mouth's lips as he looked at me in contempt.

They have already agreed on this. I stared hard at Mohor, weighing my answer.

"And nobody will be killed," he added before I could say anything.

At that moment, I realized that once Mehadin died in battle, and his city fell into Mohor's hands, I had lost some of my position, if not most of it. *The political game starts after the war ends*; I remembered Vlaicu's words. The future was bright, and there was no longer much need for an army commander. Restraining myself, I turned, leaving without a word, and went back to the castle.

"You can't leave yet," I said to Calin, after I closed the door behind me. Mara was not there, and it was easier for me to speak openly.

"I understand," Calin acknowledged with his usual calm, reminding me again of Cernat. "I prepared this for you." He took a piece of paper from his desk – an official document with Mehadin's seal. "There is a hunting house and a piece of land in Leyona Seigneury, close to Orhei, a hundred hectares. It was supposed to come into our possession for good services, but there was always a new reason to postpone it. Seigneurs are sometimes too tight with their purses, and Mehadin was worse than many. I still have my official rights in Mehadia, so I gave them to you."

"Why not to your daughter?" I asked, confused by his offer.

"It may be contested, as the document is signed by me. I dated it a month ago, when Mehadin was still alive, to avoid unwanted scrutiny."

"I will return it to you later, when things calm down."

"My understanding is that I will not leave the city alive," Calin shrugged. "But that's not so important right now. You are new in the game of power, and your position is not as strong as you think. Old faces loathe new faces. It's a normal human reaction." He turned his palms up, to underline his words. "You are a strong and ambitious young man, ready to climb in the hierarchy, but you need the right kind of luck, and a place to hide and plan your future, if things go wrong. Orban wants your head after this campaign against Mehadin. Mohor is too much in debt to Aron, who is not your friend. This is *your* place." Calin handed the paper to me while I wondered who told him that Big Mouth was not my friend. "Leyona is a neutral land for you, at least for now. Please take care of what is left of my family; a lone woman is not able to defend herself. Don't think me wrong, I am not suggesting marriage; Mara has two children with another man, and you need a wife able to step up to your place in the hierarchy – a Knight's daughter. Just keep an eye on Mara until my grand-child is able to defend himself."

"What makes you so sure that I will take care of your family after getting the land?"

"Your question." He smiled, almost for himself. "Many would have promised me anything I wanted to hear, and it seems that you like to keep your word, if not you would not try to save me. Mara can be your hidden Secretary. She is qualified – I am sure you realize that by now – and has many connections that might help you."

Not as many as you... You asked her to help me on purpose. "Then I will give the house to Mara."

"You did not listen well. You need the house. Your position is not as good as you think."

"Why?"

"There is a story about Mohor's wedding." Calin folded his arms across his chest. His dark eyes were wide-set and calm, his mouth was firm, and his voice revealed a good control. "Mehadin wanted to snub Mohor in a subtle way, so he decided to send a high servant instead of a family member. I could not go for obvious reasons, and our Chief of the Guard had the pleasure of participating. When he returned, he told us a strange story about some fools and a young man and, even stranger, he recognized the young man in our negotiations."

Are you playing me against Mohor? "Just an old story," I said, coldly.

"Maybe. Keep the house. Give half of the land to Mara if that makes you feel better. And one more thing; there is a second vault in the Secretariat, not a big treasure, just two thousand galbeni. The amount is at my disposal, as I am also Mehadia's Vistier. It's a small court," he shrugged. "Take the bags, and split them with Mara, so she can buy a house later. No plan works without money. The higher you rise, the more secure my family will be." He stood up, and came to my side of the table, putting one hand on my shoulder. "I trust you."

"I will think about it," I said, getting up to leave.

With surprising speed for a wounded old man, Calin grabbed my hand. "Codrin, please take the paper."

In silence, I took the document, it did not make sense to deepen his worries, and anyway I would not have kept that house and land, even when he was right that I might need a hidden place to plan my next moves. "Thank you for your trust, Calin," I said and left the room, feeling the need to clear my mind.

જ્જૂ

"You know why I had to join this campaign." Mohor's voice was calm, almost pleasant. We were alone in his tent, the next morning, and both of us knew that some disagreeable things would be said. The camp was quiet.

"To have a pleasant country journey," I mocked him in a stern voice, matching the content of our talk.

"Winning a war is a pleasant thing; not that I really won anything by myself, but a Seigneur's duty is to find the right man in the right place. Which I did." He smiled, but as I knew from the past, his smile could be as thorny as his temper. "The war is now past. You won it for us. I now need to organize

Mehadia's absorption into my lands. Well, the parts that don't go to my good friend Orban. That's a different errand, for different skills."

"And for a different man."

"That's why we are here now. Aron has more experience in controlling the Knights and organizing the land. He will take over from now on."

"Whatever Big Mouth wants to organize, it doesn't concern me or the army."

"The Spatar is the head of the army, and Aron needs it to bend Mehadin's Knights to my will. As you already know, a Seigneur must sometimes take the right, not the just, decision." A veiled reference to the month I spent in his jail, but it was not a threat, just a reminder of what he considered the right state of things.

Is this what my father failed to do? To take the right decision? Our fall began after my cousin Jan raped the daughter of a minor Knight. Father tried to punish Jan, and my uncle started the revolt, yet from Dochia, I learned that things were more complicated than I thought. "Ah, it was the Seigneur's decision," I said, and Mohor stayed silent, his face bland. *Father took the right decision, it doesn't matter what happened after that,* I reassured myself. *Father's mistake was to let Baraki, Jan's father-in-law, stay as commander of the Royal Guard. The same mistake Mohor is making. Baraki wanted to become regent. Big Mouth wants something too. To take Mohor's place?* The situation seemed somehow similar, and I remembered how Big Mouth lost the battle against Mehadin. *Was it really a mistake?* "Misplaced trust is dangerous." For a moment, I thought to reveal the letter announcing Saliné's wedding to Mehadin. I decided against it; alone, Mohor would not be able to act against Big Mouth; I needed Jara and Cernat to be involved too.

"Aron is for me what you are for Jara. He saved my life and made me Seigneur, so everything I have, I owe to him. Trust is important; when you become a Knight in your own right you will understand. Don't try to judge me until you are in the same position. Let's go on to more pleasant things." Mohor ended our discussion, which was going nowhere – each remained unmoved with his own understanding, but he was the Seigneur. Slowly, he unfolded a document carrying his seal and handed it to me. There were fifty hectares of land granted in my name, in the south-east of Severin, on the border with Mehadia and Leyona. "After we sort things out here," he gestured around, "the other fifty hectares we promised will come to you and the Half-Knight anointment. And this is a scrip for five hundred galbeni. It will take time until the land ownership produces some revenue."

"Thank you," I said, bowing slightly.

"We want to give you the governorate of Corabia." Mohor handed another paper with his seal to me. Corabia was the second most important city in Mehadin's land after Mehadia, a moderately rich place that could give influence and revenue. It was a good offer, and it was close to the land I had been given. "If everything goes well, Corabia would become Vio's dowry."

This comes from Jara. And for the first time, I realized that if I was to lose Saliné, for whatever reason – her forced marriage with the young Devan or her new attachment to Bucur – the other girl I could love was indeed Vio. My feelings were still for a young sister, but Saliné was the same for me at her age. In a mysterious way, after a month of avoiding the slightest thought related to Saliné, Mohor's decision to sort out my future according to their political needs, brought my mind back to her. *What if Jara's message was true? She came to my house to deliver it.* "I need to think about it," I said, unwilling to refuse him directly, becoming his governor would have ended my independent game.

"You have two months to think about it. The gold from Mehadin's vault will leave tomorrow for Severin. I am counting on you to make sure it arrives safely."

"I can lead the caravan until the turning for Leyona." Up to that point, the road would match my own route toward the place Calin had given me in temporary possession, which by chance was also near the land I had received from Mohor. Two roads of approximate equal length linked Mehadia to Leyona, both passing through Orhei. "It's close enough to Severin to be safe from there." It was just a day and a half travel at a caravan's pace.

Mohor looked at me, a hint of displeasure in his eyes, but nodded slowly. "Your payment will accord with the importance of the charge."

"I don't work for money with you," I said, and Mohor glanced at me, then at the paper money he had given me. "That's not payment; it's a reward."

"As you wish." He shrugged. "We are done now, go and arrange the gold shipment."

"I don't think we are done."

"Calin is free to leave the city." Mohor looked at me, a trace of a smile on his lips, and now we were done indeed. There was a long pause. He could not think of anything more to say. Neither could I.

❧

In the evening, Mara joined me again in Calin's office, and she opened the vault, revealing the little treasure it was hiding. There were four bags of money, some papers and three small boxes with elegant decorations. I took out the papers and looked at Mara.

"Some personal letters belonging to my father," she said without claiming them directly, and I gave them to her.

The first box I opened contained necklace, earrings and rings. Crafted in Tomis, their beauty rivaled the necklace I returned to Jara. The medallion was an emerald with many facets shining in the light coming from the window. The green reflection brought me a flash of Saliné's eyes. We were in the garden, and she was looking amused at me. I tried to remember the joke I had made, but my memory failed, and I did not realize the silence flowing between me and Mara.

Mara's black eyes glittered with amusement as she asked, "A girl's green eyes?" pointing to the emerald I was still staring at, and I nodded absently. "It belonged to Mehadin's wife. She died four years ago from despair, after losing her daughter in an accident; the girl who owned the other box," she pointed to the bluish one, "so why not take it for the girl you love?"

Struggling to hide my irritation, I opened the other two boxes, and they revealed turquoise gems and black pearl sets. "This should be yours." I stared into Mara's black eyes and gave her the box with the pearls.

"That was my wedding gift, but I will keep nothing to remind me of the nightmare that was my marriage." Her voice was suddenly edgy, and her eyes turned sad, recalling her lost pregnancies because of her violent husband.

"Mara, I understand you, but you have a daughter with beautiful black eyes. She will grow, and she deserves her heritage."

"No." Mara rejected the box with a brusque gesture, and I no longer insisted. "I want nothing from him. Nothing. My children will take my father's name, and me too."

Later, I gave the box to Calin without letting her know, so he could keep it in his family. One by one, I carried the four heavy bags with galbeni that were half mine to the coffers waiting outside the office. *I have enough money to buy a hundred mercenaries for three months.* Not mentioned in the treaty, the vault was my Winner's Right.

The next morning, Calin's large carriage, which in fact belonged to Mehadin, and his own wagon, followed the five wagons hauling Mohor's gold, and whatever else he thought of value in the castle. There was also a coffer containing the fifty or so books I had found. The most significant diplomatic papers received by Mehadin were hidden between the books. Thrilled, Mara's children were looking from the carriage's window, and I guessed that it was their first trip outside the city. Ban led the ten soldiers he had picked, as Vlaicu stayed with Mohor. A young family joined Calin, the woman and her two-year-old girl climbing into the carriage. The man, a soldier from the guards, had his own horse, and he tied another two to the wagon – they belonged to Calin and Mara. Calin was well prepared to leave Mehadia.

Chapter 26 – Codrin

Calin's house was inhabited by a couple with two children, Moros, the sturdy thirty-year-old man a former soldier. With two soldiers to guard the house, their safety was no longer a concern, as much as it could be in troubled times. While large, the hunting house was half the size of the one I knew so well in Severin, and there was a barn for horses, too. Dinner passed almost in silence; everybody was tired, and the bath that followed was marvelous.

"You look better," I laughed at Calin in the morning, after breakfast.

"You know, at each turn of the road, I looked back to see if Aron's soldiers were coming upon us. That man is a mule, obstinate and stubborn. Big Mouth," he laughed softly. I could not remember anyone apart from Mohor, Cernat and Saliné, each for a different reason, who refused to use the name once they'd heard it – it described the man so well.

"Today, I must go to register the house and land in Orhei. You should come with me, to arrange the bogus sale of the land."

"Thank you, Codrin," Calin said, and I observed Mara's gaze, fixed on me, intense, like she did not believe I would fulfill my promise. "Mara will go with you; there is no need for an old man."

"Carriage?" I asked Mara.

"Such a weak woman you think I am. It's less than fifteen minutes ride to Orhei. Let's have a race." She challenged me with an amused stare, then went for Moros to prepare the horses.

We left an hour later than expected; it took Mara more time to dress than for Moros to prepare both horses. When the road became straight and level, Mara had the race she wanted, and while her mare was of good quality, she could not compare to Zor, but I took care to be only half a horse's length in front when we finished.

"It's not fair," Mara complained, pushing me with her shoulder after we dismounted in front of the gates. She was a tall woman, even taller than Jara; she took after Calin, who was taller than me.

Looking at her, I could no longer observe the sadness that marked her in Mehadia, and she looked younger. From Calin I had heard that she was twenty-seven years old, not the thirty-something I thought in the beginning, and now her looks matched her real age.

"Men, they never know how to treat a woman properly." She passed her arm around mine, so we walked arm in arm, through the gates, toward the Visterie, where we found a bald clerk.

"Good morning, sir, I have come to register a house and some land."

The man raised his left eye to acknowledge me, frowning as if I had disturbed him. His office was elegant; the sign of a wealthy position, and that explained his self-importance. "Well, I am the Vistier, and always ready to take your money." He looked with both eyes this time. It was unusual for a Vistier to be directly in charge of taxes and property registration, but Orhei was a small city. "Give me your papers. Hmm. Mehadin's hunting house. He is too old to use it anymore."

He doesn't know that Mehadin is dead.

"Big house, a lot of land." He rubbed his chin, reading the paper again. "How did you get it?"

"Some services to Sir Mehadin, in the past."

"Quite a good service it must have been. The old man is a scrooge. It will cost you ten galbeni."

"Your services are not cheap," I said, taking out my purse to pay.

"Cheap men don't stay in the job for too long." He laughed, lining the coins up on the table, one by one, for his own pleasure; it was not so difficult to count up to ten. "The papers will be ready in an hour. Anything else?"

"I need some money to maintain the house. Lady Mara wants to buy fifty hectares from me."

"Excellent," he rubbed his palms. "That will bring another twenty-five galbeni in taxes from your pockets into mine. Well, that is to say, most of it goes to Sir Leyonan. It's half a galben per hectare," he said, probably seeing the negative reactions on our faces. "The regular tax. The buyer has to pay." He glanced at Mara, evaluating her status, without stopping to record the sale in his register.

"A lot of money," Mara said, surprised.

"The official tax list is on that wall." The bald man pointed abruptly at it, some irritation passing through his voice, even though he was still smiling.

"Please, sir, don't misunderstand me. It's just that I came unprepared." Mara opened her purse and lined up all her money on the table: sixteen galbeni. She glanced furtively at me, and we emptied all our pockets to gather the money. It took some time, and Mara said with a charming smile, "I hope we are not inconveniencing you too much." She placed the coins on the table, deliberately slow, to offer him a longer view of the gold, but the perfect display of her body seemed to influence him even more; there was a certain elegance to her.

"Lady ... Mara." The bald man lost a few moments to look into the papers and find her name. "For another smile like that, I am ready to help you anytime. Do you or your husband want to buy more land in Orhei?" he asked, frowning slightly. As with the Seigniorial cities, Orhei was also the name of the region.

"My husband is dead," Mara said, in a stern voice.

"I apologize for my ignorant rudeness," he said, unimpressed. "From your presence here, should I understand the war is not going well in Mehadia? There were some setbacks, as I remember."

"The war ended two weeks ago. Sir Mehadin and his sons died in battle and S'Severin is now the master of Mehadia."

"Interesting news." The bald man rubbed the top of his head, without looking at Mara. "In the way that it was ... both important and unknown to me until this moment. Then I understand your need to use your father's name." He pushed forward the papers validating the sale to be signed – there were three copies, one for each of us.

"Thank you for your consideration." Mara signed the papers before handing them to me. "May I ask you to keep my real identity quiet? Of course, I understand that you have to warn Sir Leyonan about Mehadins settling in his land."

The man nodded to her, then turned toward me. "Do you plan to sell more land, and the house too?"

"No. Some repairs are needed, but it's a fine house."

Perhaps his real question was if Mara would stay in my house too, but he decided not to press further for the moment, and we left the office. He had probably guessed that it was a fictitious sale. On the way back, we rode at leisure, talking all the way to the hunting house.

"How did you get the land?" Mara imitated the bald man accurately when we dismounted. "Some services to Sir Mehadin, in the past," she imitated me this time, and I could not say how well; you know all the voices in the world bar yours. "Excellent," I heard the bald man's voice again, and we entered the house still laughing.

Calin raised his head from the book he was reading. "It looks like you had a good day."

"The Vistier was curious why Mehadin gifted Codrin with the house and land," Mara said, fighting hard to keep her laughter in check.

"And the answer was...?"

"For some services to Sir Mehadin, in the past." Mara imitated my voice again, and Calin struggled to keep his composure. "I think that I have met that bald man in the past."

"Six years ago, we received an embassy from Leyona, led by him, when he still had most of his hair. The man you met is Dobre, the governor of Orhei, not just the Vistier. Don't be fooled by his placid appearance; he is a cunning man. Orhei is a strategic border location at the intersection of two main commercial routes. No Seigneur would place a fool in such a position. An hour ago, I sent Moros with a letter to Leyona, to my contacts there. It should arrive in two days."

"Your letter was meant to arrive before someone else informs Leyonan," I said, guessing at his real intentions.

"Information is important."

"So is trust."

Calin nodded, and after dinner everything that happened in Dobre's office was dissected; yet I was sure that he still kept some things hidden from me.

"You should have presented a fictitious name on those papers," I complained. "Leyonan may ask uncomfortable questions about me."

"I apologize for not taking this into consideration in Mehadia; the circumstances gave me no time to consider everything, and Leyonan's interest might open some new doors for you. You should not rely on Mohor, after losing your position as commander. I agree that everything appears to be on a knife-edge, like many other things in our lives."

"I would prefer to decide for myself what doors to open."

"A valid request. We had some agreements in Mehadia." Calin moved away from my complaint, and I had to let it pass too, even though my double identity was becoming more dangerous; a knife-edge, as Calin had said, without realizing how right he was. "I have to play the Secretary for you. What is your first question?"

"The Circle."

"What do you know about the Circle?" he asked, in a bland voice, but his fingers gripped the edge of the table.

"It exists."

"A secret society founded almost six hundred years ago, after the Alban Empire's self-destruction. The Circle aims to create a new one. Their first step went well; after one hundred years, nine kingdoms were created on the ruins of the Empire, and they expected to have a new one two hundred years later. Do you know of any empire that exists out there?" He gestured toward the window, and there was scorn in his voice, as if he did not consider the Circle good enough for the task.

"What went wrong?"

"The person who knows the answer to that question will become Emperor. I don't see it happening in a man's lifetime, though," Calin shrugged. "It may be that the game is too complex; there are many competing Circles, one in each kingdom. Look at the chaos we have now in Frankis."

There is no Circle in Arenia. Even when I was too young, I should have learned something about it at my father's court. *Maybe it stayed hidden because we had a king.*

"We always have a new king in the making here. Now it is Orban, but his chance died some time ago. The Circle is made of Secretaries and First Mesters, and they elect a leader every ten year. Sages, they name themselves: Sages of the Realm."

Balan is part of the Circle... The implication let me understand once more how little I knew about Frankis.

"Orban's first term started badly; Cernat refused him his daughter's hand. I don't know why Cernat snubbed the Circle, but the Sages will never forgive him or lady Jara."

I couldn't help but notice that, while all other Seigneurs were accorded their Seigniorial names, Cernat and Orban were not. In quite different ways, they were unique, and did not need a particular title to reflect their importance.

"The Circle wants her daughters. The eldest one is already marked, and the youngest will be tested in two or three years. After that, lady Jara and Cernat are no longer needed. Do you know about marking?" he asked, and I shook my head, just to oppose him to Balan, unable to grasp that *no longer needed.* "One reason for the fall of the Alban Empire was degeneration from too much interbreeding. Promising men and women of strong lineages are marked by the Circle, and they are not many."

"Are you a Sage?"

"Only the Secretaries working for Dukes and Grand Seigneurs are accepted in the Circle. A very select club," he said, gruffly. "But I undertook some services for them in the past, and it was a good time to learn."

"You still provide some services."

"If they ask me, yes, but my value has decreased."

"What we lost in value, we gained in other ways," Mara interjected quickly, and she smiled at me.

"Yes, you recovered your liberty. It's late. The old man needs to sleep."

"The Assassins and the Wanderers are playing the same game as the Circle." Even before I finished, Calin gaped in silence. His black eyes glinted beneath fiercely furrowed brows, and I saw a flicker of genuine concern, then a slow-unfurling look of wonder.

"I have not much knowledge about the Assassins," he whispered. "They come from Arenia." His realization came full circle: my birthplace, curved swords and black clothes. For the wrong reason, I became one of those terrible monsters.

"They are not from Arenia, and I am not one of them. There are no Assassins in Frankis either, but some Wanderers settled here."

"It's a secretive order," he said evasively, looking at me, then bit his lower lip long enough to make some teeth glisten.

"That's why I've asked."

"I underestimated you." His tone was composed, but he felt the need to clear his throat.

"Such was my thought," I said, setting my eyes on Mara, then back on him. "As I mentioned in Mehadia, the information game will play both ways, but it's not horse trading. There is no bargaining."

"The Wanderers can see the future, through their Visions, but they like to stay in the shadow. They opposed Orban's selection as Candidate King and, because of that, there is a rift between the Wanderers and the Circle right now; it threatens to grow wider and destroy Frankis," Calin said, as if he was more on the Wanderers' side, and his voice thickened midway through the words. "The Circle is fractional, and some Sages are wise; others are wicked, greedy and plain stupid. I know nothing more." He stood up abruptly and left the room in silence.

Amber. It came to me as Calin passed and I held my wine glass at eye level, my hand resting on the backrest of the sofa, and his body, seen through the glass, took on a strange color. Until that moment, I had not perceived the wine's perfect color. It often happens that we see things repeatedly without really noticing them.

"Tell me about your girl." Mara's voice softened to a deep whisper; we were sitting beside each other on the sofa.

"What makes you think there is a girl in my life?" I asked, struggling to hide my irritation; my girl and the many issues I had with her were not for Mara to comment on.

She did not answer, but gently took my chin between her fingers, turning my head until we were face to face. Confused, I asked myself what was in her mind, and how I should react to such familiarity, which was not unpleasant. "You don't look so bad, so you must have a girl." Her lips twitched with a trace of humor, and I chose to do nothing, not necessarily because of some sudden logical considerations in my mind. "With emerald eyes. Why is it so difficult to talk about her?"

"It's complicated."

"I see." She moved her fingers over my face, much like Jara used to in the past, and I decided to consider that resemblance the reason for my lack of reaction. "How old are you?"

"Nineteen," I said, subdued by her subtle fingers still tracing my face. "Almost nineteen."

"So young," she whispered, and I thought I could hear regret in her words. Her fingers moved away from my skin, though their ghostly presence lingered for a while. "Let's talk about me, then. I was eighteen when I married Mehadin, and it was not quite yesterday. What looked like a good step at the time turned into a nightmare. He was the firstborn of the secondary Mehadin family and a Knight. What better option could I have? My father was a fugitive and had lost all his lands in Severin. My nightmare started on the wedding night, with the first beating. I learned later what many others knew, but we had failed to learn: his body could not be physically ready for a woman without beating her first. A twisted, sad man; I am sure that deep in his mind he despised himself. The second time I lost an unborn child, I had to stay in bed for two months. Yet, I considered myself lucky that two children had been born healthy, as I never became pregnant again." She sighed, and I tried to say something to soothe her, but nothing came to my mind, so I just touched her hand. "That's when Seigneur Mehadin intervened, not out of kindness, but because he was afraid of losing his valuable second Secretary. In time, you learn that a tool is used and discarded when it's no longer useful; so, you must pretend to ignore what you really are and remain useful. I was useful; therefore, my husband was kindly advised to be more ... gentle with me – meaning violence was acceptable if it didn't leave me bed-ridden – and use some common women for his more extreme pleasures..." She could not finish, and I took her hand in mine.

"Mara, this is hurting you."

"It's helping me," she said, her voice edgy. "After a while, the kidnapped women started to die, and people started to whisper; some of them were relatives of our merchants and soldiers. Mehadin sequestered my husband for one year in one of his smaller castles, and released him when the war started – the best period of my adult life until now. As you have noticed, I have never pronounced his name, and I will never do. Never. Mehadin's fall left us insecure and vulnerable, but I feel alive again, and I have you to thank for it. So, that was my story, but it's too late to hear yours today." She stood up abruptly, and we left the room in silence.

Before I fell asleep, I thought again about Saliné, maybe because of Mara's annoying question; or maybe because she never really left my mind, even though I sometimes pretended to myself. The scene with Bucur's hand around her shoulders came back to me – not that I asked for it, the vivid images just came, silent and frustrating, as usual. '*Some things are not what they seem. What happened on that corridor was a self-preservation façade Saliné thought necessary for both of you, nothing else.*' I remembered Jara's words. *Was she right? Did she tell the truth?* Unsure, I tried to imagine why Jara might lie to me, and found no adequate reason – by that time, I had already agreed to lead their army. Troubled and unable to sleep, I left my bed for the window. A full moon, the size of a chariot wheel, shined over the land with a warmth that I could not feel. *Like that evening...* The evening of our first walk hand in hand in the garden.

Saliné was just a bystander, I went back to her walk with Bucur, the mind's predilection for choosing bad memories over good, and it came to me that Saliné was a dead woman walking, a bystander in her own life – there was no reaction on her body or face from being so close to Bucur.

Why did I not observe it that day? Or is just my imagination?

The next day, it was late evening when I remained alone with Mara. "I will not ask again about green-eyed girls." She said and touched the small scar at the base of my jaw. "It gives you a mysterious look." Her fingers moved over my face, to underline her words.

Unconsciously, I leaned forward to kiss her. A moment later, I forced myself to stay still; it would have been improper – I loved another woman, and I would have offended Mara; she was just being friendly. My body was already inclined toward her and, slowly, I moved back, as if unable to find a comfortable position.

"Women appreciate mysterious men." She laughed, leaving me unsure if her reaction was for my lost control or just a joke. "Is that not curious? A small scar like this enhances a man but diminishes a woman. It's not fair. Tell me about Arenia."

"A country far from here," I said, in that serious voice someone would use when revealing an important secret, and she pushed me playfully – her reactions were sometimes exuberant, underlining the truth in her claim about *living again*, taking life in its full colors, to compensate for her long years of despair. "It's true."

"Really? Then I would like to hear about your long journey from there to here." There was a moment of silence, memories

I wanted to forget coming back to me in swift succession. "Another bad question," she sighed. "Tell me whatever you want, mysterious man."

I told her some parts of my journey toward Frankis. My voice was bruised from recalling what I had lost, and in a reverse duplication of the evening before, Mara placed her hand over mine.

"Are you still living with Cernat?"

"I have a small house," I said, hiding how I had received it; not that I was ungrateful to Jara, but it was too early to reveal all my bonds with her and her family. "I live there with Vlad."

"This is your house, too. Why not stay here?"

"Mara, the house is not mine, and I travel a lot," I said, awkwardly.

"When you are not traveling. In the winter. I will have a mysterious man to keep me entertained with stories. Vlad can stay too, there is enough room," she gestured around, "and two good swords will keep my children safer. See? I am not hiding anything. I know we can't match your value, but the long winter evenings can be pleasantly spent in company over a bottle of wine. There is no need to answer today." She gripped my hand stronger to enhance her plea, and our eyes locked. "Time to sleep now."

Alone in my room, I realized the truth in her words; the evenings here were a pleasant reminder of my first year in Jara's house. *Just that Saliné and Vio are missing.* It was surprising how much Mara was able to replace Jara in such a short time. *Maybe because their names rhyme,* I smiled. And there were many resemblances between Cernat and Calin. There was something slippery about Calin, making me uneasy sometimes, but I needed him to reveal the underground political world of the former kingdom, and it was useful to contrast his and Cantemir's interpretations of the political landscape.

The more I thought of that first year spent in Jara's house, the more I realized that nothing could compare to it. Even if all of us moved back there again, we were now different people, and many things would just feed on our memories – we had changed, and maybe I had changed the most, yet how could I really know how Saliné was affected by everything that had happened? That cursed wedding, the aftermath, and losing Saliné, had changed me in a more insidious way than losing my entire family. I became hardened and sometimes unable to feel the beauty of life. *I have to learn from Mara...* At a deeper level, she had the same problems as me, but she seemed able to overcome them.

❧❧

On my last evening there, Calin left me alone with Mara again, and our conversation went on longer than in the days before.

"The real war will begin next year, and you will be asked to lead Mohor's army again. You will find it difficult to refuse. I am afraid that..." Her voice wobbled, and she remained silent.

"I am a soldier. Why should I refuse, and why are you afraid?" I was oddly irritated by her concern. *That war is my only chance to gain status and start the recovery of my crown. And Saliné...*

"Because I care. Mohor is just a pawn in the great game, as are you. But who cares about him?" She shrugged while our eyes met, and she smiled sadly, just for an instant.

"Tell me," I said curtly, unable to control my voice.

"That's what we've been trying to do, but you are not listening. Well, you are listening, but your mind is already settled, and you hear only what it suits you to hear. Mohor was framed by Cantemir, who is the Master Sage, the chief of the Circle. Everything was planned in detail. The Devans will step back, and they have the strongest army in the *alliance*. They accepted the marriage and alliance because Cantemir allowed them, and to hide the rapprochement between Devan and the Duke of Peyris. How Cernat could be so blind, I don't know. His granddaughter has the highest rank among the marked girls. She may be given to the new Candidate King the Circle selects next year or to some other important young man. And the Sages will make sure Cernat and Jara can't refuse anymore, by killing them."

My mind twisted from one thought to another, calculating, devising. It produced nothing useful. "Cernat trusts Devan. They are friends," I said, only because I had to say something. *Cantemir ... the Master Sage of the Circle.* A past conversation with him unfolded slowly in my mind: Cantemir's eyes flickering when I mentioned about the Circle helping Orban. *He played me. Is he aware who Tudor is? It can't be.*

"You can't trust anyone these days. Keep this in mind and be careful." Mara's voice startled me, and her eyes pleaded against my silence. I nodded, incapable to provide a coherent answer. "Thank you for training Mihail," she said abruptly, and her diversion suddenly freed my mind.

"His speed and coordination are above average. With enough training, he will become a good swordsman." Yet what impressed me the most was his seriousness, as if he was no longer a child. Told to repeat a certain move a hundred times, he would do it with no complaints. *I whined a lot when Tudor made me repeat the Assassins Dance.* My training started at Mihail's age. "Why is our son so serious?"

"He was old enough to understand some ... things that were happening in my marriage. When that bloody man came back three months ago, Mihail tried to defend me. You know well how," she smiled. "He was kicked hard by his father, but I escaped another night of miseries. It's late now," she abruptly ended the conversation, standing up, and I had to follow her. "You want to leave early in the morning, and you know what a lazy woman I am, so we must take our leave now." She embraced me gently and, with a small hesitation, I answered in kind. "Codrin, this is your house," she whispered in my ear. "I am not talking about a few papers." Her head moved back, her arms still around my neck. Our eyes locked, and I felt wordless. "Without you, my father would have been dead, and I would have been forced to do ... many things to save my children. Come back and stay for the winter."

"Yes... Perhaps..."

"I wanted to tell you something. You are the kind of man I wish I had met a long time ago. Now, it's eight years and two children too late. All those years of misery gifted me with two wonderful children. They are my life now, and I will not marry again; it wouldn't be fair to them and to my husband – I can't have children anymore. You will find the wife you deserve, but until then..." Her voice was gentle and edgy at the same time Our eyes locked, and her hands laced tighter around my neck. Her lips came closer, red and attractive, and a little moistened. A faint scent of peppermint came to me, and I could no longer control myself. Gently and little cautious, I pressed my mouth on hers, splitting her lips. She answered me warmly.

Pausing for breath, she pulled her head back, and our eyes met again. "Isn't that strange?" she asked, sadness filling her voice. "I was married for eight years and have two children, yet this is my first kiss. I feel so young." She smiled, and that chased her sadness away. "If I don't take into consideration the beatings and how well they were spread, my husband was interested in only a small part of my body."

Without thinking, I pulled her closer, searching for her lips again – my hands were still around her waist – but she stopped me, her palm touching my mouth.

"I will join you for breakfast tomorrow. Such a lazy woman you think I am," she laughed. "We couldn't have our peculiar farewell in the morning, could we?"

I kissed her hand, and we left the room in silence. What could I say?

Chapter 27 – Codrin

On the way back, my thoughts turned more and more to Saliné, the narrowing distance stirring my mind, and I let Vlad take care of our safety. Mara disturbed me too; there was no way to deny that I enjoyed our moments together. *How strange that I never kissed a woman twice.* Inside the small mountains around Severin, I woke up suddenly and felt watched, the same way I felt when I met Boldur and the Mountes. The forest was quiet. There was no noise. No birds calling, no wind shooing. Nothing moved, and I reached for the Wing Talisman. It pulsed in my hand, and the forewarning became stronger. Vlad glanced at me but remained silent.

"Let's go through the forest." I pointed to the left; on the right side, the terrain was more rugged and filled with deep ravines.

After a minute, through the trees, two riders in ring-mail appeared on the small mound from where the road was going down to Severin. In plain view, they were obviously bait that might or might not be in place for us. We went deeper into the forest, around the three-hundred-foot-long black rock rising between us and the riders, trying to fall behind them. Before turning the corner, we dismounted, and tied the horses to some small trees. Heavy, the silence of the land reminded me of the Cursed Forest. The muscles round my jaw tightened rigid, and my scar stretched with a tingling. Whatever was watching us was closer than before. *Spread*, I gestured to Vlad, and we stepped cautiously toward the rock's edge. I gripped Shadow's hilt, ready to unsheathe it.

"No," the sword whispered in my mind, and I retracted my fingers.

"How predictable you are," an unknown voice scorned us from above; a voice hard to define, missing gender.

I turned slowly, keeping my hand away from my sword – we could have been already dead – and checked the rock: there was no one in sight, and we ran behind Vlad's horse, which was closer. Quiet and motionless, I let my senses absorb everything. All I could perceive was some distant birds' noise, and still nothing moved around us. Then, from behind the rock, slow steps rustled through the dead leaves of the forest. We waited, then we waited some more.

"This is witchcraft," Vlad whispered.

Invisible, the unknown boots continued their march, going round in circles, and I wished I had a bow. I freed the handle of the dagger at my waist. Vlad did the same, and bared his teeth, ready to spin and strike, just that there was nothing to strike at.

"What do you want?" I shouted.

"You," the voice answered.

"And how do you want us?" I looked around, slow and easy, just to make sure there was no one behind us, but there were only empty trees. The invisible boots were still walking through the leaves, and I had that feeling of breathless anticipation, fear and excitement, that I used to have before a battle.

"Alive," the voice said, dismissively. "For the moment," it added after a while, with unconcealed mockery, and the tip of an arrow appeared from behind a black column of basalt.

In that instant, I knew that it was a young woman's voice. Not from the tone, it was knowledge outside the common senses, and without seeing them, I knew that the other two, coming through the dried leaves, were also women.

"Avae, sisters," I said, feeling tricked by the Wing Talisman. Relieved, I released the hilt of the dagger. *How did Shadow know?* I was still unable to fully understand the power of my sword.

"Avae, Codrin," Dochia answered and appeared from the dense forest, followed by another Wanderer.

They walked, grey and silent, resembling some sliding mist. Both wore ring-mail – the first time I saw Dochia dressed like a warrior – and that explained why, at distance, I confused them with armed men. The one behind the rock remained hidden. Cloaked with grey mantles over high-quality ring-mail, and having no colors, the two warrior women appeared as entities existing in both knighthood and the common world, belonging to neither. Their armor was light and sleeveless; the Wanderers relied more on their swift reflexes, both in defense and attack. And the rumors said things about a strange anticipation of the enemies' moves in combat, if really such rumors were true. A peregrine raven was sitting on her shoulder, its dark-blue intelligent eyes fixed on me.

"Avae, Codrin," the bird said in a mocking voice.

"Avae," I whispered – it's one thing to hear stories about speaking birds, and something else to actually hear one speaking to you.

"La naiba! I have been called many things but never a witch." Amused, Dochia looked at Vlad, and his eyes widened. "Well, maybe a few times."

"How did you...?" Vlad asked, his enlarged eyes rolling between the witch and the speaking bird.

Dochia's answering laugh was light, and a childlike glow danced in her eyes. "Even at distance, the movement of lips might be easily read by trained people. It's getting stronger." Dochia moved her stare to me.

"Go home, Vlad," I said, and he reluctantly obeyed in silence. "What is getting stronger? I asked when Vlad was too far away to hear.

"Your Light." The corners of her mouth twitched with repressed amusement.

"Men don't have the Light," I retorted faster than I wanted, and I could not quite conceal my surprise from her sharp eyes. I was not even sure what I was surprised at – the same thought had come to me a few times before – only a Wanderer's acknowledgement was in some respects surprising.

"Some men have it. Just a few, and they are weak and untrained."

"That's why the Wanderers recognized me as the legitimate King of Arenia?"

"No one knew about your hidden talent at that time. I felt it when you saved the Mountes. The rush of the battle enhanced the signs."

"If you say so."

"I say so." Dochia looked at me, and there was something sharp and searching in her eyes. "Why did you leave the road?" she asked, and I just shrugged; she did not expect an answer from me. "How did you recognize the hidden Wanderers?" Her voice was almost laughing. "Why did you touch the Wing Talisman?"

I have the Light. The thought left me confused and nervous. *Like my sister.* The memory of that Night of the Full Moon came to me, thick and miserable. It was so clear, as if it had happened only yesterday. *She died because of her Light.* Fate does not grant great powers for our purposes, but for hers. If you become her tool, it is for a dangerous reason. And you are still a tool. The Wing Talisman seemed to be a weird tool too, one that I could not control. "Last time I saw my sister... Her hands glowed white."

"The White Light is not evil."

"Then why did she go back to die that night?" I snapped, glaring at Dochia.

"We don't know why. We will never know. She had her reasons. Let her rest in peace." Dochia shook her head, and her expression grew gentler. Her rich voice and veiled sadness encompassed me, warm and caring.

I will never know... Eyes closed, I breathed deeply, fighting to contain my anger. "There is a Triangle of Assassins in Frankis."

"They are not here for you, but Vlad's sword raised some questions."

"You've met them."

"I've met them, but they've already left Frankis."

"Anything else I should know?"

Dochia came closer and gripped my arm. "Things are not going well in Severin, and they are waiting for you. Your first real test is waiting in the shadows. Saliné and Vio need you more than ever," she said with barely hidden sadness, and in that moment, I fully acknowledged her warning; since the day I killed Aron's brother and started the war, events were moving too fast. She squeezed my arm and smiled tentatively. "Umbra is now aware of your house," she pointed to the raven. "He needs no paper to pass messages."

"Your bird?" I asked, involuntarily.

"Call me bird," the bird protested with a charming accent, cooking his head at me. Then the raven spread his wings, leapt into the air, flapped noisily, circling around me before landing on Dochia's shoulder again. Spread on the bird's black body, shady red stripes reminded me the dark veins on Shadow, my sword. "I am Umbra, and nobody's property."

"I apologize," I said, struggling against a burst of laughter.

The bird's expression remained unchanged, his intense eyes searching me up and down.

"Don't worry, he likes you," Dochia said cryptically, addressing no one.

"Fate will test you soon, and you must understand your path. It's not so simple as good versus evil." Umbra's accent made me smile again, despite his warning. "I know, I know," he addressed Dochia this time, leaving me thoughtful about their hidden exchange. "Don't predetermine." His voice was now dreamy and captivating. Unmoving, his eyes gleamed at me with a silent intensity.

"It's not that I wasn't tested before," I shrugged.

"True," Umbra agreed. "You must not fail. Avae, Codrin, and good luck."

"Avae," I answered, there was nothing more I could say. They left me alone and uncertain, and I followed them walking away, but it was the bird that attracted me the most. At the edge of the forest, Umbra turned his head briefly, leaving behind the feeling that he winked at me. I went home with the thought about some hidden links between Dochia and Jara. One more link in the large net spread over Frankis, a net most unknown than known.

An hour later, Cernat arrived like a storm, and asked me to come with him. "Mohor's army was defeated," he said, his calm voice contrasting his words.

"He sent me home after we conquered Mehadia." *Dochia was right. Has the big war already started?*

"Mohor was an idiot." This was the first time I had heard Grand Seigneur Cernat using an inelegant word. "His ridiculous attachment to Aron will destroy us."

"Your problem," I said, dryly.

"Jara wants to see you. She has just recovered from a long illness. She was poisoned, but she is feeling well again," he added before I could react. "Orban," he spat.

"Orban wants to capture Jara alive," I said, convinced that Cernat knew what I meant: Orban wanted the woman for his pleasure, not her dead body. *Did Big Mouth try to kill Jara?* "Was Bucur in Severin at that time?"

"Yes, he was," Cernat answered with no other comment, and I involuntarily touched the pocket storing the letter from Mehadin's vault – my proof that Big Mouth was a traitor.

Without the issue related to Bucur, everything was going well. Calin's information that Devan had no intention to honor the marriage contract and the alliance; the battles I had won for Mohor, all made my path to Saliné easier. It was not common for a Grand Seigneur like Devan, a man of quality from all that I knew, to reject his own signature on an alliance contract, but it suited me. Even Mohor's last defeat was playing in my favor. *Everything depends on Saliné.*

Down the road to Severin, we rode in silence, and I could feel the tension moving through his body.

"Mohor," Cernat finally said, then stopped as if he could not find the words. "Mohor has a strength that at times is his weakness, and you were the most affected by it. He has a strong sense of loyalty and attachment to Aron. It comes from his childhood, when his father was killed, poisoned by his uncle. Mohor was only fifteen."

One year older than me ... and uncles seem to be dangerous everywhere. Cernat stirred some bad old memories, yet I was surprised to feel them distant, almost as if they were not mine.

"Senal and Aron fought hard to save him. Aron even killed Mohor's uncle in the battle for the Seigneury. I am sure there will be some recriminations today, but try to understand him better from what I have told you. We are living in dangerous times."

You made them dangerous, but I had my share too.

We entered the castle, passing among the remnants of the army: no more than a hundred and fifty, and many wounded, yet this time they came home like an army, not some bands of disorganized soldiers. *Some may have deserted*, I thought. It was not possible to lose two hundred soldiers in a battle; even

Big Mouth was not that stupid. *Treason? Ambush?* That might have done it.

In the council room, there was only the family, Vio included. It was her first attendance at a council. Jara was pale and thinner, but her general stance was one of a healthy woman. Their fear was obvious, it was gnawing at them. I looked at Saliné, and she avoided my eyes. Vio smiled a smile that looked guilty, as if she knew that the reason for her presence was to pressure me. I smiled back, sadly, because of Saliné, and took a seat without being invited, next to Vio, waiting patiently. *I will not speak first.* Before sitting, I ruffled her hair as I had many times in the past. Under the table, her hand grasped mine, and we stayed like this for a few moments. Vio smiled again, before settling her hands over the table, and I fixed on a point on the wall, ignoring everything else in the room.

Mohor was only a shadow of himself, and he moved uneasily in his chair. *You are wounded,* I suddenly realized. His left hand was stiff and supported with a sling, tied around his neck. *You deserve it.*

"You want to know what happened," Mohor finally said, without looking at me. He stopped, waiting for a reaction from my side — there was none. "Orban's army attacked us by surprise after we left Mehadia."

"I left three squads of scouts on the northern border to watch every move there."

"It was so calm that we decided to let our soldiers rest and disbanded the teams. They were tired after two months of..."

"You never decided anything." *It was Big Mouth's decision. Treason.*

"Codrin," Cernat interjected. "Mohor understands his mistake; he has made it clear to all of us."

"You don't even know what happened there," I retorted.

"I think we received a fair perspective of everything happening there, good or bad," Cernat replied, stubbornly.

"Did Mohor tell you that Bucur tried to kill me? The coward attacked me from behind, and I was not even armed."

"I warned you when he attacked," Mohor said, annoyed.

"Bucur did that?" Vio asked, incredulous.

Speechless, Saliné was just a marble statue, unable even to blink, her eyes staring nowhere. Cernat and Jara frowned at Mohor, who just shrugged, void of will.

"Mohor, we are in a very bad situation, and you are not really helping right now," Cernat hammered at him in a velvet voice.

"I arrested Bucur, but Mohor freed him overnight and sent him here. That night you assured your own defeat, by helping a traitor," I continued, having the impression that Saliné was fainting. She slipped on her chair, then recovered a little, hardly breathing. "Each night I had to sleep with several guards, just to be sure I would still be *alive* the next morning."

"Codrin, I agree that you have a long list of vexations, but Orban's army arrives here in four to five days from Mehadia. Three hundred soldiers. We have only one hundred forty able to fight, right now. If everything goes well, we might almost match their number in two days." Cernat redirected the talk to planning, and I had to admire his determination. "The army we have is not a strong one. Our only hope is you, Codrin."

"My term as army commander has ended," I said, dryly.

"There is much anger in you. I understand it. You may not be able to decide today, and we are not asking for that. Just think how you would feel if everything were to be destroyed here." Cernat gestured toward Saliné and Vio, and the pressure was now on me; Cernat had the most subtle and intricate mind and understanding of things of all the people I knew there. He lifted his eyebrows, waiting for my response.

Only Cantemir is equal to him...

"Codrin," Jara took over, and I had the feeling of a well-prepared strategy to include me in their plans. "Do you remember what I told you when you left? That some things are not what they appear? The time is now right for you and Saliné. Do you want to marry her?"

Mohor seemed upset, his lips tightening around his mouth, but he said nothing. Clearly, she had passed over his opposition; such an important decision could not be a spontaneous thing. Cernat was calm.

And informed... And he has accepted it. Finally, my covert actions and the war I started had given me what I had fought for: Saliné. An image from the past came to me: the gracious curve of her neck bent over a lyre. I even heard her singing, yet deep inside, I had the feeling that Fate was laughing at me.

Saliné had that look I saw in wounded men. Her face was immobile, her fingers gripping the table's edge, her breath uneven. Everything in her stance was telling me to refuse, and many different emotions and thoughts passed through me, fast and confusing. What I wanted the most had been offered to me, and I did not know what to do.

"Codrin? Will you accept?" Jara woke me up gently, her voice wobbling slightly.

"Yes," I said, reluctantly.

"Then..." Jara sighed with great relief.

"It's not possible," Saliné said, her voice void of feelings.

"There is a refusal clause related to critical situations in the marriage contract. We have that kind of situation right now, and we will find a political arrangement with the Devans," Jara assured her, yet I had the sudden feeling that it was nothing to do with the Devans. "The Devans understand that if we are destroyed now, they will follow."

"I am pregnant." Saliné voice was weak, barely audible, yet the effect in the room was astounding: the air became taut like a bowstring, ready to explode.

"You...!" Vio shouted, jumping from her chair, so angry that she could not finish her sentence.

"Saliné..." Jara said with that pain that only mothers could have in their voices.

Saliné could no longer answer; she had passed out, her body sliding onto the floor. Jara jumped up and took her in her arms. Unconscious, Saliné's face was tender, and she was breathing slowly, in a room filled with disfigured facial masks. Vio's face alone was real, whitened with fury.

Unable to muster any trace of coherence, my mind twisted from one fragment of a thought to another. *I should have killed Bucur...*

That night I had the gentlest possible nightmares: picking cherries with Saliné, over and over again.

●●

"Thank you for receiving me," Saliné said formally, when I opened the door. She entered alone, her escort waiting outside. I offered a chair at the table, and she sat, visibly uncomfortable. The day before was looming over us, and I went to the window, my mind frozen. A new moon stared cynically at me, foreseeing a completely unpredictable new cycle of events in my life.

"There is something I felt the need to tell you. Please don't interrupt. It's ... hard. Everything started after you kissed me. Do not mistake me, I don't want to put any blame on you," she added hastily. "Until that day, although unhappy, I was able to control myself, and the separation wall that Mother built between us helped too. Please forgive her; it was the right thing to do. Everything changed that day. I could no longer sleep or eat. I hoped I would recover when you left for Arad. It did not happen. The only thing that helped me was Bucur's attention. He kept my mind busy with stories and jokes and, after a while, I was able to sleep again, just because I was no longer thinking of you, day and night. And I decided: as there was no chance for us to be together, I had to split us up. I used Bucur, letting him touch me in front of you. I knew you would suffer, and that it would make you hate me at first, then forget me. I needed you to forget just to help myself to forget, too."

"When Bucur came back earlier than expected, I found it easier to forget you by letting him get close to me, thinking that I was mature enough to control the course of events. I knew that he was at ease with women, but I thought them weak where I was strong. Then Mother was poisoned, and my whole world crumbled. One evening I was no longer strong, and I ruined our future. I succumbed to my pride and to my sorrow." Her voice broke, and she remained silent for a while. Unobservant, I realized only later that she was fighting hard to suppress her crying. "It never happened again, but I am now paying for that evening, even when I don't remember what happened to me. I don't remember," she repeated, her voice barely more than a whisper, and it took her a while to recover. "Tomorrow, I have to marry Bucur, a man I despise. Since I despise myself too, we deserve each other."

Until that moment, I had listened without really hearing her, yet my mind memorized everything, and later I was able to remember all that she said, word for word. My head turned, by its own will, and our eyes met. There was no life on her face, and she stopped talking. Then something flashed in her eyes, or maybe I fantasied that it did.

I have lost everything. For the second time. First my family, now... Cernat told me in the morning that Bucur had been chosen as commander of the army. He came to arrange Saliné's visit, but for some reason known only to him, Cernat briefed me about all the decisions they had taken overnight. *He said nothing about her marriage. It no longer matters if Bucur loses or wins. I have lost anyway,* I realized how well Big Mouth had planned everything, from killing Senal and betraying Mohor, to poisoning Jara – I was now convinced that Bucur was the poisoner. *If he wins the battle, all my efforts were for him. All.*

And Fate just played me... Slowly, I turned back to the window, freeing Saliné to speak again.

"For a long time, there was nothing I could do but cry for us, when no one was looking, and many times..." Her voice stumbled again, and she breathed deeply. "Many times, I thought that Fate was angry at me, and there was no situation worse than mine after the marriage contract was signed, separating us. Looking back, I wish I had been right. My condition is far worse now, and I can't even blame somebody else. With the Devans, at least I was doing the right thing to save my family. Now, I am the one ruining everything, and there is no one else to blame except me. And it's not fair that they have to suffer because I failed so miserably. Regarding you, I hope that Vio will be luckier and wiser than me. That was all I wanted to say." She stood up and stopped in front of me.

"I would like to touch you once more," she whispered, and without waiting for my answer, her palm caressed my face. "Farewell, Codrin." She left quickly, as if pushed by a strong wind.

In a curious turn, there was no evident reaction in me that day. Now and then, some of her words resurfaced, in brief flashes. My mind was acting on two parallel strings of thoughts, one conscious and frozen at the same time, feeling almost nothing, and the other hidden at a deeper level, grinding everything like a perpetual mill, trying to protect me until some solace for my nightmares could be found.

Saliné's wedding was canceled after she had a miscarriage during the night, and a strong hemorrhage kept her in bed. In the evening, a disturbed Cernat came, trying to manage a badly hidden panic – Saliné wanted to see me one more time. *She is still alive...* When I opened the door for Cernat, I thought her dead. I had never seen him so fallen; he was now just a shadow of the Grand Seigneur I knew, and there was a thin expectation in his eyes that maybe my presence could help in avoiding what could not be avoided. *She is still alive*, I repeated, unable to react in any other way. We rode in silence, all the way down to the castle, and even there I spoke with no one. It was a world filled with silence and bad feelings. Saliné was loved by everybody. In a long row, many torches were flickering on the corridor going to her room, but they only seemed to increase the gloom.

Jara grabbed my hand when I arrived at the bed where Saliné was lying. Kneeling in front of the bed, she was crying silently, her eyes pouched with tiredness. Saliné looked pale and calm, her body and face somehow diminished – death was already claiming her. Eyes closed, she was breathing slowly. A faint scent of incense briefly caught my attention. Several lit candles cast glimmers of light, and their warmth contrasted with everything else in the room.

"Saliné," Jara whispered. "Codrin is here."

"Thank you for coming." Saliné opened her large, green eyes, staring at me, and I saw the effort consuming her. Acknowledging me, they closed slowly. "Mother, leave us alone." When the door closed behind Jara, Saliné opened her eyes again.

"Our cherry tree is waiting for me – my last journey. I will not be alone there; Horia and Mugur are resting in the garden too. I had a restless mind, always craving for new things. It will be at peace between the deep roots. They say that our bodies move up in the tree. In time. Promise me to come in spring."

"Saliné..."

"Promise me," she said with surprising force, and unable to speak, I just nodded. "I will cry petals over you. Each spring... Since my father died, all my last years were mostly tears." Drained by the effort, her voice faded, yet some resurfacing memories left a tiny trace of a smile at the corners of her mouth.

"Codrin, kiss me once more."

That was all she asked, and I took her beautiful face between my palms, touching her lips gently, her breath was so weak.

"Saliné, you have to fight," I said, suddenly knowing that the bonds between us were still unbroken.

"What is there to fight for, Codrin? There is nothing left," she whispered, and tears streamed freely down her face.

"Fight for us." My hand closed around her cold, weak fingers that I knew so well, and I warmed them with a kiss.

Two days later, contrary to all expectations, Saliné was still alive, albeit unconscious, and I was leading Mohor's army in a battle that no one gave me any chance of winning, not even myself. A second S'Arad army, six hundred strong, was coming from the north, and many of our troops had deserted us. Severin was doomed to fall in Orban's hands.

APPENDIX

Arenia

Codrin, son of the slain King of Arenia and the legitimate King. After his father's death, he finds sanctuary in the former kingdom of Frankis, sometimes using the name Tudor to conceal his real identity.

Tudor, an Assassin renegade and Codrin's mentor

Ioana, Codrin's twin sister

Radu, Codrin's brother

Baraki, Chief of the Royal Guard of Arenia

Iulian, captain of the Royal Guard of Arenia

Gaspar, Knight, Baraki's nephew

Jan, the Usurper's son, killed in battle by Codrin

Severin

Jara (Stejara), Signora of Severin, former Grand Signora of Midia. She lost her castle to Grand Seigneur Orban after her first husband, Malin, was slain in battle.

Mohor, Seigneur of Severin and Jara's second husband

Cernat, former Grand Seigneur of Midia and Jara's father

Saliné, Jara's daughter

Vio, Jara's daughter

Veres (Snail), Jara's son

Mark, Jara and Mohor's son

Aron (Big Mouth), Spatar of Severin (commander of the army)

Senal, Secretary of Severin

Raul, Aron's eldest son, killed by Cernat when he tried to kidnap Saliné and Vio at Maud's request

Bucur, Aron's son

Vlaicu, Chief of the Guard of Severin

Ban, Chief of the Archers of Severin, Vlaicu's right hand

Jorn, the second Secretary of Severin and Aron's brother

Jelin, Jorn's son

Milene, servant in Jara's house

Arad

Orban (the Beast), Grand Seigneur of Arad

Cantemir, Secretary of Arad and Master Sage of the Circle

Panait, the second Mester of the Merchants Guild in Arad

Delia, Panait's wife

Vasile, Jara's agent in Arad

The Wanderers

Dochia, the last Empress of the Alban Empire and founder of the Order of the Wanderers. She died six hundred years ago.

Dochia, the Fifth Light of the Frankis Wanderers

Drusila, the Second Light of the Frankis Wanderers

Umbra, the peregrine raven bond to Dochia

Ada, the Second Light of the Arenian Wanderers

Mira, Dochia's guard

Irina, Dochia's guard

The Circle

Cantemir, Master Sage of the Circle and Secretary of Arad

Maud, Sage of the Circle's Council and the third Secretary of Leyona

Aurelian, Primus Itinerant and Maud's lover

Aron, Hidden Sage and Spatar of Severin

Balan, First Mester of Deva

Deva
Devan, Grand Seigneur of Deva
Balan, the first Mester of the Merchants Guild in Deva and Sage of the Circle
Mona, Balan's wife
Dan, Chief of the Guard of Deva

Mehadia
Mehadin, Seigneur of Mehadia
Calin, Secretary of Mehadia
Mara, the second Secretary of Mehadia and Calin's daughter
Mihail, Mara's son

Miscellaneous
Malin, Grand Seigneur of Midia and Jara's husband, slain in battle against Grand Seigneur Orban
Boldur, one of the Mountes' chieftains
Vlad, born in Litvonia, he followed Codrin to the former Frankis Kingdom
Pintea, Vlad's brother
Gran, Vlad's and Pintea's grandmother, she sheltered Codrin during his first winter in Litvonia
Movil, innkeeper of the Caravans' Inn in Muniker
Dobre, governor of Orhei in Leyona Seigneury
Konrad, Knight
Iaru, the third Mester of the Merchants Guild in Dorna
Lenard, Seigneur of Dorna
Stefan, Duke of Peyris
Cleyre, Duke Stefan's granddaughter
Manuc, Duke of Loxburg
Tardin, Knight, he betrayed Malin during the battle against Orban

Spatar, chief of the army

Vistier, administrator of a castle and coin master

Wraith, most successful Lead Protectors (only four in Frankis)

Black Dervil, mercenary captain (only five in Frankis)

galben, gold coin, ten grams weight

turn, time unit of measure, equivalent of one hour

Wanderers ruling councils

Inner Council of the Three

High Council of the Seven.

Printed in Great Britain
by Amazon

58447530R00253